The House of Wives

The House of Wives

Simon Choa-Johnston

PENGUIN

an imprint of Penguin Canada Books Inc., a division of Penguin Random House Canada Limited

Published by the Penguin Group
Penguin Canada Books Inc., 320 Front Street West, Suite 1400, Toronto,
Ontario M5V 3B6, Canada

Penguin Group (USA) LLC, 375 Hudson Street, New York, New York 10014, U.S.A.
Penguin Books Ltd, 80 Strand, London WC2R 0RL, England
Penguin Ireland, 25 St Stephen's Green, Dublin 2, Ireland (a division of Penguin Books Ltd)
Penguin Group (Australia), 707 Collins Street, Melbourne, Victoria 3008, Australia
Penguin Books India Pvt Ltd, 11 Community Centre, Panchsheel Park, New Delhi – 110 017, India
Penguin Group (NZ), 67 Apollo Drive, Rosedale, Auckland 0632, New Zealand
Penguin Books (South Africa) (Pty) Ltd, 24 Sturdee Avenue, Rosebank, Johannesburg 2196,
South Africa
Penguin Books Ltd, Registered Offices: 80 Strand, London WC2R 0RL, England

First published 2016

1 2 3 4 5 6 7 8 9 10 (RRD)

Manufactured in the U.S.A.

Cover design: Lisa Jager
Cover photographs: (temple) Marcus Lindström/Getty Images; (woman) Fotorince/Shutterstock.com

LIBRARY AND ARCHIVES CANADA CATALOGUING IN PUBLICATION

Choa-Johnston, Simon, author
The house of wives / Simon Choa-Johnston.

ISBN 978-0-670-06947-7 (paperback)

I. Title.

PS8605.H615H69 2015   C813'.6   C2015-906328-0

eBook ISBN 978-0-14-319411-8

www.penguinrandomhouse.ca

The House of Wives

PROLOGUE

CHINA
1860

A four-year-old's encounter with the devil is different from a grown-up's. If the confrontation is serious enough, the child will freeze and lock it in her mind's eye forever. The grown-up will scale mountains, if needed, to put as much distance as he can between himself and the fiend.

Such was the case for the child riding on her father's back. Her arms wound tightly around his neck. Her legs wrapped around his waist. And her face was buried between his shoulder blades. The child had walked as far as her little legs would carry her. She hadn't cried even though she was hungry. She knew she was a good girl—her father had told her so. He was a thin, wiry farmer from Kwantung—China's southernmost province. She wondered if the three-inch gash on the side of his head still hurt. It had scabbed over but was still puffy.

Fearing detection, they slept during the day, away from the hill paths. At night they walked south. She knew the direction because that is what her father had told her. After two sunrises (when they had finished the sweet rolls he had stuffed in his pockets) he picked her up and carried her on his back. She had noticed that, as they got farther from the village, other travellers emerged from hiding and were headed in the same direction. Mostly they were women with young children. But there were also men. After a long time—she couldn't tell how many days it was—they reached a river. A full moon glowed overhead. Her father told her that behind them was China. In front, only another day's walk, was the city of Heung

Gong—Hong Kong, the British colony. There they would be safe and the devils could not harm them. She was relieved but wondered how they would cross the river without a boat.

The grown-ups must have been wondering the same thing. They stood in a row on the riverbank, speaking in hushed but urgent voices. Then some of the men snapped off tree branches, waded in, and used the sticks to gauge the water's depth. The little girl didn't know how long this took because she fell asleep. Eventually, her father shook her awake and said that they had found a shallow enough crossing. He lifted her onto his back and waded into the moonlit water.

In her tiny world, the little girl was certain about two things. First, she could hear her father's heart beating against her ear. This gave her a sense of security. And second, she could feel the piece of jade in her pocket. She took it out. It felt cold in her palm. The stone was flat and oval shaped, larger than a quail's egg but smaller than a hen's. It reminded her of why they had fled their home.

As on most market days, they were in the village not far from their small patch of farm. Her parents had set up their stall—a table with a cloth over it that reached to the ground. The little girl loved to hide under the table, where she could spend all day playing with a straw horse her mother had made for her. From that womblike privacy she could peek through the folds of the tablecloth and see the wide world without being seen, hear without being heard. Her father sold vegetables and her mother took in sewing—that was what the cloth was for, to show samples of the stitching that she did by hand. Her mother was a small woman with a round face just like the little girl's. And they both had high cheekbones that were red with health. This made her mother appear younger than her twenty-two years because the red bandana she always wore framed her lively almond-shaped eyes. Around her smooth neck was a matching scarf that was also self-made. These accessories made her mother the butt of jealous barbs in this village of hard-working farmers and their wives. But the little girl didn't care. She knew that her mother was someone special, someone she would like to be when she grew up and became a farmer's wife herself.

Horses' hooves, beating a rhythmic gallop, started in the distance, then quickly grew louder and thundered into the village. Through a slit in the tablecloth she saw the soldiers dismount. They were Chinese soldiers—too many to count. They were a slovenly bunch. Chinstraps loosened and shirts unbuttoned, they steered their mounts deliberately into the stalls. Caged poultry, eggs, and cabbage spilled off tabletops. Bags and jugs, plates and cups, wine and tea flew in large and small arcs through the air, smashing, rolling, and bouncing on the cobblestone. What was happening? These were Chinese soldiers. Why were they doing this to their own people?

Her mother crawled under the table on her belly. She was half inside the little girl's womblike tent when she tore off her red bandana and hid it inside her tunic. Out of some invisible pocket her mother produced a jade stone and pressed it into the little girl's palm. "Be strong. Stay here—"

Her mother screamed and was dragged out from under the table by the ankles. The little girl started to shake. She looked at the jade, closed her tiny fingers over it, and thrust it into her pocket. "Mama!" she shouted and crawled out of her hiding place. Two Devils held her mother's arms. She kicked and yelled, tried to tear away. But she was too small and they were too strong.

"Bo Jue!" her father screamed. The little girl turned when she heard her name. Two Devils held her father back. A third one aimed his rifle at him and pulled the trigger.

Click.

Again.

Click. The gun failed to fire. Her father struggled to free himself. The Devil raised his rifle and smashed the butt of it into the side of her father's head. His knees buckled. He crumpled to the ground.

"Get her." The Devils spat out a vulgar Chinese curse and ran at Bo Jue, who dived under the table and out the other side. The men pursued her but got stuck in the small space.

Everywhere she looked there was chaos—Devils in uniform stealing things, beating people, laughing. Bo Jue ran to where she had last seen her mother. A small mud hut at the end of the lane. Its entrance had no door, just a rectangular hole and beside that an open window. Bo Jue ran to the hut and looked in.

Two Devils pinned her mother against a wall. A third one slapped her across the face. She spat in his eye. He wiped off the spittle and said something in Cantonese that Bo Jue could not understand. But she knew it was frightening. She knew that her mother was in danger. She knew she had to do something, but what?

The face-slapping Devil reached out his hand and grabbed her mother's tunic. He tore it across her chest, exposing her breasts.

Bo Jue gasped. She felt a scream travel up from some place deep in her body. But just as she was about to yell "Mama!" a hand covered her mouth. She felt herself lifted off the ground and away from the sight of her mother's captivity. In the next moment her feet were allowed to touch the ground. Hands grabbed her shoulders and spun her around. It was her father. He held a finger up to his lips. Blood was dripping from a nasty wound on the side of his head. He picked her up in his arms and ran from the village.

That was four or five sunrises ago. Bo Jue looked at the stone in her hand. She knew that every time she touched it, she would see her mother.

When they reached the other bank, her father put her down on the ground and pointed south. Mist hovered like a white blanket over paddy fields that stretched to the horizon. "There," he said. "Do you see? Way in the distance?"

Bo Jue followed the line of her father's finger. She saw mist, sky, and birds. Her father saw their future.

PART ONE

CALCUTTA
1841–1862

EMANUEL

His parents were Arabic-speaking Sephardic Jews from Basra in Iraq, and amongst the first families to settle in Calcutta. Like their contemporaries, they had been successful merchants dealing in jewellery, tea, silk, and jute who, one day, were forced to pack up and leave Iraq. They dusted the sand off their sandals at the gates of great Muslim cities in the Middle East and headed south. They had run afoul of capricious *ashraf*, who decreed that Jewish sojourners had overstayed their welcome. In other words, their businesses were too successful and an uncomfortable amount of money was owed to Jewish merchant bankers. A pall of déjà vu fell upon the Semite community. They fled in the night, days ahead of the hard smack of wooden heels and the deadly slicing of scimitars, and arrived in Bombay in the late 1790s. Sensing better opportunities, they headed east to Calcutta—a swampy enclave that the British had selected as the site on which to build a capital city and from where they would administer their colonial ambitions in India. Like their forefathers in Spain and Venice and, more recently, in cities like Aleppo and Basra, the Jews in India had mastered the art of assimilation.

Just so, in Calcutta, the light-skinned Belilios family had merged themselves into the mainstream. They adopted European dress and enrolled their sons in academies modelled after the English public school system. Proper English schoolmasters imported from the mother country cracked the whip. These reedy-looking teachers, itchy with prickly heat rashes under their heavy cotton clothes, bashed the sons of new money into shape for the good of the Empire.

At Emanuel's school, a boy's character was moulded in the boxing ring and on the cricket pitch. But for him, assimilation was not so easy. He was fat and awkward; cricket balls slipped through his hands like water through a sieve, and he was unable to defend himself against his smaller, more nimble opponents in the ring. Being thus tormented was not new to the lad. Conversations at home during dinner were often focused on his older brother, Aaron—"the handsome one"—who seemed never to set a foot wrong and monopolized Papa's attention. His Mama rarely spoke to her second born. She had never forgiven him for almost tearing her tiny frame in half at birth; when he had looked up at her with his pale-blue eyes, she had turned away. Shortly after, she weaned him and gave him to Ayah Gita, her fourteen-year-old Hindu slave whose husband had disappeared, leaving her aching for a child of her own to raise.

They were a pair, those two: the small, dark-skinned Indian girl with her black eyes, tiny nose, and thin lips carrying a large child wrapped in cloth on her back. Ayah Gita loved the boy. She indulged his every whim, even giving him the fatty foods he devoured as a balm against his parents' lack of interest.

Of all the mockeries he had endured, none shaped his character more than what happened on the day he was summoned to the headmaster's office. He was fourteen. It had all come to a head when a badly written limerick—passed from boy to boy during Latin class—landed unintention-ally on his desk.

> There once was a lad from Howrah
> Who filled his pants with flowra.
> Ayah washed it away,
> Then the whore made him play
> The fiddle on her what-cha-ma-call'er!

Each line felt like a stick of dynamite piled one on top of another. Insulting his beloved Ayah lit the spark.

Emanuel flew out of his seat, leapt on top of an adjoining desk, bounded across two aisles, and reached the limerick makers. He grabbed the two poets, one in each arm, and wrestled them to the floor, splintering desks on the way down. Students scattered. In his haste to intervene, the Latin master tripped and fell, breaking his nose with a sickening crunch.

Emanuel punched one boy in the throat. Seeing this, the other poet ran out the door and down the hall, screaming "Help! Help!"

Emanuel did not give chase. He stood in the centre of the carnage and looked around him: desks akimbo, a teacher's nose bloodied, and his classmates cowering, terrified of his sudden and uncharacteristic rage.

An hour later, in the headmaster's office, Mr. Stuart-Fox called a truce: "Please, gentlemen, and I use that word advisedly, this must stop!" He was referring to the heated debate raging between Raphael—Emanuel's father—and the father of the boy Emanuel had punched in the throat.

The exchange between the two glowering fathers was not about what had transpired in the classroom. A roomful of people had witnessed the incident and the facts were indisputable. Nor was it about who had provoked the fracas and why. No, it was about pronouncing a suitable punishment for Emanuel's outburst, which Mr. Stuart-Fox had described as "Not on." Compounding the matter was the lack of a common language. Raphael spoke Arabic and very little English. His rival, a British bureaucrat who worked in the Writers' Building issuing business licences to merchants like Belilios, spoke English and no Arabic. Thus Mr. Stuart-Fox was forced to wave his white handkerchief with one hand and slam his palm down on his desk with the other when he called for the yelling to stop. "Thank you. Now if you will both resume your seats. Emanuel is the only one in this room who is fluent in both Arabic and English. He will serve."

The two boys were seated against the wall. Emanuel's knuckles were slightly red and his victim had a large purple bruise on the right side of his neck. The Latin master had fared far worse. He was lying on the couch nursing an inflamed and swollen snout.

Mr. Stuart-Fox signalled for Emanuel to step forward. "Translate please: There are two choices. Expulsion or six strokes of the cane."

Emanuel hesitated.

"Well, go on, boy," Mr. Stuart-Fox said. Guttural-sounding phrases fell out of his student's mouth.

Raphael looked at his son and said in Arabic: *"This man is a shit. Every week I give him fifty rupees on top of the school fees to make sure you get good marks. And now he does this to me?"*

"What is he saying?" Mr. Stuart-Fox asked.

"He says he is thinking about the choices."

"Right from the start, he said fifty rupees and not a paise less. I took the offer immediately. We shook hands on it. His predecessor wanted a hundred rupees!"

"Translation?" Mr. Stuart-Fox demanded.

"My father requires a little more time."

The headmaster pulled back his shoulders and nodded.

"Emanuel, what should I do? It will be such a disgrace for you to be expelled. But I can't bring myself to see you hurt. Tell me what I should do."

Emanuel did not respond.

"Well, what did he say—look, I'm not going to keep asking!"

Emanuel cut him off: "My father chooses caning."

Raphael did not need the Arabic version. The British bureaucrat cleared his throat and looked away. The Latin master sat up, holding his nose with a bloodied handkerchief. Mr. Stuart-Fox said, "I see."

"Six of the best" were administered immediately. Emanuel bent over and held the sides of the headmaster's desk, exposing his buttocks. He grimaced with each stroke and looked straight into the eyes of the people in the room. This, he said to himself, will be the last time anyone takes advantage of me.

He saved his tears for later that night. Ayah Gita put salve on the welts that puffed up across his skin. Then she held him close. He felt comfort in her presence, as he always had—innocently and eagerly. But the sting of the cane did not compare with the hurt he harboured against a father who had watched his humiliation and done nothing.

On the day he graduated, Emanuel shook the dust off his boots at the gates of his school and walked briskly away. Graduation had not come soon enough. Now he wanted to get as far away as he could from his family's grip. He had dreamed of this day. He had done what his father had wanted. He had endured that wretched place for ten years. He was a man now, and he figured it was time for quid pro quo.

As he headed toward Bow Bazaar, Ayah Gita kept pace as best she could. She trotted behind him, waving a fan at her master's back in a vain attempt to cool him down. She had seen him like this before—his blue eyes narrowed, his lips tightened into a thin line, his large body quivering with impatience.

At the warehouse, he ran up the stairs that led to the administration floor. When they saw the master's son, the throng of male clerks fell silent. They stepped out of his way and stared with open-mouthed surprise as the two-person cavalcade strode past. The spectacle of a short, round-bellied young white man dressed in a black European-styled suit and his Hindu servant in a sari waving her fan made someone laugh. Emanuel ignored the guffaw. He had more important things on his mind. Without knocking, he opened the door to his father's private office and entered.

"I want my inheritance," he said, jutting out his chin and speaking in Arabic, the language commonly used by the merchant class. The older man, dressed in a *thwab*—a traditional Arabic gown—and turban, looked up from his desk, put down his pen, and said to his Parsi clerk,

"Shut the door."

Mr. Rustomjee nodded. He was swarthy, round-faced, and wore a *sudras*—a long muslin shirt. Cradling papers and a notebook in his arms, he walked toward the door. Ayah Gita stayed outside, closing her palms around her fan and touching them to her forehead. Then she crouched out of sight. The door made a soft *click* when it closed. Mr. Rustomjee released the knob, held his papers against his chest with one hand, folded the other behind his back, and returned to standing beside his master.

"You gave Aaron his expectations," Emanuel said. "Now I want mine."

"To do what?" his father asked.

Emanuel hadn't thought that far. Sweat beaded on his forehead just as it used to before he entered the school's boxing ring. Raphael beckoned for his clerk to come closer and whispered into his ear. Mr. Rustomjee cocked an eyebrow and nodded.

"Follow Rustomjee. He will show you the ledgers. After you have read everything, come back to me. Tell me what interests you, then we'll see."

The ledgers contained lists of dates and commodities, each accompanied by its weight, purchase price, and sale price. The data unfolded for him like a novel. But unlike fiction, which Emanuel had never appreciated, his father's businesses were revealed in a narrative of facts free from messy emotional entanglements. He surprised himself by reading the information so easily. The ebb and flow of "getting and spending," of "late" and "soon," of "profits" and "losses" swept across the pages. They were as easy to spot as *bekti* flashing their silver fins near the surface of the water in the bends of the Hoogli. At school Emanuel had loathed mathematics. He had been bored memorizing historical dates and had struggled to apply logic to philosophic arguments. Those minutiae were insufferable wastes of time as far as he was concerned. Yet his mind was now dancing with numbers. He found himself calculating percentages and doing long division. He stored the results in the folds of his mind and retrieved them as easily as pulling a book off a shelf. Shifts in the pattern of where one commodity originated, where it ended up and why this was so, occupied his imagination. His curiosity was a gigantic maw hungry for information. So engrossed was he in the mysteries of the ledgers that he had not noticed the oil lamps Mr. Rustomjee had lit and placed on his table. Raphael had gone home at six. Shortly afterward the activity in the warehouse below had whittled down to the occasional slam of something heavy. By eleven the only ones left were Ayah Gita, a middle-aged Parsi clerk, and a fleshy young man in a hurry to make his way in the world.

"Sir is wanting some chai?" Mr. Rustomjee said in English. He had two steaming mugs in his hands. Without waiting for a reply, he placed one of them on the table in front of the young master. Emanuel looked up and rubbed his eyes. Mr. Rustomjee slurped his tea.

"What time is it?" Emanuel asked.

"Sir. It is just past one A.M." Mr. Rustomjee nodded at the wall clock.

"No. That cannot be," Emanuel said, looking around.

The large outer office was vacant. Desks sat like small, silent boats floating on dark waters. Stillness had replaced the storm of activity he had witnessed hours before. Emanuel picked up the mug and sipped his tea.

"What are you doing here?" he asked.

"Sir, it is my duty to be locking up the outer office and also the back office."

"And I have kept you from doing so."

"It is not a problem, sir," he said, waggling his head.

"Have you worked here long?"

"Sir, almost all my life. Your father is being a great man."

Emanuel did not agree but kept that opinion to himself.

"How so?" he asked.

"Please?" Mr. Rustomjee said, narrowing his eyes at the challenge.

"Take a seat. Tell me why you admire him."

Mr. Rustomjee remained standing. His eyes darted from side to side like a trapped cat. He cupped his hands around his mug of chai and composed his thoughts.

"Sir, it is like this. I am from Basra—Parsi. He is also from Basra, but a Jew. The Muslim rulers there wanted everyone to be Mohammedan. We refused. We had to flee. My father worked for your father as a clerk. We were not rich like your family. When it came time to leave Basra, my father had to stay with my mother and with my brothers and sisters. I was the oldest. My father offered me to be your father's clerk. For friendship, sir took me into service. I am very lucky and sir is kind-hearted."

It surprised Emanuel to hear of his father's humanity.

"Will sir be requiring more ledgers?"

"No," Emanuel said, "you may remove them."

Mr. Rustomjee nodded. He looked relieved that his day was finally over and that he was not being pressed for more personal information. He put down his mug, stacked the ledgers in his arms, and placed them back on the shelves. He closed the cupboard doors and took out a ring of keys.

"Will there be anything else, sir?"

"Yes," Emanuel said. "Tell me about opium."

Mr. Rustomjee stopped. "Ah," he said, locking the cupboard doors. "Sir's father was right. He said you would want to know."

Just north of the playing fields of the Maidan—where Emanuel let countless cricket balls slip through his fingers—the Ezra family lived in a villa that resembled an English country estate. Only this one was larger. Like Raphael Belilios, Ibrahim Ezra was part of the diaspora that had fled Iraq in the 1790s. He made his fortune in Calcutta real estate by buying land and building houses. For all its ostentation (gargoyles and pink walls with green shutters), *la maison* Ibrahim was not out of place in this City of Palaces. Park Street and Chowringhee were lined with tall buildings festooned with Doric columns, balustraded verandas, French windows, and more architectural flourishes than a Milanese palazzo. Behind the gates of walled-in compounds, Venetian-styled facades were as commonly seen as French Rococo curlicues on porticos. And surrounding these mansions, English botanists coaxed a riot of flora from the fecund soil.

Like Emanuel Belilios, Ibrahim Ezra's daughter, Semah, spent her childhood trying to live up to the standards imported by the British colonists. Instead of a public school education, Semah's preparations were readying her to become a proper wife. Mindful of her swarthy looks, dark hair, and big brown eyes, her parents decided early on that Semah's skin must be protected from the sun at all costs, lest the harmful rays further darken her prospects of finding a husband. Dutifully, whenever she ventured outdoors, she put on arm-length gloves, European-style high-collared dresses, a wide-brimmed hat, and a veil to shield her from the brutal sun. When Semah turned twelve she had a growth spurt that made her taller than her mother. Suddenly she was able to stand eyeball to eyeball with her father. It was imperative, they agreed, that if she was going to end up large and handsome—a euphemistic second cousin to petite and pretty—then she might at least be graceful. They hired a battery of tutors who taught her comportment, music, singing, sewing, conversation, drawing and watercolour, and riding—sidesaddle of course—and any other skills that might temper her size *avec les accoutrements des élégances*. Speech instructors lined up at the gate with promises to eradicate the guttural clatter of Arabic and to smooth out the tongue rolling of Hindi. The girl would pronounce the English language as the English did. Obediently, Semah took to it all as a flower to sunlight.

By the time she was fifteen, she had become quite the linguist. At the dining table she continued to speak Arabic with her parents, and with the servants in the kitchen she still spoke Hindi—she had the common touch—while during her lessons she flitted like a shuttlecock between English and French depending on the tutor in residence.

Ibrahim and Sula beamed with fulfillment. Their strategy had worked. "Charming and accomplished" was how they had described their daughter on the day they announced her dowry at ten thousand rupees. Furthermore, Ibrahim wanted Semah to be the first bride married at Calcutta's new synagogue. Word spread quickly through the city's fledgling Jewish community and reached as far as Bombay.

While waiting for an eligible bachelor to present himself, Semah sat daily beside Sula and watched her mother run the large estate that had a retinue of servants, a garden to tend, and stables to administer. From her mother's day room, Semah was occasionally dispatched, like an ambassador, to bring reports back from the edges of the property.

For her own purposes, Semah sketched her environs on large sheets of paper that she pasted on a wall of her bedroom. The river, in blue, meandered along the left, or western border of the property, while a vast nothingness in green occupied the eastern extremity. Everything in between—the house with its many windows, the stables, the garden, the forest—was meticulously rendered and coloured. Between the Hoogli River and the western wall she had noted "Bow Bazaar," then underneath: "Most Jews live here." Dates were written in the Hebrew calendar: 24 Sh'vat when she had peered over the red brick wall that bordered the estate; 23 Iyyar when she rode her horse to the edge of the forest. There were also brief notes, such as "shabby" or "beautiful" or "needs work."

She had access to every room except one—Ibrahim's study. Sula explained that it was her papa's sanctum sanctorum and out of bounds. "Men need their own space," her mother explained cryptically, then curled her lip and continued: "He smokes tobacco in there. I can't abide the odour." But this explanation did not satisfy Semah. She thought it unfair that she could not access a room filled with books that could enhance her knowledge of the world.

The following Wednesday afternoon, Semah's painting master sent word that he was feeling under the weather and cancelled the lesson. Semah's tummy fluttered. Her mother was at her weekly visit to her family's home and Ibrahim was at the office. An opportunity had presented itself and her hands turned cold with anticipation.

She watched the door of the library from the top of the stairs. She could hear herself breathing. Her eyes darted left and right. There was no one in sight. She made her move, tiptoed down the stairs, opened the door, and slid inside.

Her eyes scanned the volumes. Some books were large, some were small, some were wide, and some were narrow. One thing was certain: they all seemed to be waiting for her to open them. She climbed a ladder to a walkway that gave access to the upper collections. From there she had a clear view of the cavernous room below: the table against the window, the rolling bar cart, the easy chair, a sofa she hadn't noticed before, carpets with coloured designs, a large globe of the world, a collection of pipes beside a canister of tobacco.

There were voices outside the door.

The door opened. Her father entered, followed by a woman she did not recognize. She watched him close the door, tear off his jacket, and fling it aside. Meanwhile, the woman struggled with the stays at the back of her dress. Semah felt, intuitively, that her father and the stranger were doing something furtive. She was watching something that should not be happening. Her skin tingled and her feet turned to stone. Blood rushed from her face. Her knuckles turned white from gripping the handrail. She pressed her back against the shelves and felt wood against her spine. She willed her fingers to let go of the handrail. Using one hand, she covered her mouth to stifle the yelp that had been building in her throat, and with the other she felt behind her back, searching for the gap she knew was between the shelves. Mercifully she found it and folded herself into the narrow cavity without taking her eyes off the scene below.

The woman yanked up her skirt and pulled down her drawers. Her father wriggled out of his suspenders and pushed down his trousers, exposing his bare bottom. Semah closed her eyes and covered her ears against the sounds of muffled grunts and rhythmic breathing.

EMANUEL

E manuel boarded a train at Howrah Station bound for Patna Ghats, a city to the west of Calcutta. His father had instructed Mr. Rustomjee to purchase a first-class cabin and to accompany the boy to teach him about the planting, harvesting, processing, and manufacture of opium. Emanuel had decided to bring Ayah Gita along because her family was *ryot*—tenant farmers of a small patch of land where they planted poppies. In exchange for her rent, her family had offered Ayah Gita to Raphael Belilios to work as a slave. It was a daylong trip uphill to the country station. From there it took another few hours by oxcart to reach the poppy fields.

When they arrived at the village, Ayah Gita's mother, father, sisters, brothers, and a cluster of aunts and uncles rushed out to greet her. Her mother, a small round woman with a toothy smile, carried a dish of sandalwood paste and a basket of daisy petals. Garlands of golden chrysanthemums were draped over her arm. She dipped her middle finger into the sandalwood and dabbed Emanuel's forehead. Then she sprinkled his head with daisy petals and looped a garland over his head. *"Namaska,"* she said. He placed his palms together and replied, *"Namaska."* Mr. Rustomjee was next to receive the traditional greeting—*my spirit acknowledges your spirit.*

Ayah Gita's family's home was a one-room mud hut with a thatched roof. Bunk beds to one side and a mattress against the opposite wall were shared amongst eight members of her family. They were proud to show off the wool covers they had recently purchased with the money from last season's harvest.

Her father took out a long-stemmed pipe from under the mattress. He was thin and round-shouldered and looked older than his forty years. When he grinned, his teeth were stained red from chewing *paan*—red betel paste. He opened a small wooden box and took out something that resembled a fig. He took a pinch, put it on a spoon, and heated it over a flame. A thin curl of smoke rose. He turned the bowl of his pipe over the smoke and held it in place. Grinning from ear to ear, he offered Emanuel a puff.

"Sir, it is opium," Mr. Rustomjee said.

Emanuel leaned over, put the pipe stem in his mouth, and inhaled.

As soon as the first vapour reached his tongue, he coughed. The pungent odour and spicy flavour attacked his throat. Sharp, dry hawking followed and he could not stop. Ayah Gita patted Emanuel's back and led her young master out the door. Mr. Rustomjee followed. Bent over and gasping, Emanuel cleared his throat and spat several times before his breathing returned to normal. When he finally straightened himself, Ayah Gita's family were staring at him as if he were a water buffalo giving birth.

"Your father is an opium eater?" Emanuel said in Hindi, wiping spit from his chin.

"In this village, everyone is—especially the men. They receive it in payment for working in the fields."

"It is good that sir has such a reaction," Mr. Rustomjee said.

"Good? How is choking to death a good thing?"

"Sir will see, sir will see. Come, you must rest. Tomorrow we must be rising early to be witnessing the harvest."

Inside the hut, Mr. Rustomjee took the top bunk and Ayah Gita the bottom one. Emanuel used the large mattress, where he lay down exhausted from the day's travelling. The displaced family initially made do in the lane outside the hut. There they huddled together against the nocturnal winds and cold, damp air that wafted over the hillside village at night. As soon as they heard Emanuel snoring, they crept back into the hut and lay beside his warm body, lined up like kindling against the belly of a sleeping behemoth.

At breakfast Emanuel drank a cup of milk tea and ate onion *naan*. Ayah Gita's father had yoked the ox to a flatbed wagon and steered the beast up to the front stoop of the hut. He spat. A glob of *paan* hit the dirt path, staining it red. Then he gestured for his guests to hop aboard. Emanuel jumped onto the flatbed and sat on the edge of the wagon with his feet dangling off the side. Mr. Rustomjee got on and sat beside his young master. A short ride took them to the outskirts of the village, where fields of green bulbs spread out as far as the eye could see.

"Sir, this crop is ready for harvesting. You see the petals have not yet opened. The bulbs are tight and hard," Mr. Rustomjee said. "They are ready to be lanced."

They got off the wagon and walked into the thick of the flowers. Ayah Gita's father slouched off his driver's perch and tethered the ox. He reached behind his waistband and pulled out something that resembled a fork with three tines.

"Sir is seeing here this man taking his knife. Now look," Mr. Rustomjee said, "look what he does." The man made an incision on the side of the poppy bulb. Immediately a milky gum oozed out of the cut and coagulated. "He will be doing this on every flower until sundown. Tomorrow, when the gum is thick-thick like honey, his wife and children will be arriving and scraping it off into bowls."

Mr. Rustomjee explained that the gummy residue is mixed with linseed oil to prevent evaporation, patted into flat cakes about three to four inches in diameter, and dried in the shade. "The farmer is selling these cakes to a local dealer, who is draining away the linseed oil. Then he is forming the cakes into balls. Every ball is being wrapped in poppy leaves and is being placed in a wooden chest—144 balls in each chest. Then they are sending the chests to Calcutta to be auctioned under the auspices of the British government," he said.

Walking and talking, they made their way down the hill to a plateau. Giant sheds, each one occupying an acre of land, were lined up four in a row. Inside, there were floor-to-ceiling shelves on either side with an aisle running the length of the cavernous space. Black balls as big as cabbages were stored on the shelves to dry. Half-naked men wearing loincloths—some with turbans, others bareheaded—loaded the balls into wooden chests.

Emanuel stood in awe. When he was a boy he had seen sheep farms, cotton fields, and jute produced on his father's many properties. They were vast, but this was ten times the size of anything he had ever witnessed.

"Who owns this?" he asked.

"Aaah," Mr. Rustomjee exclaimed. "Now I see that sir is really intrigued."

"Has my father a share in this business?"

"A share? No. You see it goes like this. Your father is owning the land here. He is getting permission from the British to grow poppies. They are crushing you if you do not have a licence." He ran a finger across his neck like a blade. "Your father is renting the land to *ryot*. Ayah Gita's father is one such farmer. You were seeing he has seven children. That is why Gita was sent to work in Calcutta—too many mouths to feed. The *ryot* is getting themself an advance from the Bengal authorities. He is fertilizing the land. He is planting the white seeds. Working very hard, oh so hard. When the poppies are ready he is cutting the petals. In the evening the women are scraping it off. Now for all the family's work, these *ryot* must be selling the poppy juice to the government agency that was giving him the advance—and he is selling at a pre-fixed price."

"I see." Emanuel's mind was calibrating all this information. "So the British can make money by setting a low price for the product even before it is grown?"

"The *ryot* have a saying: you don't get rich growing opium but you die happy. They are referring to the small amount of raw opium that they are permitted to keep. It is given to them as an incentive when they bring in a good quantity of juice. Some keep it for personal use; others will sell it. You tried some last night."

"Don't remind me." Emanuel felt a little sick shoot up his throat when he remembered the foul-tasting drug. "Where do the opium balls go from here?"

"That is exactly the right question." Mr. Rustomjee was delighted to answer. "Each chest is weighing one *picul,* about 133 pounds. On average, each chest is fetching from two hundred to one thousand silver dollars at the British auction."

"So, what you are telling me is that my father owns this land that is rented to farmers. The farmers get a loan from the British to plant, grow, and harvest the raw opium juice. The farmers then sell it to the British at a fixed price. The British process the raw material into balls and auction it off."

"Sir is very astute. Exactly so."

"And then?"

"Sir, I thank you for asking. I am preparing here a costing analysis for your reading pleasure."

Mr. Rustomjee produced a notebook from his inside pocket. He handed it to Emanuel. Neatly written in pencil was a chart summarizing opium trading activity.

Year	No. of Chests
1773	1,000
1776	1,000
1779	4,000
1802	6,000
1805	8,000
1810	10,000
1820	10,000
1828	18,000
1839	40,000

"There was a war here," Mr. Rustomjee said, pointing to the figure for 1839. "The Chinese are wanting to stop opium from entering their country. They are attacking the British warehouse in Canton. Burning all the opium. The British and the rest of the world are giving them a jolly good thrashing by golly. China must be opening ports for trading, they say. See," he said, flipping the page, "in the next decade sales are going up, up, up—45,000 chests. See here it is becoming 50,000 chests. Three years ago, 1857, the Chinese are trying again to stop opium imports. Bang, boom, another war." He slapped his hands as if he was cleaning dirt off his palms. Then he brought a fist down hard into his palm. "But the British are defeating them again! Sales are increasing to 60,000 chest and last year 78,000 chest!"

Mr. Rustomjee's eyes widened. He leaned in. Emanuel could smell his sour breath from the morning's milky tea. In a hushed tone he said, "And today, do you know the best part—oh sir, the best part, the very best part is—the Chinese are declaring that opium trading is legal—they are even collecting tax on it!" Mr. Rustomjee stepped back and stamped the ground in a little dance. "Ha ha! Yes, damn good show. Damn good way to make money fast, fast." He held Emanuel's forearm with his dark brown hand. "Imagine, if you can be selling 78,000 chests when it was illegal, how much more can you be selling today when it is legal?" Mr. Rustomjee waggled his head and flicked his hand in mid-air to emphasize each word: "Plenty, plenty, fast, fast."

"And why have you not dipped your wick?"

"Why?" Mr. Rustomjee asked. "Because I am a clerk. Jolly damn good one, by Jove. Your father is needing me."

Emanuel could not sleep that night. His mind was filled with sums. He did mental calculations on what it would cost to purchase a consignment at auction, ship it to China, and sell it there. He could see numbers tumbling upward in ever-increasing amounts. Profits swelled in the boxes at the bottom of his imagined ledger. On the train back to Howrah, Ayah Gita had curled onto the bench seat and fallen asleep. Beside him, Mr. Rustomjee snored, tuckered out from the excitement of sharing his information with the young master. But Emanuel was wide awake. His thoughts swirled with plans. His heart pounded with excitement. He had found a way to be rich and independent. There was only one impediment. He needed upfront money to achieve his goal. That, he thought, is what fathers are for.

After the library "incident," Semah wrote in her journal *Something needs to be done* and underlined the phrase three times. She imagined sprouting a pair of wings and descending upon the unsuspecting couple with a sword of fire in her hand. Or crashing through the window with a helmet on her head and a red cape like the etchings of Boadicea she once saw in the *Illustrated London News* from England.

On the following Wednesday she made an excuse to her painting tutor and returned to her father's sanctum sanctorum, where she squeezed herself, once again, in the gap between the Biology and Culture shelves. She wanted to know if the tryst was a singular event or if it was a habit. Much to her disgust, her papa and the rosy-cheeked woman burst through the door, ripped off their clothes, and slammed against each other, their bodies fusing into a blob, arms and legs flaring out in different directions like an octopus falling off a tree.

The next week, she elected not to return to her hiding place. Instead, she took her sketchbook and announced to her tutor that she wished to make drawings of the mansion. From a reasonable distance, by the edge of the forest, she drafted various parts of the house as a pretext for keeping an eye on it. She saw her mother depart and, a short time later, her father and the woman arrive in his carriage and rush through the front door. Semah broke the charcoal in her fingers, tore the paper off her sketchbook, and crumpled it into a ball.

Later, she spent the evening pacing in her room. She needed to talk with someone. Someone who could help her think things through. But she had no friends, no siblings, no one really except her tutors. No acquaintances, save those she met weekly at Shabbat, before they disappeared into their own lives. Semah realized how small her world was and how big it appeared when she had laid it out on the map pasted on her bedroom wall. Staring at it, she came up with an idea of how to tell her mother without actually telling on her father.

Just as she had recorded the dates of her visits to various locations on the estate, she now listed the last three Wednesdays on the map. Then she drew an arrow pointing to the window of her papa's study. Two stick figures, one with a triangle for a skirt, floated above the arrowhead. She stood back and admired her work. The following day she went to see her mother.

"I want to show you my map," she said to her mama in Arabic.

"You made a map?"

"Yes, it is very large. It almost covers the wall. Will you come for tea?"

Semah knew that afternoon tea was a ritual her mama had practised for years, ever since she discovered that it was what the English did.

"What a lovely thought," her mama said. "Tea in your room." And then in English, "Yes, that would suit," remembering how the Marchioness of Dalhousie, wife of the Governor General, had replied to an invitation when she visited Bengal the year before.

Semah was ecstatic and recorded the entire conversation in her journal. The next day, her plans played out perfectly. Her mother arrived and Semah showed her to a seat by the window that was strategically placed so that she could admire the map in its entirety. Much to Semah's delight, her mama appreciated the shapes and colours and recognized the different locations instantly: the stables and horses, the garden brimming with flowers, the canopied entrance, the honeycomb of boxes that represented different rooms of her house.

"This is not just a map, my child, this is a work of art!" she said, applauding her daughter's accomplishment. "There is so much to see."

"Take your time, Mama," Semah said. "May I top up your cup?"

"Yes, yes," came the excited reply.

Her mother leaned forward, her elbows on her knees, staring in wonderment at the map. She reached out and found Semah's hand. Clutching it, she sat silent and smiling while her daughter bathed in the glow of her approbation.

And then her mama saw it.

Saw what she was supposed to see. Saw why she had been invited to tea. Saw what the map represented. There in the bottom corner was a list of dates and an arrow pointing to the study. Her eyes focused on the schematic. She let go of Semah's hand, stood up, and walked closer to the map. She crouched and touched the paper with her finger, then recited each date quietly. She looked at Semah and said,

"Wednesday. They are all on Wednesday."

Like an uncoiled spring, she stood and grabbed her daughter by the shoulders. "What happens on Wednesdays? Why are you in Papa's study every Wednesday?" Then she let go and sat on the chair, one hand on her stomach and the other covering her mouth. "Oh, my G-d," she said, "that is why ..." She didn't finish the sentence. Instead she rose, swallowed hard, then walked out of the room, leaving the door wide open. Moments later a door slammed and Semah winced.

Over the next few days, Semah didn't see her mother, not even at meals. She had sent word that she was ill and would stay in bed. The following Wednesday, from her position at the edge of the forest, Semah watched as her mother left the house at the usual time. Shortly after that, the lovers rushed surreptitiously into the house. Semah clenched her fist and kicked over her painting easel. Her tutor rushed to reset the kit, but Semah ran off toward the forest, stopping only when she reached the treeline. She leaned her back against a trunk. Her leg muscles burned from the run. Tears stung her eyes. She was convinced that her clever plan had failed. Her mother was not going to do anything. Clearly, it was up to her to expose the tryst.

The next Wednesday she hid in her usual spot. As expected, the lovers entered, ditched their clothes, and headed for the couch with gleeful abandon. Semah pursed her lips and took in a deep breath. She was about to scream "Stop!" when suddenly the door flew open. And there was her mother, incandescent with rage.

The lovers leapt to their feet, covering genitals with whatever came to hand: a trouser, a skirt, a shoe, a hat.

Semah covered her mouth with her hands.

Her father and the woman froze like statues, their mouths agape.

For a moment no one moved. Then her mother walked briskly to her father. She hauled back an arm and with all her might slapped him across the face.

Her mama looked at the rosy-cheeked woman and said in English, "This is the end of it." And with that she walked out without closing the door.

Semah felt fresh air rush into the room, liberating it from the choking, squalid atmosphere of mendacity.

That evening Semah took down the map. She considered burning it, but decided instead to fold it carefully and put it in the chest where she kept her childhood toys. She thought it belonged there with all the other remembrances of innocence and the time before she became a grown-up. She was fifteen, after all. Closing the lid put paid to an ugly chapter in her journal, and she looked forward to a renewal of the status quo.

But in the days that followed, her mama refused to speak with her papa. And her papa, despite all the books he had read, could not find the right words to ameliorate his wife's hurt. Semah was convinced that this icy consequence was her fault. After all, it was she who had engineered the discovery of her father's affair; she had set in motion the events that followed. She hated feeling like a snitch.

She hoped and prayed that somehow her parents might find reconciliation. When none came, the atmosphere around her became stifling. She found it hard to breathe. One night, the pressure was unbearable. It felt like a cloak of iron squeezing her from head to toe. She wanted air and space. She rose from bed. Without changing her nightclothes, she ran out of her room, down the stairs, and through the front door in her bare feet. Moonlight lit a silvery path across the lawn.

At the stables, she pushed up the latch and pulled open the door. A fresh smell of hay greeted her. She strode purposefully past several stalls to the Paso Fino at the back. The horse recognized her. It whinnied and pawed the ground. Semah caressed the diamond-shaped tuft between the horse's eyes and said gently,

"There, there, boy. That's my good boy. We're going for a ride."

She reached for the reins hanging on a hook and put the bit between the horse's teeth. Then she led him out of the stall, took down her saddle from the wall, and threw it on the horse's back. The buckles dangled under its belly.

"Memsahib?" She turned and saw the stable boy holding a lantern. He was as tall as she, reedy and with skin as dark as midnight. A *patka*—Sikh scarf—covered his head. "I heard a noise from upstairs," he said, rubbing his eyes.

"Veer Singh," she said, buckling the saddle. "You need not worry. I'm just taking Chocolat Cream for a ride."

"But Memsahib, it is late."

"And what of that? He's my horse," she said, putting a stool beside Chocolat Cream's left side. She stepped onto it and was preparing to mount when Veer Singh put his lantern down and grabbed the reins.

"Respectfully, I cannot allow it."

"Since when do I need permission from a stable boy?"

"Memsahib, it is dangerous at night. You cannot see."

But Semah was deaf to his concern. She footed the stirrup and pulled herself onto the seat of the sidesaddle with one leg curled around the pummel. She snapped the reins. Chocolat Cream whinnied.

"The master will kill me," Veer Singh said, adding his other hand to the reins.

"Let go, let go at once."

"I must not" came the desperate reply.

Semah heeled Chocolat Cream's flank and the horse stepped forward. Veer Singh held on as the trio exited the stable into the moonlit night. Another heel to the flank drove the horse into a canter, forcing the Indian groom to let go his grip. He trotted beside horse and rider, attempting to keep up.

But Semah loosed the reins and smacked the horse's rump. Startled, it broke into a gallop and ran faster and faster. She tried to pull up but the horse would not respond. She leaned forward, grabbed a tuft of the horse's mane, and held on for dear life. She was terrified now and screaming. Her cries scared the beast and it ran faster still. She clung to its mane, bouncing painfully. Ahead, she could just make out a wide thicket of gorse, the moon illuminating its yellow flowers. A thick web of spiky branches lay beneath.

Chocolat Cream jumped. Horse and rider sailed through the air. But the thicket was too wide. It snagged a hoof and the horse landed hard, bending a fetlock. Semah was propelled off the saddle and thrown to the ground.

Chocolat Cream stumbled and fell on Semah's leg, snapping the bone of her shin in several places.

Winded from the chase, Veer Singh doubled over to catch his breath. His lungs were aching but he willed his tired legs to move, heading in the direction he'd last seen the Memsahib, through the forest until finally he found her, shattered and unconscious. His heart pounded wildly. Frightened at the sight of Semah's bloody body (but more terrified for the whipping he would surely receive), he ran from the scene. Eventually every muscle ached. He crouched under a tree and wept. When there were no more tears, his pounding heart returned to its normal beat. He summoned what courage he had and ran to report to his master that Mem-sah had suffered an accident.

When they found her, Semah was lying on the ground, twisted and bleeding and still unconscious. Shards of bone poked through her skin like needles in a pincushion. Insects had piled onto the maroon-coloured wound. White bone and the gaping crimson hole looked angry and unforgiving.

Veer Singh, terrified of his master's wrath, backed away from the rescue party. Then he ran into the forest and disappeared.

Semah was carried home on a makeshift stretcher and Dr. Syme sent for immediately. He told Ibrahim and Sula that there was no alternative but to sever the limb to prevent gangrene. Sula gasped for air. Her knees went limp and she leaned against Ibrahim, who closed his arms around her. They held on to each other in a close and long embrace.

In the days that followed, the written word proved inadequate. Instead Semah filled her journal with pencil sketches. Initially, the shapes were perfectly drawn: two uniform arcs tapered to a point at the bottom, making the shape of a heart. But as page followed page, the shapes began to twist. Then the curves elongated into grotesque parodies. Dissatisfied, she crossed out every page, slashing the sheets with such ferocity that her pencil drove holes through the paper.

EMANUEL

With a belly full of enthusiasm and the energy of a religious convert eager to proselytize, Emanuel laid out his plan to sell Indian opium in China for his father. He did so as though he were the first person ever to think of it.

In the outer office, clerks clustered in twos and threes to whisper about the dumb show being played out on the other side of the glass walls of Raphael's "private" office. The old man sat behind his enormous desk. Mr. Rustomjee, as usual, stood beside his employer. Emanuel's hands windmilled and his lips moved swiftly. His arms gesticulated and his pudgy body shook with energy. Providing an underscore were the familiar sounds of noisy workmen and food hawkers from below.

Inside the office Emanuel finished his peroration with a dizzying flourish: "Thirty percent margin!" he exclaimed. "Nothing else makes that kind of money." He sat down and pulled out a handkerchief that Ayah Gita had scented with rosewater that morning. He mopped his brow and wiped the edges of his mouth.

Raphael let his son's conclusion dangle for a moment and then leaned over his desk, interlocked his fingers, and said, "No."

Emanuel stood, stiff with surprise. He felt as though a shaft of steel had plunged down his throat, come out his anus, and planted itself on the floor. Mr. Rustomjee hung his head in empathy.

"But why?"

"Why, you ask? I'll tell you why. Go to Chinatown. Go and see. You," he said, pointing at Mr. Rustomjee. "You take him. Let him see for himself. Go! Now!"

The prosthetic was made of wood and fitted with straps, buckles, and buttons that fastened to her thigh. It had the hard, cold feel of a tool or gardening implement clamped rudely on skin. But that was the least of her concerns. Shortly after the accident, Semah's body was rocked by another growth spurt, and over the next year she grew to almost six feet in height. During this period, longer and longer prosthetics were needed. The new false legs were always a step behind her growth, so to speak. Her good leg was always longer than her mechanical one and forced her to walk with a pronounced limp.

On the brighter side, Sula's maternal instincts yanked her out of the self-pitying fog in which she had been mired since catching Ibrahim *in flagrante*. The first thing she did was to promote a Hindu servant named Bharmini from water carrier to Semah's "body woman." Bharmini was *Shudra*—an unskilled labourer, one level above her *Dalit* inferiors. Sula had selected her not for her intelligence but for her brawn. A sturdy-looking young woman about Semah's age, she had thick arms and wide shoulders. Lifting ewers weighing one hundred pounds every day for years had given her impressive arms and a powerful upper body. Sula wisely believed that her daughter, who was now a head taller than everyone, would need a sturdy body woman to catch her in case—*Lessim Allah,* G-d forbid—the false leg should collapse.

With Bharmini on one side and Sula on the other, Semah took her first tentative steps in her bedroom. The spacious room, denuded of excess furniture, provided a safe environment in which Semah could relearn what two-year-olds knew instinctively. She had to recalibrate the subtle weight shifts of every movement. With each effort she felt a tearing sensation where the scar of her stump chafed against the leather pocket in which it sat. "Stay with her," Sula instructed.

Bharmini waggled her head and said in Hindi, "Yes, Memsahib."

After days—no, weeks—of agony, strapping on the false limb and standing and tumbling to the floor like a puppet whose strings had been cut, Semah finally got the hang of it. Months passed before she was able to walk unassisted. Semah looked at her body servant and started to cry and laugh at the same time.

Ibrahim and Sula were thrilled with Semah's progress and their own tortured journey toward reconciliation. Semah was the glue they had needed to cement their shattered relationship. The parents joined their daughter for meals that were taken in her bedroom during the recovery period. But now that Semah had renewed mobility, Sula suggested, without a hint of irony, "It is time we took meals in the dining room *as before*."

The enigmatic words *"as before"* hovered over their heads. Before what? The riding accident? Or the other event?

It was almost sundown on the following Friday when Bharmini pinned up Semah's hair for the first time. For years it had hung loose, in the fashion of most English girls; now the dark tresses were combed up and fastened to the top of her head in a more womanly style, revealing her ears and the smooth nape of her neck. Bharmini put some rouge on her young mistress's cheeks and spread the colour to give her a healthier glow. Semah attached the prosthetic limb herself, as was her wont. She never allowed anyone to handle the limb. Bharmini turned her back to show respect for Memsahib's privacy.

"I'm ready," Semah said in Hindi. Bharmini opened the bedroom door for Semah, who stepped out for the first time in months and walked, without help, to the top of the stairwell. Fifty steps curved down to the foyer below.

"Mem-sah to take my hand please?"

"No," Semah said.

She held the banister with one hand and moved her wooden foot forward to take the first step. Buttery-coloured beams from the west-facing windows flooded the place. Shabbat was approaching.

Below, the servants had come out to watch. Ibrahim and Sula stood like statues looking up expectantly—expecting what, Semah could not say.

"Slowly ..." Sula called out. Ibrahim put up one hand to stop her from saying anything more.

"She knows, Sula. Just let her ..." He didn't finish. He didn't have to.

Their hearts pounded in unison.

Masters and servants held their breaths.

Somewhere a grandfather clock ticked loudly.

Tentatively and leaning heavily on the banister, Semah took one cautious step after another. Her wooden foot, hitting the marble stairs, sounded loudly against the silence like a stranger knocking at the door of an empty house. Finally, she reached the centre landing and breathed out. She looked at her parents and smiled.

Ibrahim held his wife's hand. Semah's eyes misted at the sight.

Filled with confidence, she proceeded down the next flight, this time with only one hand on the banister. Three steps from the bottom, the heel of the wooden foot caught the edge of a stair and buckled under. She lost her balance. Quickly her right hand reached up and joined the left. Everyone gasped. Bharmini looped her arms around Semah's waist. Sula stepped forward but was held back by Ibrahim. Someone tittered. Bharmini cursed in Bengali between her teeth. Semah peeled Bharmini's arms from around her waist, righted her leg, checked the strapping, and continued safely down to the bottom landing.

Ibrahim released Sula's hand. She ran to her daughter and smothered the girl with kisses. The servants applauded. Ibrahim dismissed them with a wave and joined his wife and daughter. He wrapped his arms around both women and hugged them. There were enough tears to drown a city.

Wordlessly they walked arm in arm into the dining room. Sula took two candles from the sideboard and placed them on the dining table in front of a loaf and a cup of wine. She lit the candles just as the final rays of the sun died out. She placed a veil on her head and waved her hands over the little flames to welcome Shabbat. Then, covering her eyes, she intoned the blessing:

"Barukh atah Adonai, Eloheinu, melekh ha'olam ..."

Through the open door Bharmini's angry voice could be heard scolding the titterer. Ibrahim looked up. Annoyed by the disturbance, he walked toward the dining-room door ...

"Asher kidishanu b'mitz'votav v'tzivanu ..."

Then came a sharp slap and a yelp of pain before the doors closed gently on the outside world ...

"L'had'lik neir shel Shabbat ..."

The blessing was concluded. In unison, the family intoned *"Omein"* and sat down to Shabbat dinner.

Semah felt that the next words from anyone's mouth would be a test of the glue's effectiveness. Ibrahim breached the silence:

"I wish to announce a new dowry—at Shul."

Mother and daughter looked at each other and then at Ibrahim. Sula spoke:

"I agree," she said.

Ibrahim pointed his finger at the ceiling: "Fifteen thousand rupees!" he declared.

Sula gasped. "That is higher than mine!"

That night, Semah picked up her journal—the book of lacerated hearts—but did not open it. Instead she put it in her trunk on top of the folded map. She imagined that the brief exchange at dinner had mended the tears on every page and that every heart had been made whole.

Yet despite the return of peaceful coexistence (her parents walked arm in arm to Shul) and Ibrahim's generosity, no suitors presented themselves that year or the next or the one after that. Huddled in whispered conversation, they feared that Semah would soon be considered—No, they dared not use the phrase that described unmarried women. How could they? There was still hope. Wasn't there? But the child, the girl, the woman would be twenty next year! Something had to be done, and quickly.

EMANUEL

To the east of the City of Palaces, a world away from the beautiful mansions and verdant parklands of the Maidan, lay Chinatown, an area strangled by a labyrinth of filthy lanes. Emanuel's landau was set aside for a fourth-rate *tikki-gharri*, pulled by a sad old horse as ancient in animal years as its driver was in human ones. Soon paved roads narrowed into potholed streets. A web of muddy lanes branched into nameless tracks edged with a jumble of lean-tos—sheds bunched together like rusted tins and stained boxes tumbling out of an overturned garbage can. If he believed in hell, this is what it would look like.

Mr. Rustomjee told the ancient driver to stop his *tikki-gharri* and pressed some coins into the old man's leathery palm. He said,

"Sir, we are getting off here and walking."

Emanuel followed his guide down an alley that was little wider than his shoulders. One-room shacks lined either side, their occupants looking at him with blank stares. The soles of his boots slipped on damp ground streaked with black residue accumulated from years of neglect. Everywhere he saw naked children running wild, loosed from their mothers who were too busy picking through refuse to provide rudimentary supervision. He wanted to take a bucket of lye and a hard bristle brush to the place. With some luck a monsoon downpour would sluice away the effluent and rotted food. He noticed that denizens of this maze were inured to the sour mélange of smells. Only strangers like him noticed the reek.

They turned down several lanes before stopping at a metal gate that opened into a small courtyard. Inside, an ancient two-storey red-brick building rose up like an island of calm above the squalor of the neighbour-hood. Moss and vines sprouted on the wall between green shutters and black pipes. Mr. Rustomjee knocked on the wooden double doors. Moments later, a dark-skinned man with high cheekbones answered the door.

"Sir, this man is Mr. Yuen. He is being the headman here."

The Chinese man nodded and waved them in. Emanuel looked him up and down. Yuen wore a collarless brown tunic and flared trousers rolled up above his ankles. On his feet he wore cloth slippers. He was about Emanuel's height, bald, and had two wisps of black moustache that hung like insect wings on either side of his upper lip. Yuen nodded and grinned. A gold tooth sparkled in the dim foyer.

"Sir is mystified to see a Chinaman?"

"I've seen Chinamen before in the ghats, loading and doing the washing."

Yuen parted a beaded curtain and the men stepped into a wide window-less room. It was a squalid space illuminated by two oil lamps that hung precariously from ceiling hooks. Along the entire length of one wall were platforms on which several men and one woman lay on rattan mats. One of the men wore European clothes; beside him was the woman, in a dress. Beside her were swarthy men who might be Indians or Lascars. He could not tell since their faces were in shadow. At their feet, tiny flames flickered in oil lamps. They appeared to be dozing. Some were on their sides, others on their backs or propped up against a wall. The air was redolent of the sickly sweet odour of opium.

"Sir, this is being the deluxe suite—very fresh, AAA-quality opium here is used—fresh meaning of similar quality to Patna opium—very fine. Here customers are paying two rupees for the pipe and four rupees for each pinch."

Just then one of them pushed himself up on his elbow. He picked up a long knitting needle and poked a bit of opium out of an ivory dish at his feet. He heated the bead over the lamp's tiny flame. Soon, the opium glowed red. He turned the bowl of his pipe over the thin column of smoke, inhaled deeply, and held his breath. He took in three more puffs and was about to go for a fourth when his eyes rolled into his head and he fell back on the rattan mat like a sack of laundry. Yuen took a pebble out of a bowl and tossed it into a basket at the smoker's feet.

"That is how he counts what is owing."

"How do you know this place?" Emanuel asked.

"Sir, it is one of your father's properties. Mr. Yuen is being one renter. Jolly good man. Always pays on time."

"Plis," Yuen said, holding out an arm indicating they should move down the dingy hallway. Emanuel followed his guides. Through another beaded entrance was a larger room. This one was lined with bunk beds, twenty of them by Emanuel's cursory glance. Almost all were occupied and some by sailors, he deduced, from the flared hems of their trousers.

"In here is the middle quality. Smokers pay less. Opium is mixed with tobacco."

"How many rooms are there?"

Mr. Rustomjee turned to Yuen and asked him something in a language Emanuel could not understand. His guide turned back and said, "Sir, he is telling me twenty-six."

"Plis," Yuen said and motioned as he did before.

"I don't need to see any more. The point is made."

"Oh, but sir, I am being instructed to take you through the entire establishment. It is what your father desires."

The upstairs was divided into three large halls. Each one was filled with men and women in various stages of undress, lying down, sitting, and crouching on the floor. No platform beds here, not even a rattan mat and certainly not "AAA-quality opium." Upper-room smokers paid a few paise for a residue collected off the ashes in the deluxe and middle-quality rooms. Ribs jutted out of waxy translucent skin, cheeks were sunken, mouths were toothless. The choking stench of people who had been sweltering in the heat of windowless rooms made the place reek. Mr. Rustomjee waggled his head and said,

"Sir is witnessing Calcutta's dirty little secret."

Emanuel said nothing for the rest of the tour.

That evening he spoke with his father. "In for a penny, in for a pound. You own the building in Chinatown where opium smoking takes place. Why not own the supply?"

Raphael was seated in the salon wrapped in a shawl, wearing a floppy hat to keep his head warm. A snifter of brandy sat on the side table waiting to be sipped. He was riffling through a stack of envelopes that had arrived in the afternoon post. "If I don't rent to the Chinaman, someone else will."

"My point precisely," Emanuel said.

"And what is that point?"

"If we don't sell opium then someone else will. I only want to supply something the market wants to buy—like tea, or jute or cotton or real estate for that matter."

"Not the same thing."

"How is it not? Tell me father how-is-it-not?" He emphasized each word as though he were driving nails into wood.

"Because it kills people."

"If that is so—"

"It is," Raphael interrupted.

"If that is so, then they have brought it on themselves. No one is forcing the user to smoke opium. I just want to give the public what they want. Why can't you help me?"

"Three reasons," Raphael said. He held up three fingers, closing one with each count: "One, the Sassoons, two, the Sassoons, and three," he said, holding up his middle finger, "the Sassoons."

They were the elite of the Jewish community. Sephardic and hailing from Baghdad, they too had been expelled from their Middle Eastern comforts and joined the diaspora that fetched up in Bombay in the 1790s. There they had cornered the market in Malwa opium. From the west coast, seven brothers branched out to other parts of India and China, most recently obtaining a foothold in Calcutta, where they were now well established.

"What about them?" Emanuel said.

"They have enough money to buy up the auction every year, and they are in with the Parsi ship owners who transport their goods to Hong Kong. From there they sell to the British companies or peddle it themselves along the China coast. No, no, it's too late for a newcomer. They have it all sewn up. Forget it. Do something else." The old man took a sip of brandy and turned his attention to his correspondence.

Emanuel ran his fingers through his hair. He felt trapped. Stuck in this house, stuck with being the chunky second son forever in the shadow of his brother—the handsome one.

"Father," Emanuel said, standing up and towering over the older man.

"What? I owe you? I owe you nothing. I brought you up. I gave you the best education there was. More than I had. Look at you. You could pass for British. Make something of yourself. Be like your brother."

Emanuel clenched his teeth and swallowed hard. He turned on his heel.

"Wait," Raphael said. Emanuel stopped. "Here is an invitation from the Ezra family. He is giving a party to announce his daughter's new dowry. Ho-ho," he said, "twenty thousand rupees, up from fifteen! How guilty he must still be for cheating on his wife."

SEMAH

Excited at the prospect of a ball in her honour, Semah counted the days and busied herself with every detail of the event, contradicting her mother on almost everything, from the choice of musicians to the champagne to the theme. For Sula, the occasion would be theme enough—Vice-Regal levees required no perceptible leitmotif, so why should theirs be any different? But Semah, influenced by the modern balls depicted in illustrated journals, averred that modern guests enjoyed the challenge of having to dress for a theme such as an "all white" evening.

"Gracious, child," Sula said, "would gentlemen be obliged to wear white after dark?"

"No, mother. Our theme will be 'A Night of Light.'"

Sula wondered if Semah realized that this occasion might very well be the last opportunity for her to attract a suitor. Was now the time to stray from convention?

But Semah was determined to have her way, and took over the reins of the event. Since that Shabbat dinner a few years before, she had discovered a galloping sense of confidence in her own abilities. She had mastered scaling staircases and eventually dispensed with walking aids such as crutches or canes. However, the ever-cautious Sula had ordered Bharmini to remain at the ready, to always be just a step behind.

In preparation for the Night of Light, Semah worked on the waltz; after that, she attacked the polka. The practice sessions were not flawless. She did fall. But as Bharmini was quick to point out, it is not the fall that is important but rather the ability to get up and continue. Determined, Semah put all her energies into commanding her body to perform as a normal one should. But there was a price to pay. The skin of her stump chafed against the leather restraints. Most days it looked red and angry. Bloody patches appeared where the wound had been stitched. Her hip muscles hurt. Her spine curved to compensate for the stress. Her neck ached. All these discomforts showed on her face, especially around her mouth and chin because she pursed her lips and set her jaw grimacing with anxiety. A small dose of laudanum at bedtime helped to ease the discomfort. She did not take the painkiller often because it gave her bad dreams and left her dozy the following morning.

Despite the side effects, she persevered. Not only was this upcoming celebration meant to dispel any gossip that Semah was "abnormal" (there was a story going the rounds that she would never bear children because of her accident) but it was also an opportunity to show there was no truth to the rumour that Ibrahim and Sula's marriage was on the rocks due to his *hemulcha*—his folly. Ibrahim declared that Semah was still "virtuous, of good demeanour and a graduate of Mrs. Anderson's tutelage." And to dispel the other thing, well, he was confident that everyone would see that a good marriage had prevailed. After all, did not King David and other patriarchs have a ding-a-ling or two in their time?

The Night of Light would set everything to rights.

EMANUEL

The invitation that his father had waved in front of his face contained a handwritten addendum from Ibrahim Ezra that read, *"I shall announce a good dowry—20,000 Rs.—more if the right man proposes. I.E."* How serendipitous, Emanuel had thought.

"It is fate," Ayah Gita had said. "You must embrace your destiny."

He spent time studying the invitation with the same zeal and attention he had given to the ledgers in his father's office. This party would be *"formal"* and would feature an *"orchestra"* that would play the *"latest dance music from England."* These affairs were new in Calcutta. Up until then, parties amongst the upper-class Jewish families comprised a sit-down dinner followed by a Bengali theatre performance and then another lavish meal at a second residence, where they might enjoy a concert or parlour games. The concept of having a single gathering at one house was borrowed from the British practice. The fledgling Jewish community was eager to embrace all things English in its ever-vigilant effort to blend in. He had two weeks to master the polka and the waltz.

But to whom could he go for dance lessons? There was only one person he could think of—Mr. Stuart-Fox, the headmaster at his alma mater. Setting aside the knot in his gut, Emanuel went to see the man and leavened his request for dance lessons with an envelope containing a week's wages. Mr. Stuart-Fox cocked an eyebrow, closed the book he was reading, and placed it over the baksheesh. And with that they tacitly agreed to set aside remembrances of things past and turned their attention to the chore of transforming mutton into lamb.

Emanuel would arrive after school hours. Desks were moved aside to clear a central space and a broom used to substitute for a dance partner. The old master banged out melodies on the piano without subtlety. His choreography demanded a clear downbeat more than it did musicianship.

Often Emanuel would stumble and sometimes he would fall, unaccustomed to putting one foot over the other when doing the polka. But his purpose was never blunted. And after sessions at the old schoolhouse, he rushed home to practise on Ayah Gita.

"You must hold your hands so," he said, placing one of her hands on his shoulder and the other in his palm. "Now walk backward, right left together. One two three, one two three."

Ayah Gita tried. But it was beyond her. She had to double-step to keep up. Her hand fell off his shoulder. She stubbed a toe on his shoe and he lost count. The two looked more like Punch and Judy puppets colliding into each other than dance partners.

Inevitably, he trod on her foot.

She yelped and swore in Bengali, pushing him away.

"What is the matter with you?" he demanded.

"I am trying my best."

"Well, your best is not good enough," he said and slammed his fist into the wall. He screamed. It was a strangled cry of pain and frustration in equal parts. Ayah Gita limped to him. She kissed his red knuckles and covered them with the palm of her hand.

"You are troubled," she said. "Let me comfort you." She led him to the bed as she had on other occasions. But he pulled away.

"No," he said, "I want to practise some more."

It was the first time he had refused her favours. Ignoring her pathetic gaze, he took out a handkerchief and wrapped his injured hand. Then he pushed her aside, picked up a chair, and counted out a waltz. Ayah Gita crouched against the wall and felt like the slave she was.

Cabriolet followed landau, disgorging gentlemen in evening wear and ladies in gowns in front of the Ezra mansion that sparkled by the light of a silvery moon. Flickering yellow flames from torches lit a path to a front door festooned with garlands. Stepping into the foyer through this floral entrance, guests found themselves in a reception area. One Indian manservant wearing white gloves took coats and hats. Another—also sporting white gloves—indicated, with opened palms and a slight waggle of the head, that "ladies and gentlemen should proceed this way." Double doors opened to reveal a great room where a quintet made up of *sepoys*—off-duty Indian soldiers—played Mozart and polkas to a crush of people far too eager to gossip than to hear the magnificent music.

Over two hundred couples answered invitations that had been sent far and wide. Some respondents were well known to the Ezras; others were less so, but selected judiciously upon the advice of a renowned *Shad Chan*—matchmaker. She had wisely encouraged the inclusion of upper echelons of British expatriates, notable members of the Indian and Parsi merchant classes, and the Jewish elite. There was never any question that Semah's future husband would be a Jew, true, but this was more than a debutante's ball. It was also an opportunity to show an ambitious city how well the Ezra family had done in life.

Bharmini oiled her young mistress's shiny black hair and pinned it up on top of her head. Jewels made of diamond shavings from Ibrahim's cutters were sprinkled on her hair like stars against a night sky. She wore pearl-drop earrings with matching bracelets and rings on her fingers. Her nails were shaped, filed, and lacquered to make them gleam. Her gown was a long silk affair with an empire waist and an organza overskirt shot through with gold and silver threads. A thin tiara that Sula had worn on her wedding day was a subtle signal to those who recognized it that her daughter was prepared to take on the responsibilities that her mother had so admirably fulfilled.

"You look like an angel," her papa said when he came to her bedroom.

She twirled to give him a full view of her dress, completing the pirouette without losing her balance. He pulled out his handkerchief and dabbed the corner of his eye. Then, dismissing his sentimentality with a snort, he extended his arm. "Shall we?" he asked.

The *sepoys* struck up a fanfare. The cavalcade descended. Bharmini was in the lead, wearing a red sari threaded with gold. She had a gold ring in her nose and a ruby-coloured bindi on her forehead. Father and daughter followed, arm in arm. Behind them, a little Indian boy held her train. On either side, tall barefooted Indian men, dressed in *kurti,* held candles. Small silver shields surrounding the flames reflected light off her jewellery.

The crowd gasped as one. Semah Ezra was incandescent. The girl had her grandfather's height, they said. It was as though, unable to grow in the leg, her body had compensated by growing in every other direction. She was a giant. But an elegant one. Here was not the bunched and broken gargoyle of their imaginations but a young woman ready to take her place in the world. Ibrahim led his daughter to the bandstand, where Sula joined them. Bharmini stood to one side. Then Ibrahim signalled for silence.

"In honour of my beautiful daughter, I raise her dowry to twenty thousand rupees."

Mothers, aunts, cousins, and matchmakers crowded Semah, jostling each other for proximity to bestow their kind wishes and congratulations. The quintet struck up a polka—a signal for the room to dance. The throng around her parted, waiting to see which bachelor would be the first on her card.

A young man stepped out of the crowd. He was about Semah's age but shorter, pudgy-cheeked, and portly. "Ask her to dance," an invisible man's voice rasped.

Semah held out her hand. The young man looked at it for a long time, then extended his own. It was bandaged. Their palms met. He extended his other and she took it. Tentatively their shoulders bobbed to the rhythm of a polka, but their feet remained still. He looked down at his feet, willing them to move. She looked over the top of his head. Then, thankfully, they moved in tandem with little hops and skips in time to the energetic dance. The crowd smiled and applauded politely. Other couples joined in. The dance floor filled with a swirl of guests.

"What happened to your hand?" Semah asked.

"A wall ran into my knuckles," he said.

She laughed, which made him relax a little.

"What's your name?" she asked.

"Emanuel," he replied and stepped on the hem of her dress.

She torqued in one direction and he stumbled in the other, causing her to fall to the ground, pulling Emanuel with her. The false leg, freed from its belts and buckles, slid out from under her skirt. It came to rest in the middle of the dance floor. It looked like an ugly private part exposed to the glare of the crowded room.

The quintet stopped playing. Other couples on the dance floor turned their heads and gasped. Bharmini was at Semah's side immediately. Together Ibrahim and Sula rushed to their daughter. They lifted Semah from the floor and, supporting her on either side, walked her out of the room. Bharmini threw the veil of her sari over the prosthetic limb, picked it up, and held it close to her body as she followed her young mistress.

Upstairs in her bedroom, Semah sobbed uncontrollably. More than humiliation, it was the guests' pity that hurt the most. They had looked at her with the same sense of superiority that one might have over a wounded animal.

Sitting on a cotton mat on the floor by the open French windows, Bharmini sang tuneful ditties, hoping to bring joy back to the room.

When the giant girl fell, the awful thing shot out from under her skirt. It had spun like a windmill and eventually stopped with its foot pointed accusingly in his direction. His fingers curled into tight fists. Blood drained from his face and his chest heaved.

The other guests surged abreast of him to gawk at Semah sitting on the dance floor. Her skirt was hiked up to her knees. The white stocking on her good leg showed a thick calf and a slim ankle.

Emanuel stepped back and was swallowed by a whispering crowd. Without anyone noticing, he turned and shot through the French doors, leapt over the veranda rail, and scampered past the landau he had arrived in. His carriage driver looked baffled. The chubby *sahib* was moving with uncharacteristic speed. Emanuel ran from Ezra's mansion and on into the night.

The dress, dammit, the length of the dress was something he should have considered. But how could he have known, for G-d's sake? The only dance partners he had had before that evening were a chair and a slave.

Emanuel reached the ghats, where he hailed a rowboat. He got in, sat under the canopy of the tiny boat, and covered his face with his hands. When he arrived at Howrah's banks, he ran up the path without bothering to pay the boatman. At his father's estate he bounded up the stairs to his rooms. Ayah Gita, who had been dozing in the vestibule waiting for his return, woke up. Just as she was about to follow him the boatman arrived, waggling his head violently and shouting that he was owed money. Ayah Gita dismissed the man, telling him to come back in the morning and that he would be paid double. She slammed the door in his face and went up the stairs two at a time. Emanuel was in his rooms, hunched over a chair and panting. Ayah Gita touched his shoulder. He turned and looked at her.

"Is there anything I can do right?" he asked. His eyes darted wildly. He grabbed her by the shoulders and pressed his mouth against hers, then pushed her onto his bed. He tore off his *"formal"* clothes and decanted his frustration, rage, humiliation, and cowardice. The frenzy, the fevered spasms surprised her. But she did not resist. His energy finally spent, he rolled over on his back. He felt empty and unpardoned.

He had a dream that night.

He was running naked through a forest. A layer of moss clung to his skin and he was trying to scrub the unnatural layer off, using a fistful of poppies. Lightning cracked overhead. Diagonal raindrops pelted like needles. The earth became soft and he began to sink into the ground. His feet, calves, thighs, torso, neck, and head stiffened. His arms folded over his chest. His hands clasped the bouquet of poppies like a corpse being laid to rest. As he sank, raindrops turned into paper money—first one banknote, then two, then four, then eight, multiplying. A shower of rupees, American dollars, and British pounds poured out of the sky in such abundance that they obscured the stars. But the banknotes evaporated when they touched the soggy ground. In block capitals he wrote in the air: "I am lost." Suddenly he awoke and found himself lying in a pool of sweat.

News of the previous evening's debacle tore through the community via the *matzo* telegraph. Cruel reviews of the principals involved in the display on the dance floor led to comments that *"something was not right with the Ezra family."* In the days that followed, Ayah Gita reported to Emanuel that there was *"talking,"* then looked around furtively as though the walls had ears. In the bath, smoking a cheroot from Goa, he stared at her. When she did not elaborate, he said,

"What talking?"

"They say it is a curse upon the Ezra family," Ayah Gita whispered, the latest gossip she had picked up from the servants of Jewish families.

"What kind of curse?"

"He did wrong with his wife. He had a lover. This is his punishment."

"That is nonsense."

"Still, the girl is a cripple because of him. He bought her a horse. She fell from it. They say her woman's parts are damaged. They say she cannot bear children. The fates have done you a service. She is not suitable to be a wife."

If he had felt bad before, he felt worse now. He suddenly realized that the horror he had experienced—his clumsiness and his cowardly flight from the Ezra family ballroom—paled in comparison to what Semah must have been feeling. He got out of the tub. Ayah Gita wrapped a towel around his waist and followed him to the bedroom.

"Her father knows she is damaged," she said. "Her dowry is now 25,555 rupees! A husband can buy anything with that kind of money. But he will have no children."

He stopped in his tracks and cocked his head. His ears pricked at hearing what a great sum awaited the right man. He headed for his desk and sat down to compose a letter to Semah. He would apologize for his clumsiness, explain that he felt ... what? What exactly did he feel about her?

Hours later several drafts lay balled at his feet.

Damn, he wished he had paid more attention to essay writing at school, learned more clarity from poetry, practised better penmanship. But none of that would have helped. Writing was an unbearable torture. It required more than just craft. It required him to reveal his true feelings. And that he couldn't do—would never do again because the last time he did so—

Hang it, he thought, stabbing his pen back in the holder.

SEMAH

Images of that night's glittering start and its mortifying end played over and over in her mind. Every night she had the same fitful dream in which her movements were replayed slowly and soundlessly. The tug on the hem of her dress, the feeling of moving in one direction while her leg turned in the other, the endless tumble toward the floor, the sensation of losing her leg—again.

Each morning her jaw hurt from grinding her teeth. She felt as though she had been hit in the face with a cricket bat. And speaking of wood, she refused to strap on her leg, opting instead for two crutches that dug uncomfortably into her armpits.

She wrote in her journal, *My prospects as a desirable bride ended that day.* The rest of the page was blank. There was no more to say. Her future was as white and as empty as the wall. She grabbed her crutches and stood up. She reached for her pen, dipped it in the inkwell, and put the penholder in her mouth like a pirate with a blade between his teeth. She hobbled to the wall and eyeballed the centre point. She drew a black dot on it at about eye level. She hobbled back a step and stared at her handiwork. She took a few more paces back. The dot got smaller. When she was at the other end of the room, the dot was hardly noticeable. It had disappeared, swallowed by an ocean of nothingness. That's me, she thought. When she looked around the room, everything appeared devoid of colour. The brown uprights on the four-poster bed, the bright yellow counterpane, the green wingback chairs, the reddish ebony desk—all had jettisoned their hues. They appeared in drab shades of black, white, and grey. Her image in the mirror on the wardrobe door stared back at her. There were black circles under her eyes and her hair resembled an abandoned bird's nest. Her shoulders were set in a permanent shrug because the saddles of her crutches were buried in her armpits.

Sula burst through the double doors of Semah's bedroom. Dressed for the day—a high-collared dress with a brooch at her throat—her hair was perfectly coiffed. Sula released the handles and entered without closing the doors, her hands in constant motion, caressing her palms, interlocking her fingers, knitting one into the other.

"What is it, Mama?"

Sula stopped fidgeting and faced her daughter.

"He's here."

"Who?"

"Him."

"Him who?"

"The boy—that young man ..." She waved her hand in the direction of Semah's hem as though she were shooing away a small dog.

"Emanuel?"

"Yes."

"What does he want?"

"He is speaking with your father. I listened at the door. I believe he wishes to ask permission to marry you."

Semah's face reddened.

"He is from a good family," Sula said, then immediately corrected herself. "No, he is from one of the most prominent families in the city, and a Jew, of course, and educated at the academy." She hesitated a second time. "He is younger than you—by one year."

There was another pause, then: "He is ... neat ... and although he is not the eldest in line for an inheritance, he is very well connected." Even in her excitement, Semah noticed that her mother had not said that he was handsome or gifted in any way. Here was this man, if not the architect of her misfortune, then certainly the cause of the accident. How did she feel about this person who was now speaking with her father? Should she strap on her leg and go downstairs? Should she use her crutches—or would that scare him off? Surely not. If he had returned with a marriage proposal—after having witnessed her prosthetic skate across the marble dance floor—then he couldn't have been that disgusted.

Sula watched with alarm as Semah raced toward the bedroom doors on her crutches. "Where are you going?"

"Down to Papa's study. I wish to see Emanuel—hear what he has to say."

"No," Sula said and rushed to bar her exit. "No. No. NO!" Semah backed away. Her mother had that look. Though smaller than Semah, her presence was immutable. Her tone had an unchallengeable finality that was as solid as a wall. "That is not how it is done." It was the same tone that had put an end to her father's Wednesday afternoon trysts. The same look that had declared no further discussion would be permitted on that spicy domestic hiccup. "Your Papa will send for you—for us—when the matter is concluded." Her mother put her hands on Semah's shoulders. "Come, let us sit."

Semah followed her mother like a duckling.

She documented the following twelve months, not in her journal but in watercolours on the wall of her bedroom, where she had drawn the black dot with her pen. Like a seed planted on fertile ground, pictures flowered in every direction, rippling out from the single dot. There was no order or method to the collage, no logic or time sequence, no labels that dated the events portrayed. A word or phrase was written here and there like a summation to thoughts: *"Perfect," "Outsiders," "Together."* There were miniature scenes as small as a palm, large ones occupying a quarter of the entire space, and others in between. One of these, a medium-sized painting, showed what happened that day when Emanuel had come to call.

The perspective is over her shoulder as she gazes across the veranda past a pot of chrysanthemums and down to the circular driveway at the front of her father's house. A portly young man with his back to the viewer is stepping into a landau. You can almost hear the *clip-clop* of the horse's hooves as he drives away and smell a whisper of dusty leaves floating off the spiky petals in the pot.

The largest scene is a bucolic that fills the upper left quarter of the wall. It is an idealized Eden showing a vast park at the foot of Fort William's glacis. Mottled clouds hang like fluffy cushions against a pale-blue sky.

Anchoring the centre is the majestically domed Governor's House with colonnaded buildings stretching out on either side. The shorter buildings are bathed in the shadow of taller ones. They all have multiple rows of windows on white and yellow walls and look as sturdy as hillocks. To the left, a smartly attired couple is having a picnic. Dressed in European clothes, they are seated on a large cloth laid on the grass. Indian servants pour tea. There is the portly young man again. And there beside him is a large woman. She is touching the man's chin with her napkin. On the right side of the picture is a cluster of cattle and two goats. The ewe is nursing her kid. An Indian water carrier stands nearby with a pole on his shoulders. Clay buckets hang off ropes dangling from each end.

Floating off the edge of the above scene is a small still life. It is an enlargement of the picnic's food items. There is a pigeon pie, a collared calf's head, a cold cabinet pudding, a blancmange, a bottle of sherry claret, and an empty bottle of champagne lying on its side beside two flutes still dripping with effervescence. Had there been an audio accompaniment it would certainly be something exuberant like Offenbach—that thin-lipped romantic, renowned for silly operettas.

Myriad other scenes are scattered willy-nilly: the young portly man, drawn in profile, looking professorial with a cheroot between his lips; the same face painted from the front, all puffy cheeks and blue eyes searing with energy and ambition; a section of his back office where the young man's desk and chair sit; another section of the front office with swarthy-looking Indians in various stages of undress loading cargo onto flatbed wagons; the riverboats; the clippers with folded sails strapped to yardarms; Chowringhee Street wide and welcoming; the facade of Calcutta's Strand Theatre; an interior sketch of the balcony boxes with two figures, a large woman and her escort—the same portly young man with the icy blue eyes; the greenish Hoogli River that separates her father's estate in Bow Bazaar from his family home in Howrah.

Semah's black-and-white life had burst into watercolours. In the course of a year, the mural became a dizzying kaleidoscope representing the courtship of two people bound by their oddities—he rotund and hairy, she a cripple.

The most affecting scenes occupy the middle area of the wall. It is divided into three parts: two smaller circles hover over a larger one.

In one small circle is the exterior of Bethel Synagogue not two hundred yards from her home. Painted pale yellow, it dwarfs the buildings beside it. Above the arched entrance is a large glass panel with an elegant gold pattern flanked by columns bearing the Star of David and the Menorah. Above this is a clock with a black dial, its hands set at ten minutes to two.

In the other small circle are two hands. One is a woman's and the other is a man's. He is placing a gold signet ring bearing a Magen David on her finger. You can tell by the energy of the brush strokes, the depth of colour, and the confident use of sepia tones that this couple is happy and proud. You can feel that in the next moments he will stand on his toes and kiss her on the lips—a soft and true touch of surrender given as willingly and as smoothly as a ring slipping effortlessly onto a finger.

Below these two smaller scenes is a larger one showing the interior of the synagogue. Up the wide and welcoming marble stairs and through the double doors is a large hall with a curved ceiling. Blue tiles decorate the pillars and white stars are sprinkled against blue patches on the walls. Gleaming chandeliers, a checked marble floor, and arched windows decorated with stained glass give the place a hushed and holy ambience. A raised marble podium occupies the middle of the room. Up ahead is the altar set in an arched alcove. Above this is a semicircular dome. In the dome, etched in red glass, are these words: *Know before whom you stand, it is before the king, the king of kings, blessed be his name.* Prayers from the Torah are inscribed on one stained-glass window, the Ten Commandments on another.

A *chuppah*—wedding canopy—stands a little below the altar. The groom is handsome in his frock coat, holding his white gloves. His top hat is tucked under his arm. His father and mother stand to one side, hers on the other. The bride towers over him and everyone else for that matter. Her white dress has a long train, the only extravagance required. She needs none of the diamond flakes, the candle shields, or the sparkly ostentations that bedecked the gown she had worn on the Night of Light. No, the woman glows in her simple and elegant dress.

Stare at this picture long enough and you can hear the voices raised in song that Wednesday 27 Kislev. You will see that, moments before, he smiled as his wife-to-be entered, escorted by his mother and hers. Servants preceded them, sprinkling the path with poppy petals scattered from the baskets they carried. Semah was paraded seven times around Emanuel to re-enact the seven days of creation, since they will soon become involved in the creation of new lives. Blessings were given. Wine was drunk from the same cup. Then he put the signet ring on her right index finger and said in Hebrew, "You are sanctified to me with this ring according to the Laws of Moses and Israel." *Kiddushin* was complete—a bond for life. A glass wrapped in cloth is placed on the floor. Emanuel stomps on it with his right foot, a reminder that even on the happiest of occasions Jews must remember the destruction of the Temple. Huzzahs rise in unison. The guests shout "Mazel tov" to the newly married couple. But listen carefully and you might hear the bride think that, to her, the shattered glass means her love will last until the shards come back together again.

Semah and Emanuel leave the hall arm in arm, beaming at their guests. A camera is set up on a tripod. A flash of powder and a *click* freezes the moment. Semah is grasping Emanuel's arm proprietorially, like a cat with its paw on a bird it has just caught.

The scene under the *chuppah* was painted later than the others on the mural. It was as though Semah had returned to the room deliberately to finish the mural after the wedding had taken place. Perhaps it was painted a few years after; it is hard to say. What is clear, though, is that it is the only scene on the wall that had been shellacked. It was as though the image required extra protection lest its significance fade.

Semah moved into Emanuel's home where there was no blank wall for her to express herself on. And even if she had found a suitable surface, a hodgepodge mural would have been considered madness, attributable to a fall from a horse that snapped her tibia and fibula. Of course, those leg bones were connected to her brain—or so the chattering classes believed. No, from then on she would have to confine her perspectives to writing in her journal. Her first entry filled several pages. It detailed what happened on her wedding night in the *darkened bedchamber lit by the light of a hoary moonbeam.*

There, in the wordless ambience of night, she had allowed her newly minted husband to lift the skirt of her gown above the knee. She watched as he examined the unnatural-looking straps, hinges, and brown wood. She took his hands and put them on the top buckles. He undid them and removed the false limb. She felt comfortable, grateful for the care he took. He held it in both hands like a log and carried it to the hassock at the foot of the bed. She was eager to please her husband. But, try as he might, the bread remained *unleavened*. He rolled off and lay on his back. Moments later, he left her abruptly. He shrugged on his robe, reached for a box of cheroots, and disappeared into the veranda through an oblique beam of silver.

Semah curled into a ball. She bit the white top sheet and pulled it tight in her teeth. The whisperings had come true. She would not be able to have a child. Not because her lady parts were damaged but because her husband would not lie with her. Was it her leg? Had she misread his gentleness? Was the sight of her stump repugnant? Her disappointment made her hyper-aware. She could feel each thread of cotton against her skin, smell the jasmine and lavender from the garden and the pungent sting of tobacco that floated in from the veranda.

But what was that above the screech of cicadas and frogs?

Whisperings.

Muted voices floated in on the smoky vapours of a cheroot. Emanuel was speaking with someone.

Semah wanted to get closer to hear what was being said.

The prosthetic lay at the foot of her bed. Using it would have created sound and movement. No, her best strategy was to focus on the direction from which the voices emanated. She squeezed her eyes closed and leaned an ear toward the soft roll of Bengalese. The other voice was a woman's. She had an insistent tone. Semah recognized words like *wife,* and *must,* and *now,* and *look at me.*

Minutes passed like hours. Eventually, Emanuel returned.

"Who were you talking with?" she asked.

She saw his eyes lit by a splash of moonbeam. He knelt on the bed, hovering over her. He took off his robe and lowered himself. She felt his ample belly touch hers. But his eyes looked past her head, past the headboard and out the French windows. Whatever he was looking at had leavened his passion. She accepted him. She wanted to. She was determined to silence those who blabbered their doubts with the kind of pity she loathed.

EMANUEL

Raphael was very pleased to see his son settle into his new position as a senior clerk at Belilios & Sons. Emanuel was put in charge of collecting rents from the establishments his father owned in Calcutta and in the neighbouring countryside. Mr. Rustomjee was assigned to train the younger master, who took to his office like a fish to water. He was innovative, too. Ayah Gita was brought along. Her knowledge of Bengali and its unique Hindu customs provided the necessary balm when Emanuel decided to increase the rents that year and the one after that. This delighted his father. His son appeared to understand that the fundamental goal of business was to make money. Seeing that Emanuel was headed for a steady future and that his wife was an angel—albeit a large one— Raphael did not interfere in his son's day-to-day activities, so long as the money kept coming in.

This left room for the young man to plan—or rather to plot. Which is why, at the end of a year, he found himself face to face with Yuen. They were in the uppermost floor of Yuen's opium den in Chinatown. That day, Emanuel was not collecting rent but asking for a loan.

"Fiddy per sen." Yuen rapped the table with his knuckles. A cockroach scurried off the edge and dropped to the floor.

Emanuel leaned back in his rattan chair and looked at the bald Chinese man with the stick-thin body. The smell of old grease limned the air. It competed with scents of yesterday's rancid garlic and noodles. Mr. Rustomjee stood behind Emanuel. Ayah Gita was crouched in the corner, waving a fan to cut the still air. Yuen was grinning, which made his eyes narrow into slits. A gold tooth flashed off the yellow flame of the oil lantern hanging from the ceiling.

"You wan me to lend to you some moolah? You pay fiddy per sen inter-lest," Yuen said, and looked away toward Ayah Gita. He stared at her and ran his tongue over his teeth under his lips. Ayah Gita saw this and pulled her sari over her bare arms.

Weeks before, Emanuel had spent hours digging into back issues of *The Calcutta Chronicle*. He went at it with the diligence of a worker bee. Stacked on his desk by Mr. Rustomjee, the *Chronk* described the story of opium trading in numbers. Sale prices for Malwa and Patna opium were printed in ant-sized type in the centre section.

This is what he learned:

  – The average auction price of one chest was 200 silver dollars.

  – He had a budget of 25,555 Rs., or 5,111 silver dollars.

  – Therefore he could purchase only twenty-five chests.

"A drop in the bucket," Emanuel said, putting a cheroot in his mouth. Mr. Rustomjee struck a match for the young master.

"Sir is needing more capital?" Mr. Rustomjee said with a waggle of his head.

"Much more," Emanuel replied.

"And what, may I be asking, is sir's conception of 'more'?"

"Factoring in shipping, insurance, and other costs, at least double. Fifty chests will make it worthwhile."

Mr. Rustomjee whistled between his teeth. "That is being a damn lot of moolah, sir," he said, waggling some more and waving his hand.

"And there is another thing—the Sassoons."

"Yes sir, they are everywhere."

"Look," Emanuel said, pointing to an article in the newspaper. "And here, and here," he said, stabbing a fleshy finger into the sheets. "They purchase hundreds of chests—close to one thousand last year alone. And they control the prices, too. When they don't want to pay the asking price, they won't bid. They just walk away and wait for the price to drop. The Sassoons have made a fortune this way."

"The big cats have come to Calcutta. Why don't they stay in Bombay?"

"For Patna opium. Chinese clients are no fools. They can tell the difference."

"What can sir do?"

Emanuel was jettisoned back to the present when he heard Yuen say,

"She have nice skin—so smooth." Yuen was looking at Ayah Gita. "You lie make pokey-pokey into her?"

"Shut up," Emanuel said and stood up. Ayah Gita did as well.

"Hey, where you go?" Yuen said.

"Don't speak about her that way."

"Yessie, yessie. Come come, sit sit. All lite. I mick you good offer."

Emanuel remained standing.

"I tell you some ting, I mick a lot, a lot a moolah here for people to *geow loong*—how you say, 'chasing dragons.' I got lotsa cash money. I bin here ten, twenty year, long time. I ask you father sell me this house, he say no."

"Chinamen cannot own property in Calcutta," Emanuel said.

"Leffer mind, leffer mind, I buy. Put you name on paper all for show. Now you wan me money—I charge you fiddy per cen inter-lest. You mick money flom me many many year. Now my turn mick money fum you. You like to do business?"

"Ten percent," Emanuel said.

"Ten?" Yuen laughed and cursed in Chinese.

Emanuel walked away.

"Forty," Yuen called out.

Emanuel stopped and turned to face the usurer.

"Fifteen."

"Firty," Yuen said, holding up three fingers.

"Twenty."

"Aiyah!" he said and screwed up his face as though he had just sucked on a lemon. "Twenty-five, all lite, all lite. You clay-zee bugger, fuck me in the ear."

Emanuel made mental calculations. Mr. Rustomjee took out a stubby pencil and a slip of paper that he filled with numbers. Emanuel finished first.

"Agreed—twenty-five percent interest if you cover all my bids."

Yuen spat in his palm and held it out.

Emanuel spat in his and shook the Chinese man's hand.

"My maximum bid will be at $180 per chest."

"Clayzee—average price be 200 dallah! How you gonna buy for one fiddy? *Chee seen ah?*"

Mr. Rustomjee stopped scribbling and looked up with the same questions in his mind. Emanuel tapped a finger on his temple.

"With this," he said. "I've figured it out."

"Waah! You surely one clayzee bugger."

The next morning, at the British auction house near the Strand, chests of opium were displayed, stacked one on top of the other to form a wall on either side of the auctioneer's podium. Each was stamped with a crest to show that it contained Patna opium—the finest quality in India and arguably in the world.

At the entrance to the large warehouse, Indian dockworkers were standing by to haul the goods to various go-downs—storage places—as soon as their masters had purchased a consignment. The auction was open to anyone. But a tacit rule made it clear that only those in business attire were welcome. Emanuel strode through with Mr. Rustomjee at his elbow. Ayah Gita, being a woman and a slave, sat on her haunches in the street.

Inside, small windows high above their heads lit the vast room. Merchants in clusters of two or three or more girded their loins and sharpened their wits for a day of haggling. What they purchased at this auction would be what they could sell for the rest of the year. On the sellers' side, each consignment had been harvested, processed, and prepared at different poppy farms in the hills near Calcutta. An expert eye, touch, and tongue could tell the drug's provenance in the same way a vintner might discern a bottle of wine. Merchants interested in opium—and which of them wasn't?—crowded the place shoulder to shoulder. The auctioneer introduced each consignment, giving details of its place of origin and the amount of pure opium contained inside the waxy balls.

AAA was the highest grade and therefore cost the most. It also commanded hefty margins in China, where a superior smoke was highly valued as a status symbol. AA was the middling variety and A was the lowest grade, though still of acceptable quality. Even the worst Bengal opium was superior to all others on the market.

The Sassoon family from Bombay on the west coast knew this and desperately wanted a piece of the east-coast action. Joseph, a scion of the family, attended the auction wearing a dark European suit with a *tibba*—Arabic cloak—over it. He was a handsome man in his thirties, hair parted in the middle, with brown eyes and light, beige-coloured skin. He aimed to dominate the Calcutta opium trade just as they had done in Bombay.

The auction started with consignments of A grade and worked up to the highest AAA lots. On this day, the reserve price for the first lot of A was set at $140 per chest. But for gifted businessmen like Joseph, the reserve price (the point below which the auctioneer was not authorized to go) meant nothing. Joseph's goal was to force the cost down. And he did this by simply declaring loudly, "Too high."

The auctioneer—Mr. Ballard from Ballard & Sons Auctioneers, established 1806—couldn't believe his ears. He was a short Scot with a receding hairline and white mutton chops that curled under his rosy cheeks. His face went crimson. His pince-nez lost their balance and tumbled off the bridge of his nose. A reserve bid was never questioned. Dammit, it was a reserve bid, man. And if that effrontery was not enough, Joseph added insult to injury by walking out of the auction house.

"Let me be called at the tea house when the price is more reasonable," he had yelled before striding off.

The crowded room fell silent. Thought bubbles over the heads of the merchants were set aflame with options. Do they jump in now and bid for the largest consignment knowing that Joseph Sassoon is not in the room to outbid them? Or should they walk out as well, hoping that the seller would fall for Sassoon's ploy and lower the reserve bid once the hall was empty? It would be a gamble either way. Where did the odds lie?

Out of the rumbling ruminations, Emanuel yelled, "Too high!" and egged the room on. Another merchant joined him, and then another and another until there was a multi-voiced chorus of "Too high!" that made the rafters tremble. The merchants vacated the auction room en masse, headed for the tea house. Opium's loss was tea's gain.

The situation was a thorny thistle for Mr. Ballard. His face went from crimson to a shade deeper than an aubergine's. He suddenly felt very hungry. Or was that empty feeling in his ample belly something akin to panic? Regardless, as the dark-suited merchants quit the room like a flock of crows, Mr. Ballard felt his mouth dry out, his bald pate spritz with moisture, and his arsehole slam shut.

Hushed but spirited meetings were held behind the auctioneer's dais. Mr. Ballard huddled with the mid-level British bureaucrats who were in charge of selling the opium consignments. With their heads bent in a scrum, they debated what to do. After much discussion, the group came up empty-handed. That Jew, Sassoon, had got the better of them. And who was that new man? The one who rabble-roused the crowd? What was his agenda? More importantly, what was his name? Was he a Jew as well?

"Dammit," Mr. Ballard sputtered, "who gives a devil's shanks what he is. Lower the price and let's get on with it."

Had he been anywhere but Calcutta, Mr. Ballard might not have been as eager to compromise. Prickly heat rash covered his inner thighs in red blotches of angry-looking pustules. That and the wretched trots made this assignment intolerable. But he earned more dosh in one month here than he did all year in his grotty Aberdeen shoppe. His timely intervention gave everyone a sanguine nudge toward what one bureaucrat described as a "confluence of mutually beneficial prerogatives." Nodding sagely all round, they wrote the phrase in their notebooks. They would later reference it in reports filed in triplicate. The reserve bid was lowered to $120 per chest. A new breed of crafty businessman had outwitted the bureaucrats with engineering degrees from Oxbridge—the ruling class.

The new price was announced on a chalkboard outside the auction house. Immediately, a flock of messenger *wallahs* padded off in their bare feet to give their *sahibs* the news. Within minutes the auction room returned to its original congestion. And that was how Joseph Sassoon bought 512 chests of grade A at $129 per chest—only $9 above the new reserve price. He left the smaller lots for his colleagues to squabble over like a lion stepping away from a deer carcass after he had eaten his fill. Joseph looked in Emanuel's direction and caught the younger man's eye. The men nodded to each other in tacit acknowledgment. Joseph doffed his hat. Emanuel responded in kind.

"What a man!" Mr. Rustomjee said, leaning over and whispering into Emanuel's ear. "He could be purchasing all the lots. But look, he is silent. He is deciding to let his fellow merchants have a go. Fine gentleman."

But Emanuel knew better.

"Don't be fooled," Emanuel said. "Joseph Sassoon's display of magnanimity is not generosity. It is strategic. He is reserving his moolah to bid on the AAA lots. He wants all the good stuff. I mean to stop him."

Emanuel had studied Joseph's modus operandi, as reported in *The Calcutta Chronicle*. Walking out and persuading other merchants to do the same was what had made the house of Sassoon the largest opium trading company in India.

"He has much moolah. What is sir going to do?"

"Wait and see," Emanuel said, tapping his temple. At the same time, he felt a tablespoonful of acid pour into his belly.

After all the A lots were sold, Mr. Ballard moved on to the AA group. The largest number of lots available was in this middle category. Joseph purchased over four hundred cases. Emanuel watched him with awe, like an acolyte admiring his rabbi. Joseph was calm. He was patient. Most of all he was in control. Here again a strategy was in play. This time, Joseph did not dispute the reserve bid. Rather, he deliberately pushed the bidding upward. The other merchants kept overbidding him, fearing they would leave empty-handed. Then, when the price was sufficiently high, Joseph backed off abruptly. This allowed someone else to win the bid. In this way, merchants spent the majority of their budget on AA lots.

"Sir has not made any bids. Why?" Mr. Rustomjee asked. He hooked a finger into his collar and ran it around his neck.

"This is exciting," Emanuel said. He looked across the room and caught Joseph looking back at him. Emanuel lifted a cheroot to his lips. Mr. Rustomjee lit it with a match trembling in his fingers.

"And that concludes the disposition of all grade AA lots," Mr. Ballard announced. He wiped his head with a sodden handkerchief stained with yellow patches. Things weren't that bad after all. With two-thirds of the opium auctioned off, Her Majesty's coffers were enriched and his commission secured. The wife would be able to buy that new hat she'd been nagging him about. Mr. Ballard sniffed at the thought. He blew his nose into his handkerchief. He looked at the secretion, folded the cloth into a ball, and returned it to the warmth and safety of his inside pocket. Then he raised his voice:

"Gentlemen! We now come to the AAA lots, of which there are two. Lot #1 is a consignment of fifty chests and Lot #2 a consignment of one hundred chests. The reserve bid for Lot #1 is $250 per chest."

The room hushed.

"Do I hear an offer?" He had hardly gotten the words out when …

"Too high!" Joseph's voice rang out from the centre of the crowd.

"Now see here," Mr. Ballard exclaimed. He wasn't sure what else to say. Behind him the mid-level bureaucrats rose in unison, mouths agape. Again?

Down on the floor, shouts of "Too high!" popped out of the assembled merchants. They required no prompting this time.

"Order!" Mr. Ballard shouted. He banged his gavel and called for order once more but the shouts of "Too high!" only got louder, drowning out the small man's best efforts.

Joseph Sassoon led a second exodus from the auction house with the confidence of Moses leading the Israelites out of Egypt. He shouted over his shoulder, "You know where to find us when the price is more reasonable!" The crowd of men laughed.

Emanuel heard the sounds of bonhomie retreat as the merchants headed toward the tea house once again. Except for the auctioneer and his bureaucrats, he was the only one left in the room. Behind him, Mr. Rustomjee wiped sweat off his forehead. Emanuel took a deep breath. He strode up to Mr. Ballard, who was cleaning his pince-nez while engaged in a déjà vu conference with the engineers. Emanuel cleared his throat. Mr. Ballard looked up.

"I bid $150," Emanuel said in a conversational tone.

"I beg your pardon?" Mr. Ballard put his glasses on for a closer look.

"I bid $150."

"But this is absurd. There is a reserve bid of $250 per chest. What is the matter with you people? This is not the way it's done. You just can't …" He ran out of words again. The three bureaucrats stepped in behind their auctioneer and peered over Ballard's shoulders. They looked like tourists watching monkeys at a zoo.

"Sir," Emanuel said, pulling back his shoulders. "You are in a pickle."

"Pickles Sahib!" Mr. Rustomjee shouted, then lowered his eyes.

"You must either take my bid or declare the sale closed. Those are the rules, are they not?"

"But, but ..." was all Mr. Ballard could muster. The bureaucrats remained silent. G-d forbid they say anything that could compromise their position in any way. "Who are you?" Mr. Ballard asked.

"Emanuel Belilios, at your service."

"Well, Mr. Bulbus."

"Be-lil-i-os!" Mr. Rustomjee shouted, poking the air with a finger.

"There is no underbidding. The price is $250 per," Mr. Ballard averred.

"Clearly that is not what the market is prepared to pay. I am the only one in the room with a serious offer."

Mr. Ballard jutted his jaw and said, "I shall close the sale."

"And risk the wrath of your British employers who have invested heavily in planting, harvesting, and producing the finest opium in India? Is that prudent for you? Is it a wise career move for any of your colleagues? Do you wish to be known as the ones who were not able to sell AAA— the most desirable harvest of the season?" Emanuel let his rhetorical questions weigh on his listeners' ears. "My bid is $150 per."

Mr. Ballard caucused with his pack. Each one in the conclave sneaked furtive glances toward the young merchant and his swarthy companion. Eventually, Mr. Ballard resurfaced.

"200," he said.

Emanuel smiled. The argument had been won. Now they were just haggling over the price. "160," he countered.

"Oh sir ..." Mr. Rustomjee looked up. A long drop of perspiration ran down the side of his face. A fly buzzed above everyone's head.

"190!" Mr. Ballard exclaimed.

"180," Emanuel said. Mr. Rustomjee dug his fingernails into his young master's arm. No one spoke. The fly zigzagged at eye level.

"On one condition," Mr. Ballard said. "I'll sell this batch for 180 per if you will bid up the price of the next lot to 320 per. That way, I'll make my money back and stick it to that Jew Sassoon. Two birds with one stone, as it were."

The fly buzzed on Emanuel's left side.

Mr. Ballard leaned back with the satisfaction of a cat that had just deposited a dead bird on a doorstep.

Quick as a frog's tongue, Emanuel snatched the unsuspecting fly out of mid-air.

"Agreed," he said, and proffered his hand. The auctioneer took it.

"Sold," Mr. Ballard shouted, "for $180 per chest. Fifty chests in total!"

The bureaucrats let out a collective sigh of relief.

"Go find Yuen," Emanuel said to Mr. Rustomjee. "I need more money."

As the Parsi trotted off to Chinatown, other messenger *wallahs,* alerted by the sound of the gavel, ran to the tea house to tell their masters that someone had purchased the first lot of AAA. Clay cups of tea fell out of their hands and shattered on the ground. There were cries of "What?" and "Who?" and "How much?" as the merchants ran back to the auction room.

"Just in time, gentlemen," Mr. Ballard said when they entered en masse. "The second lot is open for bidding. The reserve is $180 per. Do I hear a bid?"

"180," Emanuel started.

"190," Joseph countered eagerly.

"195," Emanuel called out.

Who *was* this young man? Was he the one who had purchased the first lot of AAA? Was this boy a goer—someone who would go for the entire batch of AAA? In the time it took for Joseph to think this, two more bids were proffered.

Mr. Ballard said, "205. I have 205. Do I hear 210?"

"210!" Emanuel shouted. A shiver ran through his stomach like a cold stiletto blade. He had no funds to cover this bid. He had spent all he had and more on the first lot. But he had to bid up. It was the condition he had shaken hands on.

The bidding climbed to 240. Some merchants dropped off. Now only three bidders remained: Joseph, Emanuel, and a tall, dark-skinned man in a white linen suit sporting an impressive moustache.

Out of the corner of his eye, Emanuel saw Mr. Rustomjee return with Yuen in his wake. He signalled them to join him.

"245," Joseph called.

"250," from the white linen suit.

"260," Emanuel offered.

Mr. Ballard waxed eloquently on the quality of the product and looked warily out onto the quiet room. "Do I see 265? 265 anyone?"

Mr. Rustomjee and Yuen stepped in beside Emanuel.

"I need you to cover me."

"You clayzee."

"Cover me—I know what I'm doing."

"How muchee you need?"

"I'll close at 320 per."

Yuen produced a small abacus from under his tunic. "With inter-lest, waaa!" His eyes bugged when he saw the total.

"265" from Joseph.

"270" from the white linen suit.

"275," Emanuel shouted.

"How you gonna pay? If you win dis bid, if you can't pay, they kill you. If you dead, now who pay me?"

"Please sir, I am begging you to stop." Mr. Rustomjee was close to tears.

"C'mon, Yuen. You need me alive. The only way is to spot me now."

"280."

"290."

"300!" Emanuel called out. The merchants rumbled.

"Aiyah, you clayzee bugger."

"Sir, I am praying to you … stop."

"I have 300. Do I hear 305? 305?" Mr. Ballard shouted.

"305."

"310."

"Cover me," Emanuel said to Yuen again. "315," Emanuel called out. Then he turned to Yuen: "I know something you would like to have." He pulled Yuen away from Rustomjee and hissed in the man's ear. "Look at her, over there leaning against the wall," he said, pointing at Ayah Gita. "You like that black skin, don't you. *You like mick pokey-pokey into her?*"

"320," Joseph shouted.

"320," Mr. Ballard repeated. "I have 320. Do I hear more?"

"You can have her," Emanuel said.

"Gentlemen, I am looking around the room." The white-linen-suited man shook his head, no. Mr. Ballard's eyes wandered over to Emanuel.

"Yes. I lie dat," Yuen said, staring at the young Indian woman.

"She's yours if you cover me now and reduce the interest of my first loan to ten percent."

"You clayzee."

"Yes or no?"

"320 going once …"

"Yes," Yuen said.

"Make your mark here," Emanuel said, pulling out a slip of paper, hastily scribbling on it and handing it to the Chinese man. Yuen made his mark.

"320 going twice …"

All eyes were on Emanuel.

He shook his head, no.

"Sold to Mr. Joseph Sassoon for $320 per chest. One hundred chests in total."

Applause filled the room. Mr. Rustomjee fell back against the wall and loosened his collar. Emanuel felt Yuen grab his arm.

"Hey, what you do? You not bid?" Yuen said.

"I never intended to buy at 320, you fool. The only reason I asked you here was to make you lower your interest rate to ten percent. You've got to think with this," Emanuel said, pointing to his head, "and not with these," he added, grabbing Yuen by the dumplings between his legs. "I would never part with Ayah Gita. Never."

"You liar. You cheat me!"

"It's just business, Mr. Yuen," Emanuel said. He walked out of the auction house, away from Yuen's barrage of Chinese oaths that bounced off his back like toothpicks.

SEMAH

When Emanuel told her that he was departing for Hong Kong by week's end, Semah received the news like a punch in the stomach. She had suggested that she accompany him. But Emanuel and her parents rebuffed that notion. A young woman travelling thousands of nautical miles to a new colony stuffed with inscrutable Chinese? No. G-d no. What would she eat?

Then on the eve of his leave-taking, they sat in the salon adjacent to her bedchamber. She kneaded the palm of one hand with her thumb and listened to the clock ticking on the mantel. The atmosphere was thick with taciturnity. Finally she said,

"So soon? Must you?"

Emanuel let his head hang and said nothing.

She knew the answer. Delaying the sale of his merchandise would only put off his inevitable departure. Even as the words had tumbled out of her mouth, she knew the question was a foolish one—a wifely display of selfishness. Why even ask? Well, she wanted to start a family. His occasional visits to her bed would now be interrupted by an absence of months.

But Semah had little option. She would do what was expected. Later she would write in her journal, *They also serve who only stand and wait.* Then add, *Clearly Milton had two good legs or he would have written "sit and wait"!*

She was thinking these thoughts when the clock struck eight. She stood up and crossed to her secretary nestled against the window. She picked up a parcel wrapped in brown paper and tied with string.

"This is for you," she said and gave it to him. He pulled the string off and parted the paper to find a red velvet box about one foot in length. In it was a shiny brass telescope. The metal, polished to a bright gold, reflected off the lamplight. "I had it engraved," she said, pointing to the lettering. He read it aloud: *"For Emanuel, my Husband, from your Loving Wife, Semah."*

"I shall use it," he said.

"I'm glad. You will be able to see a long way into the future— perhaps even your destiny," she said and stood up. She touched his cheek. "Kiss me," she said.

He put the telescope back in its box and stood up slowly. She closed her eyes. He looked at her and kissed her on the cheek.

"Thank you," she said, touching her cheek with the back of her hand. She walked to the double doors that led to her bedchamber. She went through them and left one door ajar.

The *Cowasjee Family* had weighed anchor at dawn. With Emanuel and his cargo aboard, she headed toward the open sea.

He took a deep breath, pulled open his new telescope, and ran a thumb over the names etched in the brass. The salty air larded the metal with a layer of moisture. The smudge left by his thumb made the grooves of the lettering look deeper, more permanent. Against his chest, he could feel the pendant stick to his clammy skin.

He lifted the telescope to his eye.

He could see the ghats on the riverbank. Farther inland, the sun glinted off a flagpole surrounded by the crenellations of a turret on Fort William's roof. The Union Jack rose slowly to a bugler's reveille that he could hear bleating a mile away. The hopeful melody wafted down the citadel's glacis, across the Maidan, and over the Hoogli. A steady wind billowed the fo'c'sle. The *Cowasjee Family* glided silently over the water at the gentle pace of a bicycle.

She was a sleek, twelve-gun American clipper built for speed. Just over a hundred feet long and weighing three hundred tons, she could cut through ocean waves at fourteen knots. With her sharp bow she ran the waters like a greyhound, leaving the larger Indiamen to bob in her wake like floating castles.

As luck would have it, a certain Mr. Cowasjee (a Parsi trader known to Mr. Rustomjee) had purchased the vessel while she was being refitted in

Calcutta before repositioning to Hong Kong for short runs along the China coast. Mr. Cowasjee owned thirty-nine ships and traded primarily out of Bombay, but had recently expanded his business to Calcutta, where the merchants were in great need of sea transportation. His latest acquisition, then called the *Lady Smith*, was a speedy ship built in California for opium runs across the Pacific. He had purchased it from Mr. Delano, an American opium trader whose grandson would one day become president of the United States. As was his wont, Mr. Cowasjee had ripped off the plates that carried the clipper's American name and replaced them with the more parochial *Cowasjee Family*.

The shiny flyer had been in her final stages of a fit-up when Mr. Rustomjee introduced Emanuel to Fincher, the ship's master. A sandy-haired old tar, he wore his sea years on every line of his leathery face, reddened by decades of exposure to sun and wind. He was on the dock.

"Well," he said. "She can take up to seventy-seven chests."

"I have fifty," Emanuel replied, then added, "It's *Mister* Belilios to you."

Fincher's eyes narrowed and his cheek twitched. "Half now and half on arrival."

"Done," Emanuel said, proffering his hand. Fincher shook it half-heartedly.

"We sail at dawn. Be laded by then or I weigh anchor and keep the advance."

The terms concluded, Emanuel turned away and smiled at Mr. Rustomjee. "Thank you, my friend." Mr. Rustomjee's eyes brightened when he heard the word "friend."

"Oh, sir is giving me a great honour."

"I wish you would change your mind and come with me."

"Sir is very kind. But I am not of your world. I can show you the ropes, as Mr. Fincher *wallah* would say, but I am not taking the ropes by the horns."

"It is a standing offer."

"Sir must be understanding. I have taught sir all that I know. And yesterday, yesterday I saw with my own eyes: the student was teaching the teacher. No, no, sir, my heart is not being strong enough to be doing what you must do. Go with God."

"I'll go with the wind. If G-d wants to come along, he's welcome."

As the clipper slipped out of port, Emanuel felt released from his father's grip. His last contact with the old man the day before his departure had not gone well.

"The Sassoons will eat you alive," he had said. "This is a foolish thing you've done. Go to them—there is still time—apologize, sell the fifty chests to them, make a little profit if you must, but let them have it or get their permission to sell in China." The older Belilios was pacing in his study, a shawl around his shoulders and a cigar thick as a banana between his fingers. Clouds of smoke billowed above his head like a train engine. When his diatribe ended, he sat on the edge of his desk and waved a finger at his son, who was seated in front of him. "Don't be reckless."

"Father," Emanuel had said, standing up and moving away from the finger and the murk of tobacco fumes, "assuming I do as you say— then what?"

"What? I don't know what. Make sons. Work for me. This is a family business. You have a wife, settle down; you don't need to take risks. I did that for you, for your brother, so that you wouldn't have to. Can't you see that?"

"Yes, I see that you want me to have the same boring life that you have. You want me to be defined by others, like you are."

"What are you saying? You speak to me like this? How dare you?"

"How dare I? Father, you never supported me. It has always been Aaron—"

"Nonsense. I gave you an education just like your brother."

"And then you watched when the headmaster beat me—"

"I had no choice."

Emanuel's fists curled. His chest heaved in short, audible breaths. Eyelids slammed shut, and in that moment of blackness he saw himself bent over the headmaster's desk, felt the sting of a bamboo cane slash across his buttocks while his father watched.

Emanuel opened his eyes, cancelling the memory. He turned on his heel and walked out the door. Behind him, Raphael shouted, "I only want to protect you. I warned you. Let this be on your head!"

On board the *Cowasjee Family*, he let his telescope wander down from the Union Jack. The flag had reached its apex. At the same moment, the bugler hit the final C note. Emanuel focused his lens on the docks.

There she was, towering over the small crowd of dockworkers. Dressed in a white Victorian day dress and a wide-brimmed hat, she held an open parasol. It was more for show than necessity—the sun was hardly a threat at that time of day. Semah was elegant and graceful; he'd give her that.

Ayah Gita stood two steps behind Semah. He tried to move his memory from what had happened the night before. But the recollections were too insistent.

He had walked to the door that Semah had left ajar. Through it, he saw his wife sitting at her dressing table brushing her hair. She stopped when she saw him reflected in the mirror. She looked over her shoulder. He put his hand on the doorknob and pulled it closed between them. Then he walked away, out of the house toward the shed, at the end of the garden, where he met Ayah Gita.

And when they had finished their tumble of backs against walls—first hers then his, of hands holding the underside of a thigh, of mouths squashed and lips disappearing, of the slapping and the tickling, of the grunts teeming with a wild abandon born of desperation—who knew when they would do this again—they lay against sacks of feed. Outside, the cicadas clicked and an owl hooted to accompany their steady breathing of contentment.

"What am I to you?" she asked. "Am I a nanny giving a little boy the love he cannot find in his parents? Or a slave you cannot resist?" He didn't answer. "Perhaps you just like the danger? I have raised you but I do not know you. Do you love me?"

Yes, he thought, whatever love means. He stood and put on his clothes, looking out the small casement above the door into a moonlit sky. Across the yard he could see the house and his wife's bedchamber window. An amber glow backlit a figure silhouetted in the window frame looking down on the shed.

"You push everyone away who cares for you," Ayah Gita said. "One day, someone will come into your life that you will love more than she loves you. And when she betrays you, pray G-d the rest of us are still here to give you comfort."

Ayah Gita reached for her cloth sack. She pulled out something small wrapped in cotton. She opened it. "I do not know lettering. So there is nothing written," she said, showing him the necklace in her palm.

He picked it up. Hanging from one end was a pendant in the shape of a six-pointed star, the Magen David—the Shield of David. He kissed it. She put it around his neck and said, "Who you are is how you will be remembered."

Emanuel lowered his telescope. He pulled a handkerchief out of his inside pocket and blew his nose. He cleaned the lens at each end of the tube that had misted over. Then he lifted it to his eyes again.

Semah was waving a lace handkerchief high in the air.

Ayah Gita was holding her palms together tightly against her chest. She looked up, staring at the clipper slipping downriver away from her. He saw her lips mouth the word "goodbye."

These were the people in his life, he thought: a wife and an illiterate slave girl. His father, Raphael, was conspicuous by his absence.

"To hell with him," Emanuel said and collapsed his telescope.

He turned his back on the ghats, put one foot up on the port rail, and breathed in the early morning air. It caught in the back of his throat. He hawked up a loogie and spat the lung cookie over the side.

Peering out over the bow, he thought, I can see forever, even without a telescope.

PART TWO

HONG KONG
1862–1875

EMANUEL

A cannon shot rang out.

Emanuel sat up in his bunk. His shirt clung to his back, glued to the skin with sweat. The cabin was dark. He rubbed his eyes and blinked several times, trying to bring the dimly lit room into focus.

Quickly, he swung his feet to the floor and lurched across the cabin. He undid the clasp on the only porthole in the room. The cover swung down like a drawbridge. Immediately his head snapped back from the powerful stench—rotted fish, effluent, and salt water warmed by the noonday sun. He reached for a handkerchief from the inside pocket of his jacket that was hanging on a peg by the door. With the other hand he grabbed a bottle of rosewater beside the basin. He pulled out the tiny cork with his teeth, upended the bottle onto his handkerchief, and pressed it to his nose.

Light poured in through the square porthole. Dust flickered in the wide yellow beam. Humidity from days at sea had limned every surface with a shiny veneer that made everything sticky to the touch. The small room came into focus: a single bunk bed against the far wall, a washstand with basin and ewer, some cotton sheets for towelling, his trunk opened like a book, a small table and two chairs with his writing box on it, his shoes on the floor and beside them a ceramic cuspidor. Mercifully, a lid covered its contents but not the sour odour that made his stomach turn. He looked out the porthole again.

He had arrived in Heung Gong—Fragrant Harbour.

His ship was stationary. Across the water, a puff of grey smoke rose over the hillside, a residue of the cannon blast from moments ago. In the dock area, a Union Jack fluttered merrily atop a mansard. Massive white-washed buildings with colonnades and terra-cotta roofs lined the coast. Some were two, three, no, four storeys high. Behind them, steep hills rose in the shape of a massive prehistoric creature, making a verdant backdrop to an emerging city. How long had he been asleep? He could only guess. His first taste of prawns the night before had given him a bad case of the trots. It was shellfish—a forbidden food. He shouldn't have eaten it. But there was nothing else. (Fincher had correctly eschewed weighing anchor in Singapore to pick up stores. Instead he opted to complete the Calcutta–Hong Kong run in twenty-six days—a dizzying speed.) He had self-medicated with a tablespoonful of lauda-num that put him into a fitful sleep. He had dreamed of a cannon aimed squarely in his face and had woken up when it fired.

He looked again in the direction of the puff of smoke. It had dissipated in the humid air. A signal? he wondered.

Voices—men's voices that he hadn't noticed before, muffled but excited—wafted in. He recognized English words. But mostly it was that horrible guttural Lashka tongue used by half-breed Indo-Portuguese labourers. A smattering of singsong Chinese folded into the polyglot sounds from above. Bangs of something heavy on wood and the footfalls of people walking to and fro thrummed on the ceiling.

Emanuel peeled off his shirt and moved to the washstand. He splashed water on his face and looked at himself in the mirror. Blue eyes stared back at him. He ran his fingers and palms through dark, curly hair to slick it back over his ears. It parted naturally in the middle. He had a month-old beard. Shaving had been impossible in the cabin of a ship that was constantly in motion. His temples and cheeks were red, his nose almost maroon from exposure to sun and wind. He turned sideways, hoping to see a flattened stomach from all the retching and bum diddles of the last few days. But, alas, his pear-shaped body persisted. He shook his head with disappointment, reached for a fresh shirt he had reserved for this occasion, and slipped it on.

Emanuel emerged from below decks and immediately pressed the handkerchief to his nose again.

"You'll get used to it in time," Mr. Fincher said.

"Good day, Fincher."

"... 'day," he replied, refusing to use the word *sir* or *Mr. Bil-bos*.

"What the devil is that smell?" Emanuel asked.

"*Fragrant* Harbour," he replied with a smirk, opening his arms theatrically, "alias: night soil. The shite is emptied at dawn and, depending on the tide, the floaters come from the island yonder, across the harbour headed to the peninsular—like little brown salmon going upstream." He made an undulating gesture in mid-air like a fish. "On their way across, they cozy up to the side of the ship."

Amidships, a bevy of brown-skinned men, naked to the waist and barefoot, were hauling cargo up from the hold. Emanuel saw his lading stacked in neat rows on deck. While he was counting his inventory, he saw men lowering jute netting into the hold to retrieve the remaining chests.

"I need to get my lading into storage ..." Emanuel didn't finish.

"That you will. Grab yerself a few coolies and they'll see to putting your load on a sampan," Fincher said, jerking a thumb over the side.

Surrounding the clipper were single-oared dinghies made of mismatched driftwood, blacked with barnacles. Dark-green seaweed, shimmering with moisture, clung to their little hulls. A rounded canvas shelter at the rear of these vessels provided a cave-like room where the owner would store his meagre belongings. The black-brown colour and shape made them look like cockroaches ringed around a chunk of lard. They were manned by barefooted coolies dressed in wide black pants folded at the waist and long-sleeved, collarless tunics. All of them had toothy grins. They shouted to the *gweilo,* indicating with their fingers how much they would charge for their services.

Emanuel ignored their cries. He had learned from dealing with inferiors in Calcutta that it was best not to even talk to them, let alone hire them, unless you absolutely had to. He pulled out his telescope and scanned his new surroundings.

Cowasjee Family had anchored in the middle of the harbour, a wide, natural waterway between the island of Hong Kong to his right and the peninsula called Kowloon on his left. The port was teeming with sailing ships of all kinds: clippers like the one he was on; *countrymen,* large three-mast floating castles; gaff-rigged schooners with their four-cornered masts; *lorcha,* Chinese bat-winged sailing boats built with clipper hulls; and *centipedes,* long, narrow boats oared by fifty men on either side that carried cargo and passengers from the island side to the peninsula. His heart raced. Before he left Calcutta he had, of course, read all about the trading frenzy of Hong Kong, but the reality was overwhelming. Everyone was in a desperate hurry. The edges of his mouth curved into a smile and his body tensed with anticipation. This was clearly where he was meant to be.

Moving his scope across the bow, he saw what he was looking for. It resembled Noah's ark. Anchored about two hundred yards away was a massive ship—perhaps ten or twenty times the size of the clipper he was standing on. It had no sails. Instead an A-framed longhouse took up the entire deck area. It was two, three, maybe four times larger than any other ship in the harbour. This was a floating warehouse, dead anchored and built specifically for warehousing opium.

Emanuel collapsed his telescope and called out, "Fincher!" The Irishman looked up and jutted his chin as if to say *Whaddyawant.* "Do you speak Chinese?"

"I have a few words," Fincher said.

"Will you translate for me?"

Fincher didn't reply. He put two fingers in his mouth and whistled a shrill tweet across the deck. The coolies turned in unison and immediately crowded around Emanuel, shouting in different languages, raising fingers and knuckles to indicate the price they would work for.

"Don't need Chinese here. They all speak moolah," Fincher said, rubbing his fingers and thumb together.

The coolies' voices got louder. Words shot out in different tongues, all of them foreign to Emanuel. Bald heads and leathery arms, gnarled fingers and filthy palms, eyes eager for custom and bodies shiny with sweat swarmed him. Out of the crowd a voice hollered *"Sa bat Sa-lom!"* It came from a Chinese man craning his neck above the crowd. He was slight of build and bald. There was a nasty-looking purple scar on the side of his head.

On the day her husband departed Calcutta, Semah had stood at the dock waving a white handkerchief, towering over the Jezebel standing behind her. No, that was too elevated a name. Jezebel was a princess and this creature was a slave. Semah was convinced that Ayah Gita had watched them on their wedding night. And the harlot had watched them on other occasions as well. There were three people in the marriage. She knew, first-hand, what her mother had experienced. For months she had felt a knot twisting in her belly and she could not get rid of the bitter taste on her tongue. Without realizing it, she had gnawed the cuticles of her thumbs until they bled. This was not his fault—he was weak. It was she, Semah. Her truncated leg made her undesirable. Yet this was a marriage. Only two people were needed. And she had chosen the day of Emanuel's departure to amputate the unneeded chunk.

So, when the clipper had sailed well past the marker buoy and shrunk to a dot in the distance, Semah turned her back to the sea and said to Ayah Gita,

"Your services are no longer required."

The Indian clasped her hands to her mouth. She looked frightened.

Semah turned away from the small brown woman and said, "I have known for a long time."

"Memsahib—"

"No. No words. It ends now."

Semah climbed into her landau. The knot in her belly unravelled. The sourness on her tongue disappeared. Behind her she heard the soft *thump* of something hitting the ground. She had ordered a servant to bundle up the woman's belongings. He had just tossed them at Ayah Gita's feet. She was lucky she had not been thrown out the window and her flesh eaten by stray dogs, thought Semah.

Then she burst into tears.

EMANUEL

He sat sipping a brandy on the fourth floor of the Hong Kong Hotel. Overhead, a *punkah*—a wide fan—hung motionless.

He looked through his telescope past the French windows and scanned the wharves a few hundred yards away. Condensation steamed off the roofs of the buildings. Low clouds trapped the air and humidity hung over the colony like wet wool. A noonday gun blasted somewhere to his right. A puff of smoke balled against the green hillside and stayed there. On the Praya that ran along the harbour, recently erected Greco-Roman style buildings brought to mind the picture of Venice that hung above the fireplace in his father's study—a reminder of where his family had come from.

But here there was none of the ordered efficiency of palazzos and piazzas. The city of Victoria—Hong Kong side—was still a fishing village. Not far from the gleaming white multi-colonnaded buildings were shanties and lean-tos. Small and ashen-coloured from mildew, worn down by years of humidity and exposure, their flat roofs were covered with salted fish drying in the heat.

On the roof of one hut, Emanuel picked out a lad fighting off seagulls. Wafer thin with a large head and sandy-coloured hair, the boy leapt from one roof to another.

At street level, fisher folk who lived cheek by jowl and hand to mouth were only steps away from the whitewashed buildings. In the harbour, he saw the storage vessel where his opium was kept. It had been one week since he had hired the Chinese man with the purple scar on his head.

"What is your name?" Emanuel had asked.

"*Nam?* Li," he said, slapping his palm on his chest. "You nam?"

"Belilios."

"*Bay-lay-low-see?*"

"Sir will do."

"*Sir Wil-do Bay-lay-low-see.*"

Emanuel was not about to waste any more time with pleasantries. "How much?" he asked, rubbing his fingers and thumb together.

"*Me tikkie one dallah,*" he said, slapping his chest to mean himself. "*I tikkie six forgay—six man,*" he added, holding up a thumb and pinky finger like horns to indicate six. He pointed to the other men. "*Six for-gay. One dallah each. Seven dallah toe-toe.*"

Through sign language and pidgin English, Emanuel agreed to the fees. It was up to Li to hire others for the cartage job. If he hired them for less than one dollar each, he could pocket the difference. Hiring completed, the opium chests were shouldered onto a chute that hung over the port side and lowered with ropes to waiting sampans. Emanuel climbed down a rope ladder and stepped aboard Li's boat. Single oars were lowered off the stern as the sampans headed for the giant storage boat dead-anchored mid harbour.

On the way, a little girl peeked out from behind the makeshift curtain of the small cabin on the sampan's aft. Emanuel looked at her and smiled. She saw the *gweilo* and disappeared from view.

In the crowded low-ceilinged hall of the storage vessel, a Chinese man with a waist-long pigtail sat on a wooden stool. Dangling from the ceiling in front of him was a large iron scale. Emanuel estimated it to be four feet long on either side of the fulcrum. Brass *picul* weights, about a foot tall, stood at the assayer's feet like enormous pawns of a giant chess set.

Merchants and coolies filled the hall shoulder to shoulder, jockeying for attention from the English manager for a scrip—a six-inch piece of sandalwood that recorded the freight deposited for storage. Emanuel's lading was opened, inspected, and weighed. He was given one scrip for each box. Emanuel tied the wooden receipts with string and threw the bundle into his grip.

"*Tikkee, Hong Kong sigh?*" Li asked with his toothy grin.

"Yes. Hotel," Emanuel said, dreaming of a hot bath and a brandy chaser.

"*Yessie, Sir Wil-do Bay-lay-low-see—long name, ha-ha,*" Li laughed.

Emanuel climbed on board and sat facing aft. As they pulled away, the little girl emerged from the compartment. She briefly looked over the side at her reflection in the water then got up and ran to Li, grabbing hold of his leg. Emanuel stared at her. She stared back. Emanuel winked at her. The girl giggled and hid her face.

At the wharf, Li tethered his sampan.

"*I tikkie bag? Ten cent. Hotel dis way. Plis, come, come.*"

As they made their way past a sea of people—half-naked labourers with filthy sweat rags slung over their shoulders, European managers jotting in notebooks, rickshaws and chairs used as palanquins—the noisy jibber-jabber of a port city surrounded his every step. A sandy-haired urchin ran through the crowd and bumped into Emanuel. Man and boy held each other in an awkward dance for a few moments before the scrawny lad slinked away. Li said,

"*Aiyah, lo prob-lem, lo prob-lem. Hotel dis way.*"

For the rest of the day and for the days that followed, Li was always close at hand. He squatted at the steps outside the hotel waiting for Emanuel.

"*Rickshaw? Chair? What you want I get for you,*" he would say whenever Emanuel emerged. Thus, a rickshaw or chair was called.

Emanuel took his bag with the scrips in it and made daily trips through a warren of streets lined with shops to wait for an audience with Mr. Jardine at the Scotsman's brick-and-stone office building in the Central District. Jardine was the largest opium trader in China and the first to be known as *Tai Pan*—big boss. Emanuel's plan was to sell Jardine his lading of fifty chests and establish a supply chain from Calcutta to Hong Kong for the veteran China hand.

Li trotted ahead of the rickshaw like a herald, calling out Chinese obscenities, yelling for pedestrians to get out of the way.

But Emanuel was turned away from Jardine's office every day, forced to return to his hotel room to simmer with impatience like so many young men desperate for the *Tai Pan*'s attention. Here in Hong Kong,

Emanuel was just another nobody—another greenhorn with something to sell but with no connections.

Today was the seventh time he had made the trip and the seventh time he had returned to the hotel with nothing to show for it. He reached for his glass and emptied the brandy in one gulp.

A pebble shattered the windowpane and fell near his right foot. Startled, Emanuel spilled brandy on his shirt. "What the—?" he muttered, pushing open the French windows. He looked down to the street. Li was signalling for Emanuel to come downstairs.

"Jardine go-down, Jardine go-down. He wan you come now!"

There was no time to change. This was the moment he had waited for. He grabbed his bag. He needed to check that the storage receipts were still there, to touch the reality of his destiny. But the scrips were gone! Replaced with a small bundle of sticks.

Outside, Li yelled, *"Plis to come, Sir Wil-do Bay-lay-low-see!"*

Emanuel seized his coat and hat and ran down the stairs two at a time. Li had a rickshaw waiting. Emanuel climbed aboard and felt his shoulders hit the back of the seat as the chair pulled away. Li, as usual, ran ahead, waving wildly at pedestrians to open a path. Emanuel clutched his bag with its useless contents to his chest. Overhead, grey clouds turned black. Humidity thickened around him.

When they arrived, Li had quite forgotten himself in the excitement and had preceded Emanuel up the stairs, shouting, *"Bay-lay-low-see! Bay-lay-low-see!"* He ran headlong into a phalanx of Sikh bodyguards, who tossed him back down the stairs. Li sprang to his feet. *"No ploblem, no ploblem,"* he shouted. Emanuel's instinct was to help. But a clerk—a young, pock-faced English lad about Emanuel's age—called out his name.

"Mr. Bil-bos?"

"Belilios," Emanuel corrected him.

"This way." The scab-cheeked young man knocked and opened double doors.

Emanuel entered the inner office. Behind him, the doors closed.

Jardine was seated on a high chair at a small desk more suited to a clerk than a man of influence and wealth. He wore an ink-stained white glove and was writing in an oversized ledger with a penholder and nib.

It was a large room with windows overlooking the harbour and tele-scopes pointing out to the eastern and western passages. On the left hung a chalkboard that covered the entire wall and contained the names of vessels along with their destination, lading, dates of departure, and return. To the right a well-used wingback sat like a throne beside the fireplace. Emanuel curled his lip—these English and their need to make everything like home. On the side table beside the chair he saw a small plate on which a line of ants and a cockroach competed for biscuit crumbs and bits of cheese. A crystal decanter half filled with red wine stood beside the victuals. The room's dank quality and a lingering sulphurous odour seemed designed to make visitors uncomfortable. Without looking up from his writing, Jardine leaned to his left and broke wind. It burst with such ferocity that Emanuel was surprised the man's britches did not tear off.

"Come closer," Jardine said.

Emanuel stepped into the miasma and coughed.

"Catching the ague?" Jardine said. "Try a hot bath, not a cold one as so many griffins think, but a hot one; it opens the pores."

He took off his ink-stained glove, stepped off his chair, and let out another wallop of wind as he walked toward the crumbs on the table. Emanuel followed.

"Stay," Jardine said, as though to a dog. Emanuel stood still. "I judge you to be a, how shall we put it, a compliant fellow. Are you?"

Emanuel did not respond.

"What?" Jardine said.

"Nothing, sir. I said nothing."

"Nothing comes from nothing—mend your speech lest your tongue mar your fortune." He cocked an eyebrow, wondering if his guest had recognized the quote. "Shakespeare, dear boy—*Twelfth Night*."

"Mister Jardine—" Emanuel began.

"You have the scrips?"

Emanuel hesitated. He felt the handle of his carpet bag in his sweaty palm. He wondered if he should come clean and say they were missing. But he may never get another opportunity to speak with Jardine. Make the deal first. Then find the little turd who lifted them.

"Well, do you?" Jardine growled.

"Yes, sir. I do."

"My offer is $100 per chest."

"Surely sir, you jest," Emanuel said.

"Take it and be off with you," he said, reaching for a morsel on the plate. He brought it to his mouth. Emanuel saw a red ant on the crumb and said,

"No!"

"No? What do you mean, no?"

"There is an ant on your food."

Without taking his eyes off his visitor, he placed the morsel into his mouth, chewed, and swallowed it. "And you, sir, are an ant in my world," he said. "You have come to feed at my table from the scraps I choose to leave behind and now you will do as you are told."

"Now see here ..."

"You are not cut out for this life because you are timid just like the rest of them out there, looking for the easy way into this trade. You arrive with lading, look for someone like me, thinking to make a quick sale. I have spent thirty years laying the foundation for my business. I have fought wars and lost fortunes—I have made a commitment to this place, boy, and that has cost me a lifetime of struggle. And you want to achieve what I have in one week!" His face reddened and his hands shook as he poured himself a draught of wine.

"Sir, I ..."

"I what? You will do as you are told. I made you wait in the anteroom and you did. I made you come without prior notice and you did. I made you stand there and take in the sweet aroma of my emanations and you did. Now you will take my offer and return home, unless of course ..." He left the thought dangling.

"Unless what, sir?"

"You can try selling to Sassoon. They have a trading house up the street. One Jew to another might be better suited ..."

Emanuel felt his face redden. *"King Lear,"* he said. "That quote was from *King Lear,* not *Twelfth Night,* you stupid old man."

He ran out through the crowded anteroom, down the stairs, and into the street. Li waved him toward a waiting rickshaw but Emanuel ignored it and headed to the hotel on foot. He flung the useless bag into the gutter. His hat fell off and rolled down his back but he couldn't have cared less. Lightning flashed in the distance. Moments later, thunder cracked over-head. All he had worked for, all he had dreamed about—gone.

Images of his youth, mocked by others, friendless and alone, entered his mind. He elbowed through a wall of gawkers, quickening his pace until he was running like a deranged fellow. He did not notice Li chasing him, nor did he see the sandy-haired lad stick out his foot.

Emanuel tripped and fell, rolling like a barrel on the cobblestoned street.

PEARL

When she peeked out from behind the curtain at the *gweilo*, she was not looking at him so much as she was interested in the pendant that hung around his neck. It was a six-point star. She wished she were brave enough to reach out and touch the shiny thing, but she was a little afraid of his blue eyes.

This foreigner must have come from a blue country, she thought. Looking at blue trees, blue mountains, and blue rivers must have turned his eyes blue as well. She retreated into the cabin. Quickly she looked around for a mirror. She had an urgent need to look at her own eyes. They were brown, she thought, but she was not certain because she had never noticed. In fact, it suddenly occurred to her that in all her six years she had never properly examined a reflection of herself. She was not at all certain what she looked like. She ran her fingers over her hair, her forehead, her cheeks, her little nose and small mouth. Did she look like her mother or her father? There was only one way to find out. She exited the compartment and looked over the side. But the water undulated with the motion of the sampan and she could not see her face clearly. Frustrated, she stood up and threw her arms around her father's leg. She looked at the *gweilo* again. He returned her stare, and then he winked. Her little heart beat faster. What a strange sensation, she thought. It made her want to laugh. So she put her face behind her father's knee. She remembered what her mother had told her: *It is rude to show your teeth when you laugh.*

They reached the wharf and the stranger got off. He was a large man with a big belly. Her father carried the foreigner's bags. She wondered what was in the cases. When they reached the big white building, the man gave her father some coins and disappeared through a swinging door. *That is a rich English gweilo,* he said, jerking his head in the direction of where the fat man had disappeared. And now they were rich too because of that man with the blue eyes and the star dangling from a string around his neck.

On the way home, they stopped to meet up with her uncle who was guarding salt fish on the roof of a fisherman's hut. He had been up there all day chasing off seagulls. He was a thin man with a large head, brown, almond-shaped eyes, and high cheekbones. She knew he was not a real uncle. But her father said she should call him by that name. She liked him. He would tell her stories and speak to her in different languages. She wondered if Uncle could teach her some English so that she could speak to the *gweilo* and maybe she could be rich, too. She walked between the two men, holding their hands in hers. Uncle's left hand was never used and he tucked it into his belt. He said it was like that since birth. She liked feeling these men's palms, calloused and hard, rough and warm. Her little soft hands felt safe in theirs, as though she were wearing gloves made of rocks.

With the coins he had earned that day, her father bought them each a bowl of noodles from the street vendor across the road from where they lived in Wanchai. This wasn't just any bowl of noodles. She found a piece of pork in it. The three slurped their meal happily, sitting on wooden stools at a square table. All around them, customers mingled with hawkers. Food sellers peddled smoked pork, steamed fish, and more dumplings than you could imagine. There was a laundry beside the food stall. Behind them was a net-mending shop and across the street the herbalist was busy consulting with a client. She loved that shop. There were counters on either side containing dried roots, flowers, barks, and reptiles. Pieces of animal soaked in liquid inside big glass jars while sacks of seeds, grains, and nuts stood side by side in the street. On the walls were dozens of small drawers from where the herbalist scooped out powders and herbs that he pulverized with a mortar and pestle. He was doing that now for his client, who sat patiently on a high stool. Sweetness from the smoked pork, the saline chicken stock, the egg-flavoured noodles, acrid salt fish, mixtures of oils, and fried dumplings filled the air.

A staircase next to the herbal shop led up to their one-room apartment. She was tired and wanted to go home. But the two men were talking excitedly in Cantonese. They mentioned the *gweilo* and his "opium." Uncle said,

"There is a curse upon those who sell it."

"I know about that," her father said with a dismissive wave of his hand.

"Carrying chests from ship to ship or from ship to shore is fine, but you are talking about selling it to Chinese people."

"If we don't someone else will. Why shouldn't we profit?"

"The mothers of addicts have put a curse on opium traders. Your sons will all die young for three generations!"

"Aiyah! You Christians are so superstitious."

"You are not afraid?"

"I have a daughter and no sons—and I don't intend to remarry. C'mon, Aleandro. This *gweilo* is our chance to make a fortune."

On and on they talked and talked. Bored, she put her arms on top of the table and nestled her head on them. With a stomach full of hot noodles, she soon gave way to sleep.

When she woke up she was in the apartment, lying on a kapok mattress that her father had placed under the window. She sat up and rubbed her eyes. *Ba-bah* was asleep on one side of the room and Uncle on the other. Both were snoring. The herbalist was boiling something below. She could hear the gentle popping of bubbles and smell the pungent aroma of something rotten mixed with the sweetness of honey. She reached into the pocket of her tunic and grasped the piece of jade she always kept there. She squeezed it in her palm. It was cool to the touch and as solid as ever. Reassured, she stood up and looked out the window onto the empty street bathed in moonlight. When she looked up at the night sky, a star twinkled as if it were winking at her. She leaned her cheek on her arm and stared up at it. One day, she thought, I'll have one just like that.

EMANUEL

Face down and winded from running, Emanuel heard a raspy voice in his ear:

"Can you stand, sir?"

Slowly Emanuel got to his feet and dusted himself off.

Li, doubled over from having given chase, handed him his hat.

A small crowd had gathered to ogle. Chinese men, street urchins and hawkers, and a European or two formed a small arc around the *gweilo* who had collapsed on the front steps of the Hong Kong Hotel.

"Aleandro Remedios," the lad said. It surprised Emanuel to hear the name. "Mulatto—half Portuguese," the boy said, indicating his hair. "Half something else."

"You!" Emanuel growled and lunged at the robber with both hands. Aleandro feinted to one side then darted through the crowd. "Stop! Thief! Thief!" Emanuel yelled as he shouldered onlookers out of his way. The crowd turned in the direction of Aleandro's escape.

"There! There!" they shouted, pointing across the street.

A crack of thunder, a streak of lightning, and a sudden downpour made the crowds scatter. The torrential rain acted like a curtain, obscuring his vision. Emanuel screamed in frustration. Water soaked his hair and trickled over his brows. He wiped his eyes, and in the few moments of clarity he saw Aleandro across the street holding something in his hands. It looked like a bundle of wooden sticks. Emanuel recognized them immediately. His scrips! Then, strangely, he saw Li walk up and stand beside the little shit.

"Hold him!" Emanuel yelled at Li. But the two turned and sprinted east. Emanuel gave chase past the Venetian buildings of Central District and past jetties crowded with fishing vessels of every shape and size.

Emanuel felt a stitch in the side of his lower abdomen but was determined to catch up. The miscreants plunged into a warren of lanes. Emanuel lost sight of them momentarily. He stopped, steadied himself against a wall, and panted.

"Bah." He spat out the word and flung his coat aside. It landed in a puddle. He ground his teeth and clenched his fists. "I'll squash them like bubbles."

He rushed in the direction he had last seen them, through increasingly narrow alleyways, past huts and mud shacks, brick buildings and lean-tos, crammed one against the other on both sides of the tight lane. Chinese men, women, and children were everywhere, huddled in open doorways against the rain—not a European in sight.

Then he saw them.

They were looking at him as though they were waiting for him to catch up. He took a deep breath, ignored the stitch in his belly, the rubbery feeling around his thighs, and the collapsing ache in his lungs. He ran toward his targets. They fled, threading between food stalls, wooden tables, and stools toward a herbalist shop. He reached it just in time to see them scamper up the stairs, open a door, and enter. He pursued them and burst through just as the door was closing.

Emanuel found himself in a dimly lit room. An oil lamp sat on a wooden table against the far wall. The little girl from the sampan was under it—hugging her knees to her chest, eyes wide with astonishment.

Standing across the room, Li held the scrips. Emanuel heard the door slam behind him. He turned around. Aleandro looked at him. He had a knife in his hand.

"Senhor, we wish to help you sell your opium."

"By sticking me?"

"No. We have a proposal—a business proposal."

"*Plis, plis.*" Li bowed several times and indicated a wooden stool.

Keeping his eyes on the blade in the mulatto's hand, Emanuel sat down slowly. His body tensed. His heart raced. Outside, the downpour had abated.

The little girl stepped in front of him. She held a tin cup in both hands. It smelled of chrysanthemum. He took it from her. She ran and hid behind her father's leg.

"*Say Tai Pan to the gweilo,*" Li ordered in Cantonese. But the child was too shy. "Bo Jue," Li said, pointing at her.

"Senhor, her name is Bo Jue—'Pearl' in English. She is his daughter," Remedios said, sheathing his blade.

"A beautiful child," Emanuel said.

"No, not beauty. Bad girl," Li said, gently stroking his daughter's head.

"Like most Chinese who are given a compliment, my friend is obliged to diminish it so that she will not grow up arrogant and with a swelled head."

"I see," Emanuel said. Clearly these scallywags were not interested in harming him—yet. The mulatto had on a dirty shirt, yellowed at the collar, wide trousers, and leather shoes—one of which was open at the toecap. He took a seat across the table. Li stood beside him. Emanuel stared at the purple scar on Li's head and sipped his tea. The warm liquid was sweet and soothed his parched throat. He set the cup down. That pungent reek of fear he sensed upon first entering the room had been replaced with the stale tang of chicken broth and pork that larded the air. He made a face.

"Give me back my scrips and let me go," he said.

"Yes, we shall. But first give us a moment of your time to explain our proposal."

He was out of breath. His muscles burned. He was tired from the chase and from the disappointments of the day. In hindsight, it had been rash of him to pursue the thieves. He was in unfamiliar territory. Could he defend himself properly against these ragamuffins, thin and small as they were? The little girl—she was a modifying presence in the room. And Li was clearly a proud father. Aleandro had sheathed his knife. Where was the threat? Emanuel felt his body unwind, a spring slowly relaxing its coils.

"You have one minute," he said, pulling out his pocket watch and setting it on the table. Immediately he regretted doing so. It was made of gold.

His hosts looked at it and then at Emanuel. Aleandro broke the silence.

"Jardine *Tai Pan* controls opium trading along the China coast up as far as Shanghai. He has his own army to protect his interests. He won't give you fair market value for your cargo. You are out a lot of money, my friend."

"You tricked me into coming here to tell me something I already know?"

Aleandro ignored the tone and continued. "Opium is greatly desired in China." Emanuel shifted in his seat, impatient for the young man with the big head to come to the point. "Those who live inland have to pay extra to have it transported to them by mules and camels. And the stuff they get is cut—good opium mixed with inferior sap."

"I am a wholesaler. I export to the highest bidder. How it is distributed in China is not my concern."

"Oh but it is, Senhor. The game has changed. You cannot sell your lading here in Hong Kong. So, why not go directly to the customer?" Aleandro paused to let the idea sink in. "They will pay 320, 350 per chest; and in *real de ocho. Peso de ocho?* Pieces of eight. Silver coins, my friend—without punches."

Emanuel raised his eyebrows. If this mulatto was telling the truth, he could almost double his investment in silver. He had not considered this possibility, having assumed that Jardine would pay him with a draft that could be drawn on banks such as the Oriental or the Chartered. Silver was mainly used for larger consignments, not small ones like his. *Real de ocho,* or Mexican silver, was especially prized because of its purity. So esteemed that it could be traded for cash at rates above its face value. Three hundred and twenty silver dollars would be worth far more when it was converted to cash. Not only that, but individual coins could be "punched." That is, a small amount of silver could be extracted and sold separately without diminishing the coin's face value or its potential market value. This was why foreigners liked trading with the Chinese. If he could do the same ... but that would be a great risk. There would be no turning back. Going head to head with the Jardine *Tai Pan,* braving waters infested with privateers—pirates—and walking into untapped Chinese territory with Li and Aleandro, two dockside coolies ... Emanuel rubbed his chin and ran his fingers through his hair.

"Go on," he said.

"I know people. Inland. West of Macau. They want good opium—Patna triple A, like yours—and they are willing to pay in silver. Good money for the good stuff. Simple," he said with a shrug.

"Who are these people?"

"A warlord and a priest," Aleandro replied without a hint of irony.

PEARL

Was there no end to the fascinating things that this *gweilo* had in his pockets? Already she had seen the six-pointed star that hung around his neck, but now the man produced a round gold-coloured thing that looked like a small version of the clocks she had seen on the face of a tower. It ticked loudly. The grown-ups were so involved in talking that they did not notice her moving away from behind her father's knee. Without taking her eyes off the gold thing, she reached the opposite side of the table. It had a white face on which two black needles pointed to strange back letters. She wanted to reach for it, give it a shake and put it to her ear to hear the ticking sound. But she resisted the urge. It was clear that the men were discussing something very important and she did not want to disturb them. Aleandro took out a sheet of paper and pointed his finger, saying words like *Victoria* and *Macau*, new sounds that she committed to memory. Clearly they were names of places because Aleandro translated from English to Cantonese, telling her *Ba-bah* what he had just said to the *gweilo*. The foreigner had a hairy face and beautiful eyes. His feet were as large as sampans.

The three men never stopped talking. No matter how many words came out of their mouths, more and more seemed to grow inside them. They must have talked late into the night because the next thing she knew she was waking on her little mattress not having remembered getting under the cover. She sat up and rubbed her eyes. The three men were still at the table. The oil lamp was extinguished and a candle had melted down to a lump, its small flame struggling to stay alive.

Eventually, the *gweilo* stood up and extended his hand. Her father put a small bundle of sticks into it. The foreigner counted them and smiled. Her father said, *Part-nah*. He lifted one of the stools and turned it upside down: *Flee leg, one chair.*

"He means—" Aleandro began.

"I know what he means," Emanuel said. "Three legs, one chair."

"Hai," Li exclaimed with a wide grin.

"We'll go upriver and we'll trade with your people. But have one over me and ..." Emanuel didn't finish his thought but wagged his finger at the men.

"We won't, Senhor, you have my word."

The *gweilo* left.

She could hear him going down the stairs. She ran to the window and saw him walk north toward the harbour. Dawn had illuminated the streets. Hawkers and food-stall workers were already busy with activity. Her father and Aleandro crowded in behind her. Once the *gweilo* was out of sight, they broke into a joyful whoop. They hugged each other, slapped their palms on the table, whooped some more, clanged tin cups against bowls, and erupted into a high-stepping dance. Were they crazy?

In the next moment, they were all down in the street headed for the chop shop. There, her father ordered half a soya sauce chicken. It came in a clay pot over a bed of rice. Not only that but a plate of steamed *gailan*—delicious and leafy, shiny and green—came with it. She had never seen so much food. And, after they had eaten every piece of chicken (except for the bones, which the two men sucked dry), every bit of vegetable, and every grain of rice, a large bowl of almond soup appeared. Her father ladled it into three smaller bowls.

"You drink it like this," he said.

Bringing it to his lips, he slurped loudly and drained the entire bowl in one gulp. "Aaah," he said, patting his stomach. Then Uncle did the same. Then it was her turn. The soup was cold and sweet and fragrant and tasted like the happiest day in the whole world.

Her father opened his mouth and belched loudly. Uncle did too. Both men turned and looked at Pearl. It was her turn to show appreciation for the meal. She opened her mouth and made several attempts but no sound came out. Finally, she managed a tiny cough. Watching her effort made the two men laugh so hard they almost fell off their benches.

The following day and the day after that were filled with activity. Her father and Uncle rolled up their bedding and tied string around it, threw their metal plates and wooden chopsticks into an old sack, and swept out the flat above the herbalist shop. Pearl put her own things in a bundle and tied the edges together in a bow, leaving enough room to thread her arm through the top. When they exited the flat, her father nailed two pieces of wood across the door. Across the slats, Aleandro wrote in Chinese: *Returning soon.* Her *Ba-bah* drew the character for peony—his wife's name and the only pictogram he knew.

At the harbour, they boarded a *lorcha*—a vessel with one large sail in the centre and smaller ones in front and at the back. Pearl had seen many of these sailing in the harbour. It was much, much larger than her father's sampan and she could run up and down the top deck that was as big and as wide as the Praya or the avenues in Central District. While her father and Uncle supervised coolies who were loading the ship with large chests, Pearl explored. She opened a door at the rear of the vessel. A ladder stretched down below decks. Her heart pounded. She wondered whether she should venture into the darkness.

Her father and Uncle were helping the *gweilo* on board. Once on deck, the three of them started talking, pointing at the sky, holding fingers to the wind, and inspecting the chests. If the day before yesterday was any indication, these men would be engaged in talking and talking and talking. They would not notice her absence. Her heart raced as she descended. When she reached the bottom, her eyes adjusted to the dimness.

It was a large room. To her left, hammocks swung from the ceiling. In front, a series of benches lined the walls, and sticking out of the port-holes were long oars. She had seen such a ship before but only from a distance. This vessel could run fast, driven by wind and rowers.

"Bo Jue!" her father yelled. And again, "Bo Jue!" He sounded angry. She ran back up the ladder and opened the door.

"I'm here, *Ba-bah*," she said.

"Aiyah!" he yelled, wagging his finger in her face. His eyes bulged with annoyance. He shook his finger at her. "I thought you had fallen overboard. You scared me to death. What if you fell into the water? Do you think you are a fish? Bad girl."

Holding her by the wrist, he walked briskly to the front of the ship, Pearl stumbling behind him. He opened the door to a storage locker and pressed her into it. "Stay in here until we reach our destination—at least I will know where you are."

The door slammed shut. A metal bolt was thrown.

Inside, it reeked of jute ropes and seaweed. Luckily there were several small holes just above her head. She could look through them if she stood on tiptoe.

She saw coolies loading chests from their sampans onto the deck and from the deck into the go-down below. Oarsmen climbed aboard and took up their positions. Then ropes were pulled. The large centre sail rose and caught the wind with a thump. She felt the ship lurch forward. From below decks, she heard muffled chanting. It was the sound of oarsmen pulling and releasing their paddles to the rhythmic pounding of a drum.

What had she done that was so bad? And how long would she have to stay in this place? Forever and ever? Her eyebrows narrowed and her mouth shrank into a pout, its corners turned down at the edges. Her face felt hot. She banged her little fists on the door: *Let me out, let me out,* she shouted in Cantonese. But the door did not open. She sat down on a pile of damp ropes and kicked the door with her heels. It bowed but would not break. So she kicked some more, yelling at the top of her lungs until exhaustion made her stop. She sniffed and licked salty tears that had reached the sides of her mouth. Her feet hurt from kicking and she was hungry.

Outside she saw Uncle and the *gweilo* talking to *Ba-bah.* She could not hear what they were saying but it looked like they were pointing in her direction and arguing about something. This renewed her energy.

She sat down on the ropes, raised her legs, and stomped on the door as if she was running on the spot. The drumming rang like thunder inside the tiny space. She didn't care that her feet hurt, she didn't care that the noise was deafening, she didn't care that she sounded like a crazy person. She yelled at the top of her lungs: *Let-me-out-let-me-out!*

The bolt was thrown and the door opened. Pearl saw her father and ran to him. He wouldn't look at her. Instead he stood facing the open sea, steadying himself with one hand on the rail and the other fisted on his hip. When she looked up at her father's face, she saw a little tear trickle down his cheek. She reached out and held on to the hem of his tunic with one hand. With the other, she reached into her pocket and clutched the piece of jade her mother had given her.

Daughter and father stayed immobile for a long time, waiting for the enmity to change from its hardened edges into something softer. She is just like her mother, he thought. I shall have to fight her for the rest of my life.

As for Pearl, she no longer felt she needed to hold on to his leg, nor hide behind it when she was embarrassed. The hem of his tunic felt rough. It was all she required for comfort at that moment. That and the green stone she held in her palm.

Later, when they gathered for a meal, they sat, the four of them, on stools surrounding an upturned wooden crate that served as a table. On it was a fresh steamed fish and a plate of vegetables. Each had a bowl of rice and chopsticks, although the *gweilo* ate with a fork. No one spoke. But more importantly, her father refused to look at her.

The *lorcha* pitched and jawed gently. Water lapped against her hull, her wide bow cutting steadily through the waves. Pearl noticed that out at sea, the air was different from the steamy harbour. It was cooler and lighter. Also, there was so much more room than she was used to on a sampan or at home. Here, she could actually feel herself growing.

They continued eating in silence. Using her chopsticks, Pearl cut off a piece of fish, reached across the makeshift table, and put the morsel in her father's bowl.

He looked at it. Without a word, he picked it up with his chopsticks and put it in his mouth. Pearl felt a smile on her face. In her head, her mother's voice reminded her that women should not show their teeth in public. So, she covered her mouth.

Standing on the riverbank, he tossed a flat pebble at the water and watched it skip across the surface.

"Simple," Emanuel said aloud and let fly another stone. It bounced off the water like a frog hopping off lily pads.

The proposal that Aleandro had laid out a few days ago was straightforward: for the cost of a *lorcha,* her crew, and some provisions, they had sailed forty nautical miles east and anchored off Coloane Island near Macau. From there they had loaded the chests onto *centipedes*—rowboats manned by local fishermen—forded the slough, and made a three-day trek upriver into China. Their destination (where he was now standing) was a remote village in the middle of nowhere. Here, the mulatto's priest would introduce Emanuel to the local warlord, who would buy the opium for a pile of silver, and then they would all return to Hong Kong as rich as Croesus.

Simple.

They had sailed, they had forded, and they had trekked, but they had not sold anything. Emanuel flung another stone. It hopped once and disappeared.

They had set up camp days ago on the beach. Steps away were the remains of a once flourishing parish. It now comprised a few uninhabited bamboo huts. Leafy vines, like a network of spindly arms, embraced the outer walls of these pitiful shacks. A large building stood at the centre. On its roof, a small bamboo cruciform sat askew.

When they went inside, they had found the priest dressed in his vest-
ments lying face down on the floor in front of the altar. Empty bottles of
rice wine were strewn about. There had been no congregants that day—
nor had there been for years.

When they turned him over, he was snoring. The sour aroma of vomit
and day-old alcohol wafted up from his skeletal face. He had collapsed: a
bump on his temple looked ready to burst. His rosacea nose was swollen
like a small tomato on his pale face. But it was his sandy-coloured hair
that Emanuel found interesting. And the man's cheekbones! Except for
the red nose, the priest resembled Aleandro.

They lifted him up and sat him on one of the pews. It was just a rough
bench that had somehow survived in a room that had been picked over
by thieves. Aleandro shook the priest by his shoulders.

"Father," he said in English. "Father, wake up!"

Li poured water into a tin cup and splashed it in the man's face. It was
enough to startle him awake. The priest opened his eyes. They were
brown like the mulatto's.

"Father, it's me, Aleandro."

The priest looked blankly at the people surrounding him and stopped
at a recognizable face.

"Aleandro, my son," he said and embraced him. "You've come, you've
come."

Emanuel recognized the accent—Portuguese.

"I said I would, Father. These are my friends. This is Father Remedios."

Father Remedios tried to stand but sat back down.

"I'm not at my best," he said, looking up at them with rheumy eyes.

"How is my mother?"

"The same, the same … did you bring …?"

"Yes, Father. I did. You will be free, soon. I promise."

They helped the man out of the church, walked him across the
yard to one of the huts. A beaded curtain instead of a door, a mud floor,
and a Bible, table, and cot with a crucifix on the wall were his only
belongings. Aleandro put him in the bed and signalled for the others
to parlay outside.

"What the hell is going on?" Emanuel demanded. He pointed a finger at Aleandro. "Your priest is a drunk. I warned you, if you try to put one over on me, I'd—"

Li grabbed Pearl and held her close.

"Senhor, had I told you, you would not have come."

"Damn right. Is there even a buyer? Are you going to stick me now?"

"No, Senhor, no. I am no liar. Hear me, please. Let us sit and discuss this calmly."

At the word "sit" Li let go of Pearl. He scurried over to a fallen tree trunk, dusted a small area with his hands, and indicated that Emanuel take a seat. He took out his water bottle, filled the tin cup, and held it out with two hands.

Emanuel ignored it. Instead of sitting he put one foot on the tree trunk and said, "This better be good."

"Once this was a thriving village," Aleandro began. "Father Remedios came to this place to be amongst the fishermen. He arrived with crates of books, wanting to convert the natives to Christianity. He found some success. The church was often filled. It was a happy place. My mother, Sophia, was very beautiful—a mulatto, half Chinese and half something else—she was his housekeeper. They fell in love. Yes, men of God fall in love—they are human too, no? They kept their feelings for each other secret. They had to. In time, I was born.

"I came out with brown eyes and straw-coloured hair. I was, all at once, proof of their loving union and a reminder to the congregation of their priest's shameful loss of self-control. The congregation felt betrayed. Parishioners deserted and before long the pews were empty. We could not leave. Where would we go? So we stayed and lived on fish and clams.

"Father is a Jesuit and very well educated. He taught me English and Portuguese. Cantonese I learned from Sophia and Macanese too. I also learned arithmetic. When I was fifteen, I went to Macau to find work. No one would hire me. To the Chinese I looked like a half-baked European. To Europeans I looked like an unfinished Chinese. So, I learned to steal—I became good at it.

"About one year later, I had some money and I returned here to find Father alone, dressed as he is today and saying mass for nobody. When he was finished, he told me what had happened. He hadn't eaten for a long time. Whatever possessions he had left he had traded for drink. You see, Generalissimo Wong had taken my mother."

Aleandro grunted and curled his lip. "Generalissimo," he said and sucked his teeth, "whatever that means! Wong gave himself that title when he killed his boss, the previous 'generalissimo.' Take away the title and his gold-braided uniform and he's just another thug with a small army of bullies."

He repeated what he had said in Cantonese.

Li spat, pointed to the scar on his head, and uttered something.

"He says that arsehole generalissimo attacked the farmers in his village and killed his wife when they could not pay protection. Now he wants payback ..."

"Meaning what?" Emanuel asked. "An eye for an eye?"

"No, Senhor. My friend is no killer."

"Then what?"

"Face," Aleandro said, running his knuckles several times across his cheek.

"I don't understand," Emanuel said.

"Patience, Senhor. Let me continue. Wong extorts money from villagers by providing 'protection.' If you don't pay, he will destroy your house, your boat, anything you own. He demanded money from Father. Of course he had none. So, Wong took my mother. Remember, she was young and still beautiful.

"'Bring something I want and you can have her back,' Wong said.

"When I heard this story, I vowed I would set my mother free. I walked back to Macau. From there I stole aboard a clipper and landed in Hong Kong. The only work I could get was to chase seagulls from the rooftops. One day I fell off the roof. I broke my arm. No one would help me except this man," he said, pointing at Li.

"Hai," Li said, pointing to himself.

"He made a splint and put it on. He took me to his home. He said he had seen me before and had heard me speak in English and in Cantonese when I was begging in the street. He wanted me to teach his daughter some words, maybe to write her name so that she could be a seamstress and be able to keep some records to make a living when she grew up. I agreed in exchange for a place to live. We pooled what money we had.

He purchased some medicine from the herbalist shop and nursed me back to health. But my arm did not heal properly, as you can see.

"Over time, I told him my story. And he told me his. Together, we looked for an opportunity to make some money—me to ransom my mother and he to regain face."

"Me, I chased seagulls and did a little pickpocketing. Every day he loaded opium off ships and rowed them to the storage boat. He learned to tell by their clothes, by the little hat on their heads, which ones were Jews and which not. Some had a ring with a star on it or wore a pendant around their necks. I taught him the only Hebrew I knew—'Shabbat Shalom'—that I heard your people say to one another in Central District.

"Then, one day he saw you. No bodyguards for protection like the other Jew merchants, no assistants, and no office, nothing except for the bundle of scrips in your bag. You were new to Hong Kong. So, we hatched a plan …"

"Bastards." Emanuel spat out a lump of phlegm. He drove his fist into the palm of his hand. They had played him from the beginning.

Aleandro paused to take a breath. He continued:

"Generalissimo Wong is an opium smoker. He also sells the stuff. He will pay silver for your goods."

"You fools!" Emanuel shouted at the sky. "This is a trap. What makes you think he will pay anything? He has an army. Guns. He will rip the cargo out of my hands and kill us all."

"No, he will not."

Emanuel cocked his head. Are you that naive or just stupid, he wondered.

Aleandro saw the look and stepped in closer: "There is a saying: *Feed the cow and you will always have milk.* We," he said, circling his finger to include them all, "we will supply him for years into the future."

"And if *we* don't convince this thug?"

"Then he will release you. And keep us. One day, when you are at home in Calcutta, you will receive a box. Inside you will see our heads."

Silence fell.

"I need this from you, Senhor," the mulatto continued. "Generalissimo Wong can make a fortune selling this opium. He knows it. If I show him how he can make more money he will release my mother. I will take her and Father with me back to Macau. I will support them. You can take your silver and buy more opium from India. Again Li and I will sell it to Wong. Again he will pay in silver—from Hong Kong to China to India and back to Hong Kong. Everybody wins. Senhor, do this and I am your devoted servant for life."

Emanuel looked at the two men. The little girl stood behind them. Her mouth formed a tiny O. He felt a rush of excitement ripple through his body. He could say no, pack up and return to Calcutta and face the embarrassment—the "I told you so"—of a failed ambition. Or he could take a leap of faith.

He kicked the ground. Sand sprayed the air. A gust of wind blew it back like tiny arrowheads hitting his face. "Let's do it," he said.

The following day, Aleandro packed two balls of opium in a cloth bag that he hung over Li's shoulder. The idea was to give them as samples for Wong to smoke. They were convinced that its excellent quality would be an enticement to make a deal.

Father Remedios had drawn a crude map to the Generalissimo's compound. Aleandro embraced his father and tucked the chart under his shirt. Li knelt down in front of Pearl. He smoothed her hair and hugged her tight. Then the two men walked away. Before disappearing into the thick green forest, they turned and waved.

Emanuel watched this dumb show and thought, If the plan works we will be set for life. If it doesn't … The prospect made his stomach turn.

Father Remedios made the sign of the cross and retired to his shack.

Pearl watched the two men disappear into the greenery. She turned and looked at Emanuel with a "what now" expression on her pretty little face. He walked down to the riverbank and sat, looking out onto the water. She followed, keeping a few yards of distance between them.

A day and a night and then another day and night passed. Pearl followed him wherever he went. At night, when he slept fully clothed on the floor of the church, she curled up against the opposite wall. At sunrise, when he stretched his arms and yawned, so did she. When he washed, so did she. When he picked raw clams from the shore to eat, so did she, breaking them with a rock just as he did. In the afternoon when he rolled up his pant legs, took off his shoes and socks, and sat under a banyan to get out of the heat, she did as well. Then toward evening when he tossed a pebble at the water, she watched with awe as it bounced across the surface.

He didn't know that he had spoken the word "simple" out loud. Nor did he realize until he had said it that Pearl was standing beside him.

"Simple," she repeated.

"Well yes, it can be once you know how."

She picked up a pebble and handed it to him: "Simple?" she asked.

"No, this is a pebble." He pronounced it deliberately for her: *peb-bell.*

"Pebble," she repeated flawlessly.

"Excellent. Now the important thing is to find a flat one." He picked one near her feet. "Flat, see," he said, showing it to her.

"Flat pebble," she said.

"That's right, a flat pebble. You are a clever girl. Now it's all in the wrist," he said, cocking and releasing his wrist. "You have to snap at the wrist, see. That creates speed and speed creates distance." She mimicked his action. "Now watch," he said, and threw the stone. It bounced across the water.

Pearl's eyes bulged with excitement.

Immediately, she reached into the pocket of her tunic. Her fingers felt the cold flat piece of jade she kept there. It would be the perfect stone, she thought. Her heart raced. But a little voice in her head told her not to use the memento—not yet. She sensed that there would be another opportunity and withdrew her hand from her pocket.

She turned her attention to the stones around her feet. Finding one, she imitated the *gweilo*'s stance, wound up the pitch, shifted her weight, and snapped her wrist expertly. The stone skipped across the water, over and over as though it would never stop.

Emanuel was amazed and clapped his hands. Encouraged, she searched for another stone to toss. Again it skipped on and on, even farther than the first one.

"Well I'll be ..." he said and laughed out loud.

His delight made her giggle at first, then she burst into a triumphant and full-throated laugh, completely forgetting to cover her mouth.

Shouting interrupted their fun. It was Aleandro's voice. Emanuel picked Pearl up and, carrying her on his hip, they rushed back toward the church. Father Remedios was there before them. Aleandro was alone.

"Where is Li, what happened?" Emanuel asked.

"Ba-bah," Pearl shouted.

"He is all right. He is fine. Uncomfortable but fine," Aleandro said. "The good news is that Wong is interested—" Pearl broke away and ran toward the path where she had seen Li disappear days ago.

"Ba-bah!" she yelled, plunging into a thicket of palm fronds and greenery.

The men sprang into action and chased her. They stopped abruptly when they saw Pearl back out of the jungle, her arms pressed rigidly to her sides. In front of her was a soldier in a khaki uniform and peaked cap. His rifle was aimed at her head.

She walked backward, her eyes on the Chinese devil—they were dressed just like the ones that had attacked her village on market day long ago.

When she got close enough, Emanuel reached out and pulled the girl behind him. She clutched his hand and peeped out from around his waist.

No one breathed.

The soldier saw Aleandro. Slowly, without taking his eyes off them, he lowered his rifle and yelled in Chinese over his shoulder, aiming his voice toward the jungle from where he had just emerged.

There was movement amongst the foliage. One dozen soldiers with slung rifles appeared in single file. Each one led a donkey tethered to a rope on their wrists.

"This is the captain who will escort us and our cargo to the Generalissimo," Aleandro said in English, then repeated it in Cantonese.

The captain looked them up and down, spat to one side, and slung his rifle. He was a stout, round-faced young man with beady eyes that made him look like a pig. He took off his cap, wiped the inside of it with a handkerchief, and mopped his bald head. Sweat stains darkened his armpits. He ordered the squad to rest. They did so, stacking their rifles in tripod formations, uncorking their canteens, and lighting up cigarettes. Then he sat on the ground and leaned his back against a tree—one leg pulled up to his chest, an arm resting languidly on his knee.

"What happened?" Emanuel whispered. "Did you see Sophia?"

"Where is Ba-bah?"

"He is at the Generalissimo's compound. He kept Li to ensure my return. These are Wong's troops. They will pack the chests and together we will all go to him. We leave tomorrow."

"I knew it," Emanuel said. "We will be killed—all of us."

He turned on his heel and took no more than a step when the captain stood up quickly and yelled a command. His troops sprinted into action. Within seconds, a dozen rifles were aimed at Emanuel's chest.

Aleandro, showing his palms, said something to the captain, who smirked and lowered his weapon. He commanded his soldiers to do the same. Then he hawked a glob of phlegm that hit the ground like an oyster and sauntered back to the tree, where he sat as he did before.

Aleandro motioned his friends to follow him into the priest's cabin.

Emanuel sat in the corner and started to shake. He gripped one hand over the other, trying to stop it from trembling. His mouth was dry. He hated the feeling. It was not fear that made him quake; it was the loss of control.

Aleandro watched Emanuel. "All will be well," he said. "Trust me."

"Ter coragem, não tenha medo, faça o trabalho," Father Remedios added.

"Portuguese," Aleandro said. *"Have courage, be not afraid, and do the work*—a passage from the Bible."

It was a fitful night. Aleandro spent most of the time talking to Pearl in Chinese, which Father Remedios translated for Emanuel. They had taken a wrong turn that delayed them but eventually they found the Generalissimo's compound, he explained. It was only one day's walk from here. They had been received well and the Generalissimo was happy with the gift of two opium balls. After Pearl fell asleep, Aleandro continued his tale. "Wong wants more. Li is a hostage, and if we do not show up tomorrow with the consignment, bad things will happen."

The journey to the Generalissimo's compound took all day. The captain led the way riding bareback, his legs dangling like elephant trunks on either side of the donkey. Behind him, walking single file, were Aleandro—Pearl on his shoulders—followed by Emanuel. Father Remedios, not well enough to make the trek, remained in his cabin, where he said he would pray for their safe return. He blessed them. Emanuel gripped the Magen David hanging around his neck and felt the spikes of the six-pointed star dig into the palm of his hand.

Emanuel was surprised by what he saw when they arrived at the compound. He had expected a military encampment with tents and bivouacs such as he had seen in the north end of Victoria. This was like a walled city.

A drawbridge lowered at the captain's command. Inside, the place was designed in three concentric circles. The outermost circle was the wall with its turrets. The second were barracks for the soldiers. The innermost area, surrounded by its own wall, was a tranquil compound made up of brick and clay bungalows with green tiled roofs.

A series of footpaths, edged with flowers and shrubs, wound between the bungalows. Here a eucalyptus tree, there a banyan spread its multiple trunks like a mini forest. They walked past aloe bushes, pots of chrysanthemum, hillocks of lilies with white and yellow petals, ponds full of golden koi, small bridges that forded rivulets, a waterfall, and an eight-tiered pagoda. The air was redolent of sandalwood incense.

The Generalissimo was rumoured to have thirty-two wives and concubines and ninety children. No wonder the man smoked opium.

And for this delectable pastime, he had built a special chamber overlooking a pond. It was a plain room compared to the ornate indulgences found in other areas of his realm. Two dark-brown teak cots lay separated by a bedside table, also made of polished teak. There was no decor on the walls, no flowers, no incense. Why go to the trouble when the point of *chasing the dragon* was to escape earthly things and submerge yourself in the splendours that awaited you behind eyelids hooded in exquisite reverie?

The Generalissimo received his visitors in this austere room, where he lay on his side on one of the wooden divans. He was thin, dressed in a traditional Chinese gown and mandarin collar. He had white hair and a bushy moustache, a long face and thin lips. His wire-rimmed glasses sat low on the bridge of his nose. When he spoke, he peered over the top of the frames with black eyes. Surrounding him were servants, women (wives, Emanuel guessed), and hangers-on, all of them alert as dogs waiting for a treat.

Pearl took an instant fear of him. Aleandro held her hand. She hid behind him and tried to make herself very small. Emanuel stood beside them, tapping his toe. They had had to wait for Wong to arrive. When he did, he had said nothing for a long time. Then he asked for a report from one of his servants on the recent plantings in the north garden. Wong listened, asked some questions, gave some directions, then dismissed the gardeners.

Emanuel watched all this with growing impatience. The place had an oily ambience. A sickeningly sweet aroma clung to the air from the previous day's smoke. Two servants prepared Wong's pipe while he spoke in Cantonese. Finally, Generalissimo Wong turned to Aleandro.

"*That is a pretty child. How old?*" He had changed his tone to a high-pitched voice unlike the one he used when ordering his servant around.

"*Seven or eight I think,*" Aleandro said.

"*Mmmm ...*" Wong nodded and sniffed the air.

"*This barbarian smells,*" he said, pointing at Emanuel. His hand was large and wide, like one belonging to a farmer or a labourer. The baby fingernail was so long it curled downward.

"*Your Excellency said you wished to see the foreigner. This man can supply—*"

"*Yes, yes, I know, I know ... it all depends on price ... very difficult ...*"

"What is he saying?" Emanuel hissed.

"Just being polite, nothing, it's nothing," Aleandro replied.

"Is he going to smoke or does he want to do business? Let's get to the point."

"*Apologies, Excellency, the gweilo, he is—*"

"*Is just being a barbarian. I know the kind. No manners.*"

"*Your Excellency is right of course. No manners ... I am ashamed to ask if your Excellency has enjoyed the gweilo's gift?*"

"*A trick question. If I say yes, the price goes up, if I say no, you will think I am a tasteless peasant because we both know this is Patna triple A.*"

"*Sincerely, it was an innocent question.*"

"*There is no such thing.*"

"*No, of course not.*" Aleandro bowed, acknowledging his interlocutor's wisdom.

"For heaven's sake." Emanuel rolled his eyes. "The price is 350 silver dollars a chest," he said directly to Wong. "Yes or no?"

Everyone was stunned by the outburst.

Wong stood up.

"*Excellency,*" Aleandro said, "*I beg you not to take offence. The man is from India—he does not know how to behave.*"

Wong waved his hand. A servant appeared with a chair that he put down in the centre of the room facing the pond. The courtiers now shifted to stand in an arc behind the chair. Wong rested his elbows on the arms and let his hands dangle.

"We exchanging politeness," the General suddenly said in English. It was heavily accented but understandable. "You are surprised I speak English? I receive military training in Russia. I speak also Russian, some French, of course Cantonese and other dialects. You? How many language you speak, Mr. Bil-lice?"

"Hindi, Bengali, English," Emanuel sputtered.

"Hindi—useless, Bengali—also, English very good—like me."

"Now see here," Emanuel said.

Wong said something in Chinese and everyone laughed.

"All right," Emanuel said, "go ahead, have your amusement. I want—"

"You want?" the Generalissimo said. "Why so serious? Have some fun. Doing business must be fun."

Emanuel hung his head.

"You sad? Why for you sad? Aw-lie, aw-lie—sun almost come down. We parlay now. Two hundred silver dalla per chest."

"Ridiculous."

"*Aiyah,* two hundred silver dalla very good price."

Emanuel looked directly at Wong. The courtiers took in an audible breath. No one looked directly at the master.

"Are you a betting man, your Excellency?" Emanuel asked.

"Excellency? Ah Mr. Bil-lice, now you have manners. You want to be betting? You mean wager? You want to have some fun! What you like cards, dice, hey I know what. Turtle! We make wager on turtle run?" He translated what he said and the room burst out laughing again.

"Stones," Emanuel said.

"Stone? How you make stone to race?"

"Not to race, Excellency," Emanuel said and walked to the pond. He selected a pebble and threw it. Everyone watched. Six hops.

"I know how to do. I do when I a boy. I can make eight, ten, twelve time!" He repeated his boast in Cantonese. The courtiers applauded and nodded.

"Care to take a chance?" Emanuel asked and added, "Excellency?"

He let the question dangle in mid-air. Then he said: "We can stand here for a week, me asking for 350, you countering and so on. Why not settle it with one toss of a stone? If I win, you buy my opium for 350 per chest. If I lose, I'll take 200 per chest."

The Generalissimo translated the offer to his people, whispering the terms to *oohs* and *ahs* of interest. Aleandro pulled Emanuel's sleeve and said,

"Please Senhor, are you serious?"

"Deadly."

The Generalissimo shouted an order. Moments later, Li was brought out in stocks—a wooden yoke on his shoulder, his wrists in holes on either side.

"*Ba-bah!*" Pearl shouted. She tried to break away but Aleandro held her tight.

Li smiled at his daughter. He looked weary but did not appear to be hurt.

Wong's tone changed. Gone was the high-pitched politesse. He growled, "Throw, one time. I win, 200 dallah per and I kill stupid farmer. You win, 350 dallah per and you tik stupid farmer home. Now you still want to have some fun, *gweilo*?"

"Senhor, this is crazy," Aleandro said.

Gambling is the bastard's weakness, Emanuel thought.

"Hey, you want to wager or you want chit-chat to your friend?"

"I'll do you one better," Emanuel said. "You have with you a woman—Sophia. You win, 200 dallah per. I win, 350 dallah per chest plus that man and Sophia."

Wong translated quickly. The whispering turned into murmurs amongst his courtiers then into rapid exchanges flung excitedly between them. Advice was given, rejected, reworded, and considered. Finally,

"I like you. You know how to gamble. I tell you what. I give you what you say: I win, 200 dallah per. You win, 350 dallah per plus stupid farmer and the woman. I no like her anyway. Too skinny." Wong translated and the crowd laughed, nodding their heads. "But before you answer, *I want little girl to throw*," he said.

Wong grinned and jutted his jaw. One of the courtiers, his head like the mask of a skull, leaned over and whispered something lewd in his master's ear. He made an obscene gesture, poking his finger into his palm and sliding it back and forth. Wong wiped saliva off the edge of his mouth. He opened his hand and gestured to Emanuel as if to say, "Your move."

Silence descended.

"Agreed," Emanuel said. He nodded his head.

Wong shifted in his chair, surprised by the response. The child could not possibly out-throw him. The wager was won before it even began.

"But," Emanuel added, "perhaps the Generalissimo would care to up the ante to 400 per chest?" He raised four fingers.

Wong laughed. *"This is more than I have ever paid,"* he shouted in Cantonese and looked at Emanuel. Their eyes met. Emanuel saw him blink.

"Hai," Wong said and slapped his hand on his thigh.

"Senhor, this is crazy. What are you doing?"

Emanuel ignored him and took Pearl by the hand.

Wong swaggered to the bank, shaking his head and looking around his feet for the perfect stone. He found one, picked it up, and shook it in his fist. He blew on it, placed it just so on his fingers, wound his arm back, and let fly. It skimmed the surface for quite a distance before bouncing once, twice, three times—six, seven, eight, and a short hop for a ninth before disappearing. His flunky with the skeleton face yelled jubilantly and applauded. His entourage followed suit.

When the noise settled down, Emanuel led Pearl to the bank of the pond, crouched down, and picked up a pebble. He held the girl by the shoulders. "Remember what I showed you?" he asked. She looked at the stone, then at him, and nodded. "It's going to be all right," he said and placed it in her palm. He looked deep into her eyes. She looked back into his. He touched her cheek and stood up.

Pearl's heart started to pound. She knew what was at stake because she had heard the Generalissimo brag and the cacophony of side bets on her father's fate. She pulled back her arm to wind up the throw. Suddenly, she stopped. She opened her palm, looked at the stone, and then looked at Emanuel. He nodded his encouragement. She then saw her *Ba-bah's* face. He looked at her with pleading eyes—the same look her mother had that market day. But it didn't terrify her this time. Instead, she felt a warm and comforting embrace, as though her mother was present and giving her courage.

With her free hand she reached into her pocket and pulled out her mother's green memento. She heard her mother say, *"Be strong."* She placed the jade beside the stone she was about to throw. Cupping her hands together, she shook them as if they were two dice. They made clicking sounds like crickets calling to each other. Then she opened her palms, put the jade back in her pocket, weighed the pond stone in her hand, wound up the pitch, shifted her weight, and flung it over the water with a sharp flick of the wrist.

All heads moved, following the stone whipping across the pond—one skip, two, three—six, seven, eight—and four more in quick succession for a total of twelve.

Wong stared in disbelief.

Emanuel, Li, and Aleandro screamed with joy. Emanuel freed Li from the stocks. Pearl ran to her father, who grabbed his daughter and held her close to his chest. Jubilant, Aleandro performed a little jig of delight.

"She is a witch! Take your money and go!" Wong said, waving a finger at the skull-headed courtier who shuffled off to do his master's bidding. "Never bring her back," Wong screeched. He wagged his finger: "I tell you this: you want to play some games? I make the rules. You bring me Patna triple A—five hundred cases every year! You trade with no one else in China. Me only. If you do not bring to me or if you try sell to others in China I go and I find you—in Macau, in Hong Kong, in India— where you go I find you. Then I kill you. You do this ten year and I let you live. You want to play?"

"Why not a thousand cases? Why not fifteen years?" Emanuel said.

Wong sniggered. *"Gweilo* like to gamble," he said, touching his nose. "I like you. I promise, if I have to kill you, I make it fast."

The men loaded the silver dollars into sacks, slung them across their backs, and walked out of the walled compound. Sophia was released as promised. She hugged Aleandro and clasped her son's hand, refusing to let go for the entire journey. When the group reached the jungle, they stopped to rest and then continued the following day, reaching Father Remedios's parish by nightfall. The priest came out of his shack and saw his lover. They stood still, fifty paces apart, looking at each other in disbelief. Slowly they walked toward each other, closing the gap that had separated them for so long. When they embraced, their cheeks were awash with tears.

The following morning, Aleandro walked to the nearest fishing village and found someone willing to lease him a *lorcha*. He sailed back to fetch Emanuel and the others, and just as the sun began to set they headed for Hong Kong.

En route, Emanuel settled into a deck chair. Li and Aleandro sat on the floor, their backs against the port rail. Pearl snuggled in the space between them.

No words passed. None were required.

He was on his way to Hong Kong and from there he would journey back to Calcutta. What would he be going home to? Was it home any longer? What was home anyway—a place with a wife and a child? Or was home more than that?

He opened his eyes and looked around. Li and Remedios were asleep. Pearl was watching him. When she saw that he was awake, she got up from her nest between the two men and went to Emanuel. She climbed up onto his lap and put her head on his chest.

The boat rocked. Its hull slapped the water. He felt safe here. He felt content. He felt himself smile.

Above the horizon, lightning split the reddening sky like a flash of joy. Then thunder cracked. But the little girl did not stir.

Emanuel felt his body move from side to side, rocked by the bat-winged *lorcha* cutting through a gently undulating sea, gliding past steep bluffs of shadowed hills on one side and vast dim waters on the other.

When he stepped off the *wallah-wallah* and onto the ghats, Semah was there to greet him. He looked the same—a little thinner in the face perhaps but still round in the middle. And he seemed happy to see her. She leaned forward, beaming with happiness.

But there was no embrace. He gave her a chaste kiss on the cheek, his eyes looking over her shoulder.

"Where is Ayah Gita?" he asked.

"She's gone."

"Gone where?"

"She left. Stole some silver and disappeared."

"Ayah did?"

"Yes. Gone, just like that."

On the ride home in the landau, he sat to one side on the narrow bench. The space between them felt like ice. That same chilly rancour that had hung like a mantle over her estranged parents years ago was dragged by an invisible hand and dropped over her and her husband. But her mother's disillusionment had been sparked by her father's betrayal—here there was nothing concrete to substantiate this sense of separation. Semah struggled to discern a reason for his behaviour—the lack of an embrace, the silence, the distance between them. Perhaps he was just exhausted from travelling.

"Was it a successful journey?"

"Yes."

"And did you sell all your goods?"

"Of course I did. Did I not send you money to purchase and fit up a new house? Why do you pepper me with questions?"

She had that tendency—"peppering" people with questions. She had been a curious child—she knew that—and was now an even more curious woman. But "peppering"? Was she really that annoying?

His instructions had been succinct: *A mansion in Calcutta that befits a man of position, larger than the Sassoons', decorated as befits an English gentleman of means, with a salon for receptions, stables, and a landau* ... He wrote that he had to stay on for a few weeks to finalize his banking needs *"etc."* and would be on a clipper returning to Calcutta *"soon."* Semah had set about the task of finding such a house immediately, settling on one in Bow Bazaar that had belonged to the Danish ambassador, who had just vacated it for lodgings closer to Fort William. Days of shopping and decorating followed. Workmen, plasterers, whitewashers, window cleaners, furnishers, decorators, servants, and groomsmen flowed like schools of fish in, out, and about the mansion.

When they arrived, Emanuel got out and looked up at the house. It was wide and white. It gleamed with newness. Shrubs and flowers had been planted at the entrance. The home's green shutters were opened and welcoming. And he said ... nothing. Instead he walked in and up the stairs, each footfall echoing off the walls. He opened doors until he found the rooms he assumed to be his and went in.

He ordered a bath. Semah could hear the muffled sounds of water sloshing through the wall of her dressing room. She had followed him into the house and climbed the stairs then retired to her own rooms, where she stood now in front of a full-length mirror.

Perhaps she had changed, too. Maybe she could not see it in herself. But others might. Had he noticed something? Yes, she was certain there were subtle transformations, but nothing serious. If she were to be hypercritical, she would have to admit she was a little wider around the hips and that her cheeks were not as sculpted as they had been. Too much sitting around eating bonbons and not enough exercise, she thought. She ran a hand over her belly and turned sideways. It was flat and cinched at the waist by a corset. She scanned her face. Thank goodness for her blue velvet-lined *table de toilette* that contained secret concoctions in small corked bottles ordered especially from Watson's, the new apothecary on Park Street. Her favourite was *crèmes célestes*. It was a blend of white wax and spermaceti, mixed with sweet almonds and diluted with rosewater. When applied, it gave the skin a smooth, shiny complexion. A soupçon of beet juice dabbed sparingly made her cheeks glow. All in all, she was pleased with what she saw. Her hair was a riot of black curls piled elegantly on top of her head. "If you are tall, and you are, then make the best of it. Stand up straight, shoulders back, and dare anyone to comment," her mama had said.

No, she thought, if she had changed, then they were small, physical alterations. Her heart remained constant. She loved him. He had danced with her when no one else would. He had courted her, and together they had flummoxed the gossipers. He was a successful merchant despite his family's opposition. Emanuel was a good man. He had stuck by her and she would stick by him. She was convinced of that in the deepest part of her being.

What did it matter that he was acting a bit strangely? He had come home to her and now it was up to her to make it worthwhile. After his bath, there was silence from his rooms, which were adjacent to hers. He was resting in his bed, she surmised. She spent the rest of the day seeing to the meals and wondering what she could do to celebrate his return.

She had expected him to visit her bed at nightfall. In fact she was eager for it. Clean sheets scattered with rose petals, sandalwood incense, a bottle of Chablis, and one hundred candles illuminating her room. She had imagined this so many times when he was away. He would knock softly and she would reply, "Come in." The candlestick in his hand would show his face bathed in a buttery yellow. He would stride over to her, put the candle on the side table, and sit on the bed where she lay. Slowly he would lift her nightgown, inching it up over her shin, her knee. He would stop. Unbuckle her prosthetic limb and slip it off. Then he would bend over and kiss her on the mouth.

But he did not appear that night.

Lying alone in the flickering pall of candlelight, she said a little prayer. The only insight she gained was that patience was required. Now that he was back, there would be plenty of opportunities for them to make a baby—a boy and an heir. Yes, that is what she wanted. She would talk to him about this. Not now, of course, but when he was ready.

The following morning over breakfast she split a boiled egg and removed the crown, then spooned a dollop into her mouth. Emanuel, seated at the opposite end of the table, was deep in the middle pages of *The Calcutta Chronicle*.

"I thought we might host a reception," she said.

He lowered the newspaper and looked at her.

"A party," she added, revising the noun to make it less formal.

"A reception would be ... appropriate," he said. Semah beamed and set down her spoon, dabbed her mouth with her napkin, and said,

"Who shall we have? Your parents of course, and mine—"

"I shall give you a list," he said and returned to reading his newspaper. Semah felt her face drop. She rolled the napkin into a ball and threw it at the newspaper. It fell out of his hands. He stared at her, looking as if he had just been slapped in the face.

"Talk to me," she said. Then softer: "Why won't you talk to me?"

He stood up so quickly his chair fell over.

"I ..." he said and stopped. He looked at his watch then left the room.

Semah clenched her fist. She wanted to slam it on the tabletop but arrested the action in mid-air. What had she done wrong? Was the house not to his liking?

She had no idea how long she sat there at the breakfast table. Stunned by her husband's coldness, she shifted her mind deliberately to quotidian things, like the meals for the rest of the day and the pimple that was beginning to sprout on her neck. Was there someone else in his life? Could he have, in the short time he'd been in China, would he have found ... Dare she even use the word? No, she thought, slamming a door on the possibility. She picked up her napkin, folded it neatly, and placed it beside her plate. Then she reached for the bell to summon a maid to clear the dishes.

She stood when she heard a horse neighing outside and walked to the window. A groom had made a stirrup with his hands. Emanuel stepped in it and got up on his mount. He hung the sack he carried on the pommel and glanced toward the window where she was standing. When he saw Semah, he touched the brim of his hat and tipped it in her direction. Instinctively she raised her hand to wave. Then he rode off toward the railway station.

It was a Herculean effort not to rush out. She wondered what she would do were she to run after him. The servants were doubtlessly watching and listening. They would see their Memsahib chase after her husband and hear the plaintive howl that was lodged in her breast fly out of her mouth like the wail of a wounded heifer. How undignified. And besides, Emanuel had acknowledged her. He had tipped his hat—that counted for something. Didn't it? She replayed that instant in her mind's eye and it gave her hope. All would be well, she assured herself. Let time heal, as it had for Mama and Papa.

Three days ago, he had ridden into town with his wife's rebuke ringing in his ears. He had dismounted a block away from his father's warehouse and waited behind a pillar for Mr. Rustomjee to arrive. He had no interest in seeing his father—only his father's clerk.

The district was just waking up. River traffic stirred from its nocturnal silence and grew gradually to a dull roar as labourers arrived. Some squatted against the wall waiting to be hired for the day. They chewed *paan* for breakfast—a wad of betel leaf used like chewing tobacco—expertly rolled into spitballs and expectorated with gusto on the ground in front of them. The juice induced just the right amount of euphoria to help them through another muscle-busting morning of heaving and lugging goods from one conveyance to another. It was the day after Deepawali Puja and the men were eager to chew, hoping for blessings. Across the street food sellers unwrapped their stalls, their *chatties*—small wood-burning stoves—already fired up. Fish and onion patties sizzled in pans for eager customers stepping off the riverboats.

Mr. Rustomjee rounded the corner and stopped at the chai wagon across the road from his workplace. There he paid a few paise to the tea *wallah,* who handed him a clay cup of sweet milky liquid. He reached to take it. Emanuel spun him around by the shoulder. "Shush," he said, covering Mr. Rustomjee's mouth with his hand. "I don't want anyone to hear. Come with me," he whispered, leading the Parsi down a nearby lane. The tea *wallah* looked away as though the event had never occurred.

In the lane Emanuel asked Mr. Rustomjee if he knew where Ayah Gita had gone.

"Please sir, perhaps her family in the Hill Country is knowing?"

So Emanuel travelled to Patna and returned with nothing to show for his trouble. That was three days ago. Now it was night and he and Mr. Rustomjee were alone in the back office, upstairs in his father's warehouse.

"Dammit man, we are more than employee and the boss's son. I thought we were friends. Why did you send me on a wild goose chase?"

"Please sir, sir's father is making me not to tell. I am hoping her family could be spilling the beans for you so that is why I suggested you go to see them in Patna."

"I will pay for information."

"No, sir. That is not what I want. I am an honest man—a man of principle. I take pride in my loyalty. Your father is a great man. I cannot break promise with him."

Emanuel hung his head. Think man, think. How do you get the answer you want? You ask a different question, one that does not require an answer.

"All right my friend, let us do this: I will ask you yes or no questions. If you say no I will accept that, but if you remain silent I will assume the answer to be yes."

"Sir, I am not understanding."

"You'll see as we go along. Let's try it. Are you ready?" Mr. Rustomjee nodded. "Is Ayah in Calcutta?"

Mr. Rustomjee's eyeballs searched the ceiling. His mouth turned down at the corners like a tragedy mask. He remained silent.

"Good," Emanuel said. "Is she far from here?"

Mr. Rustomjee looked down at his lap and dusted his trouser leg with the palm of one hand. But he remained silent.

Emanuel leaned forward with his elbows on his knees. He put his fingertips together to form praying hands and started to name the city's districts alphabetically: Ballygunge, Barabazar, Beliaghata, Bowbazar, Chowringhee, and so on, pausing after each one to wait for an answer.

Mr. Rustomjee avoided the young master's eyes. He looked to the left and to the right. He glanced at the ceiling and then down at the impeccably shined toecaps of his black boots. In reply to each district named, he said a soft no.

When he got to Vidyasagar, Emanuel leaned back.

"I've named them all. Is she here or isn't she?"

Silence.

"Dammit, dammit." Frustrated, Emanuel stood up and wiped his face with his palms. He ran his fingers through his hair and massaged the back of his neck.

"Sir is naming only official districts ..."

Emanuel turned. Mr. Rustomjee was looking up at him like a cat that wanted to be held. He closed his eyes and conjured up a map in his mind. Starting from Howrah across the Hoogli River, he checked off the areas he had named that covered every part of Calcutta. And yes, there were districts within districts in the rapidly growing city. The Jews clustered around Bow Bazaar and were spreading south toward Park Street. The Parsis found settlements in pockets on either side of Chowringhee Street— the long, wide avenue that ran north–south, like a river bifurcating the town. Suddenly, Emanuel's heart beat a little faster. He felt his eyes widen.

"Chinatown," he said.

Mr. Rustomjee crossed his hands over his mouth and let out a muffled whimper. Emanuel rushed out of the office, down the stairs into the street. Mr. Rustomjee called out: "Sir is not to be going in the dark, sir! Sir!" Emanuel could hear his friend stomping down the stairs behind him. Then a clanking of gates and keys as Mr. Rustomjee struggled to lock up hastily.

Emanuel ran the few blocks to Chowringhee, where he saw a chair-cart. The only one left on the deserted avenue. Its owner had a stick-thin body. He looked as though he couldn't pull a hair out of his balding scalp, let alone a cart with a large man on it. Dark skinned and shallow cheeked, he was chewing his gums like a cow munching its cud. Emanuel leapt on board.

"Tangra District," he commanded.

Shocked into action, the man shrugged on a harness and pulled hard. They moved south. Emanuel looked behind him and saw Mr. Rustomjee arrive where he had just left. Winded from the chase, the Indian bent over

and rested his hands on his knees. Then Emanuel saw him straighten up
and mop his brow with the back of his sleeve.

The cart-puller's legs worked like pistons. His bare feet slapped the
road, making the sound of hands clapping. Emanuel and his beast of
burden plunged into the deserted main street of the city. The farther south
they went, the more he could smell the greasy aroma of cattle hides. He
was headed toward Tangra—the tannery district built on low-lying marshy
land where Hakka Chinese ran factories dedicated to making leather.
Because they used cattle hides, Hindus did not always favour the area.

They turned east off Chowringhee and headed deep into a warren of
lanes that twisted and turned, braiding into each other like a web made
by a drunken spider. The cart-puller stopped and set down his yoke. He
turned to his passenger and mumbled something in Bengali. He was not
prepared to go any farther into the apostate zone. Obviously he was a
Hindu—a scrawny, slope-shouldered island of principle standing barefooted in a morass of quotidian opportunism.

Emanuel stepped off the chair and tossed a few paise onto the seat. He
quickly got his bearings, and recalling his first and subsequent visits to
Yuen's establishment, he walked toward it.

Behind him the chair-cart wheeled away. The sound of its owner's feet
slapping the road was drowned out by the cries of Chinatown at night,
where voices came alive as the rest of the city slept. Down narrow lanes
lit only by ambient light from lanterns shining out of windows above his
head, he followed his instinct toward his destination. Darkened doorways
were almost all loaded with couples—she an Indian prostitute, he a well-
dressed European, or a rent boy and his renter. Chinese men with Chinese
women, young with old, doing things that required fingers and hands
fiddling under flaps and folds of clothing. He heard grunting and huffing
and flesh slapping. A scream shot out of a darkened alley, where he saw
silhouettes of people lined against scuzzy walls in the shadowy recesses of
the city's anus.

Eventually the familiar compound of Yuen's opium den came into
view. Every window was shuttered. Lanterns flickered between the slats.
Opium fumes larded the air. The broad gate stood ajar, just wide enough
for a person to sidle through. He went in sideways, pulling in his belly,

then climbed up the stoop. The double green doors were locked. He knocked several times. "Yuen," he cried. And again, "Yuen, open this door. I want to parlay." He knocked once more, this time with the flat of his hand. The door bowed slightly but did not open. A flake of dry paint came off and stuck to his palm.

He heard footsteps inside. A bolt was thrown and the door opened. A Chinese woman's face appeared. Her eyebrows narrowed and she said in English, "What you want?" She looked him up and down. He guessed she was middle-aged and was about as tall as his chest. Her hair was slicked back into a bun. A round face and wide nose showed off two impressive nostrils.

"I want to see Yuen," Emanuel said.

"Yuen not here. You want smokee? Four rupee one time. You wan?"

"No," Emanuel said, "I want to parlay with Yuen."

"No parlee. Smoke," she said.

The woman said something else in Chinese and waved her hand dismissively. She pulled her face back inside and tried to close the door, but Emanuel put his foot between it and the jamb. The woman slammed the door against his foot. A string of expletives flew out of her mouth. She got more vocal with each frustrated attempt to close the door.

From inside, a voice called out. She stopped her slamming. Instead she opened the door wide.

Emanuel stepped in. The oil lamp in the woman's hand cast a dim light. He heard the door close with a thud behind him. As she shuffled past, her cloth slippers flip-flopping off her heels, she handed him the lamp. He took it, cocking an eyebrow at the surprising gesture. Then she motioned for him to wait and slouched away down a shadowy hallway, her arms dangling like an ape's.

"You looking for me?" a familiar voice said from above. Old smoke coated with the tang of fresh honey made the place reek. Emanuel held up the lantern. Yuen was at the top of the stairs holding Ayah Gita with one hand and an oil lamp in the other. "Maybe you like some pokey-pokey?" Yuen laughed. "Fat Boy look so serious."

"Let her go," Emanuel said. He felt a chill ripple down his spine. At the same time blood rushed up from the pit of his belly. His cheeks turned crimson.

"Lo plob-lem. I let her go," Yuen said and released Ayah Gita. She crumpled to the floor. "See, I do what you tell me. You tell me come to auction house give you money. I come. You say you want me give you ten percent interest. I give to you. So now what else you want?"

"Ayah Gita," Emanuel said to her. She covered her face with her hands. He climbed a few steps up. She moved back and hid behind Yuen's legs.

"She not go anywhere, Fat Boy. Better you give me my money plus interest then go home. She mine now. She make good pokey-pokey for my customer. Good earner. Make back money I lose when you trick me into giving you ten percent!" He screamed the last sentence. A spray of spittle arced overhead.

Emanuel walked up the stairs holding the lantern in front of him. When he got to the top, Yuen moved to one side. The lamplight found Ayah Gita.

She was huddled against a corner of the landing. Slowly her hands slid off her face. It was skeletal. Her eyes had sunk into her head. Her cheek-bones protruded and her lips were chapped and raw. Her arms looked thin and frail. It was dim but he could see that her sari was the same one she had been wearing when he had left Calcutta.

"What you think, Fat Boy?"

"Ayah, take my hand." She looked at him then at Yuen. "He can't harm you anymore. Take my hand and I'll carry you." She curled her hands under her armpits.

"She comes to me. She soooo sad when you leave. Big missy, you wife, she sack this *more-law-cha*—black person. She no sleep. She no eat. She askee me give her some smoke. She smoke and smoke. But she no money to pay," Yuen said, slapping the back of one hand into the palm of the other several times. "So I say all right, never mind, you do pokey-pokey with customer, I give you smoke."

"You bastard." Emanuel could feel his whole body stiffen with rage.

"You fuck with me, I fuck with you. You Fat Boy, you ugly. Now you give me my money and you get out!" Yuen pushed Emanuel on the shoulder.

With one sweep of his arm, Emanuel brought the lantern up diago-nally. It hit Yuen's jaw with a sickening crunch. Yuen reeled back and dropped his lamp. It shattered on the wooden floor and burst into flame. Emanuel brought his lantern down. It missed Yuen's head but hit the wall behind. Oil splashed over Yuen's cotton shirt, which caught fire. Emanuel let go his broken lamp. It fell beside the other one, adding fuel to the blaze. Old and dry from years of wear and tear, the floorboards burned quickly, igniting the hem of Yuen's trousers. Flames devoured old flakes of paint, travelled across the landing and up the stairs.

Ayah Gita fled.

Yuen tried to tear off his clothes. But flames engulfed him. *"Help!"* he shouted, again and again.

Dumbstruck, Emanuel watched. He was rigid as though his feet had grown roots. A man was burning in front of his eyes. Help him! Do something!

Yuen pirouetted like a dancer, slapping his clothes, trying to tear them off his body. He lurched against the banister with such force that it split. He plummeted through the stairwell to the floor below like a flaming meteor hitting the earth.

Downstairs, the slouching woman with the big nostrils emerged. Seeing her master in flames, she ran out the door. Pandemonium followed. Other servants emerged and fled past Emanuel, running for their lives as the fire spread.

Emanuel heard him before he saw him.

"Sir, sir," a voice came from below.

It was Mr. Rustomjee. He had entered through the door left open by fleeing servants. He stopped when he saw Yuan's steaming corpse curled in a black ball. He reached for a handkerchief. "You must be leaving at once!" he shouted up the stairs.

"Please sir, you must be coming now!" He coughed at the stench and pressed his handkerchief over his nose and mouth.

Emanuel came to his senses. He looked down and saw Mr. Rustomjee staring at the black and bloodied mess. He looked up to where Ayah Gita had run. Somewhere bells were ringing.

"Sir, they are putting out the alarm. Authorities will be arriving. They will see you, sir. Sir must be coming down right away."

Mr. Rustomjee ran up and grabbed Emanuel by the arm, pulling him down the stairs and out into the night. A crowd had gathered in the street to look at the burning building.

Mr. Rustomjee pulled the young master through the crowds until they were behind the throng. Emanuel stopped, wrenched his arm free of the Indian's hold, and looked back. The crowd's attention was directed at the rooftop, at a tiny woman standing as smoke billowed around her ankles and flames shot out of the upper-floor windows. She pressed the palms of her hands together against her chest and tipped forward.

The crowd gasped. Their heads followed her flight downward like a long, slow collective nod until she fell out of sight.

SEMAH

"*A Real Hero*" was the headline on the bottom right-hand corner of page three in *The Calcutta Chronicle*.

In the early morning hours, a fire broke out in the Tangra District that razed a three-storey building to the ground. Calcutta Fire Brigade attended the scene. The municipality's newly installed Inspector of Safety, Chief Constable Fitzroy, late of Northumberland Fusiliers (ret.), wrested success out of what might have been a catastrophe.

"This could have been the start of the great fire of Calcutta had we not intervened," the new Inspector of Safety was quoted as saying.

The blaze was contained by sunrise some four or five hours after it started. There was no loss to the adjoining properties save for some smoke damage. The fire brigade under Mr. Fitzroy's resolute command stayed to the very end, making certain that every ember had been extinguished. Only then did the brigade retire from the scene. Though exhausted, they were no doubt happy in the knowledge that they had acquitted themselves with distinction.

It is this reporter's opinion that a special medal should be struck to honour the bravery of those who provide such selfless service to the neediest parts of our city. Were such an approbation minted, its first recipient should be Chief Constable Fitzroy.

Semah read the account in the afternoon edition. Just a few paragraphs that conveyed none of the horror and urgency she knew had gripped the onlookers the night before. It did not mention any deaths or how the fire had started or who might have been responsible. She closed the newspaper, folded it in half, and returned it to Chief Constable Fitzroy, who was sitting across from her in the solarium.

He was a tall man, one of the few whose eyeballs were at the same level as hers. A ruddy complexion from constant exposure to the outdoors, thick blond hair, and a straight back gave him the look of a toy soldier when he was wearing ceremonial reds. Alas, the municipality had prescribed a sober navy blue coat (with brass buttons) and matching trousers as more appropriate to his duties as the head copper of the city. Still, the man's bearing, pencil-line lips, and blue-eyed stare made him a formidable presence.

Her husband, she had told him, was having his afternoon nap. Fitzroy insisted he be awakened. The matter was urgent. Semah had sent a servant to summon Emanuel.

Meanwhile they waited, seated on buff-coloured rattan chairs. On the table between them were two pots, one with Indian tea and the other with green Chinese tea. He chose the former without lemon or sugar or milk. "I am a plain man," he explained, "and I see no need for mixing foreign things into good quality tea. Ceylon," he pronounced, and took another sip before setting it down. "Excellent." He took his watch from his waistcoat pocket, opened the cover and looked at the time, then snapped the lid and replaced it. He put his hands on his thighs and patted his kneecaps.

"What is this about?" Semah asked.

"I prefer to wait until your husband arrives," he replied. "I am not in the habit of interviewing wives without their husbands present."

"I see. Something to do with the fire?"

The question was redundant. Why else would he have handed her the afternoon edition of *The Calcutta Chronicle* and pointed his little finger at the article? The little finger that had a ring with a Masonic crest on it: a V-shaped carpenter's square overlaid with the inverted compass. Except for the absence of horizontal lines, it resembled the Magen David—the six-pointed star on her signet ring.

The Chief Constable did not reply. Instead he took up his cup again and brought it to his nose, made a great ceremony of smelling the tea before sipping it. Semah stood up. Fitzroy stood as well. She walked over

to the boxes of bougainvillea and looked out at the front yard through
the glass windows. A bee clung to the pane, its legs heavy with pollen
collected from flowers in the window boxes.

Semah felt her stomach tighten. A little sick caught in her throat. She
swallowed hard and suppressed an eructation.

The sun had just been rising when Emanuel returned home. He had
flung the front door open, startling her from a fitful half-sleep. She had
leapt out of bed, grabbed her cane, and stepped out into the hallway.
Sunlight flooded through the doors and side windows of the foyer below.
Emanuel and Mr. Rustomjee looked up at her. Their faces and hands
were stained with soot and both men heaved for breath as though they
had been running a long distance.

"What happened?" she asked, coming halfway down the stairs. A servant
came into the foyer to shut the front door. Semah ordered him out.

Emanuel stumbled up the stairs. "She didn't steal any silver. You lied
to me." He walked past, leaving a scent of smoke.

His bedroom door slammed. Her heart pounded and she felt her solitary
knee weaken. She lowered herself slowly on the stair. Mr. Rustomjee ran
up to her, fearing she was about to faint. When he saw that she was all right,
he told her what had happened.

Once he started, he could not stop. His eyes darted. A line of snot ran
down his lip and he wiped it off with the back of his hand. He trembled
like an animal spooked by unnatural noises.

"Sir is being very upset," he concluded. "He blames himself most
terribly for the fire. He wanted to look for the girl's body. But I prevented
him. The Chinese housekeeper, she recognized me ..."

"Good day," Emanuel said.

His voice brought Semah back to the present.

Washed and changed into day clothing, he stood for a moment framed
by the doorway of the solarium as though he were posing for a portrait.
He saw the visitor. Fitzroy rose. Emanuel scanned the man's navy-blue
uniform and its line of shiny brass buttons. The gold stripes on his shoulder
flaps matched the ones on the cuffs.

"Emanuel Billy-oz?" he said.

"I am he. What's this all about?" Emanuel said, walking into the room.

"Chief Constable Fitzroy is here about the fire last night—" Semah began.

Fitzroy cleared his throat and interjected: "Madam, if you would allow me." It was clear from his tone that he was not seeking permission.

"Mr. Billy-oz, where were you last night between, say, three A.M. and sunrise?"

Silence filled the room. The bee pushed off from the windowpane and landed on Emanuel's shoulder.

"You must help me," Emanuel said in Hebrew to Semah.

"What?" Fitzroy asked.

"Hebrew," Emanuel said. "We speak Hebrew here."

"But you must respond in English."

"Why? This is my house."

"And this is a police investigation. I'll ask you again: where were you last night between three A.M. and sunrise?"

"Why do you ask?" Emanuel said.

"There was a fire. Arson is suspected. Lives were lost."

"I see," Emanuel said. He looked at Semah. She returned his gaze and held her breath. Her heart pounded so hard she could feel it in her ears.

"We have a witness," Fitzroy continued. "A Chinese woman who says she saw you enter the property that is owned by your father and rented out to—"

"Me?" Emanuel said. "She saw me?"

"Yes. The description she gave matches yours."

"Do you speak any Chinese?"

"No. But we have translators—"

"And what description did she give?"

"About your height, black hair, beard—"

"That could be any Jew in our community—don't we all look alike?"

Fitzroy cleared his throat and said,

"Yes, except that your eyes are blue."

The bee flew off Emanuel's shoulder. Frantic to get out, it rammed the windowpane, bashing its head then buzzing back a few feet and rushing the pane again and again: buzz, bash, buzz, bash. Semah couldn't breathe. No one moved. She had had that sensation once before when she was sitting in the nook of her father's library—the cold sweats, the clammy palms. The last time she had this feeling, she revealed a painful truth that had almost ruined her parents' marriage. This time she would have to lie.

"My husband was here," Semah said, "from midnight onward."

Fitzroy turned his head toward her and so did Emanuel.

"He was away on business and returned on the midnight train to Howrah Station. He did not leave the house after he came home."

Semah drew herself up to her full height and looked Fitzroy in the eye.

"I see. You'll swear to that?"

"Yes," she said. How does a person swear to something? she wondered. With a Bible? A Torah scroll?

Fitzroy looked at the couple and narrowed his eyes. Emanuel turned away from the stare and opened a window. The bee flew out and disappeared. Fitzroy reached for his hat and stuffed it under his arm as though he were trying to squeeze the life out of it. He gave a cursory nod. "No need to see me out," he said. His meaning was clear: he could not wait to leave.

Semah sat down, pressed the palm of her hand against her stomach, and watched Emanuel close the window. They looked at each other. "Thank you," he said and sagged into a rattan chair. Hearing him say the words allowed her to breathe normally again. Between them, there were a million things to say but no fitting way to say them. Semah stood and crossed the room toward Emanuel. She kissed him on the cheek, then sat at his feet and put her head in his lap.

"… I …" he said, just as he had when, days before, she had asked him why he would not speak with her.

"No," she interjected, looking up at him, "I don't want to hear it. Not anymore. Whatever passed between you and her, it's over. This much I know: You are my husband. I want to have children and build a family for you to come home to. There is nothing else."

They stared at each other for a long time. Then he leaned over and kissed her on the mouth. In that moment she felt confident that however far away he travelled and however often he did so, he would always return to her.

Five years after the *gweilo* first arrived in Hong Kong, Pearl's father had saved enough money for them to move out of their cramped apartment in Wanchai. The money he had made helping the *gweilo* sell his opium was now enough to build a big house. And so her father hired a geomancer to divine an auspicious setting for the new lodgings. The man chose a large piece of land on the plateau overlooking Happy Valley. The location was a matrix where universe, earth, and man met in harmony. From here, a man could expect continued health, wealth, and happiness—not to mention fecundity for future generations. The geomancer, a thin Chinese man from Toishan with shoulder-length hair and a long white beard, had made this pronouncement while staring at Pearl and fingering his compass. Li saw the man's leer and stepped in, blocking his view of his eleven-year-old daughter.

The new home was, by anyone's standards, a palace. It had two floors and many, many rooms. There was a dining room and a sitting room and one large room where her *Ba-bah* slept and another that he told Pearl *"is for you alone."* Pearl had stretched her arms out to either side and spun on the spot like a top. She ran and touched one wall then ran twenty paces before she reached the opposite one. In it she had a giant bed with a feather mattress and two large pillows covered with cotton. Near the washstand there was a dressing table on which were an assortment of combs and brushes. On the floor was a carpet and against the wall a desk with an inkpot, pen, and paper where she did her lessons. Beside that there were two large shelves filled with books that Aleandro Remedios had brought for her from Macau. There was also a couch by a large window where she liked to curl up to read when she was not helping her father in his office.

Outside there was a large front garden with many bushes and trees. Her favourite was an old banyan with a thick centre trunk and smaller ones that grew down from its many branches. It resembled a big octopus guarding their home. Beside it was a stone bench. Pearl loved to sit there because she could see all the way down the valley across the water toward the Kowloon hills that she and *Ba-bah* had climbed when they had escaped China. Somewhere, on the other side of the range, was where she had last seen her mother. Secretly, Pearl fantasized that perhaps one day she would see her again, standing on the crest of those hills and waving to her. Whenever such ephemeral thoughts popped up in her mind's eye, she would reach for the jade talisman in her pocket, taking comfort from its solid and unchanging form.

Every morning, Pearl entered her father's bedroom with a tray of hot tea, a steaming pork bun, and a dish of tangerine slices. She would find him still asleep on a rattan mat on the floor. He had refused to use a bed, complaining that it was too soft. Besides, he had slept on the floor since he was a child and saw no reason to change. She would place her hand on his shoulder and gently shake it to wake him. Then she would set his tea on the bedside table and open the windows to let in some fresh air. She would walk to the small altar her father had built in memory of his wife, light a joss stick, and bow three times. When this was accomplished, she would leave him to drink his tea and eat his pork bun.

After breakfast, he would take out three joss sticks from a box beside the little altar. He removed the spent one, cleaned off the ash, and lit the fresh joss sticks with a match. He fanned the sticks to produce a glow at the tip and watched smoke curl up and evaporate. Then he bowed three times and placed the incense in the holder on the altar. He replaced the fruit on the offering plate with the fresh tangerine slices that Pearl had brought in on the tray. (The old ones he put on the windowsill for the birds to take.) He practised this ritual every day to keep alive the memory of his beloved wife. Only then would he wash, change, and go to his office.

Even before they moved to this new mansion, Pearl had noticed that her *Ba-bah*'s attitude toward her had altered. It was around the time the geomancer had selected the perfect location for the house. From that day onward he no longer allowed her to go with him on voyages to China where he, the *gweilo,* and Uncle went to sell their opium. She was made to stay at the one-room apartment in Wanchai while the new house was being constructed. And when it was completed, he wanted her to stay there, indoors.

"But *Ba-bah,*" she protested, speaking to him in his Chinese country dialect, "What shall I do by myself and who will take care of you and Uncle?"

They were in his office on the ground-floor wing. It was a spartan room: a large teak desk dominated the centre with two straight-back chairs set in front of it for visitors and a cushioned bench behind it for Li.

"You need not worry. We have many men working for us now. It's not good for you to be in a ship full of men." Pearl could not understand why not. She had gone on many voyages before. "And as for being alone all day," he continued, "I have hired a handmaid. She will keep you company. You are a lady now and you must act like one."

"And what about my lessons with Uncle? He teaches me English and mathematics every day—"

"No, no, no," he said, wagging a finger, "No more lessons."

"What? Why?"

"Aiyah, little daughter, you can read and write Chinese and English and you can do sums, can't you?"

"Yes, *Ba-bah.*"

"So what more do you need?"

"But I like to learn new things."

"No, no, no, too much education is not good for a woman. How can you find a husband that way? If your head is full of education there won't be any room left to think about him."

It was the first time he had spoken of a husband. She did not know any boy her age. In fact, she did not know any girl her age.

"Who will be my husband?" she asked.

"Who?" he said and started to laugh. "I don't know. But there will be many suitors. I am a rich man and you will have a good dowry. Don't worry, they will all come sniffing around like hungry dogs soon enough."

Ba-bah shouted toward the door. After a moment, it opened slowly and a young girl stepped in. She was dressed in a servant's white tunic that was buttoned up on the side. It had long sleeves and a mandarin collar. The tunic reached down to her knees and covered long black pants. A white handkerchief hung loosely from her tunic's buttons like a fluffy tail. Pearl couldn't see her face because the girl was looking down at her hands.

"This is Ah Gum," he said, pointing to the servant. "She will be your handmaid." Then in a gruff tone as though he were scolding her, he said: "Come on, come on, say good morning to your young mistress!"

"Good morning, young mistress," Ah Gum said dutifully.

"Look at her," he instructed the servant. "And stop mumbling. *Aiyah*, these country girls are all the same."

For the rest of the day Ah Gum followed Pearl everywhere she went, walking two steps behind but leaping in front whenever there was a door or window to be opened. And for the entire time, Ah Gum did not once look up. Pearl had no way of telling what her handmaid looked like nor how old she was nor what she was thinking.

The days folded into weeks and the weeks into months. Pearl continued with her morning routine in *Ba-bah*'s bedroom and also spent time in her father's office. There she massaged his back while visitors came to see him. Usually these were Chinese merchants who sought his advice or had something to sell or wanted him to invest in some new enterprise. She patted his shoulders with the soft part of her fists and looked over his shoulder at documents on his desk. From time to time she would whisper in his ear, telling him the content of the paper that a supplicant had placed before him. She did this because *Ba-bah* was illiterate and conducted business verbally. His word was his bond and he was renowned for this, clasping his clients' hands in both of his as a way to seal verbal agreements. Pearl saw that he was this way with money, too. He did not trust paper money or promissory notes. For business transactions, he preferred using silver coins that he kept in a safe locked in a special closet in the mansion's basement.

While Pearl was with her father in his office, Ah Gum waited outside. Pearl would not permit her handmaid to interfere with these intimate moments. The servant obeyed Pearl and performed her duties flawlessly. Pearl's bedchamber was always spotless, her bed always made and her clothes washed and pressed to perfection. She was up and ready for work before her mistress and went to bed only after Pearl was asleep. Ah Gum was everywhere, head bowed, always waiting and ever ready.

A year later, Pearl had grown taller than her father. She had felt her body change with alarming speed. Breasts the size of persimmons sprouted and gave her chest a swollen look. She required a new wardrobe because of it. Her hips and bottom filled out too and gave her the shape of the hourglass that her *Ba-bah* kept on his office desk. She wondered if Ah Gum had similar curves under her loose and shapeless garments.

Then, one morning while still in bed, she felt something sticky between her thighs. She put a hand under the sheets. When she pulled it out, her fingertips were stained red. Immediately she threw back the covers and screamed. There was a patch of blood on her nightdress.

Ah Gum opened the door and ran in. She saw the blood and closed the door behind her. She leaned her back against it to prevent anyone else from entering.

Peal was sitting on the bed, her eyes wide with horror. Ah Gum ran to her and looked her in the eyes.

"Young mistress, don't worry, it is the time of your moon," she whispered.

"What?" Pearl sniffed. She felt a tear run down her cheek. Ah Gum reached up and wiped it away with her thumb. "Is it blood?" she asked quietly.

"Yes," Ah Gum replied.

"Am I dying?"

"No," Ah Gum said, putting her arm around her young mistress's shoulders.

Ah Gum removed Pearl's soiled nightdress and helped her into a robe. She explained that all women experience this flow monthly and showed her how to prepare for the event. Pearl listened intently, fascinated. Nothing in the books she had read, either in English or in Chinese, had ever mentioned anything like this. It suddenly occurred to her that men had written those books. Clearly what had happened was a secret that only women knew.

When they had finished cleaning up, Pearl saw Ah Gum in a new light. Ah Gum was prepared for what had happened. It was as though she had been waiting for weeks for this bloody event. Her explanations were lucid and her instructions about what to do in future months were practical. She spoke with confidence, looking Pearl in the eye when she did so. She is older than me, Pearl thought, but not by much, probably sixteen—seventeen at most. She looked closer. Ah Gum's black hair, tied back in a bun, gave her an open look. She had a high forehead, black eyes, a moon-shaped face, and a perpetual smile.

"Congratulations, mistress," Ah Gum said, patting the bench in front of the dressing table. Pearl sat down and looked in the mirror.

Ah Gum let down her mistress's long hair. "Now the master will look for a husband for you because today, you have become a woman," she said. Then she brushed Pearl's hair one hundred times until it shone as bright as her eyes.

EMANUEL

In the years following his first opium run into China, Emanuel poured himself into work, which helped him purge that miserable night in Chinatown from his memory. Ayah Gita disappeared little by little from his mind's eye, as did images of that horrid conflagration and the odour of burning flesh. The only thing that remained of her was the silver necklace with the Magen David pendant that hung around his neck.

He purchased hundreds of chests of opium and sold them all. When that did not slake his hunger for profits (nor quench the demand from Chinese smokers), he upped his itinerary to two trips a year and then to three and eventually four. Although he never quite got used to the sea-sickness or the length of the journey, he liked the thrill of the bargaining and the profits. As the years ticked by, the demands of his business caused him to spend more time at his Lyndhurst Terrace offices in the British colony than in Calcutta.

It was a heady period during which he (together with other Jewish merchants from India—the Sassoons, the Kardoories, the Hardoons) was on the ground floor of an export bonanza that seemed would never end. Emanuel developed a system that was as simple as it was elegant. He purchased opium from Indian auctioneers in Calcutta and sailed with the goods to Hong Kong, where his partners Li and Aleandro hired coolies to offload the chests into one of the many bloated storage vessels that were dead-anchored in the colony's harbour. Soon those floating warehouses became inadequate for the amount of lading. So Li, on his partners' behalf, purchased land on the shores of Victoria Island and built large Quonset huts—go-downs made of metal and constructed in the shape of a half-pipe—to house the increased inventory. Locked and surrounded by fencing, these facilities were guarded by Aleandro's fierce-looking gang of itinerant, headband-wearing mulattoes whom he had brought in from Macau—a small, private army loyal only to him. Thus the trio relied on each other like a three-legged stool.

In the first two years of the 1870s, Emanuel was selling two thousand chests per year. Each chest was valued between five hundred and one thousand dollars. Payment was in silver dollars—*real de ocho.* These were rolled in wax paper to make tubes of twenty-five coins, placed in strongboxes, and guarded by privateers whom Aleandro Remedios had pressed into service aboard the company's own ship, which now sailed regularly up the Huangmao River. The route snaked up the west side of Macau to reach untapped areas and avoid the traditional paths used by other merchants.

For their service and loyalty, Emanuel was wise enough to make Li and Aleandro his equal partners. In consideration of which, they reinvested some of the profits to purchase more opium. Together, their money made more money. Their profits were so vast and so rapid that they couldn't spend them fast enough. Li built his house in Happy Valley. Aleandro constructed a compound in Macau where he housed four concubines, each occupying one of four bungalows he had had built on either side of a central *palão*—palace—that was his primary residence. And Emanuel? His home was in Calcutta, so he opted to rent a modest red-brick building on Lyndhurst Terrace in Hong Kong with simple living quarters above his busy street-level offices.

Quick and abundant profits allowed merchants like Emanuel to diversify into shipping, warehousing, and underwriting businesses and to acquire real estate in a colony where banks were eager to take their deposits. Within a few short years, the three partners had netted over one million dollars and had their photograph taken standing in front of the Hong Kong and Shanghai bank. The picture was printed in the local weekly under the heading *Three's Company.* The caption described them as *Opium merchants in Hong Kong,* and a more unlikely looking group you would not see. Here on the left was a fleshy, pear-shaped man wearing a morning coat and top hat, his square face half-covered with a thick moustache and beard, scowling at the camera with those pale eyes caught in black and white. In the middle was a small Chinese man wearing a loose-fitting *chang pao*—a one-piece silk gown with a mandarin collar— and the traditional round skullcap on his head. On the right a short, sandy-haired, dark-skinned fellow, hatless and with high cheekbones, stared down the camera like a hungry wolf looking at easy prey.

Two thousand miles away there were other photographs that also mapped a life's journey over that same decade. There on the front page of *The Calcutta Chronicle* is Semah, her hat atop a pile of hair that made her look even taller than she was, standing with her arm threaded through Emanuel's on the steps of a building. Above their heads a large Magen David is etched into stained glass. Alas, none of the bright-yellow walls or the deep blues of the cut-glass windows show in these grainy black-and-white pictures. The caption tells of the family's thousand-dollar donation to the new synagogue's building fund.

Another issue of the newspaper shows Semah dressed in the latest Victorian dress and seated in what appears to be a classroom. Young Indian girls in school uniforms stand on either side of her, their hands held prettily in front of their waists. A brief caption reports another donation of an undisclosed sum of money for the first girls' school in Calcutta. Semah noted in her journal that she was very proud of that day and had wished to smile for the camera but was told not to do so by the photographic artist. Apparently such abandon was not desirable in society. There were other portraits: one of Emanuel holding the reins of a horse, his wife mounted upon it, holding a strop in gloved hands and wearing a stovetop riding hat.

Having made pots of money, he became independent of his father's influence (and the envy of his brother—the handsome one), and he had leapfrogged over the backs of his schoolyard contemporaries, most of whom had taken jobs as mid-level government bureaucrats working in the Writers' Building on BBD Bagh North.

But these pictures show the veneer of his life and not the rootless, fearful creature he was inside. Pulled by history and obligation to Semah but addicted to the world he had created in Hong Kong, Emanuel was stuck between the two. In the weeks that followed Fitzroy's visit to his home, when his wife had lied to save her marriage and his neck, he tried to be a husband to her. He tried to find the desire and love for her that she so clearly had for him.

Every evening, she left the door of their adjoining bedrooms open. First just a crack allowed muted candlelight to cast a beam onto his bedroom floor. He closed the door on it. As the weeks progressed, the opening widened and he could see her on the other side, standing in the centre of her bedroom lit by a forest of candles. The sliver of light had become a broad yellow path that invited him to enter. But fearful that he could not perform without sight of Ayah, he still closed the door upon her. Then one night, the door was not open. He hated being denied access to anything, and especially to things he considered his. He tried the handle. It turned. He put his ear to the door. He heard water sloshing. Semah was humming a melody. He opened the door and stepped into her bedroom. A whiff of rosewater and lavender scented the air. A solitary oil lamp glowed on the bedside table behind a three-panelled bathing screen to his left.

He walked slowly toward it, hoping the floorboards would not creak under his weight. As he approached, the humming got louder, as did the sound of a towel being soaked in water and wrung dry. At the screen, he looked through the slit between the panels. Semah was naked with her back toward him. He had never seen her like that. To steady herself she was standing with her legs apart, the prosthetic attached like a cage to her thigh. Her buttocks, creamy and rounded at the hips, flowed into a small waist and then curved upward. Her hair was down and thick black curls draped over her shoulders like a veil. She had raised one arm as she ran the wet towel under it, leaving a veneer of moisture on her flawless skin. Her body was taut and athletic. He shifted from one leg to the other and the floor creaked. Semah stopped humming and turned her head in profile. He could hear his own breathing. His heart pounded. Fighting eagerness, he reached for the side of the bathing screen and collapsed it like an accordion. He stepped in and heard a short intake of breath as he clasped her from behind, pulling her body against his. He reached one hand around her waist and pressed it on her soft belly. His other hand climbed up and cupped her breast.

He tore at the buckles and straps, ripping the false leg off her thigh, flinging it aside. She balanced herself by holding his shoulders before he lifted her up. With her thighs wrapped around his waist, he scurried to the bed and threw her on it. She landed with her arms and legs splayed out, her eyes searching his, her hands reaching for the buttons of his shirt. He pulled off his clothes, manic with heat. She caught a finger on the chain around his neck. The Magen David fell off and drowned in the roiling mess of clothing flung this way and that. Then he leapt on top of her eager body.

Afterward, lying in bed, watching her as she slept, he wanted to feel something more than relief. Here was his wife, someone to whom he owed his life. She was willing and patient and understanding. And all he could feel was emptiness.

He got out of bed. Her prosthetic limb lay on the floor.

He picked it up and laid it beside her on the bed so that she would not have to hunt for it when she woke. He dressed quickly, picked up the oil lamp, and walked toward his rooms. On the way, he saw a leather-bound book lying on her desk. He looked at the sleeping figure in the bed. Then he sat down, put the lamp on the desk, opened the cover, and flipped through the journal.

Pen-and-ink sketches, bordered by written narratives, filled every page. A landau, the facade of their house, the dining room, the salon, and other areas were rendered in exquisite detail, ending with the caption *A house but not a home*. A bed with a faceless woman lying in it, her arm draped over the bed's empty half; a woman's back, her hair piled on her head, looking into an ornately framed mirror—her reflection without a face; a burning building; Emanuel's head resting on a lady's skirted lap, someone's (a woman's?) hand stroking his hair.

Then his eyes landed on this passage:

> *Everyone has a role: the gardeners, the grooms, the cook, the servants, the gubbai and schamash—synagogue caretakers—they all know their function, their responsibilities, but I do not know mine except that I am a wife. And what examples do I have? My mother*

and others of her generation who are reflections of their husbands?
Is that what I am—a reflection? Do people look at me and see
him—a flawed man? Do they look at me and see him—a person
who needs more love and less fear? Do they scan my eyes and see
his soul as something that needs a bit of fixing? Is this my role? To
be a safe harbour where he is not challenged, just a place to rest and
to sleep? I am like a bird in a gilded cage, singing a song that no one
wants to hear.

He didn't read any further. Like him, she was unhappy. The cicadas
rattled in the garden. A cool night breeze came through the open window,
bringing with it a faint scent of jasmine. He looked toward the bed.
Semah was breathing deeply.

He stood. Something metallic fell on the floor with a soft *clink*. He
crouched and felt the floor with his hands. It was the necklace with the
Magen David pendant that Semah had ripped off in the heat of their
lovemaking. He picked it up and held it in his palm.

What could he do to free them both from their unhappiness? he wondered. Could he give her freedom and by so doing liberate himself?

The world changed for Pearl the day she learned she had become a woman. To disguise the shapely bulge of her chest, Ah Gum discarded the childishly tight shirts and replaced them with a new wardrobe of loose-fitting silk tops (edged with embroidery) and ankle-length skirts. The roominess of this style of clothing was designed to keep her new curves hidden as befitted a modest young lady of means. Her hair was dressed in a bun at the back or coquettishly bobbed to one side. From the stalls in Central District Ah Gum brought up shopkeepers who displayed their wares on the grass in front of the veranda. Her mistress could shop in private away from the indecorum of the downtown markets. Pearl selected a series of decorative ivory and jade combs to keep her chignon in place as well as matching earrings and bracelets from an array of shiny things. (She considered having her mother's jade piece refashioned into a pendant. But after due consideration she jibbed on the idea. It remained in her pocket, where it was always within reach.)

At thirteen, Pearl was petite with an oval face, small nose, and black, almond-shaped eyes. But it was her skin that one noticed first. It was smooth and white like the inside of an almond, almost like coconut milk. And Ah Gum was determined to keep it that way. Wherever they went she held a parasol over her young mistress's head. She also produced a pair of white cotton gloves, a wide-brimmed hat, and a silk scarf that covered her face except for a slit through which those beguiling eyes peered. Li approved of such precautions because they were designed to prevent Pearl's skin from darkening in the sunlight. Men, he thought, valued white, unblemished skin on a prospective bride. It meant that she was a lady and did not have to toil in the fields like a peasant. Gone too were those carefree adventures that she took with her father, Uncle, and the *gweilo*. Li didn't want a repeat of the geomancer's leer; for weeks he had replayed the image of the old man ogling his daughter and wetting his lips while his tongue darted in and out of his mouth like a hungry snake staring at a mouse. No, she was to stay at their house now, out of sight of men. He had hired Ah Gum to see to his wishes (and, as he had explained to the maid, to *provide the requisite instructions regarding women's matters*).

Pearl acquiesced to her father's demands, but when he was away in China selling opium, she was able to commit small acts of rebellion. His trips had become more and more frequent, which gave her more opportunities to foray out of doors. Ah Gum huffed and puffed her indignation. She tried but was unable to resist her young mistress's determination. She had no choice but to remain at the girl's side and keep their wanderings a secret from Li. At first, the outdoor expeditions were commonplace—a walk down the hill where there was nothing much to see. But as time progressed Pearl got more adventurous: a chair ride down the hill then a rickshaw to Central District; a visit to the St. John's Cathedral on Garden Road; a ride by the old apartment above the herbalist shop in Wanchai; a stroll through the Botanic Gardens; a shopping spree at Watson's where she charged her first purchase—a bottle of 4711 eau de cologne; a long mule ride along the mountain path and down the south side of Victoria Island, where they sat on a deserted beach and watched fishermen cast their nets out to sea. She loved to run barefooted in the frothy wavelets that broke on shore, ignoring her handmaid's warnings of infections from exposure to the sun and salt water. Back at home, Ah Gum insisted that her mistress soak her feet in a basin of hot water mixed with baking soda. She also prepared an infusion of *sun gook cha*—chrysanthemum tea—as a preventative against the mung she was convinced had already started its insidious invasion through the soles of Pearl's feet. Pearl giggled at her handmaid's exasperation but allowed her feet to be scrubbed. She also drank the tea, breathing in its sweet curative aromas as she pondered what other adventures she could go on.

To assuage Ah Gum's continued agitation—*What would the master say if he found out?*—and to demonstrate her gratitude, Pearl decided that Ah Gum be named the mansion's housekeeper—the majordomo with authority to hire and fire all the other servants—and keeper of the household accounts. Furthermore, Pearl gave her the honorific of Gum-ghee, which roughly translated as "sister." When she told her father about these ideas, Li approved. He was proud that his daughter was taking such an interest in household matters and saw that her handmaid was having a positive influence on Pearl's passage into womanhood. Yes, he clapped his hands triumphantly, this is exactly what he had hoped would happen. Thus Gum-ghee indulged—with pursed lips and the required amount of mock indignation—all of Pearl's whims. All except one. Gum-ghee wanted to dismiss Ah-Fook, the gardener, but Pearl intervened.

"May I ask good mistress why?" Gum-ghee asked in Cantonese, her native tongue. They were on the veranda off the dining room, where Pearl liked to have her afternoon tea and sweet cakes.

"He has been with our family ever since we moved into this house."

"He is lazy. He sleeps all day and does nothing. Look at the garden. Look at the grass on the lawn. Lazy. And he still expects to be paid."

"We are responsible for him. What will he do if he loses his job?"

Gum-ghee was silent for a moment, then:

"Mistress, the man is an opium smoker."

Pearl knew that her father, Uncle, and the *gweilo* sold opium, but it had not occurred to her until that moment that people smoked the substance.

"So what?" she said.

"It has made him incapable of work."

Pearl thought about this. True, the garden once bloomed with magnolias, camellias, hibiscus, roses, and carnations, all framed by palms and green shrubs. But recently things had gone to seed. Not knowing much about gardening, she had put the decay down to the dry weather. But really it was lack of husbandry.

"Where is he now?" Pearl asked.

"Probably in the shed, snoring and dreaming."

"I want to see him," Pearl said. She put down her teacup, left the table quickly, and strode toward the opposite end of the garden. Gum-ghee rushed after her mistress, stopped, and returned to the table to grab her parasol. She opened it and ran. When she caught up, she held it over her young mistress's head.

Pearl looked through the window of the shed.

Ah-Fook was inside, asleep on the floor. Gunnysacks of fertilizer and seed were tucked under his head and arms like rough brown pillows. An earthy aroma cloaked the hut. She gagged, not from the smell but from the sight: the man was skin and bones. This was not the gardener she once knew, the robust, muscular man who worked naked to the waist, his thick neck, rounded shoulders, and sinewy biceps shiny with sweat. Pearl had watched him from her window as he ladled fresh water from a bucket and poured it over his head on a hot day. He didn't towel off but let it drip in rivulets down his wide chest and over his stomach.

Surely this was not the same man. It looked as if the life had been sucked out of him. Here was a breathing skeleton. Undulating triceps and biceps had completely deflated to leave a veneer of skin as thin as rice paper covering his stick-insect limbs. She turned away, ran back to the house, and then up the stairs to her bedroom. Gum-ghee followed as closely as she could.

Pearl flung open the doors and headed for the washstand basin, where she vomited up the tea and sweet cakes. She never returned to the shed, nor would she allow Gum-ghee to get rid of the man. And when her *Ba-bah* returned, she confronted him.

Li and Aleandro were just finishing dinner; the *gweilo* was not with them that evening. She had decided to wait until they were well fed before she told them what she had witnessed. If what she saw was the effect of opium smoking, then surely they should cease selling the commodity.

"Aiyah, daughter. Don't meddle. These matters are for men to decide."

"But Ba-bah, do all opium smokers look like Ah-Fook?"

"No, most are quite healthy. If you can afford to buy opium and buy food, then you are in good health. But if you do not buy food, then, of course, you die."

"Little one," Aleandro said in English, "everyone is selling opium these days. If we don't sell it then someone else will. Why shouldn't we make some moolah?" Then he repeated what he'd said in Cantonese for Li's sake. His partner nodded in agreement.

"We only sell to people who want to buy," Li added. *"What they do after is not my business."*

An icy silence fell over the room. Pearl knitted her brow and looked down at her plate. She had not touched her food. Dead eyes of the deep-fried minnows on her plate stared back at her. Aleandro lit a cheroot. Li tapped his fingertips on the tabletop.

"You should stop selling opium," she said softly.

"What?"

"You should stop selling—" Before she could finish, Li tore the napkin off his chest and threw it on his plate.

"Look around you. Look at all the things you have. Look at all the fine things I have given you. Aiyah, all of this is from trading opium. Without it we would still be hauling luggage from ship to shore."

Aleandro patted the air with his palms, trying to calm his friend down. Li folded his arms and sat back in his chair. Aleandro spoke:

"It's too late," he said. *"We couldn't stop if we wanted to. There are buyers who would do bad things if we did stop. We have to live with it."*

For how long, Pearl wondered, but didn't dare say it aloud.

Her *Ba-bah* had decided, after that evening's exchange, that too much education had given his daughter an insolent mind and a disrespectful tongue. He was not concerned about what she said to him so much as what she might say to a future husband. To correct her behaviour and to demonstrate his displeasure, he made several decisions.

First, she was no longer permitted to sit at table with them. This meant that she would no longer be able to converse with the *gweilo* when he visited. Li knew that she enjoyed these visits, and had removed the privilege deliberately as a punishment.

Second, he cancelled her account at Kelly and Walsh booksellers. She could read and write well enough to keep house; what more does a girl need anyway?

But these edicts didn't prevent Pearl from getting her way. She missed talking to Emanuel, but she did see him, albeit from a distance. As time went by, she began to regard him with more and more curiosity. Here was a white man from far away who had a strange name and who had made her father and Uncle rich. She deduced that, if so, then he too must be rich—and yet he did not seem happy. Quite the contrary; she noticed that every time Emanuel was in Hong Kong, he appeared to be more and more sad. He was stoop-shouldered, as if he were carrying a great weight. He never smiled as he used to and his eyes were always looking out at the middle distance, as though he were trying to decide what to do about some important question.

As for the second edict, she was determined to continue learning new things. With Gum-ghee's help and abetted by Aleandro (he had a soft spot for this surrogate daughter), books were smuggled into the house and up the servants' stairs into her room, where she secreted them under her bed. Every afternoon when Li took his nap, she read widely in English as well as in Chinese. And of course when he was away, she would read all day.

As for Ah-Fook, Gum-ghee didn't have to dismiss him. A few weeks after Li's argument with Pearl he was found dead in an opium den in the Wanchai District. Gum-ghee informed her mistress and watched Pearl's face turn even whiter than it already was.

From that year on, Li received many supplications for his daughter's hand. A veritable procession of young men and their cohorts made the steep climb up the hill to the house in Happy Valley, swaggered into his office, and laid out gifts as an enticement: whole pigs, sedan chairs, silks, jade, and assorted cakes. But he refused them all. His reasons varied: too old (the oldest was seventy-two), too young (the youngest was eight), too ugly, too stupid, too poor (that is to say, poorer than he), too rich (richer than he), wrong family name, and so on. In short, the bar he set for his precious daughter's hand was too high for anyone to leap over.

Pearl and Gum-ghee watched the proceedings from the veranda off her rooms as the aspirants huffed and puffed up the hill. Then they sneaked looks through the crack of an open door that led to her father's office while he interviewed them. They regarded each overture seriously at first, but as time rolled by, the search for her perfect mate became a source of great hilarity for the two young women.

Then, when she was approaching her sixteenth birthday, Pearl experienced a growth spurt. She grew to her full height of five feet three inches. She was almost as tall as her *Ba-bah,* certainly taller than Aleandro, and the same height as Gum-ghee. The tight, budding body of a young woman had completely replaced the child's figure. Her face changed, too. Gone was the cute little girl. She now had an expectant look, as though she were eagerly waiting for something wonderful to happen. She didn't mind these changes, except for one aspect. She hated her feet. She thought they were too big.

To mark her birthday, Aleandro persuaded Li to set aside Pearl's banishment from joining them at meals. He agreed, as long as she promised to mind her tongue.

Gum-ghee ran a bath, prepared her clothes, and laid them neatly on the bed. She combed her mistress's hair into a tight bun secured with a wide jade comb and dressed her in a red and yellow brocaded tunic.

The men were on the veranda, sitting in wicker chairs. Cicadas sounded their nightly chorus of rattling and clicking. The air had cooled, so the men did not need fans. The *gweilo* was talking. Her father and Aleandro were listening intently.

Gum-ghee cleared her throat to get their attention. The *gweilo* paused and looked up. He stood while the other men remained seated. He was dressed in a white linen suit that looked as if he had slept in it. His full beard needed a trim and his usually bright blue eyes looked sad. She noticed that his mouth was open with surprise. He turned to Li.

"Have you taken a wife?" he asked.

Li and Aleandro laughed so hard they almost choked.

Pearl felt annoyed. It was the first time anyone had laughed at her expense.

"No," Li replied. He had learned some English over the years. "My daughter. You remember?" he said, miming the skipping of a pebble.

The *gweilo's* eyes brightened. "Can it be?"

Pearl gave a small bow. "Welcome back to Hong Kong."

"How long has it been?"

"Three years at least."

"I am happy to make your reacquaintance."

"The pleasure is mine, sir."

"Please, you must call me Emanuel. May I call you Pearl?"

"As you wish." She was impressed. The man was clearly a gentleman.

Throughout dinner, she felt his eyes on her every move. It was so impolite. To watch a person eat forced them to show their teeth. And as Pearl knew, exposing teeth in public was rude. Eating was difficult. Seeing her struggle, Gum-ghee used her fan to cover her mistress's face each time she put food in her mouth. This made it easier to eat and had the added benefit of being able to steal a look at Emanuel over the top edge of the fan or through the slats.

Whenever their eyes met, he pretended that he was not staring and turned away quickly. Though distracted, he was able to keep up his part of the conversation about the new British Governor and about the *Hongs*— companies that had erected buildings along the Praya and on Queen's Street and to the east and west of Emanuel's offices on Lyndhurst Terrace. Central District was becoming more crowded. But mainly their chat was about business and the people who conducted it. Who was up, who was down.

Men had very limited concerns, Pearl thought. They want to make money and they want to make it quickly. So they talk about those who could help improve their opportunities or how they had succeeded and others had not. The conversation went on well after they had stopped eating and the dishes had been taken away. Pearl listened without comment.

Then it happened.

She yawned. It was a big one that bared her teeth in front of her father and his *gweilo* business partner when the tea and sweet cakes were served. Li's eyes widened in shock.

To cover up the indiscretion, Pearl said to Emanuel,

"Is it not time you moved out of your rooms above your office and into a house?"

The room was silent for a long time.

"Is it?" Emanuel asked, breaking the silence.

"Is it what?" she said.

"You were suggesting I move into a new house."

"Yes, Lyndhurst Terrace is so busy and noisy. How do you sleep?"

"Not well of late, I must confess."

"Must be the noise and the heat, with all those buildings so close together."

"Where do you suggest I go?" Emanuel continued.

"Do not bother our guest with your silly talk," Li said in Cantonese.

"Pardon me?" Emanuel asked.

"My father objects to my questions," Pearl translated.

"I assure you I do not," Emanuel said. "Where would you have me live?"

"You could build a new house, in the Hill District. Where all the *gweilo*—I mean foreigners—live. Perhaps near the new Peak Tramway Station. It will be cooler on the hillside and much quieter. When it is completed, you could travel on the cable car up to the Peak any time you wished."

"You think that, do you?" Emanuel spoke as if he were addressing a pet.

"Yes, you could send for your wife and start a family."

Suddenly, his eyes narrowed. Then he began to shake and dropped his head, touching his chin to his chest. He lifted his napkin and covered his face.

"Leave us," Li said.

His voice was harsh and scary. She stood up. Without looking or saying anything further, she left the table. Gum-ghee closed the double doors behind them.

Immediately they put their ears to the wood and listened. Pearl could hear sobbing. She looked through the keyhole. Her father had one hand on Emanuel's shoulder and appeared to be consoling his guest.

Before that moment, she had never seen a *gweilo* cry. They were always in such control. What could have caused him to weep? She started to tremble. Gum-ghee held her by the shoulders and led her to the garden, to the stone bench under the banyan tree.

"Sit down, mistress," she said, and then rubbed her back and fanned her face. "I will get you some jasmine tea."

Pearl sat alone, watching thousands of stars fill the sky. Gum-ghee returned and poured tea. The scent of jasmine and her handmaid's presence reassured her. She allowed herself to wonder at the *gweilo*'s sorrow. Was he covering his face because he saw her yawn? Was he so insulted?

She was so lost in thought that she did not notice Emanuel walk up beside her.

Gum-ghee whispered in her ear. She turned and looked at him.

He bowed slightly.

She stood to leave, but he said,

"Please stay."

She obeyed.

"I must apologize for my display of weakness."

Pearl did not know how to respond, and so she remained silent.

He stood beside the stone bench, one hand behind his back. The other was pressed against the banyan. There was a long silence. Pearl shuddered from the chill of the night.

"*Young mistress must go inside,*" Gum-ghee said and rubbed Pearl's upper arms.

Emanuel took off his coat and draped it over Pearl's shoulders. It smelled of tobacco mixed with sea salt. Gum-ghee looked displeased by the foreigner's brazen gesture. It was *her* duty to take care of the mistress.

"May I sit?" he asked.

"Please do," Pearl replied. Then in Cantonese: "*Gum-ghee, lay out your handkerchief for our guest to sit on.*"

Gum-ghee did as she was told, muttering under her breath that sitting so close to a foreigner was an invitation to some undefined peril. As a precaution, she stood beside her mistress and watched the man like a bird of prey eyeing its quarry.

"*Young mistress. You must go indoors. The night air is not good.*"

"*Pour some hot water into the pot,*" Pearl ordered.

"*Aiyah,*" Gum-ghee muttered as she walked away. "*This is so inconvenient. I really don't know what they are doing there sitting like statues in the dark, cold night.*" Then she said a little louder over her shoulder, "*Shout if the gweilo attacks you!*"

Cicadas clicked. Somewhere an owl hooted. Yellow light from kerosene lamps illuminated the house behind them.

"Do you know what day of the week this is?" Emanuel asked. What a silly question, she thought. Of course she knew. It was Friday. "It is the Sabbath," he added. "At sunset my people gather to give thanks to G-d. The woman of the house will light two candles and say this prayer:

> *Barukh atah Adonai, Eloheinu, melekh ha'olam*
> *asher kidishanu b'mitz'votav v'tzivanu*
> *l'had'lik neir shel Shabbat. Omein.*"

They were strange sounds and she did not understand any of them.

"Those are beautiful-sounding words," she said.

"Yes, they are."

Above their heads millions of stars twinkled. An occasional rustle of leaves on treetops provided the perfect underscore for the beauty of the night. Emanuel stretched his arms behind him and looked up at the sky.

"Did you know that astronomers are naming every star?" he asked.

She had never thought of such a thing and looked up. The sky looked like a vast canopy dotted with silver specks twinkling just for her.

"See, there? That's Orion," he said. Pointing overhead and tracing lines with his finger, he continued: "That is his belt and that is the hilt of his sword." Then he shifted his focus: "Now look down and to the left. That bright one. Do you see it?"

"That one?" She pointed, touching his fingertip.

"Yes, that's the one," he said. "That is Sirius, the brightest star in the sky."

"How do you know it is the brightest?"

"Hipparchus said so, a hundred and fifty years before Christ."

"Who was Hipparchus?"

"A Greek astronomer. He was the first to name and measure their brightness."

Was he mocking her? How can a man measure something that he cannot touch? And how is it possible to say that one star is brighter than another?

"Pick a star. Any one and I will give it to you."

Now she was convinced that he was mad. She laughed and covered her mouth. "You don't believe me?" he asked.

"No."

"Why don't you try it and see what happens. It can't hurt. Go on," he insisted.

Pearl looked up to the heavens and pointed to a star that glimmered. Emanuel reached up and covered his hand over the one she had selected.

"Hereafter it shall be named Pearl," he said as he took her hand, opened it, and placed his small star-shaped pendant on her palm.

"This is called a Magen David," he said. "It is a symbol of my people. Whenever you look at it I hope it will remind you of this beautiful evening. And each time I look at that star, it will remind me of you."

Pearl examined the gift. It had no clip so it wasn't a brooch, and not a necklace either ... then she remembered. She had seen it around Emanuel's neck years ago when she was a little girl. She looked up, unsure what to do, what to say. It was the first present anyone had ever given her outside of *Ba-bah* and Uncle.

"It needs a chain," Emanuel said. "Perhaps I can take it to Lane Crawford's—" He reached to take it back.

"No! I shall do it myself," she said.

Closing her fingers around the object, she felt its spiky triangles dig into her palm.

He smiled.

She remembered that expression. She had seen it many years ago when they were returning to Hong Kong from that first voyage to China. She had fallen asleep in his lap, her head against his chest. She had opened one eye and looked up but he had not noticed. The look of contentment he had then was the same expression he had now.

Pearl felt protected—as she had that night on the boat when she was a little girl. This time, though, she felt more than just safe. She felt warm all over.

But this new sensation did not last long once she realized that she could not return the honour he had just bestowed. His gesture was a surprise. Had she known he had a gift, she would have prepared something appropriate in return. The ledger was unbalanced. He had given her face. Now she felt obliged to return face or be forever in his debt. What could she possibly do?

He interrupted her thoughts. "My behaviour at table this evening. It was unmanly. I wish to explain myself."

Emanuel told her about how he and his wife had met, how he used her dowry to start his business, and how she had given him no sons. Try as they might, his wife was barren. He wanted to put her aside, but that would mean he could never return to Calcutta. The shame would be unbearable. His community and his family would judge him too harshly for such a decision.

She listened intently. When he finished, he took in a deep breath and let it out. Then he closed his eyes for a moment, letting silence fall comfortably around them. Seeing his chest rise and fall gently, she realized something. She could give him her ears. She could give him friendship. And as though he had heard her thoughts, he opened his eyes, looked at her, and said, "Thank you."

Then he rose. "Good night, my Pearl of the Orient. May I call on you?"

"Yes, if you wish," she said, thinking that perhaps he wanted to tell her more of his concerns. Agreeing to be a friend would be one way of giving him face, of repaying his surprising generosity. Hearing her reply, he bowed and left her in the garden.

When he was gone she opened her hand and picked up the Magen David. It had left an imprint in the shape of a six-point star on her palm.

EMANUEL

Images of Pearl's eager expression, her dancing eyes, and her ingenuous smile filled his brain and left room for little else. That face as delicate as a peony and that small, nimble body hidden under a shapeless tunic sent his imagination reeling. For days he felt excitement in the air. Flowers seemed brighter, the air felt cleaner; he had the energy of ten men and the appetite of twenty. Strangely, he found himself needing to read poetry, to attempt to write verse and to draw her image. But he could not find any poetry books, his verses sounded trite, and his line drawings failed to capture the delicate curves of her cheeks. He found he could not sit still, and planned for opportunities to see the petite and beguiling beauty again. Hong Kong was where he wanted to be forever—this place of water and ships and commerce, this new and thrilling colony where everything seemed possible.

My Dear Li,

I wish to, once more, thank you for the friendship you extended on my last visit to your gracious home and for the honour of meeting your daughter Pearl. I recall many years ago she served us tea when we first discussed our partnership. How proud you must be to have such an accomplished daughter who is fluent in English and also such a confident hostess. I am completely charmed by her.

As you are aware, we three have prospered significantly from the sale and distribution of commodities that I have imported from India on a regular basis over the last decade. My supply and its sale have allowed both you and Aleandro to live the life of moguls. Aleandro has purchased two acres in the centre of Macau on which he has built "una casa grande" for himself and four houses surrounding it—one for each of his wives. With shrewd management he has also invested in hotels, banking, and the sale of arms and ammunitions. You have built a similarly large home in Happy Valley with an unparalleled view of Hong Kong harbour—and although you have not taken a wife or wives, you are able to lavish extravagance upon your beloved daughter. You have also increased your real estate holdings by erecting go-downs and rental units and investing in Hong Kong's fledgling stock exchange. Both you and Aleandro have become the men you are much due to my initiative.

But, and I asked this of Aleandro, what will become of it all when we are gone from this life? Who will benefit from our toil? From what I can see Aleandro will have a small civil war between rival factions of his wives, for none of them is legitimate. They are, after all, only protected women and not legitimate spouses. And will you be content to leave all you have to your daughter without a man in her life to perpetuate its capital?

For my part, I have chosen to live modestly and deposited my cash and precious metals at the Hong Kong bank. I have decided to stay in the colony for the foreseeable future and have taken this respite in Macau with Aleandro to decide how I should set down deeper roots in Hong Kong.

I am not of a mind to have a harem like my host or to lead a life of celibacy like you. Not for me the life of a Jeremiah—I wish for a new beginning with a new wife who will give me a son and heir that will inherit the great fortune I have amassed thus far and will continue to—G-d willing—for many more years to come.

I find myself open to a variety of avenues in this splendid city, where opportunity abounds for pioneers such as me. As you know, I have of late been appointed to a directorship at the Hong Kong and Shanghai bank—an appellation that has given me much joy and catapulted my personal stock amongst our fellow merchants. Imagine a Jew amongst the Christian elite. As you said to me, "Such an honour makes all your hard work worthwhile!" Omein to that. Now here's to the Chairmanship one day.

Meanwhile, I intend to expand my holdings with purchases of land now available on Kennedy Road and on The Peak. I will use my influence to petition the local authorities to build roads so that others may settle in the cooler upper levels. I will underwrite advances for the stock exchange and invest in gas and oil to fuel our ships and light our streets. And of course, I will continue in the opium trade and make hay while the sun shines on the Empire. I see gains here, for we are at the ground floor, laying a foundation for all other traders who now flock to our shores and who need our influence and investment as I once needed Mr. Jardine's.

But what of this if I am to be alone? With no one to share my successes? With no heir to leave such bounty? I see no point in it unless I take a wife—a real wife, who will give me an heir. Thus, I have laid my cards on the table. Although I am an older prospect my maturity promises fidelity and I have only honourable intentions.

This is a singular proposition. I will never mention it again should you object. Meanwhile I have entrusted this intelligence in Aleandro's hand to translate into Chinese, as I know it is your custom to have Pearl read your English correspondence. Her knowledge of this most delicate matter would be cause for me to immediately nullify my offer. You understand that, in my capacity as a director of the bank, I cannot be held up to ridicule of any sort, especially in matters that may be construed as salacious.

I remain trusting of your discretion and in hope until our next meeting.

Faithfully, ERB

The following day, when her father was conducting business out of the house, Pearl ordered Gum-ghee to call a chair to take her down to the bottom of the hill. From there the two women climbed onto a rickshaw that carried them to Central District, where Lane Crawford's had their shop. Pearl handed the pendant to the European attendant behind the counter and asked, in English, that it be fastened to a suitable chain. He dropped his monocle and looked her up and down, mouth agape and eyes wide with surprise that a Chinese woman could speak English so well.

One week later, a small package from the store was delivered to her house. She tore open the paper, flipped the lid of the tiny box, and retrieved the necklace, putting it around her neck. She ran down to her father's study, knocked, and entered. In a rush of words, she told him what had happened in the garden and showed him Emanuel's beautiful gift. He looked deep into her eyes and smiled.

"Most suitable, most suitable," he said and clapped his hands. Then he said something very puzzling: "I have received a letter from Emanuel. He has decided to stay in Hong Kong. He no longer wants to return to Calcutta."

"Oh" was all she could manage. He motioned for her to sit down. He sat beside her and folded his hands over hers.

"I think, daughter, that you should learn the Jewish religion," he said.

She immediately thought of the prayer Emanuel had recited. Such a beautiful language must surely come from a beautiful religion. Her family had no formal beliefs. If this was something that would please her *Ba-bah* then she was happy to agree. But there was no synagogue—not even enough Jews to make a *minyan,* her father explained. So Emanuel would have to teach her twice each week in his private office on Lyndhurst Terrace.

Pearl travelled down the hill by chair and then transferred to a rickshaw for the rest of the journey. Gum-ghee followed behind in conveyances of her own, carrying a bundle of books loaded into a cloth sack slung over her shoulders. Gum-ghee made a great show of heaving the heavy books up onto the table in Emanuel's office. Then she stood by the door and watched the foreigner, clearing her throat whenever his hand touched her mistress's shoulder, which it did frequently.

Pearl learned about Abraham, Isaac, and Jacob, and little by little, studying each day, she learned enough Hebrew to read Torah. To her surprise there were many similarities with Chinese traditions, especially regarding the importance of family and community. Most interesting was how Jews, like Chinese, had a history of overcoming hardships. There were similar stories of persecution but never defeat, of fleeing homes but never being homeless, of being outsiders but always survivors. Both Jews and Chinese had endured for thousands of years before even the Christians and the Mohammedans had stories to tell about their prophets. And by the time they did, Jews had settled everywhere in the known world, in Europe and in India and now in China. Scattered but somehow connected through the spirit passed down from generation to generation.

At first she learned her lessons to obey her father and to please Emanuel, who had given her face. But as the months passed she embraced the stories, the laws, and the traditions and found herself ready to make a solemn promise before G-d. Seeing Emanuel regularly, she grew more and more fond of him.

Then one day, a couple of years after her lessons had started, a message came for Pearl from Emanuel. He requested her company to tea and had sent conveyances: a chair carried by four men for Pearl and a second chair for Gum-ghee carried by two men.

When Pearl's chair reached the bottom of the hill that opened into Happy Valley, a *jinrikisha* was waiting to transport her all the way to Kennedy Road, where another chair carried by four strong young men awaited to take her up to the Hill District. It surprised her that the carriers did not stop at Lyndhurst Terrace but proceeded up the hill. Pearl looked back several times. Gum-ghee was urging her porters to go faster. But they proceeded at a walking pace while Pearl's men trotted along at quite a clip. Soon, Gum-ghee fell far behind. Delighted, Pearl realized that wherever they were taking her, she would soon be alone with Emanuel. Gum-ghee would be furious!

When they rounded the corner, a huge building came into view. Its pink walls (with off-white highlights on cornices and trims) glowed as though the mountainside on which it was built was blushing. With its domes and covered verandas on three floors, the mansion resembled palaces she had seen in magazines or paintings of Florentine and Venetian villas. It was the biggest house she had ever seen—at least three or four times larger than her *Ba-bah*'s home, she thought.

The carriers huffed as they climbed the narrow path hewn out of the thick tropical bush. It wound around to an entrance on the south side. There they set down the chair.

In front of her, double wooden doors opened. Pearl entered. The place smelled of new paint with an overlay of soil and the fresh-cut flowers that had been placed in oversized vases against the walls. A grand staircase dominated the centre of the foyer and marble floors kept the air cool even though the day was hot. Above her head, crowning all three floors, was a dome ringed with windows that let in a flood of natural light. It shone clear as a diamond atop a king's crown.

"Welcome to Kingsclere," said Emanuel, appearing at her side.

"Do you like it?"

Pearl could manage only a nod.

"May I give you a tour?" he asked. Again she nodded.

He extended his arm. She had no idea what the gesture meant, so she simply stared at it. He took her hand and placed it in the bend of his elbow.

"This way," he said.

The marble floors, the grand stairway, the chandelier, the walls, the dome all felt strange to her. It was as though she had taken a ship and landed in some foreign place. Emanuel showed her the solarium, the dining room, the salon, and various other rooms on the main floor and likewise on the middle floor. None of the rooms had yet been furnished. Their footsteps echoed off bare walls.

On the third floor they walked through a room that led onto the covered veranda. A cool breeze swept up the hill. Pearl clutched the pendant around her neck and felt her heart leap at what she saw. A panoramic view of the harbour stretched from east to west. Directly ahead, on the other side of the water, was Gow-loong—Kowloon or "Nine Dragons"—and beyond that the range of nine mountains that gave the district its name.

"What is your opinion of what you have seen?" he asked.

Pearl swallowed and took a deep breath. What could she say?

"It is auspiciously placed. Water and mountains advance in this direction. It is a house most suitable for a man of your station," she said, then added, "I have no doubt your wife will be happy in such a place."

His servants had set out tea on the shaded veranda.

They sat in silence, admiring the view and sipping from English porcelain cups that rested on little saucers. Some birds had made a nest on the ledge where a pillar met the roof. Someone shouting on the path below interrupted their chirping.

It was Gum-ghee. She saw them, high up. Winded, she stopped, mouth agape and panting like a Komodo dragon.

Later that evening, when Pearl went down to dinner with her father, her *Ba-bah* instructed Gum-ghee to send the servants out of the room.

"*Geow-lah, geow-lah*—scram, scram," Gum-ghee said, brushing the air with her hands. She closed the doors and stood behind her mistress.

Li turned to his daughter.

"Did you like the house?" he asked.

"Yes *Ba-bah,* it is beautiful. His family will be very comfortable there," she said.

"My daughter, he built it to *start* a family. He wishes to marry you. Bo Jue, the mansion is a wedding gift."

October 12, 1874
Lyndhurst Terrace,
Hong Kong

J. Sung Kum-kee, Esquire;
Ford, McDougal and Sung, Solicitors,
14 A, Connaught Road 1st Floor, Hong Kong.

Dear Mr. Sung:

This will confirm the several assignments discussed in your chambers that require briefs for my reference to be completed at your earliest opportunity and prior to my departure for China to trade my latest consignment. I wish for your firm to act on my behalf in the matters requiring signatures et cetera. You will also act as my deputy for the conveyance of funds deposited in trust to your firm or expended on my behalf. I shall set down in some detail the items that require your legal opinion that you may know my mind and therefore act accordingly in my absence.

On the matter of the camel, or rather the removal of the camel carcass, I am adamant that this is not my responsibility. I do not dispute owning the beast. I have used it for transportation to and from my place *of work on Lyndhurst Terrace to my home on The Peak. The beast bolted from its stall, likely due to bats swarming it for the insects that live in its fur. Camels are not clever animals. Lost, it wandered along a road and leaned on a wooden fence that could not take its weight. The animal fell into a ditch off May Road, broke its neck, and died. Had Her Majesty's Government's Public Works Division erected proper fencing as I had recommended in my brief to them some months ago, the camel would still be alive today and continuing its yeoman service as a mode of transportation. Moreover, HMG's refusal to entertain proposals for the building of a trolley or cable car has further exacerbated the situation for those of us who live in the cooler climes of The Peak. Clearly HMG is responsible for the camel's death due to their flagrant negligence, and therefore they should remove the carcass at no cost to me. You are to proceed with my suit against HMG with the utmost prejudice.*

As for the building of Ohel Leah Synagogue, I am equally adamant that restitution be sought and that you will respond to the letter of complaint against me with a suit against the Synagogue Committee, naming Kardoorie and Sassoon as principals against whom I seek redress. The case is simple. The aforementioned and I agreed to put up one third each in the form of a gift of land and monies to build the Shul on a piece of vacant land that I own on Kennedy Terrace. As you know, work has already begun on Kingsclere, my primary residence on said property. I offered to gift a portion of the area in question for the Shul that would lie beside my new house. Kardoorie and Sassoon reacted with surprise, saying that my domicile was never part of the original agreement. I have been quite open with my intentions, as demonstrated in various newspaper articles regarding the building of homes in the mid-levels of Victoria Mountain. Because they claim my initiative to be contrary to the original intent of the agreement, they withdrew their participation. They stated they found it reprehensible that any private citizen should be landlord of the Synagogue. In their minds, land and building should be in the hands of an independent body.

Their withdrawal halted this project. But today I see that they have—together with the Synagogue Committee—purchased a parcel of land on Robinson Road for the purposes of erecting a place of worship. This is a flagrant breach of contract and greatly to the benefit of those two individuals who have conspired to estrange me from my own community. They must not prevail in this attempt to exclude me and by so doing slander my good name. I wish redress containing an apology and $10,000 or a return to the original plan to build a synagogue on the property where I am building Kingsclere.

Thirdly I authorize you, my agent, to purchase shares of the Bank. It is my intention to increase my holding to 18%, thus making me the largest single shareholder, positioning me to be nominated Chairman. Together with Mr. Li and Mr. Remedios, our deposits would make a large dent in the Bank's coffers were we to withdraw and start a bank of our own. You may put it about that such is my thinking if ample notice is not taken of our considerable investment in the Bank's future.

And lastly, I plan to marry Pearl Li of Happy Valley and wish to present Kingsclere to her as a gift for which you will draw up the necessary documents for my review and signatures. I have every confidence that she will agree to my proposal, for she is from a good family that has always been honourable in their dealings with me.

Corollary to this, you may want to give some thought to how I might proceed with an annulment with Semah (née Ezra) of Calcutta and what might constitute a suitable recompense et cetera—a return of the full amount of her dowry plus interest perhaps?

Your immediate attention is expected as I remain sincerely,

E.R. Belilios.

PEARL

When she heard *Ba-bah* say "wedding gift," Pearl's heart skipped a beat and the soup caught in her throat.

Gum-ghee squealed and immediately covered her mouth.

The idea was as incomprehensible as it was enormous. It was too big to be believable. Was she dreaming? Was the ship that had transported her into the world of Kingsclere that morning transporting her now into another dimension? Marriage? Pearl choked and coughed. Gum-ghee slapped her back. She raised both her arms to open the air passages in her lungs. Tears welled and dropped down her cheeks. Eventually she stopped coughing and sat back in her chair.

When he saw that she had recovered, he said,

"I know this seems sudden, but we must know if you will accept."

"Accept what?"

"Daughter, you are eighteen. It is time you married. This is a good offer. With our two households combined, your children will be secure for generations to come."

She had not misheard. This was real, yet how could it be? Emanuel already had a wife. If he took her into his household she would be *yee-nai*—second wife. Many male foreigners took a concubine. It was the custom for Europeans who sojourned in Hong Kong to do this.

She had always thought of Emanuel as an uncle—an older man of position, a stranger from a strange place, European-looking yet from India. He interested her only because she had a thirst for knowledge of other lands and a curiosity about other customs. She had never thought of him as someone to marry or as someone to love as a husband. Marriage must be based on love, like the eternal devotion her father had for her mother. But never mind all that—he already had a wife. What would he want with another?

"*Ba-bah,* do not be angry with me," she said. "But I do not want to be *yee-nai.* Please don't let this happen to me."

"Daughter, you do not understand. He means to put aside his first wife because she could not bear him a son." Then he paused, leaned forward, and continued. "He sincerely admires you. I can see that in his eyes. What do you say to such a proposal?"

She was silent. She cared for Emanuel, but if she were to move to Kingsclere, who would take care of *Ba-bah?* What if Emanuel tired of her? What if she could not produce a son? He had put aside one wife; would he put aside another? Who would teach her about the duties of a wife to her husband?

"*Aiyah,*" Li said. "Why are you crying? *Go, go!*"

He ordered Gum-ghee take her to her rooms.

Pearl promptly left the dining table, rushed up to her bedchamber, and fell into bed. Gum-ghee followed, hastily closing the door. She cradled her mistress in her arms, wiped her little face, and rocked her until she fell asleep.

The following day and for two more after that, Pearl stayed in her room. She lay on her stomach and stared at the wall while Gum-ghee sat on the edge of the bed and fanned the air above her back.

Her father had sent for her several times, but Gum-ghee stood guard at the door and told him that her mistress was ill with woman's matters.

Finally, after the third day, her father's patience ran out. He banged his fist on the door. "*Stop this foolishness by sunset or I will break down the door and drag you to a monastery where I will leave you to the Buddhist nuns for the rest of your life!*"

She knew well that when her *Ba-bah* made up his mind, he always got his way.

"*I have invited Eh-mun-u-wah—Emanuel—to dine tonight. You will present yourself. A father who cannot control his daughter will lose face. Understand?*"

Pearl said nothing.

"This is what education does to a woman. It makes her arrogant and too proud to respect her parents. Your mother is lucky she is not here to see this behaviour."

He yelled loud enough that the whole household could hear his scolding.

Pearl felt deeply ashamed for making him so angry. His hurt became her pain. He had never abandoned her. Even in his most desperate times he had not sold her as a slave, as so many men would have. For that alone she owed him loyalty. It was her duty to be obedient.

When she realized this, she got out of bed and ordered Gum-ghee to draw a bath. She did so willingly, and helped her mistress out of her clothes that were stiff with sweat. Then she undid her hair and let the black tresses fall about her slim, smooth shoulders.

Pearl stepped into the tub and felt all her grief leak out into the water that had been scented with mint leaves. She immersed herself to soak her hair. When she emerged, Gum-ghee was ready with a washcloth and scented soap from Watson's. She rubbed it over Pearl's ivory-coloured skin, dragging the fabric over her slim legs and between her toes.

After bathing, Gum-ghee held up a wide, cotton sheet. Pearl rose and stepped into it, wrapping it around her body. Gum-ghee towelled off Pearl's hair, sat her mistress down at the dressing table, and rubbed eucalyptus paste on her back to promote ease of breathing. Satisfied that equilibrium had been restored, she fetched hair oils, combs, and pins that were laid out on a cloth.

Meanwhile, Pearl stared at her own reflection in the large mirror over the dressing table. Was this all that Emanuel saw? Or did he care about what she felt in her heart? How she longed for a woman to speak with and to tell her what she should do.

Gum-ghee poured extract of sesame oil on her palms and worked it into Pearl's long black hair. Who was this woman, Pearl wondered. She was like a second mother to her. And if the men had their way, Gum-ghee would soon be a second mother to a second wife.

"What will become of me?" she asked, looking at their reflection.

"You must prepare yourself to be a wife and a mother," Gum-ghee said, working her fingers through Pearl's hair, reapplying oil and repeating the gesture.

"You have told me stories from the books you study. How did those women in ancient times become wives and mothers? The stories in your books tell of great houses. They are like the great dynasties in China. You can be like those women here in Hong Kong. A woman can be either a servant or a mistress of the house."

"What makes a woman become a servant? And what makes her become the mistress? Is it money? Or birth?"

Gum-ghee continued to rub until Pearl's hair shone like lacquer. Then she braided it, speaking as she did so.

"I was born into servitude. My mother was a chambermaid who was bedded by the master of the house. You see, she served in a house where the master ate opium. At first, he did so only once in a while. Then, as the drug seduced him, he indulged every day.

"As the months passed and he ate more and more opium, he was unable to do anything except lie on his side all day and all night. His teeth fell out and he could no longer chew or swallow food. Soon word of the merchant's condition spread. People took advantage and stole his money. His servants were the worst. The man soon became destitute and strangers occupied his house. My mother fled with me. We made our way to Hong Kong where she became a beggar and a prostitute. She made sure that I did not follow in her profession by paying a hairdresser to teach me some skills to prepare me to be a servant. One day, she sold me to your father."

"How old were you?"

"I'm not certain, mistress, maybe sixteen."

When she finished her story, Pearl's braids had been pulled it into a tight bun and held in place with pins and a tortoiseshell comb. Gum-ghee placed her hands lightly on her mistress's shoulders.

"Things might have been different if my mother were a man. But it is the lot for women in this world. To survive we must serve and be silent. You must make the best of the future by pleasing your father and by being a good wife to your new husband. As long as you can give him sons he will always be loyal."

This account frightened Pearl more than any crack of thunder, any wild animal that might have leapt out of the bush, or even the sight of Ah-Fook's skeletal body lying asleep in the shed. She got up, walked to the divan, and lay down on it. Gum-ghee followed, sitting at the end of the chaise and massaging Pearl's feet.

Eventually, the sun started to set and the cicadas chirped an evening song. She got off the divan and let Gum-ghee dress her. She slipped jade bracelets on her wrists, tucked a white silk handkerchief into the buttons on the side of her tunic, and pinned a white bauhinia in her hair. With each item Pearl's mind became more settled. When she was fully dressed, she took out her mother's jade stone and placed it on her writing table, sat down, and composed a list of demands that she committed to memory.

During the meal there was not much talk. Li sat at one end of the table and Pearl at the other. Emanuel was seated to her left and Aleandro on the right. Normally, the men would be discussing the state of business. But it was not so that evening.

When the dishes were cleared and the fruits were placed at table, Emanuel wiped his mouth and looked at Pearl.

She saw his gaze and took an orange from the bowl at the centre. Gum-ghee, who had been standing beside her throughout dinner, reached down to cut the fruit for her mistress.

Emanuel cleared his throat.

"My dear," he started. This was the first time anyone had referred to her with such intimacy. "I have met with your father and discussed our future. He has agreed to the match if you will accept me."

Pearl wanted a slice of orange because her mouth was dry. But she didn't want anyone to see that her hands were shaking. She lowered her head.

"Have you considered my offer?"

Now she felt her father's eyes. Without moving her head she looked up. The lines on his forehead pulled together in annoyance or anxiety, she wasn't sure which. Pearl turned to face Emanuel:

"Yes," she said.

"And your answer?"

He leaned forward with his elbows on the table.

"Out of loyalty to *Ba-bah* and out of respect for all you have done for my family, I feel it is an honour to be asked," she said and then stopped.

She took a deep breath and composed herself.

Gum-ghee opened her fan. It clicked softly as she waved it.

"*Aiyah!* Daughter," Li said, his voice bursting through the stillness. "Every day she can talk and talk but now only silence." Then to Pearl in Cantonese: "*Bad daughter to behave with such impudence.*"

"With respect, she must come to a decision on her own," Emanuel said, stopping his partner's outburst. Then, turning to Pearl: "My dear, what is your answer?"

"It is an honour to be asked," she repeated, trying to recall the speech she had written and memorized. "But while I admire the gentleman, I do not love him."

Emanuel sat back in his chair. Aleandro made a quick translation. Li's face reddened and he said in Cantonese: "*Such emotions come later. What nonsense to talk of love when there is a good prospect. You have made me lose face with my chief business partner. You are a bad and ungrateful daughter.*"

He pushed back his chair and turned away, drumming the tabletop with his fingers. "*Bad girl,*" he repeated, almost spitting the words out.

It was painful to see him so angry. Pearl felt Gum-ghee's hand stroking her left shoulder. "I desire to be with a man that I love," she said. Aleandro started to translate but Li stopped him and spoke in English:

"Too much books. Too much education," he said.

"*Ba-bah,*" Pearl said in Cantonese, "*I owe you my life and all that I have. If I cannot marry for love then I know I have a duty to obey. And I know I must not cause Emanuel to lose face.*" Then, turning to Emanuel, she switched to English: "If this is not a love match then we must have an agreement."

Seeing that Li was about to interrupt, Emanuel placed his hand on his host's arm. "What kind of agreement?" he asked.

Pearl pulled a document out of her long sleeve and read its contents: "First, I must have my own room and be allowed to hire my own servants. Second, Gum-ghee will be my head servant for life. Third, the new house will be mine if you leave this earth before me, and it will go to my children when we are both no longer alive."

Pearl had made copies and handed them to the men. They stared at the documents for a long time. Li was the first to speak. He balled the paper and threw it across the room, muttering under his breath. Then he let loose: He was furious for her impudence. How could his daughter be so ungrateful, so arrogant? Who was this child? She did not resemble anything that could have come from his blood. Thank the gods his wife was not alive to witness this … this … Words failed him.

Pearl had never seen her father so upset. He sat back in his chair, exhausted from his outburst, and pulled open his collar. Gum-ghee rushed to his side and fanned him with one hand while pouring a glass of water with the other. She put the glass to his lips, begging him to drink it and calm down. He did so, and was quiet for a moment; then he started again with another outburst even more severe than the last. Finally spent, he mopped his brow that gleamed with sweat.

During this Pearl sat still, her eyes turned down.

Emanuel leaned in. "If I agreed," he said softly, "or should I say *acquiesced,* to these demands, what should I receive in return?"

"In return," Pearl replied, "I will be devoted to only you, and G-d willing, over time I may learn to love you as much as you say you love me."

Then she looked up and straight into his eyes. "I will give you at least one son and one daughter. I promise to raise them in the Jewish tradition."

Emanuel smiled and reached across the table with his palm up. She looked at it and placed her small hand in his. Despite the staring, the open-mouthed surprise, the disbelief from *Ba-bah,* Aleandro, and Gum-ghee, she felt a deep sense of intimacy. It was a bond that travelled from the fleshy centre of his hand right through into hers, up her arm to fill her chest with warmth. She had sealed her future with a handshake.

He gave her hand a squeeze and then released it. The action needed no translation. They all felt in that moment of contact that two people had come to an understanding that would form the basis of a lifelong bond.

Li shouted for a servant, who appeared immediately. He ordered Napoleon brandy and glasses. When it came, the men sat back and drank noisy toasts—to the two of them, then to the groom and then to the bride, downing shots and grimacing as the fiery liquid coursed down their throats.

Pearl touched the rim of her glass to her lips with every toast. She steeled herself for one more codicil and felt her neck muscles tighten. Gum-ghee patted her mistress's shoulders with the soft part of her fists.

"There is one more thing," Pearl said.

They stared at her. She looked directly at Emanuel. "You must make *gerushin.*"

He stared at her for a long time, then nodded, got up, and left the table. He went out into the night, where he climbed into a waiting chair that carried him to his rooms on Lyndhurst Terrace.

"Where is he going?" Li demanded. "What did you say? What happened?

"Do not worry, *Ba-bah*. We have an agreement and you have your wish. Now he must show how much he truly loves me."

Pearl stood from the table. Gum-ghee opened the double doors that led out to the hall. As Pearl climbed slowly up the stairs to her bedroom she could feel her father's eyes watching her. He must have wondered where his little Bo Jue had gone and who it was that had taken her place. She would have loved to be able to run up the stairs and disappear into her room. But she couldn't. Her legs weighed a ton. What had she just done? she wondered. She was eighteen years old and so terrified she could hardly walk.

When she got to her room and shut the door behind her, she collapsed into Gum-ghee's arms. The handmaid pulled out a little box of eucalyptus paste and rubbed some into her mistress's temples. Then she undid Pearl's hair and helped her change into night clothing.

In bed, Pearl curled her knees up to her chest. She looked out the window and tried to locate the star that Emanuel had named after her. She could not find it.

October 16, 1874
Lyndhurst Terrace,
Hong Kong

J. Sung Kum-kee, Esquire;
Ford, McDougal and Sung, Solicitors,
14 A, Connaught Road 1st Floor, Hong Kong.

Dear Mr. Sung:

Further to my written instructions of October 12 Inst. I attach codicils received from my intended. Having spent some time reviewing the items, I am of a mind to agree to all that is contained here. The heart wants what the heart wants. Nevertheless, I value your opinion on these matters from a legal standpoint.

I have reviewed your draft correspondence to the Calcutta recipients and authorize you to forward—post-haste—these advisements through Mr. Mohan Rustomjee, Calcutta, India, to be forwarded, by his hand, to my wife with copies furnished, in like manner, to Mr. Ibrahim Ezra of the same city.

I trust that, while I am in China, you will apprise me of any *developments regarding the items above-mentioned and that you will exercise uttermost discretion. Telegraph communications are not secure from the inquisitive eyes and loose tongues of their operators. You will have to send word via runners or horsemen should any important item arise that requires my immediate attention.*

Sincerely yours,
E.R. Belilios.

Enclosures attached.

The new art of photography had arrived in Calcutta. A Frenchman named Monsieur Leroux (who had apprenticed with "le grand" Louis Daguerre at his home in Bry-sur-Marne) had set up a studio on Park Street. He was a short, round, sweaty fellow with thinning black hair, shiny with pomade. He had a round face and a thick moustache that curled up at the ends like tiny horns on an imp. As the only reputable *artiste de photographe* in the city, he was heavily booked. Mr. Ezra decided to commission a series of portraits of his family and of his estate. He had planned to have his family pose seated on his prized horses. But he lost that argument when his wife and daughter formed an alliance against such a barbaric idea. Semah had not been near a horse since her accident more than a decade earlier. Once bitten, twice shy, she would say whenever she was asked about any equestrian activities. In fact, she did not attend polo games or the race meetings at the Royal Calcutta Turf Club—arguably the most important social events of the calendar. No, they would be photographed indoors. The other snag was Emanuel. Who knew when his itinerant son-in-law would return?

Mr. Ezra decided to proceed with the family portraits indoors and without Emanuel rather than forfeit his place in the lineup of the photographer's clients. It was rumoured that the man was going to get a Vice-Regal appointment ...

A heated discussion had ensued as to the settings. M. Leroux agreed initially with Mr. Ezra that an equine scene might be appropriate, but quickly changed his mind when he discovered that Mrs. Ezra sided with her daughter in selecting interior backdrops. He had learned his syco-phancy in the salons of Paris, where artistic matters were always left to the women of the house. After all, it was the women who would hang his portraits and point to them proudly as the work of "le grand Leroux." They would do so only if the photographs met their exacting preferences. Predictably, Mr. Ezra acquiesced, and that is how Semah found herself in front of the mural in her former bedroom on the upper floor of her father's house.

She had arrived earlier that day, met the photographer, and discussed various background options. Semah was determined that her portrait would be taken in front of the mural that documented the year of courtship with her husband. She wore a pink organdy dress with a high collar, long sleeves tight to the arms, and a full skirt. Her hair was arranged like a large, beautiful nest. Pinned to the top of it was a small round hat that might have belonged to a pixie. Even though it had been some time since she had seen her courtship paintings, staring at them now gave her a chill of excitement. So absorbed was she in reviewing the events depicted on the wall that she failed to noticed M. Leroux or his Indian assistant setting up camera equipment behind her.

"Madame," he said.

Semah flinched at the voice and turned to face him.

"Ah," he sighed. *"Si charmante, si douce,"* he said, looking at his subject. Then he noticed the wall. *"Mon dieu—c'est magnifique—une peinture digne de L'Académie!"*

The man was a whirlwind of activity. First he took several shots of the mural. Semah had said she wanted a picture to keep for herself. Every time the shutter clicked, flash powder exploded simultaneously. It made a *pop* sound and blazed for an instant in the trowel-like apparatus held at arm's length by M. Leroux's assistant. At first, the phosphorescent flash momentarily blinded Semah and she whooped with laughter. But she soon got used to it.

"Ready? Be still," he said, and then pushed the trigger that caused the shutter to click and the flash to burst. One *click-pop* followed another. M. Leroux pulled a square plate out of the camera and reloaded it with a fresh one while his assistant shook powder into the flashgun. Semah watched, fascinated, as the two men worked in synchrony.

In the midst of this exciting activity, her mother entered. She was holding an envelope addressed to Semah. "M. Leroux, would you be so kind as to leave us?"

"*Mais, Mon Dieu, comment puis-je travailler dans ces conditions?*"

"Please, Monsieur …" she implored.

M. Leroux flapped his hands in the air and jerked his head at his assistant. The two men left the room.

"It's from Emanuel," her mother said. "He wrote one to your father as well. He read it aloud to me. Mr. Rustomjee just delivered them. He is downstairs awaiting a reply." She handed the letter to Semah, who was rising from her chair. "No, you'd better sit."

Semah tore open the flap, pulled out a folded sheet, and scanned the contents. Her eyes landed on the words *gerushin, set aside,* and on *dowry returned.* She read only one sentence in its entirety: *"My intention is to remain in Hong Kong permanently."*

Her heart pounded. She felt her throat squeeze in on itself. She could not speak. The air smelled metallic and her hands turned cold. She didn't even hear her mother say "Would you like a cup of sweet tea?" Neither did she see her mother leave the room or hear the door click softly. She paced, clutching the letter in her hand, stopped, opened the paper and reread the words. Then she read them again and again, letting their meaning sink in.

Increasingly, Emanuel had stayed in Hong Kong for longer and longer periods. This last sojourn had lasted over a year now, his longest absence to date. During that time his letters had been sporadic and impersonal. And now this? A letter of dismissal? No!

She sat at her writing table and pulled out a sheet of paper. She snatched the pen out of its holder, dipped it in the inkwell, and held it over the page. Her hand shook. Ink splattered on the vellum. A drop fell on her pink sleeve. Soon her whole body was quaking as though she had been immersed in a vat of ice. A scream wailed inside her head. It cleft her brain like a hot needle driven through her ears. She couldn't breathe. She left the room and went down the stairs, gripping the banister to favour her leg.

Mr. Rustomjee stood at the bottom landing. He bowed, but she put her hands up to shield her face.

She walked past the messenger and burst through the front door, gulping for air, head spinning, tears welling. She moved quickly, hoping that her prosthetic leg wouldn't twist off. But she couldn't have cared less if it did. What humiliation was worse than being put aside? She would have crawled to put distance between her and that letter.

Outside, trees, grass, and stables whirled like a merry-go-round with her at the centre. The mansion floated in front of her eyes. Papa and Mama, brows knitted and arms outstretched, called to her. But she heard nothing, their voices drowned by the squealing inside her brain. She tore open her collar. At the stables, Lucky Lady stood in her stall, attended by a groom. He was tall, a young Sikh. He had a *kirpan*—a dagger in his belt. He stared at her.

She stumbled toward the man, her chest heaving like a bellows. Reaching him, she grabbed the handle of his *kirpan* and pulled it out. The silver blade sparkled. "Use it," she said, gasping for air.

Emanuel was true to his handshake. A date was set for the signing of the marriage contract. And it would be done at Kingsclere, the largest villa in Hong Kong, its size a testament of his devotion to his new Chinese wife. Her mansion dwarfed Government House below and lorded over the urban sprawl of Central District by the shore. Behind it a hill rose steeply, capped by Victoria Peak, accessible only by footpaths that wound through dense tropical bush where eagles sat atop trees during the day and wild boar could be heard rustling in the thickets at night.

On the day of her wedding, Pearl wore a white Chinese-style silk tunic with pearl brocade and a veil that covered her face. The white was to signify her honour according to her new religion, but it was also the colour of mourning in the Chinese tradition, as Gum-ghee was quick to point out. Only the veil met with her handmaid's approval—Chinese brides wore them on their wedding day to show that they were prepared to approach their new lives blindly.

Pearl rode in her own chair carried by four men. Gum-ghee followed in a rickshaw. A walking Chinese orchestra preceded them, playing cymbals, tabors, and trumpets. En route, firecrackers popped like rapid gunfire. The cavalcade started from the bottom of the hill of her father's house and travelled all the way to Kingsclere.

There, a tall Chinese man in a dark, European-style morning suit met Pearl at the entrance. He doffed his top hat.

"Sung Kum-kee at your service, Madam," he said in elegant Cantonese. His hair was cut very short and he had a small lump on his forehead in the space between his eyes. It looked as if a horn was about to burst through it. A pencil-line moustache grew on his upper lip.

"I am Mr. Belilios's legal adviser and a notary for today's service," he said. "I am to escort you. Shall we?"

Pearl took the man's arm. He smelled of tobacco and Bay Rum—pomade that stiffened his shiny black hair. The doors opened.

Pearl felt her heart leap when she saw Emanuel waiting for her under the *chuppah*. He was dressed in a long white *kittel* over his best suit. She could see his eyes moisten as she approached.

Mr. Sung asked her father and Aleandro to act as witnesses for Emanuel. They agreed and took their places on either side of the groom. Because neither Emanuel's nor Pearl's mother was present, she had arranged for Gum-ghee to parade her, in a circle, seven times around the groom.

Then Mr. Sung asked Gum-ghee and Aleandro's chief wife to each take one of Pearl's hands. She was led to stand beside Emanuel. Once under the *chuppah,* the ceremony began. Prayers and songs were recited and all observances were completed, including the signing of the *ketubah*—a handwritten contract that set down all Pearl's conditions. Emanuel signed first, then handed the pen to Pearl for her signature. Gum-ghee fixed her thumbprint, as did Aleandro's chief wife. Then Emanuel placed a gold ring on Pearl's finger. They drank wine from the same glass, after which Emanuel laid it on the floor and shattered it with his heel.

A jubilant shout rang out from the assembled guests. The newlyweds left the *chuppah* and walked a short distance to the outdoor reception on the lawn. A small orchestra played European melodies until the sun set.

When everyone had left and the servants had cleared the tables, Emanuel said,

"My dear, you have made me happy again. Are you happy?"

"Yes," she replied. But she felt she was not being entirely truthful.

"I shall come to you," he whispered in her ear. Then he nodded a silent communication to his notary.

I shall come to you. Although she did not know why, those words filled her with dread. It was not what he said but the way he had said it. Or rather what he did when he whispered in her ear. She wasn't entirely certain but she thought she had felt the tip of his tongue lick the inside of her ear. Before she could say anything, Emanuel was gone, busy bidding farewell to a guest.

Seeing that she was momentarily alone, Mr. Sung invited her to follow him. Gum-ghee rushed to her side. Together they went up the staircase and into one of the bedrooms.

Inside, she saw a four-poster bed covered by mosquito netting. On either side were windows and slatted French doors that led out to the veranda. It was the same room Emanuel had led her to on the day he first showed her the house. Oak doors separated her bedchamber from Emanuel's.

"Does the decor suit Madam's taste?" Mr. Sung asked. "I was advised by Lane Crawford's that this was the very best. Should Madam wish, it can all be changed."

Pearl walked slowly about the room, touching a bedpost, the surface of the writing table, the easy chairs, the paintings on the wall. She looked at the notary and nodded. She didn't know what else to do.

Seeing that she had no complaints, Mr. Sung said in English, "Good evening, Madam." He turned swiftly and grabbed Gum-ghee by the arm. Ignoring her protestations, he pushed her out the door so quickly that Pearl did not have time to object. She heard a key turn from the outside. She tried the door. It was locked. Gum-ghee shouted and banged on the door. She was inconsolable.

Pearl sat on the edge of the bed and covered her ears until the wailing stopped. When her maid's cries finally fell silent, she lowered her hands. Now all she could hear was her heart thumping so hard she thought it would burst out of her chest. As night fell, the room darkened. Outside, larks squeaked and dived at invisible insects looping about the air in their unpredictable flight.

She heard a tap on the door—from Emanuel's side.

"My dear?" he inquired.

She rushed to the door and held the handle. It moved. Her grip, even with two hands, was too feeble to stop it moving. She saw a key and turned it. The lock snapped into place.

"What is the matter?" she heard him say. "Open the door." His voice had an edge.

Pearl's mouth felt dry. She backed away from the door and sat on the bed, staring at the handle that moved up and down several more times. Then it moved no more.

There was no lamp in the room, so she sat in the dark for a long time. When the house was still at last and the larks were silent, as the moon rose and the stars appeared, she felt her body give in to fatigue. She rolled onto her side, raised her legs onto the bed, and fell asleep hugging her knees.

In her dream, it was night. She was standing on the edge of a cliff looking down into a vast gorge. Her chest filled with a chilling sense of foreboding. Grey clouds lowered, lightning flashed, thunder cracked, and rain fell, but she did not get wet. She looked down at herself and saw that she was naked. Gazing into a deep ravine, she saw a man. He looked up. His eyes were blue. Then she felt hungry and wanted to eat the man. But to get to him she had to leap off the edge. She lifted a foot and stretched it forward. Her weight shifted and she teetered. Thunder roared again. Rain fell hard in sheets. She held her breath and dived into the void.

Pearl woke with a start. Sunlight flooded the room. She got out of bed and went to the door. On the way she passed a mirror and saw that she was still fully clothed. It had been a dream—a scary but exciting one. She felt her brow. It was a little damp.

She went to the door that separated Emanuel's bedroom from hers. She listened but heard nothing. Images from her dream appeared in her mind's eye. It made her feel warm, so she opened the French doors, stepped out onto the veranda, and took a deep breath. She noticed something: there was no wall separating Emanuel's side from her own. She hugged the outer wall of the veranda and tiptoed toward the neighbouring set of French doors. They were open. She looked inside.

Emanuel was lying on his back, asleep. She gasped and looked away. Then thought: last night he could have gone out to the veranda and come into her room through the French doors. But he didn't. Her heart leapt. Looking through the window again, she watched his chest rise and fall, rise and fall.

Although fully dressed, Pearl felt naked. That sensation of hunger from her dream returned. Only it was not for food. It was more like a giant emptiness in the pit of her belly that longed to be filled. Emanuel stirred. He woke up and looked at her—stared at her with his piercing blue eyes. He got up and walked toward her. It must have started to rain because she suddenly felt sodden.

SEMAH

She thrust the dagger into the Sikh's hands and turned her back. "Cut the stays," she cried.

He stood there, dumb.

"I can't breathe. I can't breathe," she gasped, and fell to her knees before Papa and Mama could reach her.

Ibrahim snatched the knife from the startled groom, slid it under Semah's bodice, and cut the stays, then the ties of her corset. When they fell open, Semah panted with relief and leaned back. Ibrahim caught her in his arms.

"My dear child," he said, kissing her forehead. Her mother mopped her daughter's brow and held her hand. Semah saw Mr. Rustomjee clench and unclench his fingers, his eyes misty, his lips tightly closed.

"Come, come my dear, let's go back inside," Ibrahim said.

He signalled the groom. The Sikh took back his knife and sheathed it. With one arm around Semah's waist, he lifted her to a standing position. She leaned on him. He felt as durable as a brick wall and smelled of straw. Behind them Lucky Lady whinnied. Slowly, her heart that had pounded against her chest like a kettledrum returned to a more normal rhythm. As they walked toward the house, Semah tried to place the Sikh. His face looked familiar.

"What is your name?"

"Veer Singh," he replied. "At Memsahib's service."

Yes, she remembered him now. This man was the stable boy who had found her twisted and broken from her fall. Then he had disappeared.

Indoors, he helped Semah onto a chaise, folded a hand over his chest, and stood beside her for further instruction. Sula had ordered a cold compress. When it arrived, she made her daughter lie back and placed the wet towel on her forehead.

"Close your eyes, dear. Try to get some rest," she said.

But Semah studied Veer Singh. Tall and athletic, he was dressed in a tight, short-sleeved undershirt, riding jodhpurs, and knee-high leather boots. Brown skin, the colour of chocolate, was drawn tightly over his biceps and the muscles of his arms. His wide forehead and patrician nose gave him an aristocratic bearing despite his lowly position. A black stubble beard dotted his face. Yes, he would do very well, she thought as she laid her head back.

Ibrahim tried to find the right words to console his daughter in the face of his son-in-law's betrayal, but they escaped him. He looked at the Sikh. "Veer Singh," he offered, "came back after your marriage. He said he was sorry and could he work off his debt to me—to you. He felt responsible for your accident ... he said that if he were not such a coward, he would have gotten help sooner ... instead ... he said he will devote his life to righting the wrong he believes he has done ... Semah?"

"Yes, Father, I understand," she said.

"Good. You see, what goes around comes around. Good comes out of bad—sometimes ..." He didn't finish his sentence. His words sounded fatuous, their meaning inappropriate, their authority limited. But he needn't have beaten himself up. His attempt to offer balm was not in vain. Semah had heard him.

After a good rest and a change of clothes, Semah ordered buckets of water brought to her old room. Servants rushed into action, thinking that Semah wanted a bath. But that's not what she had in mind. She did not disrobe. Instead she stood in front of the mural in her old bedroom. As the buckets were brought in, she ordered them placed at her feet. Once they had all arrived, she lifted one bucket and threw its contents against the wall, discarded it, reached for another, emptied that one, and so on. Bucket after bucket of water was dumped against the pictorial history. White circles appeared where a blast of water hit the wall. Gravity pulled rivulets down like tears, distorting the faces, the places, the objects.

Carefully assembled images melded into meaningless blobs, except for one area. In the middle, the picture of her and Emanuel remained immune from dissolution—it was the only area she had shellacked.

Hearing the strange noise from above, her parents rushed upstairs. Semah stood in front of her handiwork, her hands on her hips.

"What are you doing?" her father asked.

Semah was determined not to release the well of tears that threatened to burst. No! That would not happen. Emanuel was her husband. *Her* husband. If he would not come back to her then she would have to go to him.

"It's time to start again," Semah said. She looked at her father. "I want Veer Singh to accompany me—a woman alone, travelling by sea to a savage country, needs protection. Have him at my house. I shall leave as soon as possible."

In her mind, words materialized. *Money* and *Luggage* and *Passage* appeared on bits of paper pinned on an imaginary wall. For *Money* she would go to Raphael, for *Luggage* she would press Veer Singh into service, and for *Passage* she would book a cabin on the fastest clipper she could find.

After that first morning with him, the nights that followed came easier to her. Truth be told, Pearl looked forward to being with her husband. She had known the mechanics of the sex act but, until then, had known nothing of its pleasures. Nor did she realize that the act did not have to be confined to the bedchamber or the night. Emanuel's office, the study, the solarium, and other places around the house provided impromptu venues to satisfy their mutual hunger. And they did so whenever the urge came, regardless of the time of day (or night). In the weeks that followed, the servants darted out of sight whenever they saw the master and mistress enter a room. But they didn't go far—they pressed their ears against doors and walls and listened with giggling delight at the lovers' *cries of happiness*. Gum-ghee dispersed them, averring, "Only the *Lo-baan* and the *Tai-tai* have a licence to behave thusly," and adding, "They are making a son so that the family may have a glorious future." Servants young and old rolled their eyes. Regardless of the aphorism's noble intent, what they heard were two people rutting like golden-haired monkeys driven mad with spring fever.

Surely then, with such diligence, Pearl would have been able to *catch a baby*. But no, her monthly arrived as usual, which spurred Emanuel and Pearl to go at it with greater determination. Alas, another month passed and the crimson stain appeared on the cloth. Pearl wept when she saw it. Once again, she went to him and shook her head no to indicate another disappointing result. The last such message was delivered on the eve of his voyage inland to trade opium for silver. "We shall try again when I return," he had said. That night he did not lie with her. The following morning he was gone without a word of farewell, leaving Pearl to wonder, in the days and weeks that followed, if she had done something wrong. If it had been her fault that she could not *catch a baby*.

"*Tai-tai,* I have something to report," Gum-ghee said early one morning. Pearl had just finished a bowl of congee with fermented egg. She was in the solarium that overlooked the harbour where Emanuel had erected his telescope on a tripod.

"What is it?"

"I am afraid that you will not like what you hear and throw me out."

"You are silly to think such thoughts," Pearl said. "You have been with me since I was a girl. If you are gone, who will fix my hair and fan me to sleep on hot summer nights? It's impossible to train anyone else to do it properly. So don't talk nonsense."

Gum-ghee made no response. Pearl softened her tone. "Gum-ghee," she said, "what is it? What is the matter? Why don't you look at me?"

"I heard some things. I heard …" She stopped again. Her face was pale.

"Gossip?"

Hong Kong was full of scandals. Servants tattling on market days were a great source of community intelligence on all the households in the colony.

"It is about you, mistress. Please do not be angry."

"Me? Are you certain?"

"Yes, mistress. They say you have received a curse. You and the master."

"What kind of curse?"

"It is said that purveyors of opium will suffer misery for three generations during which no male offspring will survive to manhood. It is a vengeance meant to make opium sellers feel the same pain endured by Chinese women whose husbands or brothers or sons died *chasing the dragon*."

That phrase brought her mind back to the image of Ah-Fook, the gardener. The once robust and hard-working man had been reduced to skin and bones. Death was a mercy for him.

"Nonsense." Pearl almost spat out the word. "Superstition."

"It is why your father has never taken a new wife," Gum-ghee continued. "He does not want the pain of another loss. And Aleandro in Macau, that man has more wives than an emperor and yet no children. And the *gweilo Tai-Pan* traders—and the other Jew traders—same thing, no children until they stopped trading and gave to charity, then children came."

Pearl's mind raced. What Gum-ghee had said was true. Could it be? Emanuel had gone on the voyage on his own, without her *Ba-bah* and without Aleandro. Could it be that they knew about the curse but no one had thought to tell her? She didn't think *Ba-bah* would keep such a thing from her.

"Is there any method to end such a curse?"

"I do not know, *Tai-tai*," Gum-ghee replied, her eyes downcast.

"Find out. You bring me nothing but problems. Now go and find a solution." It was a surprising tone—gruff and cruel.

Gum-ghee stood but kept her eyes downturned. She was hurt that her mistress was upset.

"There is something else," she said.

"Yes?"

"The master's first wife—she has arrived in Hong Kong. Her chairs, they are coming up Garden Road."

"You are crazy. Coming up the hill now?"

"*Tai-tai* can see for herself," Gum-ghee said, gesturing out the window.

At the bottom of the hill in the forward chair sat a woman dressed in a white European-style dress and a large hat. The procession was still too far for Pearl to make out her features, but she was a large woman. The chair she occupied required four carriers, and they were walking slowly. Behind them coolies shouldered many boxes of her belongings suspended in netting hung from bamboo poles. Due to the weight of their cargo, the carriers stopped twice during their ascent. Bringing up the rear was a tall man with a turban. He carried a sack over his shoulder and seemed to be directing the coolies.

Aiyah! Thoughts whipped through Pearl's mind. Was there no end to bad fortune hitting her in the face like bird droppings? Should she run back to her father's house? Should she prevent the woman from setting foot in her home—the one that her husband had built for her? Gum-ghee offered that perhaps she could poison her. Pearl dismissed the idea; besides, how would they get rid of the body? What to do? What to do? Where was her mother now that she needed her wisdom?

Pearl left the window and went to the front door and waited. The hall clock ticked loudly, but its minute hand seemed never to move.

"Will *Tai-tai* wish me to prepare a bedchamber?" Gum-ghee asked.

"What?"

"For the *gwei-paw*—foreigner woman."

"Yes," Pearl said, then corrected herself. "No—perhaps. I don't know. Why do you ask me these things?"

Gum-ghee backed away and stood behind her mistress. Pearl opened the front door and stood on the stoop as the woman's cavalcade arrived.

The giantess was holding an open parasol over her head. Pearl watched the Indian manservant with a turban help her off the chair. Pearl was amazed at how tall the woman was. And her hat made her seem even taller. There was a long ostrich feather on one side. A netted veil covered her face. The woman walked toward the front door. Behind her, coolies deposited luggage boxes on the front yard. She spoke:

"Do you speak English?" Pearl nodded. "Good. Pay the men and give them fair baksheesh."

She closed her parasol and thrust it at Pearl. Instinctively, Pearl took it and watched the *gwei-paw* enter her house. The Indian followed on her heels. Once inside, the woman pulled on each finger of her gloves and took them off.

"Gum-ghee, pay the carriers but leave her belonging where they are," Pearl said in Cantonese. *"And take this,"* she added, handing her servant the parasol.

No sooner had Pearl done this than the *gwei-paw* handed off her gloves. Again Pearl took them. She watched as the woman removed her hat, tossed it on the hall table, and admired her own reflection in the mirror. She straightened her pearl necklace and polished the diamond studs on her earlobes with the tips of her fingers. A gold signet ring sparkled. Then she smoothed her hair, pinched her cheeks, and said,

"Where is the master?"

"In China."

The woman turned away from the mirror.

They looked each other up and down without speaking. Finally:

"When do you expect him?" she asked.

"I am not certain," Pearl replied.

"Didn't he say? Didn't he tell you?" ·

"No."

"You know who I am?"

"Yes."

"Then you will address me as Madam …"

Pearl's eyes widened and she clenched her teeth.

"… Or Memsahib."

Gum-ghee finished settling with the men outside and came in. Immediately, she put a finger to her nose and pulled out her fan. Suddenly Pearl noticed the powerful stench of body odour wafting through the air—it was from the giantess. Although the *gwei-paw* was wearing a clean linen dress, it was easy to tell that she had not bathed in a long time. The sea voyage from India took about thirty days. From what Pearl knew, there were no washing amenities for women. Likely the Sikh beside her was also in need of a wash.

"Well? Don't just stand there. Show me to my rooms. Make up a bath. You will find rosewater in one of my trunks. Have my things brought to me. Must I tell you everything? Honestly. Chop-chop." She clapped her hands twice and strode up the stairs, holding on to the banister.

Pearl flinched at the hand-clapping gesture.

"Take the gwei-paw to the guest room," she said to Gum-ghee. *"Fetch water for a bath and burn her clothes as soon as she has disrobed. She smells like a gutter."*

Pearl watched the woman ascend the stairs. She walked with a limp and took each step with a halting gait. Her Indian manservant followed her. When she reached the top landing she said, "I shall have a long soak then take tea with lemon. Fetch me food. I'm starving."

Pearl sat in the parlour, her brows knitted and lips drawn into a thin line. She could not have been more different from this *gwei-paw*, Emanuel's first wife. Not only was there a distinction in size and appearance but in demeanour and background as well. This *gwei-paw* was rude and domineering, but she was elegant and Emanuel had married her. And unlike Pearl, she was a Jew from birth, Pearl merely a convert.

Sounds of water splashing came from the room directly above. Outside the window, a small cloud of smoke rose from the composter where refuse was burned. Gum-ghee had done as she was told. For a moment,

Pearl entertained the thought of burning the rest of the woman's belongings, but resisted the urge. Instead, she ordered tea and rice cakes to be
brought upstairs.

Time passed and the giantess did not appear. Nor did any sounds
come from the room above. This was curious. Pearl went upstairs and
saw the Sikh standing guard outside the bedroom door. Pearl went into
the adjoining room, a sitting salon, and closed the door behind her. Then
she walked as quietly as she could to the veranda, opened the French
windows, and stepped outside. Hugging the wall, she peered into the
guest room. Inside all was quiet. She could see a plate with the remains
of the rice cakes beside a pot of tea and a porcelain cup. She leaned in
farther. Across the room the *gwei-paw* lay asleep on the bed with a cotton
sheet wrapped around her body. One white leg stuck out the end of the
sheet like a birch log. Pearl gasped, looked away, and covered her mouth.
Her foot was huge! She leaned in again and gasped even louder. Propped
beside the bed was another leg with straps and buckles on it. It was made
of wood. A false leg!—the *gwei-paw* was a cripple!

Taking advantage of the big-footed woman's slumber, Pearl went down
the stairs and out into the front yard. There she used a garden axe to pry
open the locks on the *gwei-paw*'s travelling boxes. Inside were clothes and
some personal belongings that smelled of camphor. She selected a dress and
some undergarments and handed them to Gum-ghee to take upstairs. The
rest would remain outdoors; Pearl had decided that the woman was not
going to stay.

Amongst the belongings was a small red leather box. It was about the
size of a sewing case. Inside were blank papers, an inkpot, pens with nibs,
and a stack of letters bound together with ribbon. All of them posted from
Hong Kong and most of them from Emanuel. Under the correspondence,
there was a book. It was her journal. Pearl took them indoors and read
them all.

Stirring came from above. Quickly, she replaced the papers, closed the
lid, and put the box back on the *gwei-paw*'s pile of travelling boxes.

Earlier she had told Gum-ghee that when the *gwei-paw* woke up, she
should be led to the gazebo for a midday meal. A rattan table had been
set with cushioned chairs on either side. Cook served an aromatic

garoupa—a sea bass steamed with ginger and scallions, fluffy white rice, and steamed bok choy with oyster sauce. When Semah was comfortably seated (with her Sikh standing close by) and about to tuck in, Gum-ghee fetched her mistress.

Pearl stepped into the gazebo. Without looking up, the *gwei-paw* said, "Why are my things still in the front yard?"

Gum-ghee pulled out a chair and Pearl sat down at the table.

"What are you doing?"

"I am sitting down for lunch," Pearl replied.

"Here? With me?"

"Yes."

"You will do no such thing. Servants do not sit at table."

"Servants do not, but I do."

"And who, pray tell, are you?"

"I am the mistress of this house. I am Emanuel's wife."

The giantess was stunned into silence. Her face went pale—as pale as the skin of a plucked chicken.

Pearl picked up a chopstick, not to eat with but as a weapon in case that *baak ghaam gei*—white-skinned chicken—decided to attack. But she didn't. She sat there as though she had turned into a pillar of salt.

"Would you like more sauce?" Pearl asked. When she did not respond, Pearl used her chopsticks to serve herself. She could feel the woman's eyes upon her. She started to eat.

"I see," Semah said.

"What do you see?"

"I see that Emanuel has taken a mistress."

"Not a mistress, Madam: a wife."

That upstart Chinese woman would not prevail. Indeed, Semah couldn't be certain if the creature was a woman at all. She judged that Pearl couldn't have been taller than fifteen hands high, and those rosebud lips were altogether too red. The rouge on her prominent cheeks made her appearance tip the scales of propriety heavily on the side of harlotry. Well, she thought, that little thing can stare for as long as she pleases.

Semah's eyes narrowed. Then as quick as a whip she lifted her skirts, descended the gazebo steps, and walked into the house, ignoring the protests she could hear coming from the Chinese woman behind her.

Once inside, she looked around and headed for the dining room, where she picked up a chair. Veer Singh reached out to help but she refused, walked back to the foyer, and placed it on the floor directly under the chandelier that hung like a luminous sword of Damocles above her head. She wanted to be certain that the first thing Emanuel saw when he arrived was not his round-faced whore but his faithful wife.

Though Semah would later regret such a childish ploy, she felt she had to do something to demonstrate her occupation of the house. Planting a flag, staking a claim where her presence would be a statement of her status, a message that she was here to stay. Veer Singh stood at her side. She felt quite safe. With him there, that Chinese woman would not dare stab her in the back with one of those ridiculous knitting needles she used in her hair.

She could feel the Chinese woman's eyes burrowing into the back of her neck, the curve of her back, her waist. She imagined those little black eyes lighting on the area where her prosthetic limb met her truncated leg. Without looking down—she didn't want to draw attention to the thing— she ran her hand over her skirt as though she were smoothing wrinkles. She wanted to make sure that there were no bumps that would betray her deformity to her tiny, perfectly poised rival.

She heard whispering. It was in Chinese—easily recognizable by its guttural quality. Her hands tightened until her knuckles whitened. She looked sharply to the right from where the voices had emanated. Four Oriental faces peered out from behind a wall that separated the foyer from the salon. Aha, she thought. The Chinese woman had called the servants to come for a look-see. Semah wanted to shout: "Fill your plates with whatever you wish! Stare to your heart's content. I will not move!"

And so she remained seated there all afternoon. A clock ticked and chimed the hours and quarter hours. Outside, coolies shouted as they arrived, making deliveries for the kitchen, the garden, the stables. One hour felt much like the next. To pass the time she debated mentally on the wisdom of her actions thus far, leaving Calcutta abruptly like a thief in the night, boarding a schooner filled with strange men, finding her husband's house only to discover that his lover … Her cheeks flushed. She felt hot, not so much from her husband's mendacity or from the impertinence of his lover, but from the humiliation of having been cast aside for someone younger, someone so perfectly pretty, elegant, and tiny. Trickles of sweat ran down from her armpits.

She took a deep breath and closed her eyes. A pungent aroma of eucalyptus mixed with jasmine wafted through the air. It was a strange combination, but not unpleasant. Somewhere there was also a vague whiff of chicken stock. Soon, the poly-redolent air had soothed her fevered mind and slowed her pounding heart. She felt a calm pass through her body.

She lost track of the number of chimes from the clock, the variety of voices outside, the sound of birds chirping, the bumps, thumps, and groans from within the vast house, and the distant tolling of church bells—the aroma of chicken soup eclipsed them all …

She opened her eyes and followed the smell. Looking down at the floor, she saw a bowl and a spoon on a tray. Her taste buds swelled with anticipation. Saliva filled her mouth. That woman stood about twenty feet away watching her. She gestured at the soup and mimed eating it.

Semah could not tell from that inscrutable face if such a person was capable of an act of charity or if the soup had been laced with arsenic. Her stomach growled and she prayed no one heard it. She wanted that soup. But she knew that taking such an offering would mean she had capitulated. Her gambit was set. She had to play through to the endgame. So, she leaned back in the chair and closed her eyes.

More time passed. In the shank of afternoon when the sun was at its highest, no one stirred; creatures were mute in the garden, in the thickets, copse, and forests. The clock ticked. Suddenly she heard shouting. Chinese words. Her eyelids sprang open. What were they saying? What was the commotion?

The front door flew open and there stood Emanuel.

Semah heard footsteps clacking down the stairs behind her. To her right a gaggle of servants clustered, eyes wide with anticipation. Emanuel's mouth fell agape; his blue eyes pierced hers. Semah stood and felt the room spin around her like she had been lifted up and was oscillating in mid-air above a cacophony of voices: Emanuel's low rumbling baritone and the Chinese woman's high-pitched squeal all mangled into a Babel of sounds, penetrating her brain like red-hot shafts of steel.

She fell, hitting her cheek on something hard. Her final thought before everything went black: Please G-d, don't let this damned leg come undone.

PART THREE

THE HOUSE OF WIVES
1875–1898

EMANUEL

When he opened the letter, addressed in Mr. Rustomjee's neat, cursive handwriting, he felt a chill run through his veins. It was early morning. He was deep in the jungle fortress north of Macau, luxuriating in a hot tub that his long-time client, Generalissimo Wong, had provided for his comfort. He only half-heard the decadent bully say something about the need for cheaper opium—he was distracted by the letter's urgency. His eyes lighted on one phrase that he had reread several times: *"Your wife is headed for Hong Kong in search of you."* Gone was the Parsi clerk's peculiar grammar. The written communiqué was as right as rain. The letter was written on the day of Semah's departure. Emanuel dressed and headed toward the *lorcha* before the ice had a chance to thaw in his veins.

Once landed on the Hong Kong jetty, he waved aside eager chair carriers and tore through the crowds on foot. He dashed up Garden Road, passing Murray Barracks, St. John's Cathedral, the Governor's mansion, the Botanic Gardens, and St. Joseph's church until, huffing with exhaustion, he barged through the front doors of Kingsclere. Semah stood up and fainted, dropping to the marble floor like a marionette. The scene immediately brought to mind that horrid, breath-catching disaster years ago when he had stepped on the hem of her dress. But that image was wiped from his mind the instant he saw Pearl.

She was on the stairs, frozen in mid-descent. Her hand grasped the banister so hard her knuckles looked ready to burst through her skin.

The sight of his two wives in the same room made him rigid as cement. His heart struck a demented rhythm, crashing about in his chest and thundering in his ears.

The tall Sikh had rushed to Semah's side. Kneeling, he lifted her into a sitting position. He patted her cheek with his hand. Eventually, she came to. He helped her to her feet. Then, as he walked beside her with one arm firmly around her waist, they climbed the stairs slowly.

Calcified, Emanuel watched and wondered if what he was seeing was a dream.

The two visitors passed Pearl, who followed them with her eyes. At the top landing they turned left and disappeared into the guest chambers.

Emanuel watched Pearl descend and walk toward him. How small she looked compared with Semah. Pearl's round face looked up at him with inquiring eyes. No, not inquiring exactly. Her brows were knit and her lips were drawn tightly together.

"She must leave," Pearl said.

He had seen that expression once before. On the day they discussed their marriage contract. There was a calm determination in her voice and a confidence in her small and perfect bearing. He didn't reply. Instead, he backed away, then walked around her and up the stairs. He knocked on the guest-room door. The Sikh opened it. He placed the palm of one hand on his chest, made a slight bow, and opened the door wider to let Emanuel in.

Semah was semi-recumbent on the chaise. She had detached her prosthetic leg and propped it against the wall. She was running her hands over the top of her skirt to massage her thigh. The muscles on her jaw tightened several times. When she looked up, he saw that her eyes were red. He took out his handkerchief, mopped his shiny brow, ran the cloth around his neck, and unbuttoned his collar.

"This ends now," she said. He opened his mouth to speak but she interrupted, holding up one hand. "Whatever she is to you, fix it," she said, leaning back on the headrest and putting an arm over her eyes. The Sikh cleared his throat. He had held the door open throughout the brief encounter. It was opened wider now—a tacit invitation for Emanuel to leave. He stepped out and saw Pearl down the hall, standing in the gap of her half-opened door. He made a gesture with his palms: *Could we talk?* But she slammed the door on him. Simultaneously, the Sikh closed Semah's door and stood guard in front of it with his arms folded across his chest.

Emanuel had never expected Semah to show up and fight for her marriage. Nor had he expected his compliant wife of a few months to be so adamant. He had remained mute not because he had nothing to say but because he was too gobsmacked to say anything. So, he thought as he walked down the stairs, tapping his fingertips on the banister, what to do, what to do?

The legalities of the situation mattered little. Semah could argue that she never had nor ever would agree to a divorce. Pearl could argue that she was married under the eyes of G-d, and who was he to dispute that? Both could sue for breach of trust, breach of contract, breach of promise, and probably several other varieties that a clever lawyer could muster. All three could be engaged in a protracted war that pitted solicitors against attorneys, providing a hungry press and the chattering classes with gossip for years to come. What a distraction, what a loss of face, how despoiling of reputations, not to mention exhausting for the mind and spirit. And besides, how would he ever produce a son and heir under those circumstances? Arguing legal standings and jurisdictions, promises and contracts would drive a private matter irredeemably into the public sphere. No, that was not the way to go. Yet his two wives were in situ, under his roof, biding their fates in adjacent rooms.

He mulled over his situation a hundred different ways and soon found himself seated behind his study desk, puffing on a cheroot and staring at a glass of brandy.

He checked his watch. Good grief! Hours had passed.

His stomach growled but he ignored it, reaching for a sheet of paper instead. He dipped a pen in the inkpot and drew a line in the centre of the page, dividing it into two columns. At the top of one he wrote *Pearl* and at the top of the other he wrote *Semah*. It took him the better part of the night to figure out what to list under each name.

In the document (pages long when he had finished), he had ascribed to each woman a portion of the house—Semah had the west wing and Pearl the east; tracts in the garden were similarly separated, as were carrier chairs, glass, silver, plate, and servants. He drew crude sketches of each floor and labelled rooms *S* and *P*. All of them had buffer zones in the centre labelled with an *E* for Emanuel, who occupied rooms in between the two so that he might have access to both. The plan contained details: meals would be taken at certain times and in a variety of locations, such as the formal dining room, the solarium, the salon, the bedrooms, and so on. There was a protocol regarding receptions, what guests would be invited and when. In some instances Semah would be seated at the head of the table opposite him; at other times, Pearl would occupy the seat of honour. The text went on and on for pages, prescribing Kingsclere's new world order. Mercifully, there was no women's gallery in the fledgling Jewish community's temporary Shul, situated in a rented house on Hollywood Road. Of the sixty Jewish families there, no women attended services regularly. Thus Emanuel was spared the need for protocols that dealt with seating arrangements there.

When he was done, he made final drafts in duplicate, sealed each one, and had them delivered upstairs. Famished from a hard day's night, he ordered food brought to his study. Servants arrived with a well-deserved meal of bread, several cuts of cheese, a bottle of his favourite, cheeky Bordeaux, and pears plucked from the garden. He ate noisily and then belched with satisfaction. He was well pleased, thinking he had done Solomon one better.

Semah reacted first.

She opened the double doors to his sanctum sanctorum—the holy of holies. Her Sikh manservant closed them behind her. Three long steps took her to the middle of the room, where she stood with hands folded at her waist. She took a deep breath, drew herself to her full, impressive height, and said: "Do you love her?"

"Yes," he said.

"And what about me? Do you love *me*?"

He had not expected that question either. But he knew the value women placed on such emotions.

"Yes," he said. "I respect and admire you. Any man would be proud to have you as a wife."

Her eyes welled up.

"But I am not enough," she said.

He stood and came around his desk. Her fingers threaded and unthreaded each other. He put his hands on hers but she tore them away from his touch, picked up her skirt, and turned so fast he thought she would fall. He grabbed her, holding her tight in his arms, their faces so close he could feel the trickle of a tear on her cheek.

"I will not let you go," she said.

He felt her disengage from his grasp. She sniffed then.

"I won't," she said and stepped away, walking unsteadily toward the exit. At the door, she turned. "I love you, Emanuel. I always have and I always will. In time you will come to realize that."

Pearl reacted differently. She consulted her father.

"This is a loss of face," he said in Cantonese.

Because she refused to leave Kingsclere, Mr. Li had to travel by rickshaw and carrier chair from his home in Happy Valley to Kennedy Road. Earlier, Pearl had sent Gum-ghee with a simple message for her father: *"The first wife is in my house."* That brief statement was sufficient for Li to drop everything, turn away the queue of supplicants waiting outside his office (and their cages filled with chickens and pigeons, tethered pigs and assorted other gifts eagerly tendered in consideration of a loan or an investment), and go to his daughter's side. Emanuel had watched him arrive, storm into the house, and climb the stairs to Pearl's rooms without so much as a nod to his *gweilo* partner. He gave Li some time with his daughter before knocking on Pearl's door and entering her salon.

Li was apoplectic. A bulging vein like a tiny blue river snaked around the maroon scar on his forehead. The cuffs of his long sleeves fell over curled fists. *"It is a monstrous injustice … how dare he do this!"* he said, looking at Pearl and pointing at Emanuel's face.

"My father says—" Pearl started to translate.

"You needn't bother. I can tell by the tone," Emanuel said.

"My husband says—" Pearl said to Li.

"You don't have to repeat. I know what he says." Li waved his hand.

"Li, this is a matter between Pearl and me," Emanuel said.

"This house is mine—" Pearl began.

"Upon my death," Emanuel interrupted.

"It was given to me as a wedding gift. This is a betrayal of our agreement."

"Betrayal," Li repeated in English. Spittle sprayed. He banged a fist into his palm.

On and on they went for what felt like an eternity. The energy needed to fuel this contretemps should have exhausted them, but the more they argued the more entrenched each became. They sat, they stood, they sliced the air with fingers and palms and arms, all without any resolution, acting out indignities that Emanuel again feared would become public were the matter litigated in court.

Finally, Li left in a huff, declaring in Cantonese: *"Daughter, you are a fool if you stay in this house for one moment longer. And as for you,"* he said, wagging his finger in Emanuel's face, *"you, you …"* He could not finish and ran, double-stepping down the stairs, out the front door, and into a waiting carrier chair, excoriating the coolies for their stupidity and laziness. The workers heaved the poles on their shoulders and trotted off down the hill.

A silence fell in the room. Neither Pearl nor Emanuel had anything left to say. Curtains billowed. Palm branches rubbing against each other produced a *clicking* sound like raindrops against a windowpane. Pearl sat in a rattan chair looking out toward the harbour. She tapped the arm with the papers he had delivered. Emanuel sat beside her.

"I love you," he said. "You are the prettiest, most precious—"

"Then why do you do this?" she said, holding up his edict.

"Because you are both mine."

Pearl looked at him. His pale-blue eyes stared back at her.

"What would you have me do?" he asked. "Drag her out? Receive solicitor's suits? Slog through the legal proceedings and be a laughingstock?"

Pearl said nothing.

"I cannot allow that. I will not be laughed at."

He noticed her slender fingers choking the papers. Her chin touched her chest and her body rocked gently to and fro. It appeared that she was deep in thought, so he stood up, kissed her forehead, and left.

In the days that followed, he saw neither woman. By some tacit agreement both his wives sequestered themselves in their rooms. Their respective servants, who sometimes passed each other on the grand staircase, brought meals to them. Whenever this happened, Gum-ghee would cover her nose and mouth, convinced that the Sikh exuded harmful vapours from his pores. For his part, the taciturn man pretended that his Chinese equivalent did not exist.

Meanwhile, Emanuel slept alone, wondering each night what more he could do. He had hurt them both. He acknowledged that, of course. But his proposal provided a way for all three to live in harmony. They would see that in time. Meanwhile he would endure their silences, put up with their self-imposed segregation, and wait. Eventually their antagonism toward each other would cool. How long could they go on like this? But after the second week of the standoff, his patience started to wane and he wondered if he had been wrong to give them such a wide berth.

As he lay in bed one evening, meditating on whether his gambit would prove to be folly, the scent of rosewater mixed with lavender wafted through the gauzy mosquito netting.

A figure dressed in white came in from the veranda and walked to the foot of his bed. He sat up and gasped.

"Shush," the figure said.

"Who is it?"

The white linen netting rolled up slowly to reveal Semah standing at the foot of his bed. She attached the mosquito net to an overhead hook and looked at him.

My, but she was tall. Her loose hair fell in a torrent of curls around her shoulders. Her face, lit by the dim lantern, was bathed in honey hues.

"I want to be with you," she said and climbed onto his bed. "I want a child. I want to give you a son."

Emanuel felt himself respond quickly. The pressures of the last few weeks, the cavity of loss, the desperate need to regain his life—all funnelled into his belly and down to sensitive places.

Semah straddled him and pulled off her nightdress. Lamplight coated her nakedness. His eyes explored her smooth skin. His hands stroked her hips. His palms pressed the small curve of her stomach. Her body was still strong like an athlete's. He groaned when his flesh touched hers.

Throaty squeals of abandon echoed through the house. Downstairs, in the kitchen, heads snapped up in the direction of the savage grunting.

Everywhere ears pricked and eyes bugged like cats spooked by sudden sounds. Should anyone have been tempted to peep through the keyhole they would have found their sortie blocked by a tall Sikh who stood guard in the hall like a lion over his pride.

Pearl could not allow such an event to go unanswered. It was on the record now—and there was an imbalance in the house. She had lost ground and had to regain it. She surfaced from her self-confinement one day and found her husband in the solarium reading the newspaper. He did not hear her enter, so when he lowered the broadsheet and saw her, he reacted with a start. She was wearing a red silk kimono-styled gown tied at the waist. It had a golden dragon pattern that snaked up from the hem, ending in a massive head near the collar. Her hair, tied in a bun, was held in place with a comb.

She reached up and loosened her hair. It cascaded in a black wave past her waist. She took his large hand in hers and led it to the bow of her belt. He pulled the tassel slowly until the knot released. Silk parted down the middle, giving him a peek-a-boo view of her tiny belly button. She took half a step back, shrugged off the gown, and let it tumble around her ankles. G-d but she was beautiful—small, perfectly proportioned, and delicately framed. Without taking his eyes off her, he tore off his clothes. She prepared herself to receive him by laying out her gown at her feet.

In all the times they had made love before, she had not been overtly vocal. Now she wanted to be loud, louder than that giantess who had come from away and laid claim to her territory. Her first scream startled him. He stopped, thinking he was hurting her. But her hands pulled him back into place. He smiled as she yelped with pleasure at every greedy lunge.

SEMAH AND PEARL

Rivalry and jealousy burned like a roaring furnace that soon subsumed every aspect of domestic life at Kingsclere.

On moving day and in the weeks that followed, each wife cast a hawk-like surveillance on the other's furnishings, linens, curtains, and decorations. If one purchased a new sofa, the other purchased a larger one. If one collected ivory, the other displayed her jade collection (that boasted a variety of colours, including her highly prized white "mutton-fat" nephrite). If one planted tomatoes, the other planted more. The air tensed wherever they moved, each wary that she might encounter the other by chance. And when they did, each ignored the other. To minimize such occurrences, Gum-ghee was tasked with confirming that the halls and stairs were free of the *white giant* before Pearl emerged from her quarters. Likewise, Semah used Veer Singh for reconnaissance. In time, Semah added Chinese servants to her retinue. Pearl, of course, judged them badly—they were rude peasant girls from the New Territories, freshly arrived from pig farms, seeking employment as servants. It was bad enough that the Sikh had horse manure on his boots from the stables he tended; these *mui-chai* had pig swill on theirs!

The entire Hong Kong community gossiped about the *"big house on the hill."* Local wags quipped about *"the foreign wife who looked out western windows at eastern skies and the concubine who looked out eastern windows at a western future."*

Regardless of their innate competitiveness and the tacit agreement to one-up each other, both Semah and Pearl knew themselves to be on shaky ground. Pearl, after all, was what Jews called a *pilegesh* and the Chinese referred to as *yee-nai,* a second wife. Worse still, some Chinese might consider her an extra wife, no more valuable than the chattel that came off one of Emanuel's ships. She could be traded on the open market like a possession. (Gum-ghee had told her of some *yee-nai* who were buried alive so that the husband could have company in the afterlife!) But customs aside, the real issue was that Pearl had not produced any offspring. She could sense her status diminishing with each barren month. Such feelings gave her headaches so severe that not even hourly rubbings of tiger balm paste on her temples could make the pain go away. And nothing short of a baby could calm her troubled spirit.

As for Semah, her insecurities lay in her age. How much longer would she be attractive to Emanuel? Would she have to fight for every inch of control over the household when she was no longer favoured? Would his attention turn solely to the China-woman? Or worse, would he take a younger third wife? Where did they stand now that the ferocity of conjugal visits had calmed? Neither one was a clear favourite.

Both wives had come to this conclusion more or less at the same time. Within days of each other, each broached the subject with Emanuel in the afterglow of lovemaking. His response was simply to redraw the lines of responsibilities held by each wife. In his new plan, Pearl ran the house-hold. All servants reported directly to her. Immediately she got rid of the mainlander *mui-chai* and sent Gum-ghee to hire new ones. She let the Sikh stay as long as he never set his filthy shoes inside the house.

Both wives were promised residency for life. Pearl's male heirs would inherit an annuity and her female heirs a dowry. Semah got the same. Thus, both wives achieved a measure of security for themselves and their future children. And with that settled, Emanuel revealed a condition of his own. The word on the street was that *"A man with two wives and no children must be a eunuch."* This could not stand.

Emanuel's home life became very busy, visiting each of his wives. And when the women's cycles coincided, as often happens when women live in close proximity, the poor man was pressed into service for days in a row, popping from one bedroom to the other. Each month after that week of fecundity, he slept for a full twenty-four hours and walked bowlegged for days. In the race to produce an heir, Semah took the lead when she announced that, three years after arriving at Kingsclere, she was *"with child."* She was almost forty years old.

PEARL

Pearl plunged into bitterness after the announcement of her rival's pregnancy. In the months that followed, she took infusions—ground-up sheep ovum and ginger teas to stimulate blood flow—and instructed Gum-ghee to massage her lower back and feet and pay special attention to the meridians in her ankles. She even purchased foul-smelling poultices and applied them to her lady parts. A meat-free diet was suggested and followed. Then she changed to a diet that was meat-heavy. She tried post-coital handstands, hoping that gravity would do the deed. Other positions, recommended by her herbalist, were also employed—*doggy style, the reverse swan, two rising crocodiles,* and *crazy monkeys*—illustrations of which were in books smuggled into the house under Gum-ghee's tunic. But nothing came of those acrobatic attempts. She was as barren as a desert. The months slipped past and Pearl was forced to watch with steely-eyed, tight-lipped resentment as Semah's breasts and belly swelled and her skin grew luminous.

When Semah's time came, they were in the garden. Pearl was at the eastern end and the giantess at the western. Pearl carried a mirror in her basket so that she would not have to turn her head if she wanted to look at her rival. In the glass, the *gwei-paw* looked like a mountain wearing a dress. Her belly was as swollen as if she had strapped on a sack of rice. The cows in the meadow looked smaller. Semah reached down to pluck a sprig of parsley. Then she straightened up, held her gigantic stomach, and twisted around to look at the back of her skirt where a wet patch appeared.

She wobbled a little on her feet and then screamed. The Sikh, who had been grooming horses in the stables nearby, ran to her side. He held her by the waist, staining her dress with his filthy hands.

"Gum-ghee!" Pearl yelled. Her servant looked up from where she was harvesting tomatoes. "*Go and help the woman,*" she ordered in Cantonese. "*Her water has broken.*" Blood rushed out of Pearl's face and she felt light-headed. Her heartbeat hastened as she watched her rival enter the house, the sprig of parsley still in her fingers.

"*Stay with her,*" she ordered Gum-ghee. The servant looked at her mistress as though she had just been asked to pick up cow turd. "*I am not a monster!*" Pearl said. "*Women must help women in times such as these. Go!*" she said, and watched her handmaid's lips tighten.

Despite her counterpart's imminent elevation in status, if she delivered a boy at least, Pearl felt compelled to do everything she could to support a successful birth. It was instinct more than obligation.

After sending one messenger to fetch a doctor and another to inform Emanuel, she went up to her own rooms and left the door ajar so that she could see the activity in the hall. She sat in a teak chair and rubbed her palm over its shiny arm. Her throat felt dry. She swallowed hard several times. By her calculation, Semah was premature. Would she live? Would the child? The long nail of her baby finger tapped the wooden armchair. It sounded like a clock ticking.

Rumblings downstairs. People arriving. The doctor? Emanuel?

Footfalls echoed on the stairs.

Mumbled voices bubbled in the hall.

Then a woman's scream tore through the air.

Pearl's body tensed. Both hands gripped the chair's wooden arms.

Then came another scream and another, followed by a brief pause before the pattern was repeated. It went on for hours.

Each bellow was like a punch to Pearl's heart. She would have traded places with Semah in a trice. Instead, she sat, feeling as hollow as an empty bucket. The mantel clock chimed. Her fingernail tapped its monotonous rhythm. The sour taste of envy started in her mouth. It caromed through her body, filling her throat, her chest, her arms, her belly, and her legs in a green wash of bitterness.

As suddenly as they had started, the screams ceased. A breathless silence replaced the sharp, piercing cries. Pearl looked up. Nothing stirred.

She heard more footsteps—hurried and heavy. Then voices—nervous and hushed. She saw through her open door that it was Emanuel—headed for Semah's room. Then ...

A newborn child wailed triumphantly, cutting the dull, stale, tired atmosphere like a breath of fresh air.

Pearl sagged with relief. She loosened her grip on the arms of the chair and heard someone pad softly toward her room. Gum-ghee poked her head around the door.

"It is a boy!" she said, beaming from ear to ear. But her smile dissolved slowly when she saw her mistress's face.

In the months that followed the birth of David, Semah could not stop grinning. She felt as relieved as someone who had been exonerated for a crime she did not commit. The baby was a joy, and her heart filled with pleasure whenever she looked at his cherubic face. But with whom could she share these feelings other than with Emanuel? Veer Singh? Certainly not! He was a servant. No, she wanted a woman friend, a confidante who could understand her success as a wife and mother and its significance in the household. In lieu of such companionship, she turned to her journal.

My dear, dear David,

You are asleep now after another restless night protesting your milk teeth. Nanny Chin collected some juice from an aloe bush that grows wild in the garden and rubbed it on your gums. I was apprehensive at first, but when she assured me that she had done the same for her own child, I relented. It appears to have dulled the pain sufficiently for you to sleep. Veer Singh has decorated your bed with fresh white bauhinia blossoms. He has done this every day since you were born. He stands guard outside the nursery but against what I am uncertain. It is his way, I suppose, of showing respect for the "prince" of the house. You are well loved here at Kingsclere.

I had suspended writing in this journal when I landed in Hong Kong because there was so much to learn, so much to adapt to in this strange and wonderful city. I was so overwhelmed I could do little else but try to get through the day. Until your birth I felt like someone learning to swim, dog paddling my way toward a shore that never got any nearer. It was difficult at first, having been away from your father for so long. But I'm getting the "hang" of it, as they say down at the Jockey Club. With your arrival I am finally out of the water, having succeeded in my primary responsibility to provide Emanuel with an heir. I am now safely on dry land. Yet life deals us strange twists. I shall explain.

She had forgotten what a release it was to put pen to paper. Her deepest and most intimate musings—the truth of how she felt—poured out of her so fast that sometimes she was unable to keep pace with her galloping thoughts.

There is living in this house a woman named Pearl who has been, how shall I say, a confidante of your father's for many years now. She is a formidable young woman. Your father and I have agreed that she will run this household's domestic staff. She is the daughter of Mr. Li, your father's business partner. She is, of course, Chinese, but a convert to Judaism. She is fluent in several languages, which is a skill that comes in handy in a city where you might encounter a dozen different tongues while walking any stretch of Central District. She seems intelligent enough, if somewhat spiteful.

I shall return to her later. For now, suffice it to say that she is a live-in occupying the east wing of this beautiful home. Never mind—she may be governess of that sector, but I shall remain queen of its entirety. You will, in time, address her respectfully as Mrs. Li, for it is what your father wishes. I shall say more about her later and turn my commentary to other matters, such as our standing in this community.

We are firmly established in society and are mentioned annually in the society register. There is not an occasion at the Governor's mansion to which we are not invited, and your father is a prominent member of the synagogue, along with the Kardoories and Sassoons from the old country. Your father has pledged land on which a new Shul will be built. Our growing community (of several hundred) will one day worship in our own temple instead of using the rented house on Hollywood Road. Your father, the Kardoories, and the Sassoons all made their mark in the opium trade but have invested also in real estate, shipping, and local transportation. "We want to make a go of it here," as your father is often quoted as saying in the local papers, boosting confidence for the recently formed Stock Exchange. His opinions carry weight because he is the longest serving Chairman of the Hong Kong and Shanghai bank and a Legislative Councillor appointed by the Governor. I must say, as an aside, that on the day his Excellency made the announcement, Emanuel danced a little jig in the salon. But that day pales in comparison to the day you were born. That morning I woke to see him sitting beside my bed with you asleep in his arms. He looked up. His blue eyes shone with pride. Without speaking, he placed you between us. Then touched his fingers to his lips and put them on your forehead and on mine.

Everyone prospers—the Chinese too. The Hong Kong and Shanghai bank was created to manage these extensive fortunes. I say this without pridefulness but merely to describe this world and our place in it. While your father toils in the vineyard of business, my work is to create a home for him and to bring a level of refinement to this town that heretofore has not experienced much of the finer things in life—unlike the sophistication of Calcutta, where our people originated.

We host dinner parties and garden affairs and jimkanahs, depending on the time of year and the occasion. Here all the cognoscenti gather to see and be seen and perhaps to curry favour with E.R. Belilios & Son! Your father's partners, Mr. Li and Senhor

Remedios, are ubiquitous. (They have both done well for themselves, having hitched their wagons to your father's star.) Ever
present, they treat me with polite reticence, be it at events outside
this house or at the Jockey Club or in the street. I cannot but
conclude that their suspicious diffidence is out of loyalty to Mrs. Li.
After all, she is the daughter of one and the de facto niece of the
other. They feel that I have supplanted her status in this household. But I have acquiesced to her position as head of Staff. What
more can I do? As it is, Mrs. Li attends every event at Kingsclere.
I shall relate one.

She wore a traditional Chinese silk gown. The top was decorated
with intricate gold threading and buttoned up the side. Her ankle-
length skirt (in matching blue) featured a slit on both sides that
revealed her ankles clad in white stockings. She glided like a swan
amongst the guests, flitting from person to person. Her shiny
black hair was combed into a tight bun. From her earlobes pearl
earrings dangled, matching the pearl necklace that surrounded the
mandarin collar of her tiny neck. Her handmaid never left her
side. I could have sworn they were joined at the hip!

It was on this one occasion—the annual spring gala—the first
since your birth—that something disgusting happened. At the start
of the evening, Mrs. Li looked pale and abruptly excused herself
from the receiving line. She reappeared when the dinner gong
sounded and took her place just as the soup was being served. The
gentlemen rose when she entered. When once she was pallid, she
now looked green. Assisted by her handmaid, she sat down. The
men did so too. She was seated at one end, your father at the other,
and I to his right. One hundred guests lined either side of the table.
Standing behind them were servants enough to serve ten courses on
china that was stamped with our family's crest. When the soup
arrived I saw her handmaid mop her mistress's brow. Then without
warning, Mrs. Li vomited into her bowl of pea soup.

Immediately, her ayah whisked her from the scene. Footmen appeared and took away the mess. In a trice everything returned to normal.

That was the last time we were in a room together. After that incident, I have kept a keen lookout to avoid her company. I have seen her often, her back to me, pruning bauhinias that border the eastern edges of the grounds. Once, as I was watching, she stiffened her back and raised a hand mirror aimed in my direction. I pulled my head back. When I had the courage to look again, she had returned to her pruning. Her presence in this house drives me, a grown woman, to behave like a child. Irritating! But I have cause to do so. That tiny woman has a vicious temper. For instance, when you were born, dear David, she demolished her own bedchamber, broke everything there was, mirrors, vases, and tables. Chairs were flung about and scissors taken to all her clothes in the wardrobe. Pillows were eviscerated and pitched out windows, where feathers dropped like snowflakes onto the grounds below. It was a strange reaction to my happy event. Much to my chagrin, your father refurnished her quarters. The woman is spoiled.

Après l'affaire vomissure, or should I say eight months later, Mrs. Li gave birth to a daughter. I pause here to say that I shall not comment except that I felt sorry for the child. You see, she rejected the baby. It had been a long and agonizing delivery, during which she had lost a great deal of blood. It was not clear that she would survive. Weakened by the ordeal, she slept for days. I made chicken soup every day for her and I was happy to see her ayah deliver it to her mistress. But in all that time, she never once asked to see her newborn. I fear she rejected it because it was not a boy.

I could not stand idle in the face of this attitude and took charge of the baby. I took her into my care as though she were my own. I found a wet nurse and let the newborn sleep in my room. Your father was very pleased to see this and praised me for my consideration. In the weeks that followed, I attempted to approach Mrs. Li through messages carried to her door by Veer Singh. When that failed to catch her attention, I went personally. I wanted only one thing—a name for the child. But all my ministrations were rebuffed with silence. It appeared that Mrs. Li had fallen into a deep melancholia. Yet she would eat soup. Curious.

It was your father's desire that the child be given a Jewish name. He suggested Leah and promptly made a generous donation to the synagogue's building fund. But I was determined to involve Mrs. Li in the naming ceremony. It was my duty as one Jewish mother to another. But what could I do when the woman refused to participate? One day, her lackey arrived at my salon door. Veer Singh led her to me. I was at my desk near the window that overlooks the western grounds below where you were playing in the garden. Nearby to me was a crib where her baby girl lay on her back, gurgling happily. The servant looked at the child and smiled broadly. Veer Singh pointed at a paper that the servant carried, indicating that she should give it to me. She did so, using both hands and accompanied by a deep bow.

The thick vellum was folded in half. Inside was a Chinese pictogram and beneath it a translation. It meant: FELICITY. The servant pointed to the word and then to the baby. I understood that this was the name to be given to the child. I asked if this was a message from Mrs. Li, but all I could get out of her was an inscrutable smile and several more bows.

I took it upon myself to provide a naming ceremony. As we had no Chazzan to sing Shir ha-Shirim—*from Songs of Solomon—I did so myself. How I wished there was a proper Shul, a mikvah, and a rabbi who could perform these beautiful and ancient ceremonies. Our community is growing and our babies need to grow up in the proper surroundings of our people.*

Your father was magnanimous toward Mrs. Li and her daughter. Against all my protestations, he insisted on lending his family name to the child. He said that this would give him a lot of face with his partner Mr. Li (Mrs. Li's father) and indeed in the community at large. I argued against such an action—argued vehemently, I should confess. Sharing a family name would make her offspring a half-sister to you, my dear David. How could I let this happen? But I was powerless to prevent it.

I sent word to Mrs. Li that a private naming ceremony would take place. I did not expect any response. But she appeared on the appointed day, bright-eyed and rouged-cheeked, having made a miraculous recovery. We gathered in the solarium together with Mr. Li and Mr. Remedios, who witnessed the occasion. Papers were drawn up and duly signed. Henceforth the child would be known as Leah Felicie Belilios. The registrar—a Chinese gentleman— misheard the middle name and misspelled it. No one noticed in the excitement of the moment. But it is of little consequence: "a rose by any other name would smell as sweet"!

I cannot help but wonder if that woman's melancholia was all a ruse. Could this be what she always wanted—sympathy from my husband, playing on his magnanimity and by so doing obtaining the man's name for her daughter?

If so, then well played, I'd say.

```
┌─────────────────┐
│    EMANUEL      │
└─────────────────┘
```

In the years that followed the birth of his son and daughter, Emanuel fell into a welcome routine. Awakened early in his own rooms by the delicate dinging of the clock on the mantel opposite his bed—a new device given him by the Board at the bank for services rendered—he made his ablutions in the adjoining bathing room. With hair still damp, he smoked his first cheroot standing on the veranda and counting the ships in the harbour, tallying the traffic and its economic significance. After a good breakfast, he rode on his camel to his offices on Lyndhurst Terrace at the bottom of the hill. Preceding his arrival, clerks, supplicants, lawyers, and colleagues packed the large, open front room. They bowed as he passed them on his way to his spacious private offices, where he conducted business by acquiring as much as he could at the lowest possible price. At five by his watch, he closed the portfolio on his desk and, bobbing his head in acknowledgment to his staff, entered the street. There an office boy waited with one hand on the camel's halter and the other cupped over his nose and mouth against the animal's foul breath. Emanuel mounted the beast, flicked a coin to the boy, and loped up Garden Road to Kingsclere. There he delighted in spending a half hour first with David in the western wing and then with Leah Felicie in the eastern. He took great care in giving both his children equal amounts of time.

Social engagements kept him busy most evenings he was in town (he still made frequent trips to his client warlord in China), and depending on the occasion, either Semah or Pearl would accompany him. He took pains to ensure that each attended the same number of annual events and that these occurrences were complementary in stature. Domestic peace, it seemed, had arrived at last. But peace came dropping slow ...

Emanuel enjoyed dusk. He liked the pall of calm that fell over the house. In the stillness, linnets winged and cicadas rattled. He looked up when he heard the knock on his door. Without waiting for an invitation, Pearl entered. He put the legal documents he was reading beside the others on his desk, adjusted his focus, and chuckled.

"My presence amuses you?" she asked.

"The black-and-white telegraph works fast," he said, referring to the gossiping amahs who wore black pants and white tunics.

"It's true, then?"

"Yes."

She was there because Semah had commissioned a family portrait from Ming Qua, an acolyte of the great Lam Qua from Macau, who was a student of the English painter, the late George Chinnery. It would feature herself, her husband, and their five-year-old son David, and would be painted in the style of the portraits she had seen in the *Illustrated London News* of Queen Victoria's family. When completed, the painting would hang in the foyer of Kingsclere and be the first thing visitors would see upon entering the mansion.

Emanuel took off his reading glasses, set his elbows on the desk, and leaned in.

"If there is to be a family portrait," Pearl said, controlling her tone, "then I want one as well." Her statement hung in mid-air. Her eyebrows were raised to the maximum height, her lips tightened.

"And?"

"And it will be a photograph, not a painting!" She proposed Wan Chik-hing and his brother Wan Leong-hoi, neither of whom Emanuel had ever heard of. "They create the sweetest pictures mounted on card stock about the size of a sheet of writing paper. These photographs can be reproduced and given to everyone who comes to the house. They will have a permanent record of their visit."

"And obviously, these photographs would feature Leah Felicie, you, and me?"

"Obviously. You think about it," she said, closing the door behind her.

He reached for a cheroot, lit it, and walked onto the veranda. A pair of crows watched him expectantly. He breathed out a plume of smoke. Linnets flitted. The cicadas made an anxious din as the sun lost its heat.

As with social engagements, he thought, there would have to be two sittings on two separate occasions to ensure equanimity. He felt foolish. Shuttling back and forth between the eastern and western wings of the house, devoting his days to a game of diplomatic chess, suddenly felt idiotic. Good grief, not a week had passed when he didn't have to arbitrate some domestic matter. No! Enough is enough!

A fog of smoke had collected around his head. He flicked the stogie at the crows. The birds flew off in anticipation of another missile.

That's right! he thought. There will be no more shuttlecocking. The women will learn to settle disputes face to face—like a family!

The following day he summoned his wives to his study.

Emanuel stood in front of the fireplace and glanced from one to the other, seated on settees on either side of him. "If there is to be a family portrait, then it will be of the entire family," he announced.

Semah's jaw muscles clenched. Pearl's eyes narrowed.

"Yes, yes, my dear, I know this, this ..." What was the word she had used? "... Sitting!" he shouted, as though it was something distasteful done in private followed by a thorough washing of hands. "This sitting was your idea, Semah, but I've given it a lot of thought ... we shall *all* be in the picture. You and David will be on one side, Pearl and Leah Felicie on the other. I shall give you one hour of my time a month from tomorrow."

Emanuel paused.

Semah twirled her ring as though she were screwing on the lid of a tiny jar.

Pearl remained still as a rock, one hand folded over the other.

"You may each decorate your sides however you wish."

He paused again.

The air turned as thick as treacle. He saw Semah's chest rise and lower like a piston. Pearl's lips disappeared. Filled to bursting, the women spoke simultaneously.

"It is impossible for painters to work under such conditions!" "This is insulting to my side of the family!" Outrage flew like a barrage of flaming arrows shot from a platoon of archers. But his decision, like a gigantic shield, repelled whatever projectiles, darts, barbs, shafts, and shots they had in their arsenals. Eventually the incendiary debate flamed out.

Winded, the women drew breath. Emanuel seized the moment.

"See here," he said, looking from one to the other, "this 'sitting' is not just for you. I see it as an opportunity for me as well. I want the world to know that, unlike so many of my peers with plural spouses, I am comfortable with our domestic arrangement. No! I am *proud* of it."

One month later, in late September, preparations began at dawn. Servants harvested flowers from the garden, arranged them in vases, and placed them behind the two padded benches that flanked a large wingback chair in the foyer. Playthings appeared: stuffed animals, a family of wooden ducks tied with string, rattles, and small leather balls were scattered on the floor. It looked as though a toy shop had exploded.

Sunlight from the sky-high casement windows streamed onto gleaming marble floors and the banister was festooned in leafy vines. A crowd of workers arrived to convert the foyer into a photographer's studio and an atelier.

Emanuel could hear the commotion from inside his sanctum sanctorum. Occasionally, he peered through the slit between the double doors and scanned the goings on. He harrumphed, took a sip from his brandy snifter, and looked at his watch for the thousandth time.

The sitting had been delayed. Not because Leah Felicie (frightened by the crowd of noisy people) would not stop wailing and not because David refused to take his thumb out of his mouth, but because Semah and Pearl discovered they were wearing the same colours—albeit one was in Western clothes and the other in a traditional Chinese gown. An hour's delay was called for, and Emanuel had escaped to his study for a drink.

He put his watch back into his waistcoat pocket. The hiatus was almost over. He spied photographers and painters discussing the angle of the light reflected off long mirrors held by their assistants, the angle of the benches, the arrangement of toys, and dozens of other picayune matters that were beyond his ken. It was enough to make a man swear like a Christian. He drummed his fingers, regretting his decision to sit for a family portrait. For heaven's sake, there were other fish to fry.

Li and Aleandro's commitment to the opium trade—the goose that laid golden eggs—had waned.

"No, no, no," Li had said, wagging his finger in Emanuel's face. "It is the golden egg that will kill the goose!" His finger punched the air. "There is a curse on the heads of opium traders. They will suffer misery. Their offspring will die before their eyes!"

The finger was long, the knuckles like the nodes of a bamboo stick. It reminded Emanuel of the switch used by his headmaster when he was a boy. Had it been the finger of anyone else but his father-in-law, he would have reached up and snapped it off.

"Utter nonsense!" Emanuel countered.

"You have children. I have a granddaughter. Think about it. We'll talk again."

He heard a knock on the door. They were ready for him in the foyer. Leaving his brandy glass on the silver tray, he tugged at the hem of his waistcoat and strode out the doors of his study. His daughter bawled relentlessly above the chatter of servants, artists, and photographers. They all made way for the large man who headed for the wingback.

Four artists in green smocks stood in front of their canvases mounted on easels placed a few feet apart. Because this was to be a one-time sitting, Ming Qua had averred that multiple artists were required: four to do studies of colour and shape and at least a dozen to capture details of expression, light, and composition. By that same precaution, the brothers Wan mounted three cameras on tripods to shoot as many slides as could be fit into the hour. Camera operators in white smocks fussed with the lenses. Photographic assistants readied their flashguns. Where were Semah and Pearl?

Semah appeared dressed in a pale-yellow off-the-shoulder dress. He had never seen her eyes and dark skin look so radiant. She sat to his left.

Pearl took her seat on the padded bench to his right. His eyes widened. Her navy-blue gown with gold trim set off her shiny black hair tied in a bun and held in place with a jewelled comb. Her face and hands looked like they were made of ivory. Emanuel's chest puffed. My, but they looked beautiful, if a little stern faced.

Next, the children were brought in by their amahs. David sucked his thumb, his eyes full of wonder at all the big people in the room. Terrified by the noise and the strangers, Leah Felicie remained inconsolable in Gum-ghee's arms. Ming and the brothers Wan led little David to stand beside Semah and instructed Gum-ghee to place Leah Felicie on Pearl's lap, thinking that that would placate the child. When it didn't, they waved a rattle in her face, bounced a ball, and made funny faces. Those attempts only exacerbated the girl's fear. She let out squeal after piercing squeal.

"Oh for heaven's sake!" Emanuel exclaimed, hanging his head. He pinched the bridge of his nose and squeezed his eyes shut. Dealing with lawsuits, cynical Jews, and weak-kneed business partners were strolls in the park compared to this. Heat rose from his chest and flooded his cheeks. Family portrait be damned. He felt an overwhelming urge to stand and leave.

He released his fingers, opened his eyes, and looked at his daughter.

Leah Felicie had stopped crying. She flashed a beautiful smile and pointed. Emanuel followed the line of her tiny finger to the object of her delight: David. David took his thumb out of his mouth, pointed it at Leah Felicie, and smiled back at her.

SEMAH AND PEARL

Bewilderment! Disorientation! Surprise rippled through their veins when the mothers saw the unexpected happen. For one special moment, their guileless children had seen each other for the first time and cut through a rivalry that had sullied every aspect of domestic life at Kingsclere.

But then the moment passed.

As the women's faces changed from shock to disbelief to bafflement, Ming Qua and his assistants caught every nuance while the brothers Wan set off flashes and reloaded several times in the course of an hour's sitting. The artists captured everything.

One week later, a box of one hundred photographic prints arrived. In her parlour, Pearl put down the book she was engrossed in, leapt up from her chair, and eagerly unsealed the box. She took out one photograph, looked at it, and curled her lip. The tinted picture (a Wan brothers specialty) showed two stern-faced women, a portly man with a smirk as if he had just found a lump of gold, and two happy children, the younger of whom could not take her eyes off her older half-brother.

A week after that, Veer Singh informed his mistress that the portrait had arrived. Semah left the western wing and headed to the solarium, where a beaming Ming Qua unveiled his canvas. She looked at it for a long time. However she tried to resist, her eyes were drawn to the angelic glow that surrounded David and Leah Felicie: cherubs of equal status. She looked at the artist and quietly said: "No." Ming Qua's grin collapsed.

After those presentations, neither the photographs nor the canvas ever saw the light of day. Pearl waved a hand dismissively at the box of photos—a tacit command for Gum-ghee to take it out of sight. But before her servant reached the door, Pearl said, "Wait. Bring it back." Gum-ghee did so, complaining about its weight. Pearl opened the box, retrieved one photograph, took it to her desk, put it in the top drawer, and locked it. "Destroy the rest," she ordered before returning to plumb the mysteries of Dr. Jekyll and Mr. Hyde.

Semah assured Ming Qua that he would be paid in full. She attempted to assuage the artist's confusion by praising his technique without telling him of her disappointment in the portrait's focus—the two cherubic children. He managed to stammer a few words. What had he done wrong? What changes might he make? But Semah held up a hand. Veer Singh knew his cue. He took the canvas off its easel, showed the dazed artist out, and closed the door, leaving his mistress alone in the solarium.

No more was said or done to capture another family portrait. It was as though the event had never occurred. Tension, taut as a tug-o-war rope, remained. Each wife continued to believe the other a treacherous usurper.

Pearl would not risk having Leah Felicie exposed to David's graceless giant of a mother. "No, no, no, her size alone would surely frighten the girl," she declared to Gum-ghee, who was only too willing to agree.

And Semah could not imagine a future in which David could regard Leah Felicie as his half-sister. Nor could she run the risk of having him come under the spell of her untrustworthy rival—that pocket-sized opportunist.

Leah Felicie, always attended by two amahs (one to ensure she did not fall over and the other to carry a towel and bag of snacks), roamed the east wing. Correspondingly, Nanny Chin restricted David's movements to the west wing.

A couple of years after the family portrait debacle, Gum-ghee disturbed her mistress's afternoon reading. A leather-bound book—a collection of short stories by Anton Chekhov translated into English and autographed by the great man himself—lay open in her lap. She had been eagerly awaiting the edition ever since she gave the young author a reception at Kingsclere when he visited Hong Kong on his Far Eastern travels. She had planned to spend the afternoon reading while Leah Felicie napped.

"The master's son," Gum-ghee said. "The master's son is in the garden!" She reported the news as though a meteor had just crashed into her bed of peonies.

Sure enough, when she went out to the veranda, Pearl saw David happily chasing a ball. His amah, Nanny Chin—a plump, tan-faced woman—was squatting under a banyan holding a fan. A few steps away, the *more-law-cha* had set up a seesaw. He stood back to admire his handiwork, then dashed behind the boy and lifted him up in the air. Surprised, David squealed with delight. The Sikh placed the lad on one end of the teeter-totter and showed him how to hold the handles. Then he sat on the opposite end. The first few lifts shocked the boy. But he quickly got the hang of it and shrieked with pleasure.

Pearl's eyes widened with surprise. David had grown. He was big for his age. He looked like a ten-year-old when he was only seven.

"It is a loss of face," Gum-ghee whispered. "The boy has more privileges than your daughter. The girl must have the freedom to play in the garden too."

Gum-ghee had put her finger on the nub of the issue. The knot in Pearl's belly tightened. The mansion—her mansion—had been divided. By letting David out into the garden, the *gwei-paw* had expanded her territory outdoors! This situation could not be a matter of record. Yet if she allowed her daughter outdoors …

"The sun," Pearl said. "It will darken her fair skin, ruin her face."

"Mistress, I will hire an amah with strong arms to hold a parasol as big as a tree over the little girl."

If she did nothing, the *gwei-paw* would notch up an intolerable victory. If she allowed Leah Felicie to play in the garden, she would grow up looking like a farmer's daughter. A dozen other equivocations rattled in her brain, not the least of which was the consequence of the two children seeing each other. How long could she reasonably keep Leah Felicie in the dark about her half-brother?

At the same time the following day, David was once again in the garden. Nanny Chin took up her usual spot under the banyan, where she squatted with her back against its trunk and flapped her rattan fan. The *more-law-cha* nailed hoops into the ground at intervals of a few feet. David watched with fascination. Then the man poured out the contents of a gunnysack. Wooden balls, each one with a coloured stripe around its circumference, tumbled onto the grass. He produced two wooden mallets, gave one to David, and showed him how to putt the balls through the hoops.

Pearl could hear the gentle *pop* of wood on wood as David putted, determined not to stop until every ball went through every hoop. When he was done, the Sikh gave the lad an exaggerated bow then touched his hand to his chest, his mouth, and his forehead in a kind of salute. David giggled and jumped up and down on the spot, excited by his accomplishment. Pearl felt herself smile at the sight.

On the third day, Gum-ghee interrupted Pearl's reading again. This boy's stupid amah—the country bumpkin—had dozed off under the banyan and David had headed out of sight with the *more-law-cha* toward the stables.

Quickly they mustered on the wraparound veranda's southern side.

Pearl peered down over the railing. Behind her Gum-ghee stood at the ready, holding a small telescope she had grabbed from her mistress's desk. They waited in silence, their eyes peeled for activity on the path below.

Gum-ghee reached under her tunic and produced a fan. She opened it and wafted the air a few inches from her mistress's back. Pearl felt a sliver of coldness between her shoulder blades. She could hear her own breathing and felt her heart throb a little faster.

She held out her hand. Gum-ghee placed the telescope in her mistress's palm. Pearl extended the tubes and looked through the lens.

At the stables, the man told the child to wait. He disappeared through the doors. Moments later, he emerged leading a brown horse.

David looked up and backed away, alarmed by the animal's size. The Sikh said something to the boy, who listened, stepped gingerly toward the horse, and raised his hand. The horse lowered his head and David stroked its nose. Then the Sikh took something out of his pocket and gave it to the boy. A carrot. David took it and fed it to the horse. The beast whinnied. David clapped his hands gleefully.

A shriek cut through the air. Man and boy snapped their heads in the direction of the cry.

"*Tai-goon*—eldest son!" Nanny Chin screeched. "Come back here. Get away from that animal!" She ran up the hill toward them, spitting words like bullets.

David stood petrified.

The amah reached them and doubled over to catch her breath. But the heaving did not stop her mouth from unleashing an avalanche of invective aimed at the Sikh. Pearl could pick out a few words and phrases. "*... I'll report this to the mistress ... you will die ... horses are dangerous ... you are an idiot ...*" Spent, the amah sat on a tethering post and mopped her brow.

The Sikh led the horse back indoors. When he emerged, Nanny Chin had dragged David halfway down the hill. He could do nothing but look at her and open his hands as if to say, "What did I do?"

She had come to the conclusion that David should not be cooped up in the house with his lessons and his toys but be allowed outdoors for an hour or so each day to play in the garden. The boy had exhibited boundless energy that had stretched his amah's capacity to cope, and *besides,* Semah mused in her journal, *he is quite wilful. I fear he will find a way outdoors anyway, so why not let him? Under Nanny Chin and Veer Singh's supervision, what could go wrong?*

But after the frightened amah woke up to find the boy missing, then discovered he had been kidnapped by the *more-law-cha* from whom she braved a daring if crude rescue, Semah set down some rules. It was important that her son understand that *with privileges come responsibilities.*

At supper, after the main courses were cleared and a sugar-glazed pudding placed at the dining table's centre, Semah wiped her mouth with her napkin. David mirrored the gesture. Then he eyed the pudding. Cinnamon and orange aromas filled the air. He did not hear his mother's carefully prepared preface, and wouldn't have heard the rules either if Semah hadn't reached out and turned his head to face her.

"First, you must not go near the horses." She held up one finger. "Can you hold up your index finger?" David did as he was told. "Second, you must not leave sight of Nanny Chin." She held up another finger. David did the same and wondered how many more rules there were before he was allowed a dish of pudding. (He could count to fifty.) "And third, you must not cross over to the eastern section of the garden." The boy looked puzzled. He cocked his head and asked,

"Why?"

Semah tapped his nose and replied,

"Because I say so."

David's brow creased. But it quickly smoothed when a slice of pudding appeared on the dessert plate in front of him.

To ensure that her terms were followed, Semah decided she would sit on the veranda overlooking the western garden during playtime—just to let her son know she was watching. There she opened her sketchpad and made eclectic studies of whatever caught her eye: white bauhinias in their pots; a Eurasian jay with blue-edged wings nesting in the eaves; the red blossoms on trees called Flame of the Forest that reminded her of India. Using coloured pencils, she captured the verdant hill that sloped down to the Tramway Station where the recently completed cable car ran up Victoria Mountain to the Peak.

Sitting *en plein air* relaxed her. She could hear own breathing. She could feel the sun's embrace as it made its languid journey west. And she could enjoy her son's unfettered pleasure as he chased a bouncing ball. She sketched him, too. One afternoon she saw a child emerge in the eastern garden, led there by an amah. Following behind, a second amah carried a large parasol. Covered from neck to toe and wearing gloves, the child wore a wide-brimmed hat made of rattan and held a rag doll against her cheek. Unsure of her whereabouts, she looked around and let her eyes wander. When she saw Semah, the little girl pointed to her with her doll.

Semah covered her mouth. Oh my gosh! It was Leah Felicie! She was taller! And walking! Well, of course she would be at her age!

The trio reached the centre of the garden, where the first amah pulled out a large white handkerchief (it had been dangling from the side buttons of her tunic) and spread it on the grass. The second amah opened her parasol, spiked it in the ground, and adjusted the angle to produce a patch of shade where the handkerchief lay. The first amah patted the makeshift seat and said something in Chinese to Leah Felicie, but she didn't respond. She was too busy watching the little boy playing about fifty yards away.

David kicked his ball. It arced through the air and landed with a hop, skip, and jump at Leah Felicie's feet. She looked at the ball, and then at the boy who had kicked it.

David ran to retrieve it.

Seeing this, amahs on both sides stood up and yelled instructions in Chinese with arms outstretched. Clearly they wanted him to stop, but he kept running toward the ball.

He halted a few feet from it.

He looked up and saw his mother looking down at him.

She heard her own voice: "You must not cross over to the eastern section …," and saw David's furrowed brow. He cocked his head just as he had done at dinner when he had asked "Why?"

David looked at the ball. Looked up at his mother, and then at Leah Felicie.

He took one large step toward the little girl. No one spoke. He took another step. The ball was within reach. He picked it up and gave it to Leah Felicie. She dropped her rag doll, took the ball, and flashed one of her adorable smiles.

As though awakened from petrifaction, the amahs sprang into action. They grabbed the children by their waists, gathered their toys, and, cawing like a murder of crows, retreated to their respective wings of the house.

As Semah drew back, she saw Pearl leaning out over the eastern veranda. The two women looked at each other. Unlike their children, they did not share any joy.

In his study, Emanuel watched as a servant poured tea for Semah and Pearl. Behind him the carriage clock on the mantel ticked. His fingers tapped rhythmically on his waistcoat pocket. With tea poured, Emanuel waved the server away. To his right, Semah fidgeted with her ring. On his left, Pearl fanned her neck.

In the past week, both his wives had made proposals regarding the need to prevent their children from contacting each other. He could think of nothing else and had even consulted his partners.

"Good fences make good wives," Aleandro chuckled.

Li, taking his daughter's side, had averred that building a new house for the *gwei-paw*—white woman—would be appropriate. Emanuel ignored the slur.

Aleandro tapped his nose. He lived with a quartet of wives in a walled compound in Macau where they each had their own bungalow. "Fences are cheaper," he offered.

"No, gentlemen, thank you for your counsel, but there will be no fence and no, we will not live separately."

Li growled and swatted the air with his palm.

There was no gain in either suggestion, Emanuel thought. The former would bifurcate the magnificent property that rose like a gigantic but handsome nose from the face of the colony's highest mountain. The latter—to build another house—would have created unbearable competition between the women. They would spy on each other by dispatching their amahs to gather intelligence about what the other wife had acquired. If one had a bathroom on each floor the other would want two, custom-made furniture would be trumped with silk upholstery, crystal goblets by plate and silver stamped with the family crest, and so on, each one collecting possessions like warlords collecting fortresses—as conspicuous demonstrations of their superiority. It was not the money—he had plenty of cash. No, everyone had missed the point.

The servant closed the doors with a soft *click,* freeing Emanuel to speak to his wives:

"These are my children," he began. "They are my blood and they should know each other as brother and sister. I never had that as a child. I had a sibling but we weren't close—" Emanuel stopped himself. No need to go on. "I want them to play together as often as they like. And, I have today written to Calcutta for the rabbi to recommend a *Melammed tinokot*—a religious teacher for children—whom I shall bring here. The children's day lessons will continue—but they will be taught together. David will attend those taught by you in reading and arithmetic," he said, gesturing toward Pearl. "And Leah Felicie will attend those taught by you—drawing, music, geography," he said, gesturing at Semah. "In time they will need more formal schooling ..." He let his voice trail off.

If ever there was a moment when the two women might simultaneously roll their eyes, it was this one. But neither actually rolled anything. Rather, they took huge intakes of breath, rose, and walked out of his study, Semah to the right and Pearl to the left.

Emanuel had hated being a side player in someone else's story. With his sovereign pronouncement, he had just wrested the narrative back. He lit a cheroot, poured a brandy, and walked out onto the veranda, smiling like the cat in a children's book.

Below him, awash in sunset gold, the city prepared for night. Lamplights flickered from Kennedy Town to Causeway Bay. In the harbour, silver streaks on the water pointed like spears toward Kowloon Peninsula, where vast tracts of empty land lay ripe for the taking. He lifted his glass in a toast. "I'll have it all," he whispered.

SEMAH AND PEARL

A bright, airy room on the top floor with floor-to-ceiling windows became their classroom.

Furniture had been removed to make way for two desks placed side by side facing a vast chalkboard. The surrounding walls displayed maps of different countries. Postcards and pictures (cut out from magazines) were pinned to the cities they portrayed like little windows onto the world. Alphabet blocks spelled the "word of the day" on one tabletop. On another, drawing paper, crayons, pencils, and a xylophone lay ready. A teacher's desk set on a dais held a mammoth book used daily by the *Melammed tinokot*. Beside it sat a tiny handbell.

Every morning started with religious instruction in Hebrew. While this was happening, Pearl sat reading at one end of the classroom. Semah took up a similar position at the opposite end, where she sketched. When the *Melammed* finished his lesson, he rang the handbell and departed.

Semah taught drawing and music and quizzed the children on the names of countries she pointed to on the maps. When she was done, she rang the handbell and resumed her seat by the window. Pearl taught sums—addition and subtraction, as well as reading, grammar, and cursive writing with nib and ink. When her lesson was over, she rang the bell and released the children to play in the garden.

Despite their initial misgivings, the women could see that their children learned quickly and supported each another. But cooperation was a lesson that they themselves could not learn. They continued their teaching regimen, icily ignoring each other. Despite their almost daily proximity (there were no classes on Shabbat or Sunday), no words passed between them. So it came as a surprise when they finally did.

One afternoon, Semah watched her son pedal his tricycle while Leah Felicie chased him in the garden. Her words rose from a heart filled with inexplicable delight at the sight of such unfettered joy:

"She's adorable," Semah said.

"Thank you," Pearl replied, a little surprised at the sound of her own voice. "David is a handsome boy," she added without taking her eyes off the children.

"Thank you," Semah replied.

Below them, David stopped. Leah Felicie caught up to him. He got off, helped her on the seat, and pushed her around the garden. Leah Felicie egged him on, squealing "Faster, faster!"

"Soon they will need to go to a proper school," Pearl said.

"Yes, David must prepare for the world. Make other friends."

"Leah Felicie, too."

"Yes, of course. Leah Felicie too."

Pearl turned and looked at Semah. "What do you draw?" she asked. Semah raised both eyebrows and faced her interlocutor. Pearl continued: "On your drawing tablet."

"I'll show you," Semah said, and retrieved her drawings from the classroom.

Pearl watched her. Remarkable, she thought. You couldn't tell she's a cripple.

"These are studies I'm making of the children," Semah said, opening the cover.

Leah Felicie's long wavy hair, her oval-shaped face, the long nose; David's round face and pointed chin—all were captured in light and shadow.

An urgent yell rose from the garden. Both heads turned simultaneously. The sketchpad dropped with a slap on the stone floor.

Leah Felicie had fallen over. The amahs (calling out a tirade of blame) rushed to her rescue. But David had already pulled the girl to her feet and was dusting off her dress. Leah Felicie looked up and waved at her mother and Semah.

The din the amahs made criticizing each other for their obvious lapse in stewardship had distracted the women from realizing that they had clasped hands in alarm. When they did realize it, they withdrew as though their fingers had touched a hot stove.

In the moments after they had let go, their palms tingled. Their hearts beat a little faster. Their minds muddled. How could they have allowed the wall of caution, built up over so many years, to crumble so easily? They had held hands as sisters might!

So foreign were these sensations that neither one was ready to acknowledge them. Rather, they turned on their heels, rushed down to the garden, and led their children indoors for tiffin, followed by a nap. Then the women—each in her room—examined their own hands. Who had reached out first?

From that day on, when they met in the classroom, they permitted themselves, by tacit agreement, to broaden their communication with comments on the weather and topics such as their children's future education. What had one or the other heard about such-and-such headmaster or headmistress? Would instruction be in English? And does the school accept Jews?

As he prepared to celebrate his son's bar mitzvah, Emanuel felt that he was a man in full. He had flouted convention by living with two wives and dismissed the so-called curse that threatened his children's lives as "blatant rubbish."

A natural athlete, David had grown into a tall, dark, and handsome lad (often mistaken for a senior) who regularly took prizes at the English School Foundation where he was enrolled as a day student. Likewise Leah Felicie had flowered into a pretty girl. She attended the Central School for Girls and had a good head for figures, just like her *Ma-mah*. Together Emanuel's children had cultivated a retinue of friends, who often turned the mansion into a riot of activity that he loved to complain about.

But he also noticed that despite their new acquaintances the siblings didn't lose their devotion to each other. Often he would see them in the garden—David seated on a swing reading about horses (he was forbidden from riding them but not from reading about them) and Leah Felicie perched nearby, sketching the world around her—both happy to be in each other's company.

At last, peace had settled upon his house. The comfort of his children and the truce between his wives gave his personal life the stability he had craved. But the same could not be said about his business affairs: by the mid-1890s opium trading had declined to a few hundred chests per year from its peak of eighty thousand a decade before. Roving crews of illiterate ne'er-do-wells used modified *lorcha* stripped down into light and nimble ships, some of them steam-assisted, to ply the South China seas like wolves. They raided opium runners regularly and caused insurance and security costs to soar, which in turn ate up profits. Additionally, cheaper harvests from the mountainous regions in China and Turkey had replaced top-quality Patna triple A. Over the years, bloated storage vessels that had crowded the harbour were up-anchored and dismantled, their wooden beams used to build smaller warehouses onshore. Some merchants, like the Sassoons and the Kardoories, wanted out of the trade altogether, and found a willing buyer in the one person who insisted that opium was still a viable commodity.

Emanuel had decided to purchase his competitors' inventories, gambling that his reading of future demand was correct. Users would prefer his high-quality brand to the cheaper, inferior stuff that had flooded the market. And when users decided to go for something better, he would be ready. Having cornered the entire local supply, Emanuel went from being *"one of the many opium traders"* to being called the *"foremost opium trader in Hong Kong."* In fact, by the mid-1890s, he was the *only* opium merchant left.

Sitting on two million dollars' worth of inventory was, at best, a pyrrhic victory. Year after year passed with no change in the public's demand. They wanted their drugs fast and cheap. Not even his old reliable client, the Generalissimo, was interested. His investment against the future remained idle. And in business, idle money is as useless as tits on a bull. Gossip spread that this was *"Belilios's folly."* The man had blundered. His rivals, the Sassoons and the Kardoories, had bested Emanuel by selling him a fortune in unwanted goods. He had to do something to silence the chattering and the chinwagging blather that reminded him of his school days. He had to show that *Belilios's folly* did not make the slightest dent in his portfolio, which now included real estate, shipping, and utilities. As a palpable demonstration of his wealth, he decided to *"give back to the community."*

Doing charitable works was not just a cultural obligation but also a handy strategy. It assuaged the guilt of having profited mightily from the sale of a drug that gave him a privileged life while it sucked the marrow out of millions of addicts in China. Following his lead, other Jewish opium traders jettisoned their old ways, shifting their focus from the aggrandizement of filthy lucre to the promotion of a brand-new image as humanitarians. This canny *giving back* initiative produced no end of willing beneficiaries. Administrators of schools, hospitals, parks, sanatoriums, and orphanages gleefully accepted the gifts. Unlike the rich, charities could not afford principles.

At David's bar mitzvah reception, held under a massive white tent erected on the western lawns at Kingsclere, Emanuel was proud to call his son "a young man." David beamed. And to honour the occasion, Belilios *père* announced a substantial donation amounting to one-third the cost of building a new synagogue. (He would have gladly pledged the full amount if his peers the Sassoons and the Kardoories had not beaten him to it when their own sons were inducted.) Furthermore, he set Leah Felicie's dowry at $10,000—double the going rate and equivalent to more than double Semah's. A chorus of applause followed nods of approval and a few gasps of surprise.

Once he had succeeded in besting his contemporaries with donations, Emanuel strove to better them in other ways, regardless of the cost. For Semah, he purchased "The Eyrie" on the Peak as a summer house. It had panoramic views of the harbour and Mount Kellet. From its front yard they could gaze down onto the Governor's own summer residence, not a stone's throw away. Gardens were cultivated across the road and a charming belvedere erected a short walk up a hillock. For Pearl, he built a castle-like pile of bricks and mortar overlooking Repulse Bay on the island's southern shores. Remote and wild, it gained in feng shui what the Eyrie had in stature. But that was not all. Getting and spending became his daily routine, his only drug.

To pay for his insatiable lust for acquiring land, he leveraged one property (or business) to raise the cash needed to buy new ones, gambling on future growth to meet his obligations. Three years after David's bar mitzvah and as the new century approached, his empire was built like a house of cards. Every piece relied on another to keep the structure erect. Remove one and …

"I don't understand," Emanuel said, scratching his head. "This is the biggest land auction in the history of Hong Kong and you're not interested?"

He was in Li's home on the hill overlooking Happy Valley. After decades, Li had become proficient in English; Emanuel still could not wrap his tongue around the Chinese language.

"They want too much," Li said, his mouth downturned, his finger wagging the air. "You ask before. Today same answer—too much!" He slapped the back of his hand on his palm.

"That's why it will take our pooled resources to make a serious bid," Emanuel said, bringing the argument full circle for the umpteenth time.

Li said nothing. He looked down at his desk blotter and fingered his moustache.

"Aleandro, what do you say?" Emanuel asked.

"I say it is risky," Aleandro said.

"Of course it is. Our business was built on risk. That's what we do!"

"No, no, no, too much," Li repeated, waving his hand in mid-air.

Emanuel wished he didn't need partners. But even if he sold all his assets, he would not have enough for this deal. He needed his old friends to kick in some capital for a venture that would make him the undisputed *Tai Pan* of Hong Kong's business elite.

"Look, I was in with you on the ground floor and we made a lot of money trading opium. I got you into investing your profits. And what happened? You prospered. We prospered. Now you, Aleandro, you practically own Macau—the real estate, the banking, the coal supply, transportation. And you, Li, you have bought up half this valley, your go-downs store goods all along the Praya, and your ships crowd the harbour. Would either of you have what you have if not for me? You owe me."

"You also do good—you have riches like we two," Li said. "Now it is time to stop—enough."

"Amigo, twenty-five, thirty years ago we were young men. We had nothing to lose. Today? We have everything to lose."

"This is a once-in-a-lifetime prospect. Three million dollars is a bargain for the land on the Kowloon side—you both know that. We'll carve it up. Sell off parcels—double the investment. One million from each and we would be the top bid. You both have it—"

"Do you?" Li eyeballed Emanuel.

The two men stared at each other for a long time.

"Don't worry about me. I can get it."

"I don't worry for *you*. I worry for my daughter, for my granddaughter." His voice was a throaty growl.

"How dare you. I know how to take care of my family!"

"Family is one man and one woman. You marry my daughter. I am witness," Li said, pointing a finger at his own nose. "Ale'dro also witness. You have tik her house and give it to *gwei-paw*—"

"I gave nothing away that was not mine to give."

"When you marry her, Pearl having whole house—now half-house. Very bad."

"I built her a castle near Repulse Bay."

"Not same ting."

"I purchased the Eyrie for Semah so that the two would each have their own homes."

"Aiyah." Li waved his arm dismissively. "You have two wives but you know nothing about women!"

Li got up and walked to the windows overlooking the valley. He opened a window. Emanuel slumped into a chair. Aleandro stood between them.

"Amigo, I have four wives and I don't understand them any more than you do."

Li took a deep breath. "They never leave Kingsclere," he said. "You know why?"

Emanuel looked up blankly.

"Mung-cha—stupid, it is up to man with no wife to tell you why," Li said, walking back to sit at his desk. He leaned his elbows on the surface and spoke as though he were a professor imparting wisdom to his dullest student. "Kingsclere is prize. Why? Because that is where you live. Possess Kingsclere, also possessing you. And whoever possessing you is winner."

He leaned back to let that insight settle.

"When first wife arrive, my daughter loses face. When daughter lose face, I lose face," Li said. "Now you come to me and you want me to give you money? *Hey-yow-chee-lay*—how *dare* you?"

Emanuel could see he was getting nowhere and looked at his watch. "I'll go it alone then," he said.

"How you do that?"

"I shall take loans using my businesses as collateral."

"Do not be rash, Senhor."

"I want this and I shall have it. Even if it means mortgaging everything I own, I shall have it."

"Amigo, think what you are saying. If you mortgage your businesses you will still be short. Where will you get the difference?"

"I shall sell Kingsclere," Emanuel said. He stood abruptly, and without looking at his former partners, said: "I shall be at the auction house one month from now. If you show up, I will know I still have partners. If you do not ..." He did not need to finish. He nodded. "Good day, gentlemen."

Emanuel headed for the door of Li's office.

"Senhor," Aleandro said. Emanuel stopped and turned to face the mulatto. "You can put up $1 million?

"Yes."

"And you still have a large supply of opium worth $2 million?"

"Yes," Emanuel said.

"It is time to put it to work," Aleandro said. He walked slowly toward Emanuel and hooked his arm around his old friend's elbow. "Let us walk and talk," he said.

SEMAH AND PEARL

At David's bar mitzvah, Semah, Pearl, and Leah Felicie (in a new white dress) sat in the front row of the women's side grinning with pride when he chanted from Torah.

"You skipped a phrase," Leah Felicie said to him afterward.

"Did not!" he retorted, just before his school friends surprised him with a shower of coconut and honey-drop sweets.

At the banquet, when Emanuel had surprised the gathering by announcing a dowry, Leah Felicie buried her face on her mother's shoulder while guests applauded and pointed in her direction.

"Mazel tov." Semah leaned in close to Pearl's ear.

"Thank you. It was most generous," she replied with a slight bow.

Ordinarily, that would have been the limit of their exchange. But this day was different.

"Would you come to tea?" Semah asked.

Pearl looked up at the tall woman. Flashes of their old rivalry popped into her mind. What does she want? Where would they take tea? In the formal sitting room where they met only for public occasions? In the solarium, perhaps? As Pearl searched Semah's eyes for the answers, she felt a tug on her sleeve.

"*Ma-mah,* say yes!" Leah Felicie said. "She has paintings on her wall!"

Semah flushed.

A few weeks prior, on a Wednesday when the school had a half-day and his mother was away shopping at Lane Crawford's, David had led his sister up to Semah's rooms. Before entering, he told Leah Felicie to close her eyes. He opened the door and led her to the mural. "Open sesame!" he said, which was the signal for her to open her eyes.

Leah Felicie's mouth fell open at what she saw. Studying the fresco, she lowered herself to the floor, sat down, and hugged her knees. David sat beside her, put his hands behind his back to prop himself up, and grinned. "Told you so," he said proudly.

Who knows how long they remained entranced before the door opened again? Semah entered, followed by Veer Singh carrying an armful of pink boxes with the initials *LC* on them. The children scrambled to their feet, expecting a scolding.

Pearl had heard through the black-and-white telegraph that the *gwei-paw* drew pictures on her walls. But she had dismissed such tittle-tattle as improbable. Now, it would appear, the rumours were true. And she was anxious to see for herself.

On the day of the tea, Semah changed her dress several times, edited the jewellery she wore, and checked her hair every time she passed a mirror. She ordered the doors of her rooms to be opened wide to create a sense of welcome. Moments before the appointed hour, she checked her brooch-watch and nodded to Veer Singh. He stood outside the doors, his white-gloved hands folded in front of his body.

Precisely at four, a grandfather clock on the landing chimed and Pearl appeared at the top of the stairs, Gum-ghee behind her. Tinkling bells, gongs, and cuckoo calls from an assortment of other time-keeping devices also sounded the hour, providing a fanfare of tintinnabulation as they walked down the hall toward the Sikh. He bowed and indicated for them to enter.

"I had thought to take tea on the veranda," Semah said after polite greetings, "but decided we should get to the main event right away."

Without comment, Pearl took in the room. Her first thought was, What a mess! Gum-ghee curled her lip.

The floor was speckled with paint. Against the far wall stood easels with canvases of unfinished paintings. Propped against another, a long table held stained rags and jars of greyish water with brushes sticking out of them. Beside these, crumpled tubes lay in a chaotic hodgepodge. A ruined chaise in need of upholstering sat in the corner. Pinned above it, large sheets of butcher's paper showed charcoal sketches of faces, hands, and eyes, and still more eyes. Then she saw it.

Semah twirled her ring and held her breath.

Pearl gasped and quickly covered her mouth.

"Do you like it?" Semah asked.

Pearl said nothing as she examined the mural. Her attention darted from one image to another, attempting to take in everything, trying to gobble up the entire wall in one bite. But that was impossible. She lighted on an image here, another there, then distracted, she panned her gaze to another part of the kaleidoscope of scenes that chronicled David's and Leah Felicie's life from birth to the present: babies swaddled, cribs rocked, a woman's arms coddling an infant, a rendering of the family portrait, David on a tricycle, Leah Felicie with white gloves, amahs holding a toddler's hand, horses, views from Kingsclere, classroom activity, the children with prayer shawls, all captured in beautiful and loving detail.

"I made one in Calcutta," Semah said, but did not elaborate.

"It is exquisite. I can see why David wished to show Leah Felicie."

"The children thought I would be angry. But I wasn't. I did say that they should keep it to themselves. I wasn't sure how you would react."

"How long did this take?" Pearl asked, but immediately waved her own question aside. "Years, obviously!" she said.

Flanked by Gum-ghee and Veer Singh, Pearl and Semah enjoyed a tea that lasted the better part of an hour. Both women made mental notes of the last time they had sat down to a meal together, just the two of them—almost a decade and a half ago! But out loud, they engaged in polite chitchat, not unlike two diplomats whose countries were once at war but now enjoyed an unfamiliar peace. The weather was covered, as was the garden and of course the children. Off-limits, by tacit agreement, were Emanuel and Kingsclere.

One week later, Pearl reciprocated. In the days leading up to the event, she had Gum-ghee set up a table with two chairs in her salon, then changed her mind and had the furniture moved to the veranda. Not satisfied with that location, everything was relocated to her private rooms. But when that didn't feel right she ordered everything removed back to the salon. Tablecloths were also changed a number of times, as were the teapot and cups, until Pearl was satisfied that the atmosphere would look appropriately relaxed.

On the day, she had her hair brushed, oiled, and rolled into a bun. She chose jade earrings to match her three bracelets and the pendant that hung on a gold chain around her neck.

Semah arrived alone. The room, neat as a pin, reminded her of a Chinese furniture store. Mahogany cupboards with brass handles, straight-backed ebony chairs with hard, uncushioned seats, vases (Were they Ming or the more recent Qing? She couldn't tell), and a screen with three painted panels depicting a village scene of fisher folk filled the space.

Pearl dismissed Gum-ghee, who knitted her brow and mumbled, but obeyed.

"I have a selection of teas." Gesturing to each pot, Pearl continued: "Chinese red, chrysanthemum, gunpowder, and India—you are no doubt familiar with that one!"

Semah smiled and chose the chrysanthemum.

"That is a most becoming pendant," Semah said, surprised by her words. Becoming? Had that sounded condescending? Why couldn't she have said she liked the necklace? Or used the word "beautiful"?

"Thank you," Pearl replied. "That is a beautiful ring."

"Thank you ..." Semah breathed in the sweet aroma of chrysanthemum.

Pearl sipped from her cup of gunpowder tea.

From the harbour, Semah heard a steamship whistle. In the middle distance a horse neighed—from the stables, perhaps? A bee buzzed over the sweet cakes then zoomed off.

Pearl's heart beat a little faster. She had wondered what she could do to restore equanimity. It wasn't a matter of competition. No! It was a matter of face! Semah had given face to Pearl by inviting her into her rooms. Now Pearl felt bound to return the compliment. The imbalance had to be remedied not only by hosting a tea but also by displaying something of equal value to Semah's paintings.

"May I show you something?" Pearl asked.

"With pleasure," Semah replied, and immediately cringed inwardly. A simple "yes" would have sufficed.

She rose and followed Pearl through doors that led to an adjoining room. Her prosthetic leg pinched a little bit of skin and made her wince. But that pinprick evaporated when she saw Pearl's library. Shelves filled with books covered the walls, except for one on which maps of Hong Kong, Canton, and Macau were pinned in a neat row. Atop a gigantic table nestled against one window were pens and inkpots. Stacked below these writing implements, well-ordered columns of newspapers, magazines, and notebooks stood in tidy rows. Arranged smartly, like a portrait gallery, were two rows of small pictures of men cut out from print journals. Below the miniature gallery, a large green blotter—without a stain on it—spread out like a verdant lawn on the teak surface of the desk. To the right, a thick stack of cream-coloured vellum sat ready. On the opposite side was a smaller stack of what appeared to be a manuscript.

"I'm interested in Hong Kong's history," Pearl said, handing over the stack.

Semah read the cover page: "From Pottinger to Robinson."

"The first Governor to the present one," Pearl said.

Semah nodded. That accounted for the maps and for the row of portraits of men on the desk. She was about to ask if she could read the book, but her thought was disrupted by the sound of footsteps running toward them.

Breathless, her cheeks flushed, Leah Felicie burst into Pearl's study.

"Ma-mah," the girl blurted out in Cantonese, *"He didn't mean to do it, it wasn't his fault, it was me, I planned the whole thing and now the more-law-char found us and he's going to tell his mother and she'll be upset with him and he'll be punished and it was all my fault."*

Pearl held her daughter by the shoulders and replied in English, "Slow down, child. What happened?"

"We went to the stables and saddled a horse. David got on and lifted me up behind him. We went for a short ride before ..."

"Before what, daughter?"

Semah let the papers drop. They scattered around her ankles.

"Did he fall?" Semah said, a little louder than she intended.

"It was my fault," Leah Felicie repeated, her eyes tearing up.

Semah rushed out of the study and hurried into the hallway. Then she stopped, clasped her hands to her chest, and exhaled.

David walked toward her followed by Veer Singh. Gum-ghee took up the rear, scolding them for the dirt they left on her floors.

"I'm a man. Father said so," David said when he saw his mother. Pearl and Leah Felicie arrived behind Semah. With his fists clenched and his eyes ablaze, David looked at his mother. "Stop treating me like a child." Semah noticed his chin quivering.

Thinking that Veer Singh was attending Semah, Leah Felicie had told David that the coast was clear. They sneaked into the stables. David saddled a horse and mounted it. Leah Felicie got on behind him. He heeled the animal's shanks and the horse walked forward out of the stable but stopped once it arrived at the mound of hay some fifty yards away. There, it lowered its head and chomped at the feed. No amount of encouragement from the children would make the beast move. As if from nowhere, Veer Singh appeared and David and his accomplice were caught.

Semah and Pearl looked at their children and realized just how much they had grown. David had inherited his mother's height. Like his father, his blue eyes shone with purpose. Leah Felicie was small like her mother. But she also had a straight nose and wavy dark hair like her father's.

"Having two wives, two children, many properties, titles, director-ships, *aiyah!*" Li had said to his daughter in Cantonese. "His name on so many charities, he has achieved enough for two, three men. Now he wishes to hang a sword over his own head!"

They were seated in a discreet corner of his favourite tea house, facing the Jockey Club's main building. Father and daughter met there regularly. The clang of dishes and over-loud voices of other guests created a wall around them. Waiters with large trays on their shoulders wove through a maze of tables selling dim sum. The manager, knowing that Mr. Li valued privacy, had set up a folding screen that partially obscured them from curious onlookers. To ensure that his best customer was not disturbed, he assigned his mother (a short, doughy woman with a permanent grimace who was deaf as a post) to stand guard beside the partition.

"A sword? What do you mean, *Ba-bah?*"

"Next month, the British will auction a large parcel of land on Kowloon Peninsula. Your husband wishes to buy it all, break it up, and sell it off in small parcels."

"So?" Pearl's impatience underlined that little word. "He has done that before with other properties in Central District."

"This time it is different."

"Why?"

Li sat back and looked at his daughter. Why? Was his little Pearl challenging him? She had changed since becoming a wife of the foreigner.

"If he wins the bid he loses!" he said.

"I don't understand."

"Emanuel is overextended—he has too many projects, owns too many properties, too many businesses. Before he has paid for one project, he starts another. He is asset rich but cash poor."

"How do you know this?"

"He came to me and Uncle. He wanted our cash to go in with him. We said no. But he is determined."

"Where will he get the cash?"

"Without me and Uncle, he will have to sell Kingsclere and most of what he owns to make up the difference."

Pearl felt a tingle up and down her spine—an army of ants with cold legs racing along her backbone.

"Why do you tell me these things?"

"Why? Daughter—you must stop him or he will be ruined."

They sat in silence. Small round boxes of steamed dumplings remained untouched. Bolei tea cooled in their cups. Pearl stared at the pale liquid and wished she knew how to read the black leaves.

Yes, Emanuel was like a dog with a bone. Once he had set his mind to an idea, he was relentless. Anything short of his goal was, to him, failure. He had been that way in everything he did. But would he sacrifice Kingsclere?

"Daughter?" She felt her father's hand on her arm. "You must leave him. Come home."

Slowly, Pearl pulled away from him.

"No," she said softly. "He is my husband. He will not sell Kingsclere. It was built for me as a wedding gift—"

"Hah," he said with a dismissive wave. "That changed when the *gwei-paw* stepped through the door. Can't you see? She is just like the British in Hong Kong—they will never leave."

"Emanuel loves me. He won't sell Kingsclere," she said, looking him in the eyes. He turned away and shook his head from side to side.

"Stubborn," he said. "Just like your mother."

Her stomach gurgled but she ignored it. She had no appetite. As they left the restaurant, guests stood and bowed toward her father. But no head dipped lower than the manager's. Li acknowledged everyone graciously, smiling and waving hello to those across the room.

Pearl watched but heard nothing. It was as though the volume had been turned off on the world around her. She felt as if she were floating. Outside, Li got into his waiting chair and Pearl climbed into a rickshaw that Gum-ghee had hailed to take them home. Father and daughter went in opposite directions.

What *Ba-bah* had told her couldn't possibly be true. But what if Kingsclere *were* sold? Where would she live? Move back in with her *Ba-bah*? That would be far too humiliating. Go to that foreboding pile overlooking Repulse Bay? Isolated on the other side of the island? An unbearable thought. She bit her lip. Words stabbed the sides of her brain: demeaning, degrading, dishonourable … No. That was not going to happen again. The worm of doubt returned. It had been asleep the last two or three years while the women had busied themselves with their children's education, but … Did Semah know of Emanuel's plans? Were they in this together?

Suddenly, the chill of insect legs crawling up and down her spine returned. Emanuel had betrayed her before. He had promised to set aside his first wife but he didn't. He had built Kingsclere for her but allowed Semah to share it. Equivocations whirled like midges swarming overhead. Out of her chaotic thoughts came a line she remembered from the Buddha's *Book of Dialects: "Embrace your enemies for they will be unable to lift a sword if their arms are wound around yours."* With this tenet in mind, she sat down at her desk, composed a note to Semah, and gave it to Gum-ghee for delivery.

"*Aiyah,* mistress," Gum-ghee said, shaking her head, "she is so big the chair will break when she sits down."

"Don't talk stupid. Do as you are told," Pearl ordered. Then, seeing her handmaid's reluctance, she added, "I must find out what she knows. I need to find out if she has any dragon honour tiles."

"You want to play mah-jong with her?" Gum-ghee shook her head. She held the note as though it had been contaminated.

Since the day Pearl showed Semah her writing project, they had alternated hosting tea every month or so. Strictly speaking, it would have been

Semah's turn. Despite the elapse of three years, their relationship had not progressed far enough to ignore such nuances. Formality still governed these occasions, with each woman making arrangements to meet at different locations—the Peak Café, the tearoom of the Botanic Gardens, or the palm court of the Hong Kong Hotel.

For this occasion, Pearl had chosen the gazebo—a fitting place, since that was where they had first sat down when Semah arrived. Also, it was situated on neutral territory, on the north side of the house near the banyan tree that overlooked the magnificent harbour. Emanuel's telescope had been mounted on a tripod there.

Pearl arrived early to ensure that everything was just so. She wore a collarless blue tunic buttoned up the side, an ankle-length skirt, and flat shoes. Her hair, immaculately oiled to a black sheen, sported a yellow bauhinia above her left ear. A long white handkerchief left a cloudlike trail from her hand.

She looked through the telescope down Garden Road past St. John's and admired the massive Queen's Building that dominated the shoreline. Kingsclere had been modelled after that structure, with its covered verandas, domed corner pieces, and wide stairways. She looked to the right where the new cenotaph had been erected in the town square. Nearby at Murray Barracks, men wearing matching white uniforms and English police helmets stood in two neat rows of six apiece. From her perspective, they looked European. An officer appeared to be barking orders at the men. They dispersed.

Moving the scope northward, she saw that the harbour was unusually quiet. No commercial ships were sailing. Steamers were anchored and still. Only British Navy vessels were plying the waters, positioning themselves at Lei Yue Mun Passage, the eastern gateway to the South China Sea. Swinging her sights to the west, she saw similar manoeuvres. How strange, she thought, the navy appeared to be blocking access to the harbour from both sides. What was going on?

She had more important matters to deal with and aimed the telescope northward to the Kowloon Peninsula. There it was—a stretch of land almost twice as long as all of Central District, empty and ripe for the plucking.

"Good afternoon."

It was Semah. Her Sikh manservant stood behind her. Although it was a warm afternoon, Semah wore gloves, a high-collared, cream-coloured dress, and a pink hat with a feather shooting out of its band. Her Sikh wore a multicoloured turban, a white jacket with brass buttons, jodhpurs, and leather boots. Pearl thought he looked like an overdecorated rowboat being towed by a floating castle.

"Please sit and have some tea," Pearl said.

On the table, a pot of tea and a tiered tray of finger sandwiches stood at the ready. Semah approached the table. Her Sikh manservant pulled out a chair. Gum-ghee did the same for her mistress. The wives sat opposite each other. Gum-ghee stood behind Pearl, fanning her back with a heart-shaped fan. The Sikh stood on the grass, his hands behind his back. Seeing this, Gum-ghee sped up her fanning to wave off any suspect vapours that might have emanated from either the giantess or her swarthy manservant.

"You are well?" Pearl asked.

"Yes I am. And you?"

"Thank you. I am too," Pearl replied.

An awkward pause fell. Rosewater and lavender merged with the sweet aroma of Pears soap. Curious sounds wafted up the hill from Central District—a yell, a neighing horse, a steam whistle, a clang of an iron hammer.

"And David?" Pearl asked.

"Oh, I fret, perhaps too much ..."

"He is doing well in school, is he not? Graduated top in his class?"

"Yes, yes, he is a good student. But he loves to ride and horses are not my ... As you know, I tried to discourage it. But he can be wilful ..." Semah blotted her upper lip with a lace handkerchief. "Anyway, I agreed to let him but only under Veer Singh's supervision." She stuffed the handkerchief into her cuff, stirred a teaspoonful of sugar into her cup, and put it to her lips.

Pearl watched, her temples throbbing.

"And Leah Felicie? How is the child?"

"Taller than I! They grow so fast."

Both women sipped their teas.

"I wish to thank you," Pearl said, putting down her cup. Semah cocked her head. Pearl anticipated her question. "For taking care of Leah

Felicie during my …" She paused to find the right word and settled on the phrase " … my great illness." Then she said, "I realized the other day that I have never expressed my gratitude."

Semah closed her eyes for a moment and nodded in acknowledgment of the words. "I did only what any mother would have done for—" Here she stopped, unable to find the right description. What were they to each other? "What any mother would have done," she repeated.

"David—he is a handsome boy," Pearl said. Semah smiled at the compliment. Pearl continued: "And he is kind to Leah Felicie. The two are like brother and sister."

Pearl took a sip of tea, put down her cup, and said,

"I hear from Leah Felicie that he is not well?"

"Just a summer cold and a fever."

"I shall make an infusion for him to drink."

"Thank you."

"Leah Felicie is so pretty," Semah said, abruptly changed the subject. "Bachelors will be lining up to offer."

"Thank you. G–d is generous …"

"Indeed He is."

"But man can be … fickle."

Semah's head tilted to one side. "How so?"

"My husband …" Pearl said.

At the sound of the words *my husband* Semah flinched. Emanuel and Kingsclere were the two subjects that both knew were off-limits.

Pearl put her hand on Semah's.

"Emanuel, then," Pearl said.

When Semah did not move her hand away, Pearl got directly to the point. "How secure are our futures?"

"Whatever do you mean?

"He has plans to sell this house—do you know anything about that?"

Semah's face paled. Her head shook. From the harbour a cannon boomed.

Both women snapped their heads toward the sound. A puff of grey smoke rose from one of the naval frigates anchored at Lei Yue Mun Passage. Two British officers dressed in white appeared at the far end of the garden.

Emanuel had sent for a team of doctors who examined David, shook their heads, and left the bedroom in silence. She watched them as they walked down the stairs. She strained to hear what they were saying. As they were about exit the front door, she called out "Wait," and ran down the stairs too quickly. Her leg buckled and she pitched forward. Grasping the newel post, she pulled herself up before falling, her face flushed with rage.

Only one week before, two British officers had arrived with printed warnings to remain indoors, to double-boil the drinking water, to scrub down all pots and clothes with lye and the floors with carbolic soap. Hong Kong had been infested with bubonic plague. It had started in the filthiest parts of Wanchai. Within days, it had travelled into her home with pernicious cunning. And David was its victim.

"What do you mean with your silence, your shaking of heads? You are medical men, are you not?"

The pack of doctors stood rigid, staring in disbelief.

"We pay you to have answers. What is the cure? What is the cure?" Hot tears blurred her vision.

"My dearest," Emanuel said, wrapping his arms around her body. "The good doctors have done their best—"

"They have not! I merely wish to know what is the cure! Is that so difficult a question for men of science? Well, gentlemen, is it?"

The bunch shifted from foot to foot. Finally, one of them stepped forward.

"Madam," he began, then paused, tapping his lips with his knuckles. "We have little information on this disease, save to say that rat leavings in water not properly boiled can cause the spread of sinister germs." The others nodded in support. He glanced at his two colleagues and continued: "We are united in our opinion that laudanum will ease his suffering. That and a proper diet may lead to recovery ..." He let his words trail off, turned on his heel, and led a hasty exodus toward the waiting sedan chairs.

"Recovery" rang in her head like a lifeline thrown to a drowning man. Recovery it would be. She sat on the bottom step and tightened the buckles on her leg brace. Modesty be hanged! Then she mounted the stairs toward the east wing. Pearl was the head of household and therefore must be held to account. Behind her she could hear Emanuel's remonstration:

"Semah. Semah, for the love of G-d, be still. Semah! Semah!" But she was deaf to his protestations. She reached Pearl's door and entered without knocking.

Inside, the air was redolent of joss-stick smoke. Incense filled the salon with an unbearable stench that stopped her cold. Everywhere in the room bunches of slender yellow sticks, clustered by the dozen, stood erect in bowls of sand. The sticks were lighted at the tips and emitted thin curls of smoke. Pots of them crowded the room so that the sum total of their emissions bathed the salon in a thick fog. Even though the green wooden blinds were closed on the French windows, some light managed to leak through the cracks, illuminating Semah from behind. Pearl was in shadow, surrounded by smoke.

The détente, the strides they had made toward it, the many teas they had enjoyed, the goodwill that had been engendered had evaporated.

"Did you boil the water?" Semah asked, and then broke into a fit of coughing. Recovering, she saw that Pearl was having a footbath. Her servant had dried one foot and was tapping the sole with her fingertips. The other foot remained submerged in a washbasin. Pearl waved a hand. Her maid quickly dried her mistress's feet and disappeared with the bowl. "Did you boil the water?" Semah repeated.

"Water is boiled in the kitchen, poured into a basin, and carried up here. I find that by the time it reaches me, it has cooled sufficiently to prevent scalding my feet," Pearl said. She stood, walked to one of the many bowls, removed some spent joss sticks, and replaced them with fresh ones that she lit with matches.

"Don't be coy," Semah said. "You know what I mean."

"Do I?"

"Yes, yes, you do. You are in charge of these things. You are to blame for rancid water. You are to blame!"

Semah left the room, slamming the door behind her to lock in the fetid miasma.

EMANUEL

The land auction had been put on hold pending the lifting of the health advisory, which had placed the entire city in quarantine. British naval frigates lined the western and eastern harbour approaches. Vessels that wanted to enter the port were turned away. Those wishing to leave were forced to remain, their passengers and crew confined on board. Police lines were erected around the district known as Wanchai. Happy Valley was also cordoned off, and a barrier erected at the bottom of Garden Road. There and in the dozens of other checkpoints scattered throughout the island, inspectors searched bags and containers, looking for rat droppings and for evidence of any kind that would lead them to eradicate the horrible blight that had invaded the colony. Streets emptied. Houses were shuttered. An eerie hush fell over the city. Everyone waited.

Emanuel waited, too. He wanted two things: for David to recover and, secondly, for word from China. Just before the quarantine was fully in place, Aleandro Remedios had sailed for Macau. In the hold of his *lorcha* was Emanuel's lading of opium bound for Generalissimo Wong, who had agreed to purchase the entire stock. If he could complete that sale, Emanuel would have enough to succeed at the auction.

```
┌─────────────────┐
│     PEARL       │
└─────────────────┘
```

Because of David's illness, the authorities put a rope around Kingsclere. The occupants became like prisoners. Guards wore white masks and inspected all foodstuffs for signs of rat leavings. But such precautions were tantamount to closing the barn door after the animals had fled.

The plague had already unleashed its malfeasance on a child. Could he have gotten it by drinking unclean water? But from where? Pearl wondered. Gum-ghee was meticulous with her instructions about cleanliness. As the mansion's majordomo, she didn't need a government advisory to insist that the servants double-boil the potable water. Why David? He was such a handsome and jovial boy. Why not Veer Singh with his filthy boots …?

Then it occurred to her. She had seen Veer Singh a few days earlier. He was on foot, following David, who was on horseback riding up the hill toward home. Quickly, images like scattered photographs appeared in her mind's eye. Her breathing hastened with every picture …

– David on a limping quarter horse arrives outside the stables.
– The animal's hind leg is lifted off the ground, its fetlock dangling in mid-air.
– Veer Singh arrives on foot, somewhat winded.
– The boy dismounts. He inspects the hoof. He runs a finger along the horseshoe.
– There is something stuck in it that had made the horse hobble.
– David picks at it with his fingers.

– Veer Singh reaches for his knife and digs it into the fetlock to loosen a
   pebble.

– It pops out and bounces on the gravel.

– The blade catches David's fingers.

– David pulls his hand away. He is bleeding. He sucks the gash.

– He submerges his hand in a trough of water and sucks on the wound.

– He repeats this manoeuvre …

Drinking fetid water mixed with mud from the horse's hoof that had
trampled manure—that was it. When she explained her theory to
Gum-ghee she ended with, "I knew it would come to no good with
that man." Her servant agreed. Seeing an opening, Gum-ghee built on
that idea and proffered her own theory: "It is the curse …"

Pearl looked at her. She remembered what Gum-ghee had told her on
the day Semah arrived in Hong Kong: *"It is said that purveyors of opium will
suffer misery for three generations during which no male offspring will survive to
manhood. It is a vengeance meant to make opium sellers feel the same pain endured
by Chinese women whose husbands or brothers or sons died chasing the dragon."*

Pearl thought about this for a long time. "Superstition. G–d warns us
not to be a part of such decadent influences. On the other hand, just
because I am a Jew doesn't make me any less Chinese."

Gum-ghee smiled when her mistress ordered joss sticks to be placed
in every nook and cranny of the eastern wing to ward off the evil. She
also had sandalwood staves placed in the foyer and the hallways of the
western wing. But Semah countermanded these orders, ignorant of their
purpose. She had Veer Singh remove the sticks and scatter them "outside
the Chinese woman's rooms."

EMANUEL

A petrifying scream rang through the halls. It was Semah's cry. A shriek so piercing that it struck terror in all who lived there.

Emanuel came out of David's rooms. He closed the doors behind him. Then he tore a piece of his coat just above his heart and fell to his knees in the hallway. Slowly he brought his hands up to cover his ears to lock out Semah's screaming. But it was impossible. Her sorrow penetrated the thickest walls. So he let his arms drop to his sides and sagged to the floor like a discarded rag doll.

He did not see or hear Pearl, who rushed to hold him in her arms, rocking him gently back and forth. Nor could he see Semah inside David's bedroom, walking to and fro beside the bed where their son lay covered with a linen sheet from head to toe.

For the rest of the day and late into the night Semah bawled. Wordless howls of pain that came from deep within her. The sounds were inhuman and terrifying. She cursed G–d in the language of sorrow. A host of angels could not have provided enough comfort for her that night.

Emanuel did not move from his position, nor did Pearl leave his side. He allowed himself to be held as he sobbed and sobbed. Around midnight, Semah, exhausted and her voice hoarse, emitted a long, guttural growl and stopped. Only then did Emanuel allow himself to sleep.

Before sunrise he awoke, moved Pearl's arm carefully from his body, and rose to his feet. He looked through the keyhole. Semah was dozing in a chair, breathing gently. The Sikh was seated beside her, his back against the wall and his head resting on his knees.

Emanuel walked down the stairs and disappeared into the night. Had he been any less numb, he would have noticed that Gum-ghee opened the doors for him, her eyes bloodshot from a night of ceaseless watching.

PEARL

Finally the sun rose. Pearl stirred and opened her eyes.

Disoriented, she sat up slowly, wondering why her mattress felt so hard on her back. She removed the blanket that was covering her shoulders and realized that she was on the floor. Looking around, she recognized the hallway outside Semah's rooms. Beside her was Gum-ghee sitting with her back against the wall. Somehow the servant had arranged herself so that her mistress could use her lap as a pillow. Then Pearl remembered everything: David covered with a linen shroud, Semah screaming, Emanuel rending his garment.

She looked at Gum-ghee, who began to wake up and stretch. Pearl rubbed her eyes, flicking away rheum to restore her morning vision.

"The master has left," Gum-ghee said softly. "He walked into the night. I was going to follow him. But I did not want to leave you alone."

From the other side of the door, Pearl heard a moan. She looked through the keyhole. Semah had awoken and was making her way toward her son lying in the bed. The tall Sikh appeared from somewhere and reached out to catch her but could not get to his mistress in time. Pearl gasped. The giant of a woman grabbed the back of a chair and sat on it. The Sikh stood at her side, looking helpless.

Pearl wiped her face several times with the palms of her hands, checked her breath, and smoothed her hair. She knocked and opened the door.

The two women stared at each other.

"Semah, I am here to help. Please, let me ..."

Semah turned away and looked down at her own hands. Pearl walked toward her, casting a glance in David's direction. He was so still and so thin. When she reached Semah, she put her hands over the woman's fingers. The face of her signet ring felt like a cold disc against her palm. Pearl said:

"May the prayers and supplications of all Israel
Be accepted by their Father, who is in Heaven,
And say Omein."

Semah looked into Pearl's eyes and mouthed *"Omein."*

"Come," Pearl said, "I'll take you to your rooms. You must rest."

Semah stood up. Pearl could feel the woman's weight against her. Gum-ghee didn't wait for direction. She held Semah under the other arm. The three women left the boy's room. Behind them Veer Singh closed the door on a bedroom that was now a crypt.

That evening Pearl held her daughter tighter than usual. The child's eyes were red and she shook with grief. Pearl cooed to her chick, reassuring her that David would always be in their hearts. Leah Felicie nodded.

Pearl made all the final arrangements. Due to curfews and restricted movements, David was first laid in the ice chamber in the mansion's basement until the following week, when the government closures were finally lifted. Only then were funeral directors permitted to take him away for burial at the Jewish cemetery on Shan Kwong Road.

Black cloths covered all mirrors in the mansion.

Semah, Pearl, and Leah Felicie sat shiva. But no one else came; no one wished to risk being exposed in a house where bubonic plague had claimed a victim.

For a couple of weeks following, Pearl sent food on trays three times a day to Semah, who had confined herself to her rooms. Leah Felicie had asked if she could bring the meals and Pearl allowed it. Each time, the young girl would hold a glass of water to Semah's lips. She drank it but she refused to eat. Pearl also directed the servants to clean her rooms, bathe her, and open the windows to let in fresh air. Semah did not resist these initiatives. Nor did she participate. She was like a child; everything had to be done for her. Each day, she had to be awoken, dressed, and fed, after which she went to David's room. It had been kept exactly as it was when he was alive. There she sat all day staring out the window. At night Semah lay in her own bed and cried herself to sleep. But most chilling of all her behaviours was her silence. She uttered not one word. It was as though she had screamed all the words out of her body on that lamentable night and silence was all that remained.

"Mistress, you should send her away. She has been driven insane and she should be in a hospital," Gum-ghee said often.

"She helped me when I fell ill. Now I will do the same for her," she would say as she ground up a mixture of herbs from her garden. "Infuse this paste and let Leah Felicie bring it to her. I have mixed it with some honey."

Gum-ghee accompanied her mistress, who fed it to Semah. Seeing that it came from Leah Felicie, Semah drank it without question. This routine took place twice a day, from the day after the funeral until, little by little, Semah improved. Gradually, with Leah Felicie's encouragement, she opened the French windows in David's rooms and finally began to eat a little on her own. But she remained mute.

Then one day, her Sikh manservant produced a pack of playing cards. He wished to engage the Memsahib in a game of two-handed bridge, but she would have none of it. Instead, she took the pack from him and, leaning one card against another, constructed a row of triangles. Then she laid cards like bridges across the apex of each triangle. Repeating this pattern, she stacked the cards tier after tier. The exercise required concentration and a steady hand. And even though the delicate structure would collapse from a sudden gust of wind or a careless bump against the table, she continued to build the house over and over. Some days she would make it to twenty-four cards, then to thirty-two before they collapsed.

Eventually, she was able to build a house using all fifty-two cards. When she was done, she sat back and smiled at her handiwork. She stared at the arrangement for the longest time, half expecting random seismic shifts vibrating from the floor to travel up the table legs and shake loose her handcrafted pyramid. But it remained intact. Her next experiment required supreme focus and rock-steady hands. She removed one card at a time to see how many needed to remain to keep the structure intact before the whole house of cards came down.

Pearl thought Semah's obsession with this game was bizarre. "But what does it matter if the woman wants to play childish games—she is eating regularly," she said to Gum-ghee. "I only wish my husband had her fortitude," she added.

Emanuel wanted nothing from anyone. Since his son's passing, he had forsaken everyone and retreated like a wounded animal into the shuttered rooms of his office in Central District. Emanuel could not abide returning to Kingsclere—that was where his heart had been shattered. "*Mo-daam*— no fortitude," Pearl called his behaviour. And with that label, she felt her attitude begin its irreversible journey against him.

Seven weeks passed. Finally Semah said,

"Good morning, child," when Leah Felicie arrived with breakfast.

The girl was so surprised she almost dropped the tray.

"I'm starving," Semah said, sitting down and reaching for her napkin.

Leah Felicie flashed a wide smile, kissed Semah on the cheek, and ran to tell her mother. Hearing this, Pearl wanted to see for herself. When she got to Semah's rooms, not a scrap of food remained on the breakfast tray.

In the days that followed, neither woman referred to the previous weeks. The loss of a child and a husband's disappearance were shared experiences that forged a tacit bond. This unspoken connection required no meetings in the gazebo, no servant emissaries with carefully penned notes delivered on salvers, no rehearsed speeches or calculations of wins and losses.

"This plant is for *fog tea*," Pearl said to Semah one morning. She was showing off her Chinese herb garden. "And these are *hare's ear root*. It clears heat from the heart. I used it after you took *fog tea,* which is to heal melancholia."

Semah bent down to sniff the plant and her head snapped back. Pearl giggled.

"It doesn't smell very pleasant—" Pearl said.

"But I suppose the results are standing in front of you."

"Just so. Ah, here we have *tangerines.*"

"They are like miniature oranges," Semah said.

"Yes, same family but smaller."

"Like you and me."

The women burst into laughter. Pearl did not object when Semah threaded her hand into the crook of her elbow. Arm in arm, they continued the tour: *Cyprus roots, Chinese rose, white peony stems,* and, "Here I have bitter orange peels on grape leaves drying in the sun. And these I use to make *emperor's tea* herbs that make you sleepy."

Semah rubbed the leaves between her fingers and recognized the aroma. She had drunk infusions of these herbs every night.

"How do you know all this?" Semah asked.

"When I was a girl, we lived in one room above a herbalist store in Wanchai," Pearl said, pointing toward the eastern section of the shore. "As often as I could, I would sneak downstairs. I loved watching the *see-fu*—the master herbalist—mixing his concoctions and poultices. As I got older, my Uncle brought me books, and when I had the opportunity, I planted this garden."

Their enthusiasm for each other's company, their eagerness to share things they were good at, had put paid to any remaining wariness between them. Conversations flowed. Much to Leah Felicie's delight, she was welcomed whenever her mother met Semah. She watched the two women, one in middle age and the other close to it, enjoying each other's company the way she and David once did.

On one such occasion, Pearl sat with Semah on the stone bench watching the sunset. Leah Felicie sat at her mother's feet. Semah looked toward Stonecutter's Island to the west. The setting sun painted her face in a golden glow. She said,

"I shall never leave Hong Kong because my David is here."

"You visit him every day," Pearl said.

"Yes. He is my constant. And when my time comes I will be buried beside him."

Pearl made no comment. None was needed. As a mother, she understood. When the sun had disappeared, Semah stroked Leah Felicie's head.

"You are fortunate—you have this child."

"You can be my aunt," the girl said.

Semah looked at Pearl: "May I?" she asked.

"Yes! Yes of course!"

"An aunt. That would make us sisters then?"

"Yes," Pearl said. "Sisters living in a house of wives."

EMANUEL

In the days after his son's passing, Emanuel tore at his garments every day until they hung like peelings off his ample frame. He ate nothing, nor would he countenance medicines for his profound melancholia. On the day of David's interment, Emanuel stayed in his carrier chair outside the gates of the cemetery. He watched the proceedings like a Nazarite who feared impurity by being near corpses, even those of his own family. He saw his wives there, the Sikh and the amahs, saw them intone the Kaddish, saw them toss dirt, saw them leave a stone remembrance, but departed before they could see him.

In the weeks that followed, those who visited him at his offices on Lyndhurst Terrace saw an ashen-faced man who looked as if he had slept under a bridge. Their attempts to offer him condolences were met with obscenities. Insomnia had clouded his mind to the point where he signed whatever papers were placed on his desk in front of him. He used his office as a bedroom and ate the occasional crust of bread there. When motivated and stoked with wine, he would sneak, unseen, in the dead of night, back into Kingsclere. He would enter David's room, sit in a chair, and stare at the empty bed. Then, before dawn, he would depart as surreptitiously as he had arrived.

Each day he would lie on the leather couch in his office and beg his G-d for some sign, some relief—a moment or two of sleep, a second's reprieve from the agony-sucking pain in his chest, an instant of psychic harmony. But all he received was silence, that deep, wide maw of emptiness that invades a parent who has outlived their child. Downing a cup of rice wine and scratching his signature on papers were never sufficient to distract him from the turbulence in his heart and mind. In time, even the thought of waiting for nightfall to begin a nocturnal vigil in David's room became meaningless and the visitations pointless, so he abandoned that routine. Other than the upcoming land auction, which had been postponed due to the recent quarantine, he had nothing to look forward to.

Silence fell when he entered the ballroom of the Hong Kong Hotel. Heads turned and necks craned to see the rumpled, portly man, hair frazzled and beard unkempt, shuffle into the room, his clothes in tatters and his shoes scuffed. Emanuel presented himself at the registration table. When asked to sign his name, he pushed so hard on the nib that it snapped and sprayed ink across the sheet of paper. Attendees murmured and shook their heads, then turned away and restarted their conversations. He took his bid paddle and looked around.

Huddled in a cabal near the auctioneer's dais were Sassoon, Kardoorie, and Hardoon. They nodded in his direction. But Emanuel ignored them, biting his lip with disappointment. Neither Li nor Aleandro was present.

"I will do this for you, Senhor, one time and the ledger is balanced," Aleandro had said. "You freed my family, now I will free yours." Emanuel had seized upon those words as his surety. The mulatto had sailed out of Hong Kong just prior to the British naval blockade. But the quarantine had been lifted for weeks and there was no sign of his return. Emanuel was about to bid everything he had without knowing whether he possessed sufficient funds to cover the purchase.

As he walked to his seat, attendees in the vicinity gave him wide berth. He sat alone, surrounded by empty chairs.

There were several lots ahead of the main event. As the auctioneer got closer to the lot containing the Kowloon properties, the air seemed to stiffen. Men brought handkerchiefs to their foreheads as the room turned warm with body heat. Emanuel too felt the change in temperature. It was exactly what he had felt that first time he attended an auction in Calcutta. He needed this. He needed to win at something. He needed to fill the giant hole that had been hewn out of his chest. He needed to feel danger.

The auctioneer announced the final lot and started the bidding at one million dollars. Increments rose by fifty thousand and soon reached one and a half million, with the Sassoon cabal leading the pack. Emanuel raised his bid paddle and called out his first offer: "Two million."

A collective intake of breath shot through the hall. But the crowd recovered quickly. Someone offered 2.1. Other bids followed in increments of one hundred thousand. 2.2! 2.3! The Sassoon cartel shouted 2.5. Emanuel topped it with 2.7.

Anything beyond three million would place him on shaky ground. Someone called 2.8. Emanuel felt a rush of excitement shoot up into his chest. It made him stand and shout, "2.9 million!" He was almost at his limit. The occupants of the room murmured. Some shook their heads and tossed their paddles to the floor.

"I have 2.9," the auctioneer said, looking around the room. "Do I hear more? I'm looking around the room. Do I see three?"

"Three!" Sassoon yelled and punched the air with his paddle.

Emanuel narrowed his eyes and focused on his rival. He felt like a young man again, suddenly transported back to the dusty floor of Calcutta's auction rooms where he had learned his trade. He was about to raise his paddle when he felt a tug on his shoulder. It was Li. He said,

"I must speak with you."

"No need for words, old friend." Emanuel smiled. "You're here, that's all that counts." Emboldened, he turned back to face the auctioneer: "3.1!" he shouted. The room roared with disbelief.

"Emanuel, come with me," Li said.

"3.2!" Sassoon yelled, face as red as a beet. His fist curled around the handle of his bid paddle, making it vibrate.

Li grabbed Emanuel's hand, thrust something into his fleshy palm, and closed his fingers over it.

"3.2 million," the auctioneer called out. "Do I have more? Mr. Belilios?" he asked, looking directly at him.

"Yes," Emanuel shouted, "3.5 million!"

Then he opened his hand. Sitting on his palm was a stone larger than a quail's egg but smaller than a hen's. It was flat and smooth—perfectly shaped for skipping on water.

"The Generalissimo has taken all the opium—Aleandro is dead," Li said.

"$3.5 million going once," the auctioneer stated cheerfully. "3.5 going twice." The auctioneer was insistent now.

"Oh my G-d," Emanuel said. "No—"

The gavel fell.

"Sold for $3.5 million dollars to Mr. Belilios!"

Blood drained from Emanuel's face—he was over two million short.

The room erupted in cheers and applause. Even the Sassoon clique joined the caterwauling hoots and whistles that accompanied cries of congratulations for the largest bid ever made in the colony's short history.

For the Chinese in the room, it was a good omen. It was auspicious that this had happened at the end of the lunar year. They had seen an abundance of money exchange hands—money that would grow as the colony grew. Everyone agreed that the business concluded on that wintery afternoon certainly augured well for the years ahead.

Cries of "*Gung Hei Faat Choy*—Happy New Year" rang out around Emanuel. The room emptied quickly and he was left to enjoy his *joss*—his good fortune—standing alone in the hall as mute as the stone in his hand.

SEMAH

A pre-dawn silence palled over the mansion on the morning after Chinese New Year. (The sister-wives had agreed that the servants should be given two days off to visit their relatives.) Semah, Veer Singh, and a mono-toothed gatekeeper—the man had no family—were the only ones in residence. As was her custom, Pearl (and Leah Felicie) had left for her father's house in Happy Valley to play hostess to the New Year's celebrations there. The stillness at Kingsclere mirrored the quiet of Central District. The occasional popping of firecrackers echoed through the narrow canyons between deserted office buildings. Everyone, it seemed, needed one more day to recover from the celebrations. In the harbour, the ships looked like flat-bottomed vessels sitting on a sheet of glass.

Semah was still in bed when she heard the rhythmic grunt of chair carriers outside. Pearl returning home so soon? She was usually away for a few days. Semah got out of bed, threw on a gown, put on carpet slippers, and rushed to the veranda. It was Emanuel. Ropes groaned as the coolies set down his chair. He climbed off. Under his arm, he carried a small box. He walked slowly to the front door, stopping once to steady himself against the wall.

It was the first time she had seen him since … Although he was dressed in a clean suit, he looked sick and old. She rushed down the stairs and out the front door. He doffed his hat when he saw her.

"Madam," he said.

"Semah, surely."

"Thank you, my dearest. It is good to see you well again. I had heard …" He let his sentence drift into silence and began again. "I have not been the best of husbands of late, but the circumstances …" He struggled to find words, but they failed him.

"There is no need to explain. You are home now."

He remained silent. His eyes wandered, searching for the right words. The flat of his hand tapped vigorously on the box.

"There are matters to discuss," he said. Semah motioned toward the house, but he signalled no with his hand. "I cannot bear to … Come with me."

He led her to the bench under the banyan that overlooked the harbour below. They sat side by side. Without setting down the box, he said in a low voice,

"We must leave this place."

"Whatever do you mean?"

"Please, just listen quietly. I have sold Kingsclere to pay my debts—"

"What?"

"Let me finish. I cannot be here. Everywhere I look I see disappointment, and I have tried, tried my very best to overcome my grief, but … it is futile."

Their eyes met.

Semah embraced him, and together they felt that sour lump of bitterness clog their throats as a flood of memories returned. It was the first time they had shared the sorrow that only parents who have outlived their child could feel.

He broke away first and spoke in great detail about his business ambitions, culminating in the overextended bid that he made only days ago.

"Here, a reputation is everything. The property will default to the next highest bidder—Sassoon and his clique. When people hear that I was unable to meet my obligations, I will become a laughingstock … and they will come for me."

"What about your other businesses, your properties?"

"Mortgaged on each other, waiting for the market to increase."

"Then why did you make the bid?"

"I needed a win."

"Are we ruined, then?"

"All but. I have found someone willing to buy me out."

Semah gasped.

"But there is a condition."

What could that be? she wondered. His eyes pleaded for understanding.

"We must both leave and never return."

Semah could not talk. Her heart raced. Her head spun. She thought she might faint and turned, reaching for the trunk of the banyan to steady herself. Behind her, she felt his looming presence, heard his voice in her ear.

"Here, in this box, are silver coins and a ticket for you. The steamer departs this evening. Dearest," he whispered, "come with me. Say you will."

Semah looked at her husband for a long time. Then she nodded.

His shoulders dropped with relief. He kissed her hand and departed in the carrier chair he had come in just as the sun rose to brighten up the world.

On the day of Emanuel's visit to Kingsclere, a loud knocking woke Pearl in her old rooms at her father's house. Annoyed, she sat up in bed ready to scold Gum-ghee for disturbing her lie-in. But it was her father who entered quickly and closed the door behind him.

"*Ba-bah,* what is it?" Pearl asked, stepping out of bed.

"I did not want to bring this matter up until today. The guests, the banquet, Chinese New Year is a special time and we had so many people ..." He waved his hand nervously. "Let me get to the point of the matter—Emanuel has departed Hong Kong with his first wife. You will never see them again."

Pearl suddenly felt hollow, her body emptied of blood, lungs, heart, liver. Her vision blurred. Her ears snatched at phrases: "... Emanuel played the Hong Kong game and lost ... liquidated his assets ... I purchased Kingsclere ... on condition that he leave with the *gwei-paw* ... for your sake ... for Leah Felicie's future ..." Pain shot through her temples. Could this be true? Abandoned? After all she had done for Semah, for Emanuel?

She had no memory of how she got dressed, how she travelled from her father's house back to Kingsclere. Time had collapsed. Space had shrunk. She walked upstairs to the west wing. Gum-ghee followed. She went into every room, but there was no sign of Semah.

"Take her clothes, her furniture, take everything and burn it in the backyard."

"Everything?" Gum-ghee asked.

"*EVERYTHING!*" she screamed and heard the word echo through the house.

When Emanuel stepped aboard P&O's SS *Bungaree*, he knew that Semah had already checked in. Her manservant, Veer Singh, was stationed outside her cabin door, his arms folded across his chest. Emanuel was glad that Semah had purchased a passage for the man who had served her so faithfully. Yes, the fierce-looking Sikh could act as a bodyguard for them both.

"Memsahib is at rest," he said. "She begs you please to meet her for supper in the dining lounge at eight o'clock."

Emanuel looked at his watch. "Very well," he replied, and retired to his cabin to freshen up and have a lie-down before dressing for dinner. At seven-thirty, the ship's horn blew three times to signal all gangways up. Ropes were flipped off their cleats and pulled in. The stacks let off thick clouds of black smoke and the vessel pulled away from its dock. Meanwhile, Emanuel had a stand-up douche and changed his clothes.

He exited his cabin. The Sikh was no longer standing guard at Semah's door. He checked his watch and saw that it was nearly eight o'clock. Obviously, she had preceded him and was waiting in the lounge as they had arranged. Other passengers were now leaving their cabins, crowding the narrow hallway as they made their way up the stairs for dinner. Emanuel followed the cavalcade, happily thinking that the worst year of his life was ebbing away. He was eager to put as much distance between himself and Fragrant Harbour as he could.

At the dining lounge, he looked about for Semah but did not see her. Nor, for that matter, was there any sign of her Indian bodyguard. So he asked for a table by the window and sat down to wait.

SEMAH

So much of her relationship with Emanuel had been forged by moments of separation. And this would be the last, Semah thought, standing on the pier and watching the SS *Bungaree* steam out of Hong Kong harbour, the last, longest separation. She had sent her trusted manservant on board as a ruse. He had delivered the message as ordered. Emanuel would now be at the dining lounge waiting for her and wondering where she was. Veer Singh had waited at his post until the last moment possible, then stepped off the vessel before the gangplank was raised.

She had no intention of leaving Hong Kong with a man who had been inconstant. Yet she felt a pang of guilt that she had deceived him. But then, she had made up her mind that her place was to be close to David. She would never desert someone she loved. And with that thought, she instructed Veer Singh to fetch a carrier chair to take her back up the hill to Kingsclere.

Nearing the house at dusk, a choking smoke filled the air. Something was ablaze. Veer Singh tried the front door but it would not open. He banged on it with the palm of his hand.

Semah looked up from her chair. Pearl was on the veranda looking down at her with folded arms, knitted brow, and pursed lips. Semah smiled and waved.

She had trusted Semah and considered her a friend. No, more than a friend, a confidante, a sister-wife. They had shared decisions affecting their children, shared a husband, and shared a home. Pearl had given face. She had a right to expect the same in return. She had a right to be the first to know about Emanuel's betrayal, not the last to find out. Semah owed her. So when the giantess waved, Pearl did not reciprocate. Instead, she left the veranda and went indoors, leaving Veer Singh to minister to his mistress.

Shortly after, as dusk fell, Pearl heard shouting outside.

Semah was nowhere to be seen, and Li had arrived. Normally servants anticipating his arrival would have opened the doors. But Pearl had ordered them to remain shut. Surprised, he yelled to be let in. He hammered on the door with the flat of his palm, backed away, looked for a stone, and threw it up to the veranda. He called out her name, swore at the servants whom he knew were cowering indoors, and threatened them with beatings. But the doors remained shut.

Pearl sat alone in her salon, the shutters drawn and the lights off. She covered her ears from the sounds of his indignation. Her father's ire sprayed relentlessly for what seemed like an eternity—*for your own good … reclaim face … why do you humiliate me*—but she remained unmoved by his entreaties. She blamed him. He was the instrument that had enabled Emanuel's abandonment and Semah's betrayal.

Hoarse from screaming, his rage in tatters, Li departed from the garden, climbed into his sedan chair, and wept like a parent who has lost a child. The curse had come home to roost and the sun disappeared, pulling darkness over the house like a carapace.

In the evening silence, Pearl crawled into bed fully clothed, reached into her pocket, and pulled out her mother's piece of jade—smoother now from years of rubbing. She held it, looking for the solace it had always given her. But it was cold comfort.

EPILOGUE

News of Emanuel's passing reached his wives first by telegraph, and then a few weeks later by a letter written in Mr. Rustomjee's neat, cursive hand. In it he explained the cause—heart failure at age sixty-seven—then ended with condolences for the loss of a man he had felt honoured to call *friend*.

Some days later, Semah looked through the east-facing window of her small suite in the King Edward Hotel, from where she could see Kingsclere perched like an enormous white nest on the mountainside. For years now she had been convinced that, if she squinted and used her imagination, at noon each day she could see Pearl standing beside the gazebo looking through the telescope that was aimed in her direction. And so, each day at the sound of the noonday gun, Semah had looked out the window, raised a white lace handkerchief in her hand, and waved. In her imagination, Pearl would return the greeting. But weekly letters, delivered by Veer Singh into the hands of Pearl's Chinese handmaid, went unanswered. Birthday gifts for Leah Felicie were returned.

So it was a cause for great excitement when, after all those years of estrangement, Pearl had agreed to visit. Semah had been agitated ever since the message had arrived. She clapped her hands and fussed about. Tottering around her rooms, she spent the day straightening pictures that did not need adjusting and running her fingertips over the mantel looking for dust that did not exist.

She needn't have worried. Although the cramped rooms were a bit dowdy, the place was clean. Veer Singh had seen to that with daily dusting, polishing, and airing. Ever faithful, he had continued his service, retiring each evening to a cot in the hotel's attic. Mindful of the special occasion, he had not scrimped on the groceries, even purchasing a bouquet of daffodils that he had placed in a pretty cloisonné vase at the centre of the table.

Precisely at three o'clock, the doorbell rang. Semah checked her hair in the mantel mirror and then nodded at Veer Singh, who opened the door.

Pearl's appearance had not changed. Her face was youthful, her skin was flawless, and her black hair (tied in a bun) still radiated vitality. Dressed in a traditional navy blue *cheongsam*—an ankle-length gown— she wore a blue wrap around her shoulders and held white gloves in one hand. Gum-ghee, eyes downcast and resplendent in a starched white tunic, stood behind her mistress.

"Pearl," Semah said, leaning heavily on her cane and holding out one hand. "It is so good to see you. Please come in."

"Thank you," Pearl said and entered, touching Semah's hand with her fingers. She looked around the room. Gum-ghee closed the door and forced herself to stand beside the Sikh. She had little choice; the room was so small. Besides, she thought it best to be near the front door in case a hasty retreat was required.

"Would you care for some tea?" Semah asked.

"Perhaps after ..." Pearl let her sentence trail off.

"Yes, of course," Semah said. Indicating the sofa, she continued: "Would you mind if we sat? My leg is not as steady as it once was."

"By all means," Pearl replied and sat down.

Veer Singh leapt into action and assisted Semah as she lowered herself beside her guest. Pearl opened her shawl to expose her Magen David necklace. Together the women intoned the Kaddish—an ancient Hebrew prayer said by mourners. When the prayer was concluded, Semah said,

"Thank you for being here."

"It is I who should thank you," Pearl said.

"For what?"

"Your suggestion that we do this—mourn for our husband. A blessing."

An awkward silence fell between them. Semah took a deep breath— who knows when such an opportunity would present itself again?

"I was never going to leave," Semah said.

"I know that now," Pearl replied. "After news of Emanuel's passing, I read all your letters."

"You kept them?"

"Leah Felicie did. She insisted I read them." Pearl looked at her fingers. "You visit David often?"

"Daily if I could. But my health prevents me now."

Those admissions breached the thick wall that had separated them. Semah talked about how simple her days had become. Writing letters, painting, reading, and visiting her son's gravesite were the sum total of her activities. She said she could not bring herself to attend the new synagogue, built on Robinson Road. Not because of her lack of mobility but because she could not stand the glares and quizzical looks of congregants who were filled with questions about her husband. Pearl offered that she felt the same and had eschewed attendance herself.

"Thank you for all this," Semah said.

"All what?"

"This," Semah repeated, waving her hand to mean the hotel suite.

"I don't know what you are referring to."

"My account is settled monthly. I assumed it must have been you."

"It was not." Pearl's tone was emphatic.

"Then who?"

Pearl raised her eyebrows and breathed in.

"More tea?" Semah offered, trying to bridge the stillness.

"Thank you, no." Pearl fidgeted with her pendant. "I, too, have something to say. I would like to ask you to come home," she said, looking squarely at her hostess.

Semah froze. Her shoulders dropped first, then her mouth opened. She covered it with her hand and felt tears welling up. Between them the air seemed to turn into tentacles of spun glass that if touched too roughly might splinter.

"Would you like that?" Pearl whispered.

Semah nodded. "Yes," she replied. "Yes I would."

Both wives reached out and clasped hands. Holding on gave them a strength that neither had felt for a long time.

"What a life," Pearl said.

"What a life indeed," Semah replied.

A sharp knock on the door made the women jump. Veer Singh opened it. Framed in the hallway was a beautiful young woman.

"Ma-mah," she said, and smiled when she saw Pearl and Semah sitting together.

With Pearl supporting her, Semah struggled to her feet.

"*Daughter,* say hello to your Auntie Semah."

"Let me have a good look at you," Semah said. Leah Felicie's dark wavy hair was tied at the back. Her strong jaw and straight nose echoed her father's looks while the high cheekbones and almond-shaped eyes resembled Pearl's. Look this way and she appeared to be Chinese. But when the light changed you would swear she was a *gweilo*'s daughter.

"A beautiful child and now a beautiful young woman!" Semah said, reaching out her hand. Leah Felicie took it, and with the other reached out to her mother, who folded hers in her daughter's palm to complete the circle.

Together, they made arrangements for Semah's return to the house the following week. Reluctant farewells were made. Cheeks touched cheeks and Leah Felicie heard her aunt say to her mother, "You should have been treasured." And she heard her mother reply, "So should you."

But Semah's homecoming never happened. On Thursday afternoon, while sitting by the window, she felt a frisson, pulled her shawl tighter around her shoulders, and took in a deep breath. As she exhaled, she felt herself falling into the sky.

Veer Singh appeared at Kingsclere's front door to bring the news to Pearl. He was watery-eyed and ashen-faced—even Gum-ghee dabbed the corner of her eye at the sight of the man's grief.

That night, Pearl walked out to the gazebo near the banyan tree and sat on the stone bench that overlooked the harbour. She put her hand in her pocket and felt the familiar coldness of the jade memento her mother had given her long ago. She clasped it in her palm until it slowly warmed. Then she stood and looked through the telescope, aiming it one last time at the window of the hotel. Though there was no one there, she raised her hand and waved, imagining that her sister-wife was waving back.

Pearl made arrangements for Semah to lie beside her beloved David. At the interment, she stood beside her daughter, Gum-ghee, and Veer Singh. At the end of the service, Pearl turned to the Sikh.

"Where will you go? What will you do now?"

"Australia, Madam. There I own many horses."

"You do?"

"Yes, G-d has been kind to me."

"But why did you stay all these years?"

"Because I loved her—with all my heart. I have done so since I was a boy."

"Then *you* must have been her benefactor?" Pearl asked.

Veer Singh did not reply. He simply put his palms together, made a slight bow, and walked out the cemetery gates.

THE END

AUTHOR'S NOTE

In 1862, my great-grandfather, a twenty-five-year-old Sephardic Jew named Emanuel Raphael Belilios, left his home in Calcutta and set sail for the still-new British colony of Hong Kong, leaving behind his young wife, Semah. In the ship's cargo hold were chests containing opium he had purchased at a British government auction. His intention was to sell his lading quickly, make a fortune, and return home to live comfortably for the rest of his life.

But when Emanuel landed in Hong Kong he was unable to sell his goods as swiftly as he had planned. Other opium traders who had established their businesses decades before had monopolized the ports of entry along the China coast. Ever resourceful, Emanuel found an alternate route. With the assistance of a comprador—a local Chinese agent—and a mulatto boatman, Emanuel accessed the Chinese interior through Macau, which in those days was a Portuguese protectorate. This strategy soon made him the foremost opium trader in Hong Kong.

Over the next two decades Emanuel's wealth increased, evidenced by the many properties in his portfolio. He had a residence at 13 Caine Road named Kingsclere, offices at Lyndhurst Crescent, and a summer retreat called the Eyrie on the Peak. The best, of course, was yet to come. He had plans to build an immense mansion—known as the second Kingsclere—on Kennedy Road and to use part of the land to build a synagogue. During this period Emanuel also found time to take a Chinese lover, a woman named Li.

Back in Calcutta, Semah tired of waiting for her husband and decided to set sail for Hong Kong, arriving there in the early 1880s. There she discovered that her husband had established a parallel family. Rather than contest the issue, she moved in and the three managed to work out tolerable living arrangements—after all, there was more than enough room: Kingsclere's four turreted storeys towered above the harbour. With Semah, Emanuel had four children: Sally, Hanna, Raphael, and David; with Li he had one daughter: Felicie Marie. How they came to regard each other and what activities formed their daily lives are questions that only fiction can answer.

This blended household seemed to work well for all concerned. The Belilios family were model philanthropists and gave generously to hospitals, public works, and schools. In 1893, Emanuel donated $25,000 to the Central School for Girls for a new three-storey building to be erected on Hollywood Road. In April 1965, the school was relocated to its present premises in Tin Hau Temple Road and is called the Belilios Public School. In business, Emanuel rose quickly to take his place amongst the early Taipans of the rough-and-ready colony, becoming a director and then chairman of the Hongkong and Shanghai Bank (HSBC). He was also honoured by the Queen and appointed a Knight Commander in the Order of St. Michael and St. George.

From 1898 onward, Emanuel spent more of his time in London, England, leaving Semah and Li behind in Hong Kong. He lived in an elegant townhouse at 134 Piccadilly, Mayfair, facing Green Park, near Buckingham Palace, until his death in 1905. A copy of his probated will shows that his "effects" were valued at less than £700. This begs the question: What happened to the fortune made from the sale of opium? If there were mansions and summer houses, enough to support two families and give to charitable causes, how did Emanuel manage to leave such a modest sum, and die so far from the bosom of his family?

Sometime after her husband's death, Semah moved to the King Edward Hotel on Ice House Street in Hong Kong. She died there in 1926 and is buried at the Jewish cemetery in Happy Valley, Hong Kong. There is no record of Li's burial. Her daughter, Felicie Marie Belilios, my grandmother, married Choa Po Sien, the son of a well-established family of traders from Malacca. Together they created a lavish home on Broadwood Road. Both Felicie and my grandfather lie in the Roman Catholic cemetery in Happy Valley. Their daughter, my mother, Pauline Choa, was one of twelve siblings born and raised in the colony. She married Thomas Johnston, a merchant from Shanghai, and together they survived the 1941 Japanese invasion and managed to escape to Macau, where they spent the duration of the war, raising three children. After the war ended in 1945, they returned to Hong Kong, where three more children were born—

I among them. Growing up in a mixed-race family, my parents had always been taciturn about my ancestors. But when I was around twelve, my father once said to me, "Remember, you are a Jew because your mother is a Jew." Curious to know more, I asked my mother how this could be because we were all baptized Roman Catholics. She answered tersely, "My grandfather was Jewish. His name was Belilios and he came from India. He lived at Kingsclere." The finality in her tone of voice and the expression on her face prevented me from ever raising the question again. In the late 1960s, I left the British colony for studies at McMaster University in Hamilton, Ontario. My parents remained in Hong Kong until they immigrated to Canada in the 1980s. Whatever they knew about my Jewish ancestors, they carried to their graves.

I returned to Hong Kong for the first time just before the 1997 handover of the colony back to China. Being there re-ignited my genealogical interest. A couple more visits in the 2000s led me to a photograph exhibit at the Hong Kong Museum of History. There I saw a photo of a colossal white mansion called Kingsclere.

Why Emanuel named this house Kingsclere is lost to history and few facts remain of its provenance. Records show that the land was auctioned in 1896 and construction of the mansion was completed in 1901—far later than the one in the novel. (For dramatic purposes, I have conflated all of Emanuel's real-life residences into the largest and most impressive one. The Kingsclere in the novel is located between the current Kennedy Road Peak Tram station and Garden Road.)

The trustees opposed Emanuel's plans for the synagogue and the idea was dropped. Instead, he erected the 14,000 sq. ft. mansion that survives only in sepia photographs. One year after Emanuel's death the property passed to a new owner, who turned it into a luxury hotel. It sustained great damage in the typhoon of 1908 and was demolished in 1923. Today, all that remains is the colossal foundation upon which several modern highrises stand.

After a decade of research in London, Kolkata, Hong Kong, and China, I found that there were too many gaps in the narrative to write a historical account of my ancestors' lives. Yet the story of a young Jewish opium merchant and his two wives carving out a life in the new colony captured my imagination and refused to let go. Inspired by these characters, I started to write a play to discover their voices. As soon as my ancestors started speaking they wouldn't stop. Before long, the play grew and morphed into the novel you hold in your hands.

ACKNOWLEDGMENTS

Fortunately I had a lot of support while researching and writing this novel or it might never have happened. My wife, Sheila, encouraged me to continue regardless of how many blind alleys I stumbled into and was the first to read and comment on every draft. The Canada Council for the Arts–Theatre Section gave me a travel grant to do research in India, Hong Kong, and China. My aunt France Choa introduced me to Judy and Michael Green, members of Ohel Leah Synagogue in Hong Kong, who put me in touch with Brenda Yi, the synagogue's Judaica librarian. John Grey, chairman and CEO (ret.) of the Honkong and Shanghai Bank, gave me permission to access the bank's archives. Also in Hong Kong, Annelise Connell, my local researcher and guide, located all of E.R. Belilios's residences and cousin Andrew Tze shared his photo archives. Later, based on a chimera of an idea, the Stratford Festival (Canada) provided me with a Playwright's Residency during which the play developed into a novel. Readers of early drafts were Natasha Nadir, my literary manager at Gateway Theatre; John Wright, artistic director of Blackbird Theatre; and my brother, William—who all commented with kindness. My early editor, Michele Ebel, in London, Ontario, and the unflappable Scott Steadman worked with me on several drafts before it was ready for submission. My agent, the formidable Denise Bukowski in Toronto, helped to further shape the narrative and placed my story with Penguin Canada and Penguin India. Amber Chatterjee, my Indian editor, provided much-needed advice on the accuracy of place names and proper names. I'm indebted to my publisher, Nicole Winstanley, who provided laser-like notes that were a joy to work on. I'm also so grateful to my editor, the always-awesome Adrienne Kerr, who has the uncanny ability to speak fluent me. I would like to thank my family: Tom, Peter, Jacquelyn, Valerie, and Andreas; John and Baya, Eva and Tova; and friends in the greater Vancouver region, Richmond, Toronto, Hong Kong, London (U.K.), New York, and Rig David in Kolkata. Thanks also to my colleagues at the Playwrights Guild of Canada and my golfing buddies. You have all been so supportive of the process. I am truly blessed to have such a tribe.